PROMISED LAND

This Large Print Book carries the
Seal of Approval of N.A.V.H.

A CHOSEN PEOPLE NOVEL

PROMISED LAND

ROBERT WHITLOW

THORNDIKE PRESS
A part of Gale, a Cengage Company

LIBRARY OF CONGRESS CIP DATA ON FILE.
CATALOGUING IN PUBLICATION FOR THIS BOOK
IS AVAILABLE FROM THE LIBRARY OF CONGRESS

ISBN-13: 978-1-4328-7603-6 (hardcover alk. paper)

Published in 2020 by arrangement with Thomas Nelson, Inc., a division of HarperCollins Christian Publishing, Inc.

Printed in Mexico
Print Number: 01   Print Year: 2020

*To all who dwell in the Promised Land
and the Land of Promises*

Come, let us go up to the
mountain of the LORD,
to the temple of the God of Jacob.
He will teach us his ways,
so that we may walk in his paths.

— MICAH 4:2

PROLOGUE

Rahal Abaza sat motionless in front of the panoramic view of the Persian Gulf. The gently rippling blue water sparkled beneath a cloudless sky. Rahal lived in a modern apartment that occupied the entire thirty-sixth floor of a skyscraper in the Al Dafna neighborhood of Doha, the capital and largest city of Qatar. He owned a half interest in the building. The other owner was a member of the Qatari royal family.

The first son of his father's second wife, Rahal found favor as a boy due to his sharp mind, skill as an archer, and literary talent as a poet. Upon his father's death, he assumed control of the family's stake in the country's oil reserves and quickly expanded into other business ventures, including several contracts with the US government at the Al Udeid Air Base located twenty miles southwest of Doha. With a population of more than eleven thousand, Al Udeid contained the largest concentration of US military personnel in the Middle East. Rahal's company supplied everything from cleaning services for bathrooms to caviar for banquets.

Five years earlier, Rahal's life had dramatically changed during a pilgrimage to Mecca. Not far from the entrance to the Great Mosque he encountered a wizened, elderly beggar. Since he was on a pilgrimage, Rahal stopped to give alms to the man. The beggar grabbed his hand with surprising strength and didn't let go until Rahal looked directly at him.

"Do not spend your wealth on pleasure but for the glory of jihad until all the earth is in submission to Allah and his prophet. Then you will be welcomed with open arms into paradise," the old man said.

Rahal jerked his hand away. The beggar threw the money on the ground and spat on the pavement.

"Take your wicked alms to the place of torment," he said.

Rahal couldn't tear his gaze away from the beggar's face. The old man's eyes were deep pools that plunged to depths far beyond anything that existed in the natural realm. Rahal desperately wanted to escape the beggar's presence, but his feet refused to move. There were over one million pilgrims in the holy city during the height of the hajj, but Rahal felt completely alone. He knelt down and slowly collected the money with trembling hands.

"What must I do?" he asked.

"Recognize Ali as rightful successor to the prophet," the old man said in a low but intense voice. "Truth flows from truth."

Rahal drew back.

"But I am Sunni," he protested. "Just like all my fathers before me. I'm making the hajj as commanded by the prophet."

"You!" the man said as he pointed his finger at Rahal's chest. "You are an infidel!"

Rahal's heart pounded. He'd been raised as a Sunni, not a Shiite. The greatest controversy between the two groups arose from the correct line of succession from the prophet Muhammad. No one but Rahal knew that for over two years he had been at war with himself over the issue. To express doubt about Sunni beliefs in Qatar, where ninety percent of the Arab population and all the political leadership were Sunnis, would cause him to be ostracized or worse. Rahal felt his soul being ripped in two.

"I have questions," he said, his voice quivering.

"Question no more!" the man commanded, raising his voice.

"But —"

"Go!" the old man ordered, pointing toward the Great Mosque and the Kaaba.

Suddenly, Rahal's feet came unstuck and he was swept along with the crowd that moments before had flowed around him like water past a rock in a river. Over the next few days, he completed the requirements of the hajj, but the old man's warning haunted his every waking thought. As the power of the beggar's words burrowed deeper and deeper into Rahal's consciousness, they exposed his previous beliefs as false. He returned several times to the place where he'd encountered the old man, but he never saw him again. Perhaps he was a *malak,* an angel.

Rahal returned to Doha and terminated the lease on the apartment in Paris where his favorite mistress lived. He began studying the Qur'an as never before, memorizing long passages and secretly listening to sermons by influential Shiite imams. Soon he was utterly convinced that the Sunni heresy was a malignancy almost as great as the moral corruption of the West. The only thing that exceeded them both was the cancerous presence of the Zionists along the shores of the Mediterranean.

12

Rahal's wife cared about nothing except comfort, and his two grown daughters were married to men more interested in horse racing than religion. Rahal had no son or men his age in whom he could confide. He carefully began to expand his network of connections to include those who shared his zeal and faith.

"Sir," said a male voice behind Rahal.

Rahal swiveled in his chair and faced a pair of wiry but strong young men in their early thirties. Khalil and Mustafa Morsi came from a well-respected Shiite family in Beirut that had fallen on hard times due to the political upheaval in Lebanon. They shared Rahal's beliefs and knew about his spiritual change while on the hajj. A sophisticated IT expert trained in Germany, Khalil was a Hafiz, the term awarded to a person who had memorized the entire Qur'an. Mustafa, two years younger, was Rahal's chief of security. Before moving to Qatar he'd served for five years in an elite military unit of Hezbollah in Lebanon. The brothers looked so similar they could pass for twins. Both of them were open Shiites, but their presence as part of Rahal's entourage didn't raise suspicions because they occupied subservient roles.

"You wanted to see us," Khalil said, bowing his head slightly.

"Yes," Rahal said. "I want to ask you a question."

Neither Khalil nor Mustafa showed any sign of nervousness or fear in his presence. It was another reason Rahal included the talented young men in his inner circle. Emotion was the enemy of courage.

"Where does the heart of darkness reside?" Rahal asked.

Mustafa was quieter, Khalil more vocal.

"In four places," Khalil answered. "The soul of an infidel, the eyes of a loose woman, the land occupied by the Jews, and in America."

"You've answered well," Rahal replied. "Let me add another — a traitor who betrays those who follow the prophet."

Both brothers nodded.

"What should we do about the heart of darkness?" Rahal continued.

"Strike it with the sword of jihad!" Mustafa moved his right hand forward as if thrusting an imaginary blade.

"And who best wields that sword in my household?"

"I do," Mustafa answered, standing up even straighter.

Khalil put his hand on his brother's shoulder. "And together we are invincible."

14

"Sit beside me," Rahal said, motioning to two empty chairs. "I want to talk to you about piercing the heart of darkness in Sharm el-Sheikh."

CHAPTER 1

It was 3:33 a.m., and the Lord gently nudged Hana Abboud Hasan awake for a night watch. Daud, her husband of six months, was out of the country on business. A sound sleeper, Daud rarely woke up when she slipped out of bed. When Hana asked him about it, he smiled and replied, "The sleep of the righteous is sweet." Hana rolled her eyes but didn't argue. Daud was a good man, the husband she'd prayed for, and the soul mate chosen for her by God himself.

Hana went into the living room of the one-bedroom house where she'd lived since moving from Israel to the US. Turning on a lamp, she opened her Bible. A low moan came from the kitchen, followed by a series of short snorts. The source of the noises was Leon, a furry, eighty-five-pound black-and-white dog who had trotted out of the woods and into Hana's life a year earlier. A random mix of big dog breeds, Leon looked like a small Saint Bernard. His thick coat forced Hana and Daud to set the thermostat on the air-conditioning unit a few degrees cooler to keep their pet comfortable in the humid heat of the Georgia summer. Otherwise the dog's long red tongue would hang out of his mouth and drip saliva all over the house.

After reading a psalm, Hana placed earbuds in her ears and listened to worship music performed in Aramaic, the ancient language spoken by Jesus and his disciples. Hana spoke Arabic, Hebrew, English, and French. She wasn't fluent in Aramaic but knew enough to understand familiar songs. She closed her eyes and listened to melodies that might sound discordant to a Westerner but captured the expanse of the star-filled skies that had beckoned her ancestors to gaze heavenward and worship the one who created all things. Hana quietly sang along in a clear alto voice. She transitioned to songs in Arabic.

As the final song came to an end, a spontaneous lyric rose up in Hana's heart. Turning off the music, she continued to sing a cappella. The new song was part prayer, part declaration. When a phrase formed in her mind, she repeated it over and over until sensing a release to continue. Phrase followed phrase, then doubled back in repetition that built on what came before. Few things nurtured Hana's confidence in the Lord's love and faithfulness more than the songs he gave her. But tonight she didn't sing in personal worship. Instead, she offered up a song of intercession — for her new husband.

Daud sat alone in a hotel room in Sharm el-Sheikh, Egypt. A US government–issued cell phone lay on the bed beside him. Through the window he had a clear view of Na'ama Bay and its glistening beach. It was late afternoon, and as the sun sank lower in the sky only a handful of people strolled along on the white sand.

It was a two-hour boat ride from the local marina to the beautiful coral reefs that made Sharm el-Sheikh a choice destination for scuba divers. Close by were places where anyone could snorkel and swim with the colorful, exotic fish. Daud was a certified diver who'd explored the reefs of Tiran Island and Ras Muhammad in the past, but on this trip he wouldn't rent scuba gear and schedule a pleasure-boat ride.

Daud glanced at his phone and waited for the text message that would send him into

19

action. Four days had passed since his arrival at the southern tip of the Sinai. Twice, orders came through directing him to begin his phase of the mission. Both times his CIA contact rescinded the order within thirty minutes. His phone vibrated and lit up.

Stand down until tomorrow at 0900 hours.

It wasn't the message Daud wanted to receive. He resisted the urge to fire back a response questioning the competency of his American superiors who seemed fixated on everything being perfect before authorizing him to move forward. Exact preparation was impossible when people were involved. Daud's years of experience working as a covert agent for the Shin Bet, the Israeli equivalent of the FBI, had taught him it was better to act when the chance of success was ninety percent than delay and see the odds rapidly diminish due to unforeseen changes in circumstances. He paced back and forth across the room in an effort to release his pent-up tension. Confined by the walls, he decided to go out for a walk and an early dinner. Putting on dark sunglasses, he left the hotel room.

Just over six feet tall with a muscular physique, Daud had celebrated his thirty-second birthday while on honeymoon with Hana in southern Spain. They spent two weeks in Seville, Grenada, and Cordoba, places where Arab culture continued to exert its influence hundreds of years after the final defeat of the Moors by King Ferdinand and Queen Isabella.

Daud and Hana's wedding in Reineh was the culmination of a weeklong celebration involving his small family and her much larger one. Because of security concerns arising from Daud's previous undercover work and ongoing threats against his life, the wedding was a private affair without any public announcements or posts on social media.

One of Daud's favorite moments was the time they spent with Anwar Abboud, Hana's aged great-uncle. The ninety-nine-year-old man welcomed the couple into a small room where he sat in a comfortable chair with a glass of freshly squeezed lemonade on the table beside him. Anwar's memory was unreliable, and Daud wasn't sure the family patriarch remembered him from a single previous meeting, so he introduced himself in a respectful tone of voice.

"I'm not like Isaac, who didn't know the difference between Esau and Jacob," the old man replied with a gap-toothed grin. "The

Lord is faithful. He often brings Hana's face before my spirit. Recently, you've joined her there. That means the Holy Spirit brought you together."

Daud felt chills involuntarily run across his shoulders and down his arms. He glanced at Hana, whose face beamed at the confirmation of what they both believed.

"Has the Lord told you anything about Daud?" she asked.

Anwar nodded. "Child, you always ask the right question. Does Daud want to know the answer?"

Daud swallowed. He'd survived multiple life-or-death situations, but never had his heart beat faster. Hana nudged him and vigorously nodded her head.

"Yes, sir," Daud answered and then held his breath.

Anwar locked eyes with Daud before he spoke. "Like your name-sake, King David, you are destined to occupy the gates of your enemies."

Daud waited for an explanation, but none came. Anwar's eyes closed, and his head dropped to his chest. Within seconds his breathing indicated that he was asleep.

"Should we leave?" Daud whispered to Hana.

"I'm not sure," she answered. "I was hoping he would pray a blessing over us."

They sat quietly and waited. Anwar snorted. He squinted and looked at Hana. "And what about you?" he asked. "Do you want to hear from the Lord?"

"Yes, Uncle," Hana replied respectfully. "I want to be like Mary when the angel Gabriel came to her and she said, 'Be it unto me according to thy word.' "

Anwar smiled. "I'm not an angel, just an old man who loves you."

He then stared directly at Hana with a fiery intensity that startled Daud. He heard Hana's sharp intake of breath.

"Did you feel that?" Anwar asked her.

"Yes, sir," she answered.

"Some promises come only through pain and sacrifice. And so it will be for you." Anwar extended his hand outward in a broad motion and ended by pointing his index finger at his chest. "There is a promised land without and a land of promises within. Both realms are yours to possess if you pass the tests."

Hana bowed her head for a moment. "Daud and I are getting married tomorrow," she said. "It would be an honor if you would bless us as husband and wife."

Anwar paused as if listening. "Be fruitful in every way," he said in a lighter tone of voice. "It is the first commandment."

The old man became silent and in a few moments fell back asleep. Daud and Hana slipped from the room. Daud reached for Hana's hand as they walked down the hallway onto a small balcony that overlooked a spacious enclosed garden at the rear of the property. People were setting up tables and decorations for a party in their honor later in the evening. Hana leaned against Daud, who looked down at her.

"What do you think about your uncle's words?" he asked.

"I'm not sure. Uncle Anwar's words are like seeds that have to lie in the ground until they germinate and sprout. And what comes up isn't always what you expect."

As he waited for the hotel elevator, Daud felt his wedding ring in the left front pocket of his pants. He slipped it on and off his finger and thought about Hana. His heart ached at the longest separation of their young marriage.

Daud's boss for this project was a man who communicated via a secure computer network and sent texts to the designated cell phone. He used the name Charlie, but Daud had never met him in person and suspected it wasn't his real name, a common practice in the intelligence world to limit the knowledge of each person about the chain of command. That way if an agent like Daud was arrested or captured, he couldn't divulge damaging information.

A Shin Bet supervisor named Aaron Levy who'd worked with Daud in Israel recommended him to Charlie. When Daud learned the purpose of the mission, he accepted the offer to be part of a team. The interests of the United States and Israel to limit the spread of sophisticated missile technology and nuclear proliferation in the Middle East were parallel, and in this instance, the US had the better logistical capability to accomplish the mission.

Their target was a Ukrainian scientist named Artem Kolisnyk who was fleeing from his homeland after being charged with selling classified information to the highest bidder. The Egyptians were one of his clients. Kolisnyk's area of expertise wasn't designing the heavy-payload rockets capable of striking any city in the Middle East, but something smaller and in some ways more dangerous — the development of short-range missiles capable of evading the Iron Dome defense system that had proved so effective in knocking short-range rockets and conventional artillery fire from the skies over Israel. Daud wasn't briefed in detail about the underlying science of the Ukrainian's work beyond the fact that the compact weapons he designed could mimic the million-dollar cruise missiles in the American arsenal by flying extremely close to the ground, thus making it difficult for the radar component of an Iron Dome battery to detect the missile and intercept it. The Egyptians had arranged to buy the exclusive rights to Kolisnyk's services. The Americans and the Israelis didn't want that to happen.

As an Arab who spoke fluent Russian, Daud was tasked with convincing the scientist to accompany him to a meeting with American officials who would offer Kolisnyk a better deal than the Egyptians, a proposal that included political asylum in the US and guaranteed financial security through a nonmilitary job. The mission would require subtlety and finesse. Kolisnyk was in Sharm el-Sheikh on his way to Cairo, so this was the last chance to intervene. A complicating factor was the presence of the Ukrainian's fiancée, a young Egyptian woman. It was assumed the couple would travel under fictitious names.

Daud stepped out of the air-conditioned hotel into the dry heat and tossed a lightweight sport coat over his shoulder. It was a five-block walk to the central shopping district of Na'ama Bay where he could have a good meal. Finding a seafood restaurant, Daud slipped the maître d' a twenty-dollar bill and was seated at a table with a view of the entire room.

Fifteen minutes later four succulent prawns arrived resting on a bed of delicately seasoned rice. Glancing up, Daud saw a man and a woman approach the maître d' and instantly recognized them from the briefing material for the mission. It was Kolisnyk and his fiancée. Encountering the Ukrainian at the restaurant gave Daud a prime opportunity to initiate contact in a public environment without interference. He took out his secure cell phone and quickly sent Charlie a text message.

A and B are in the restaurant where I am eating. No security present. Permission requested to approach and engage.

CHAPTER 2

Hana brewed a cup of traditional Arab coffee flavored with cardamom and ate a breakfast of yogurt and fresh fruit. While she ate, she anxiously watched Israeli news reports on her computer. Daud had reassured her that he wouldn't be in Israel or the West Bank, but she couldn't help worrying. She grabbed her journal and reread her prayers from the night.

After breakfast, she checked the social media accounts in Israel for her relatives and read the latest posts about her many cousins, nieces, and nephews. Hana didn't maintain a public Facebook presence and sent only private messages. Her two favorite cousins, sisters named Fabia and Farah, no longer sent out daily requests for updates on Hana's life as a married woman, but Hana knew they remained eager for any tidbits of news she could pass along. She sent them photos of a dinner of shish taouk, a skewered chicken dish she'd prepared for Daud the night before he left.

Hana put on a tan skirt and white blouse and brushed her long black hair. Office attire at Collins, Lowenstein, and Capella was a step above business casual, and she frequently participated in corporate meetings, for which it was better to be overdressed than underdressed. Leon sat expectantly at the front door.

"Ready for school?" Hana asked the dog, who flapped his big tail against the floor.

There was no need to put Leon on a leash. He walked directly to Hana's car and waited for her to open the door. He licked Hana's hand when she moved the shifter from park to drive.

"I love you too," Hana said, scratching the dog's favorite spot behind his right ear.

Once they arrived at the doggie day care facility, she snapped on Leon's leash. He matched her pace across the parking lot, but once they were inside, he pulled hard in the direction of the area where his four-legged friends waited.

"I'll take him from here," said a male worker who'd watched Leon grow into a full-grown dog from a pup. "Rusty is out sick today, so it will only be Leon, Butch, and Oscar in their pack."

"I may have to pay a late fee this evening," Hana said. "I have a conference call at six o'clock."

"Send us an email if that happens, and we'll feed him supper."

Before leaving the kennel parking lot, Hana checked an app on her phone that let her watch Leon remotely. He and Oscar, a black Labrador, were already playing tug-of-war with a thick cotton rope.

For most of the morning Hana worked on a buy-sell agreement between an Israeli software company and an American private equity firm. A key part of her job involved translating documents into Hebrew or English without changing the meaning or intent of the parties. After finishing one long section, she took a break, leaned back in her chair, and quietly sang a snippet of the new song she'd received in the night. Janet appeared in her doorway.

"Could you sing louder?" the assistant asked in her Maine accent. "I want to record that on my phone so I can sell it and make both of us rich."

"It's in Arabic."

"Which adds to the mystery."

Janet had worked at the firm for over fifteen years and took Hana under her wing when the Arab lawyer arrived in Atlanta.

"Have you listened to your voice-mail messages?"

"Not yet."

"Jakob Brodsky called."

Jakob was a young Jewish lawyer who'd associated Collins, Lowenstein, and Capella in a wrongful death claim arising out of a terrorist attack in Jerusalem that resulted in the death of Sadie Neumann's mother. While working on the case, Hana first met Daud, whom she hired as a private investigator to assist them.

"Did you listen to it?" Hana asked.

"I was curious. He said there's a case he wants to talk to you about. No details."

Hana's heart skipped a beat. The Neumann case had been a success, but she and Jakob came close to losing their lives when taken hostage by terrorists in Jerusalem.

"What kind of claim?" she asked cautiously.

"He didn't give details."

"Okay," Hana sighed. "I'd better call him. It will be hard to concentrate on anything else until I know what he wants."

Hana stared at the photo of Sadie for a moment before calling Jakob.

"Brodsky Law Offices," Jakob answered in a voice that revealed his roots in Long

Island. "How may I help you?"

"It's Hana. Didn't your phone recognize my number?"

"Of course, but it could have been Leon Lowenstein."

The senior partner initially tried to marginalize Jakob's involvement in the Neumann case but had grudgingly developed appreciation over time for Jakob's perseverance and courage.

"When was the last time Mr. Lowenstein called you directly?" Hana asked.

"To ask me for a charitable contribution a couple of weeks after my cut of the attorney fee in the Neumann case landed in my bank account. It had to do with buying an ambulance for the equivalent of the Red Cross in Israel."

"That's Magen David Adom. It means 'Red Shield of David.' "

"Yeah, but Magen David Adom sounds more legit when you say it than when Mr. Lowenstein does."

Hana smiled. Leon Lowenstein's knowledge of Hebrew was limited to words and phrases he'd absorbed by osmosis in synagogue and during a lifetime in the Jewish community of Atlanta. He'd visited Israel only once and spent most of his time on the Mediterranean coast.

"What kind of claim did you want to talk to me about?"

"Are you interested in archaeology?"

"I've visited lots of sites and volunteered for a week on a dig when I was a teenager."

"That's good enough for me. I'm going to send you a news article. After you read it, I want to introduce you to a new client named Vladimir Ivanov."

"I'm busy."

"Just read the article."

Five minutes later Hana received an email from Jakob with the subject line "Rare Archaeological Find." The email included a link to an article in the Israeli press about archaeologists discovering a miniature three-thousand-year-old ceramic head that was originally part of a detailed figurine of an unknown king. The small ceramic piece was uncovered near the modern town of Metula on the Israel-Lebanon border, close to the ancient village of Abel Beth Maakah mentioned in 1 Kings 15:20. The Iron Age artifact was only two inches in size but featured exquisitely crafted facial details enhanced by brown and tan colors almost as vibrant as they must have been when created by a highly skilled artisan. The newswriter hypothesized that the head could be of an Israelite, Aramaean, or Phoenician

33

ruler. The exceptional find was immediately placed on public display at the Israel Museum in Jerusalem. There was no mention of a man named Vladimir Ivanov. Puzzled, Hana closed the email and began working on a project for Mr. Collins. Thirty minutes later her cell phone vibrated. It was a text message from the ever-persistent Jakob.

Read the article yet?

She entered a reply.

Yes.

Jakob immediately answered.

What if the king had a queen? Can you meet with me and Ivanov for lunch? I'm craving curry.

Hana smiled. She'd introduced Jakob to an Indian restaurant that had become one of his favorite places to eat.

12:30?

The Jewish lawyer responded with a thumbs-up sign.

Daud ate a prawn as he waited for a re-

34

sponse to his text message. Kolisnyk and his fiancée sat at a table for four on the opposite side of the restaurant. The presence of a horseshoe-shaped bar made it difficult for Daud to keep them clearly in view, but there was only one exit, so they couldn't leave without him knowing it. He chewed thoughtfully. The fact that he'd not received an immediate reply from Charlie denying his request gave him hope that a frantic discussion was going on behind the scenes. His phone remained dark. He finished eating his meal, and the waiter approached with a dessert menu in his hand. Daud's phone lit up with an incoming message.

"No dessert," Daud said curtly.

As soon as the waiter left, Daud read the message.

Proceed with contact. Rendezvous point M is operational for the next two hours. Confirm.

Daud acknowledged the message. Catching the waiter's eye, he summoned him back to the table.

"There is a couple sitting across the room. The man is wearing a tan sport coat, and the woman has on a black dress. Please see what they're eating and pair it with a bottle of the best wine in your cellar."

A puzzled expression crossed the waiter's face.

"Add it to my bill," Daud continued. "And don't tell them who bought the wine. Say that it's compliments of the house."

The waiter nodded.

"Oh, and find out their names," Daud added.

"How do I do that, sir?"

"Ask the maître d' if they made a reservation. If they didn't reserve a table, then ask their names when you deliver the wine to confirm they're the correct people to receive it. It doesn't matter how they answer, but remember their names so you can tell me."

The waiter hesitated.

"You can do it," Daud continued. "I'll make it worth your while."

"Yes, sir."

Daud watched as the waiter checked with the maître d', then looked at Daud and shook his head before making his way across the room. Several minutes passed. Daud shifted in his seat. The waiter returned.

"It's done, sir. They're eating fish so I brought them an unoaked Premier Cru Chablis," he said. "Their names are Mr. and Mrs. Bakaj."

"Mr. and Mrs. Bakaj?"

"Yes. They're on their honeymoon."

"Excellent. I'm ready for my check."

Daud paid the bill with a credit card bearing the name that matched his fake Egyptian passport. Because his family had moved to Beersheba from the Alexandria region at the mouth of the Nile, Daud spoke Arabic with an Egyptian accent, which made it easy to pass himself off as an Egyptian. He added a generous tip.

"Thank you, Mr. Sayyid," the waiter said with a slight bow of his head.

Daud stepped over to the bar so that he had a clear view of the couple. They lifted their wineglasses and clinked them together. After sipping the wine, the woman leaned closer to the man and placed her left hand on top of his. A diamond glistened on her ring finger. Daud waited until they'd enjoyed two more sips of wine before moving toward their table. As he came closer the woman glanced up and saw him. Daud intentionally made eye contact with her. A curious yet welcoming expression crossed her face. When Daud reached the table, he could see a wedding band nestled beside the diamond ring on her finger.

"Excuse me," Daud said to the man in Russian. "I hope you're enjoying the wine. I asked the waiter to deliver it to you and

Mrs. Bakaj. Congratulations on your wedding."

Kolisnyk looked up. "Who are you and how do you know our names?" the Ukrainian asked sharply in Russian and then spoke to his wife in Arabic. "Esma, do you know this man?"

"He looks like someone I knew once," the woman answered in heavily accented Russian with a friendly nod to Daud. "Thank you for the wine."

"May I join you for a moment?" Daud asked in Russian.

"No," Kolisnyk shot back with a look toward the maître d' station.

"Don't be rude," his wife responded in Arabic. "You were just telling me this was a superb Chablis."

The man hesitated for a moment. "Very well," he replied. "What do you want?"

Daud sat down, leaned forward, and placed his hands on the table.

"Would you prefer I speak in Russian or Arabic?"

"Arabic," the woman answered. "My Russian is atrocious."

Kolisnyk brusquely waved his hand as a signal for Daud to continue. Daud locked eyes with the Ukrainian before he spoke.

"I'm here to inform you about a better

38

deal," he replied. "A much better deal."

"What kind of deal?" the man asked.

"Your real name is Artem Kolisnyk," Daud replied. "I know why you fled Ukraine and the reason you're on your way to Egypt."

The woman clutched her napkin tightly and stared at her husband for a moment before facing Daud. There was panic in her eyes.

"How do you know these things?" she asked.

"From the people who sent me to talk to you," Daud answered, keeping his gaze on Kolisnyk. "I was also instructed to tell you that Uri Bondar remembers the days you spent together fishing in the stream that flows through the mountain meadow."

"What does that mean?" the woman asked her husband, who was staring at Daud.

The dossier about the mission indicated Uri Bondar and Artem Kolisnyk were long-time friends and colleagues. The information had a clear impact on Kolisnyk.

"Is Uri in Sharm el-Sheikh?" Kolisnyk asked. "I haven't heard from him in over two weeks."

"Uri is here, and my job is to accompany you to the boat at the marina where he's waiting," Daud answered. "You will learn more there."

"Who are you working for?" Kolisnyk asked. "I'm not going anywhere until you tell me."

"As I said, people who want to give you a better deal than the Egyptians."

Kolisnyk was silent for a moment. "I told the Iranians I wasn't interested at any price. They can't guarantee my safety."

"It's not the Iranians. It's the Americans."

"The Americans!" Kolisnyk blurted out. "I can't trust them!"

"Uri does."

Kolisnyk looked at his wife and shifted nervously in his chair. "I need to make a phone call," the scientist said.

"Who are you going to call?" his wife asked. "Uri?"

Kolisnyk ignored her question.

"Are we in danger?" His wife turned to Daud.

"You've been in danger since long before your husband left Kiev," Daud answered.

"Go!" Kolisnyk said abruptly to Daud.

"No," Esma Kolisnyk cut in anxiously. "I want him to stay here with me. I don't want to be left alone if what he says is true."

"Suit yourself," Kolisnyk said gruffly.

The Ukrainian walked past the bar and disappeared in the direction of the men's restroom. Daud moved to follow in case the scientist was going to abandon his wife and leave the restaurant, but Esma reached out and grabbed his right arm with surprising strength.

"Please, don't leave me alone," she pleaded. "Artem is doing this for me so we can begin a new life together."

Daud felt a measure of pity for the new bride. He didn't know her background, but her future was cloudy.

"Have you seen Uri?" she continued. "What can the Americans do for us? For me?"

"I'm here to see that both of you are safely escorted to a meeting where everything will be explained to you," Daud replied as calmly as he could. "Consider me a bodyguard."

He pulled his arm loose and headed toward the restroom. As soon as he rounded the bar, he saw Kolisnyk holding a cell phone to his ear and standing in a secluded corner. Daud stepped back and glanced over his shoulder at Esma, who remained at the table with her face buried in her hands. Kolisnyk lowered his phone, turned around, and made eye contact with Daud.

From the look in the Ukrainian's eyes, Daud knew Artem Kolisnyk wasn't going with him voluntarily. Other types of persuasion were going to be necessary.

CHAPTER 3

Hana's nose welcomed the pungent smells associated with South Asian cuisine. Lunch featured an expansive buffet that included lamb curry, vegetable root curry, rabbit curry, chilli paneer, tandoori chicken, and five or six other entrées. Jakob wasn't in sight. The hostess seated Hana at a table with a good view of the door.

Hana was checking email on her phone and sipping hot tea when she glanced up and saw Jakob hurriedly enter. He was alone. Like Hana, Jakob was in his early thirties. Tall and slender, he had short, curly black hair and dark eyes.

"Sorry I'm late. Mr. Ivanov went to the wrong Indian restaurant and won't be here for at least fifteen minutes. I know you're always on a tight schedule, but is it okay if we wait for him before eating?"

"Of course."

Jakob ordered hot tea. "What's the latest

news for you and Daud?" he asked.

"Not much for me, but Daud's out of the country on business."

"How long?"

"I'm not sure."

Jakob raised his eyebrows. "What kind of business?"

"For the government," Hana replied, lowering her voice. "I don't know where he is except that it's not Israel."

The waitress arrived with his tea. Jakob took a sip. "I thought Daud was going to spend all his time developing his consulting business," he said.

"He is, but he doesn't have a website, so that business is based entirely on referrals. This other job was something he believed he should do."

"How are you holding up?" he asked.

"Struggling. I mean, after what all of us went through in Jerusalem, it's hard not to worry about something unexpected happening."

"Absolutely. I'll be praying for him and you."

Hana managed a weak smile. Formerly a secular Jew, Jakob immigrated to the US as a child with his Russian parents. He'd welcomed Jesus Christ as his Messiah the previous year while standing in front of the

Western Wall in Jerusalem. To hear him mention prayer was like fresh water splashed on Hana's troubled soul.

"No one knows how to pray better about this sort of situation than you," she said.

"I don't know about that, but I took your advice and have been spending a lot of time reading the Psalms. They contain plenty of material that's relevant to life regardless of what's happening."

For several minutes Hana listened to Jakob talk about what he'd been reading.

"Here's Vladimir," Jakob said, raising his hand in the air.

Hana turned in her chair and saw a short, balding man with dark-framed glasses coming toward them. He was wearing a white shirt and black pants. She and Jakob stood.

"No, no," the man said in Russian-accented English as he motioned for them to sit down.

"This is Vladimir Ivanov," Jakob said.

Ivanov bowed slightly when he shook Hana's hand. Jakob spoke to him in Russian.

"Vladimir's English is improving," Jakob said, "but I'm going to have to tell you most of his story."

"Eat?" Ivanov interjected, pointing toward the buffet line.

Jakob nodded. "Yes."

Hana led the way. The restaurant had mastered the art of keeping food fresh on a steam table. It helped that the place was crowded with lunchtime diners. Hana selected lamb and vegetable root curry along with saffron rice. Jakob took longer and came back with his plate piled high with multiple dishes. Ivanov took a much smaller portion of the lamb and curry. Jakob spoke to him. Ivanov smiled broadly and returned to the buffet.

"He didn't understand that it was all-you-can-eat," Jakob said to Hana. "A place like this wouldn't last long in Belarus where the economy isn't doing so well."

"Does he have relatives in Atlanta?"

"Yes. They bought him a plane ticket. He's been here for over a month."

Ivanov returned with a much fuller plate.

Jakob turned to Hana. "I'll pray," he said and then spoke to Ivanov, who immediately bowed his head.

Hana closed her eyes and waited.

"God, thank you for Hana and Daud," Jakob said. "Watch over him while he's gone and bring him safely home. Bless Vladimir and his family and what we're here to talk about today. Thank you for this food. In Jesus' name, amen."

46

"Amen!" Ivanov repeated in a boisterous voice.

Hana ate a bite of lamb marinated the perfect amount of time in the sauce so that it didn't become tough or lose its own flavor profile. Ivanov sampled the same dish from the food on his plate and closed his eyes for a moment as if savoring it.

"Good?" Hana asked him when he opened his eyes.

"Yes, yes," he said. "More."

The main selection on Jakob's plate was vegetable root curry with oven-roasted carrots, parsnips, turnips, and red onions. Roasting the vegetables brought out their natural sweetness before adding the other seasonings. They ate in silence for a few moments.

"What did you think about the article I sent?" Jakob asked Hana.

"I'm familiar with Metula," she said, wiping her lips with a napkin. "It's very close to the Lebanese border. When Hezbollah fires a mortar round at the village, the residents have about ten seconds to reach shelter. Metula is in a very fertile region, so people have lived in the area for thousands of years. It's not surprising that archaeologists discovered the ceramic head of a nobleman or king who lived in the Iron Age. But the quality of the craftsmanship was amazing. Most of the things I've seen in museums from that time period are much simpler and more primitive. The detail and coloring were also stunning."

Jakob leaned forward in his seat. "There's a queen to go along with the king."

"The article didn't mention another piece."

"Because the archaeologists don't know about it," Jakob said with excitement in his eyes. "At least not yet."

Ivanov said something to Jakob in Russian. Jakob replied, and Ivanov nodded his head vigorously.

"He heard the word 'Metula' and wanted to make sure I told you about his great-grandfather who discovered a similar fragment of a statue a hundred years ago at a place called Eyon. Do you know where that is?"

"Yes, it's near Metula. There's an ancient mound or tell there."

"Which makes sense."

"But fraud with archaeological artifacts is rampant across the entire Middle East, and there are a lot of fakes," Hana cautioned. "Proving something to be genuine is hard."

"I'm not naive. Establishing the authenticity of an artifact is like documenting the

48

provenance of a famous painting, only there's less to go on. But Vladimir has a fascinating story, and when he contacted me for help, I didn't have the heart to show him the door without digging a little."

Hana gave him a wry smile. "Is that a pun?" she asked.

"Uh, no," Jakob replied sheepishly. "But I could pretend it was."

Hana laughed. "The first step is obvious," she said. "Has a reputable expert examined the item owned by Mr. Ivanov?"

"Not yet."

"Maybe I can help you locate someone in Israel who —"

"Vladimir doesn't have the female head in his possession," Jakob interrupted.

Hana was about to take a bite of food. She lowered her fork. "Where is it?" she asked.

Jakob took a sip of tea before answering. "Vladimir and his family have lived for generations in Belarus. His background is a mixture of Russian, Belarus, and Polish, but he claims to be predominantly Jewish. He grew up in Minsk, the biggest city, and he has a niece who lives in Atlanta with her husband and kids. She's the one who contacted me because my new website mentions that I speak Russian. Vladimir's great-grandfather lived on a kibbutz on the south side of the Sea of Galilee in the early 1900s. I can't remember the name of the place, but it was one of the first kibbutzim."

"Degania," Hana said.

"Yes," Vladimir interjected with a smile. "Degania. Good."

Jakob continued. "After spending several years on the kibbutz, the great-grandfather returned to Minsk to get married. He was an amateur archaeologist and brought back artifacts that he either found himself or bought locally, including a small figurine of a woman's head and shoulders that looks a lot like the male figure in the article I sent you. The great-grandfather's wife didn't want to immigrate to Palestine, so he never returned."

"What proof exists for all this?"

"Vladimir has twenty old black-and-white photographs that he's transferred onto his niece's laptop. I've seen them. The pictures show several coins minted during the Bar Kokhba revolt against the Romans, some pottery items, and the queen's head. Vladimir claims the family always believed the woman's head was special. The great-grandfather kept a diary and recorded that he found it himself while digging at Eyon.

There's a decent sketch of the head in the diary."

"Does Mr. Ivanov have any idea where the artifacts are now?"

Jakob glanced at Vladimir before answering. "They were lost during World War II when most of the family was murdered in the Holocaust. Vladimir says two-thirds of the Jews in Belarus were killed by the Germans or the Ukrainians who worked for them. Vladimir's father and a male cousin were the only ones out of a large family who survived. They fought as partisans and were able to hide the collection in an old barn to save it from the Nazis. Unfortunately, toward the end of the war the Soviets found the cache and confiscated it."

"That's a different twist. Usually it was the Nazis who stole works of art."

"True, but theft is theft. Since all this came up about the discovery at Metula, Vladimir and his family have done some preliminary research."

"What sort of research?"

"They know the name of the Soviet colonel who raided the barn. He was a famous guy with so many medals on his chest that he could barely stand up without falling over. After the war, he lived in a big château outside Moscow where he displayed some of the collection, including the woman's head. Vladimir has a newspaper article about it from the 1950s. The article falsely claims the colonel purchased the items during multiple trips to the Middle East."

"If the Russian man's family still has the collection, any lawsuit would be filed there, not here."

"There's more. The colonel fell out of favor when Stalin died and Khrushchev took over. Shortly thereafter, the colonel disappeared into the Gulag and died at a logging camp in Siberia. The artifacts disappeared with him."

Rahal stood at the end of the flat field and waited for the young boy to remove three arrows from the target and run back to him. As he grew older, Rahal had decreased the draw on the competition bow and now pulled at thirty-seven pounds. He still practiced regularly. To him, archery was the most honorable sport on earth. Muhammad was an archer, and a bamboo recurve bow supposedly used by the prophet himself was on display at Topkapi Palace in Istanbul. One of Rahal's most prized possessions was an ancient decorative bow adorned with gold calligraphy that extolled the virtues of the archer as warrior in Islamic history.

The boy returned with the arrows. Rahal had landed one shot in the second ring from the bull's-eye and two other shots in the fifth ring from the center. Three other arrows missed the target altogether and were discarded. Rahal never reused an arrow that failed to find its mark. Khalil stood beside him. Another servant opened a bottle of water and handed it to Rahal, who took a long drink.

"Let's step up to sixty meters," he said to Khalil.

While they walked forward, Khalil answered his cell phone. They reached the sixty-meter mark and stopped. Khalil ended the phone call.

"What were the names of the prophet's six bows?" Rahal asked the boy who'd retrieved the arrows.

The young man was the son of the chauffeur who'd driven them to the private archery field on the outskirts of Doha.

"Az-Zawra, al-Bayda, and as-Safra," the boy said and paused. "But I don't remember the others. His quiver was named al-Kafur."

"Not bad," Rahal answered. "How old are you?"

"Twelve years old, sir."

Rahal looked directly in the boy's face. "What is your name?"

"Yanis, sir."

"When you can name all the prophet's bows, I'll give you a gift."

"Next time, sir. I'll be ready."

Khalil stepped closer to Rahal. "Sir, I'd like to have a word with you in private."

"After this round."

Rahal placed an arrow against the string and looked across the field at the target. He smoothly drew the bow and released the arrow. Rahal's technique was flawless. The symmetrical flight of the arrow was a thing of beauty enjoyed in the moment but never exactly replicated. It penetrated the target toward the middle.

"It's touching the yellow, sir," the boy said.

"Your eyesight is better than mine," Rahal replied.

Rahal shot five more arrows, all of which hit the target and would survive to fly another day.

A different servant handed Rahal a pair of Russian-made binoculars. Rahal raised them to his eyes.

"You're right," Rahal said to the boy. "What is the score if the arrow lands on the line between two colors?"

"You receive the higher score."

"Correct. Go!"

As the boy ran across the field, Rahal and

Khalil stepped away from the other servants.

"Proceed," Rahal said.

"Mustafa is in Sharm el-Sheikh and has located the resort where Kolisnyk is staying. The information you received about him leaving Ukraine was correct. He's traveling under a false name with a woman companion. They've rented a villa on the beach. The woman is an Arab."

Rahal raised his eyebrows. "An Arab? With an infidel?"

"Yes. Mustafa believes they married while in Sharm el-Sheikh."

"The heart of darkness widens," Rahal said. "I only wish we could recover the money we wasted on Kolisnyk. He has many enemies and is likely seeking sanctuary from them. We can't let that happen."

Rahal removed an arrow from his quiver and lightly touched the razor-sharp point. "Just revenge will be my payment. Mustafa has my blessing."

CHAPTER 4

Daud followed Artem Kolisnyk to the table where the Ukrainian's wife waited. Artem motioned for her to get up and follow him.

"We have to go now?" she asked.

"Yes," he replied and turned to Daud. "Whoever you are, leave us alone or I will call the police."

The waiter, a different man from the one who served Daud, hurried up and spoke to Kolisnyk in Arabic.

"Was there something wrong with the food?" the man asked.

Artem reached into his pocket and took out a thick wad of hundred-dollar bills. He peeled off three and thrust them in the waiter's hand.

"This should pay for the meal," he said. "And ask the manager to call the police so they can arrest this man for harassing us. That's why we're leaving."

The waiter gave Daud an apprehensive

56

look. Daud stepped back and lifted his hands.

"I haven't raised my voice or threatened anyone," he said.

Esma glanced at Daud and spoke. "Artem, I'm scared. I'm not sure you should ignore what this man told you. Remember, Uri sent him."

"He didn't say Uri sent him, and I don't believe Uri is here in Sharm el-Sheikh. He's waiting for us in Cairo."

"Did you talk to him?"

Artem didn't answer. Several people at nearby tables were watching them. Daud saw a woman take out her cell phone and begin taking pictures. The Kolisnyks continued toward the exit. Daud waited until they were four or five meters in front of him before following. Artem spoke to the maître d' as he passed by but didn't stop.

"Please, sir," the maître d' said, holding up his hand as Daud approached. "We do not want any disturbances."

A security guard stepped forward. Daud shook his head. "Do not touch me," he warned.

The young man hesitated. Daud moved past him, then immediately felt a hand seize his right shoulder. With one quick movement, Daud grabbed the man's wrist and twisted his arm so that the security guard ended up bent over with his face toward the floor. When he tried to move, Daud increased the pressure on the man's arm. The maître d' watched wide-eyed. The light on a cell phone flashed as someone took a picture. Daud released the security guard and pushed him away.

"I'm leaving," Daud said. "Peacefully."

Outside, he glanced up and down the sidewalk. It was dark, but lights from nearby shops and restaurants illuminated the street. A block to the east, Daud saw Artem and Esma Kolisnyk get into a taxi. There wasn't another cab in sight. Daud jogged down the sidewalk as the vehicle pulled away from the curb. It turned down a street toward the part of town where most of the expensive hotels were located. Daud waited almost a minute before another taxi from the same company appeared. He waved it down and opened the passenger-side door.

"Do you know who drives taxi number 467?" he asked the driver, who looked barely old enough to have a license.

"Uh, no, sir, but I can check with my dispatcher. Did you have a problem with him?"

"No, but I need to talk to the man he just picked up at this corner."

The driver hesitated. Daud took out a fifty-dollar bill and handed it to him. The young man immediately picked up his cell phone.

"He's on his way to the Four Seasons Resort," the young driver said.

"Get there fast and there's another fifty dollars in it for you," Daud replied, getting into the front seat.

The driver turned down a side street. The tires on the vehicle squealed.

"I know a shortcut," the young man said.

In less than five minutes they reached the hotel.

"Let me out here, not at the main entrance," Daud said.

The driver pulled to the curb and received another fifty-dollar bill. He handed Daud an index card on which he'd written his contact information.

"Call me if you need me during your stay," the young man offered eagerly. "I haven't printed any business cards yet."

Daud slipped into the shadows and stood behind a palm tree so he could watch the main entrance to the resort. Two taxis arrived at the same time. The Kolisnyks exited the second vehicle. Daud took out his secure cell phone and sent a text message to Charlie.

> Contact with A and B. Not yet agreed to cooperate. Staying at the Four Seasons Resort registered under the name of Bakaj. Provide room or suite number.

It was fifteen minutes before Daud's phone vibrated.

> Villa 4. Will you be able to deliver A on schedule? Any means authorized.

Trying to drag an uncooperative Artem Kolisnyk out of a fancy villa and across town to the marina would be difficult. Including the Ukrainian's new wife, who seemed to somewhat trust Daud, might make it easier. He entered a brief reply.

> Presence of B likely to increase cooperation by A. Advise.

This time he had a much shorter wait.

> Proceed.

Adrenaline coursed through Daud's body, and every sense heightened. He confidently entered the hotel lobby and asked the concierge for a map of the property. A cluster of detached villas was in a separate area from the general guest rooms. The

Presidential Villa had its own private beach with villa 4 next door. Tucking the map inside his sport coat, Daud left the lobby and passed through a pool area on his way to the beach. Now that it was night, the desert air had quickly cooled. The calm, clear waters of the Red Sea lapped against the sand. Daud saw a young couple holding hands as they strolled along.

It was two hundred meters to the private beach reserved for guests staying at the Presidential Villa. A sign marked the boundary line. Daud ignored it. There were no lights shining in the villa. Turning away from the water, Daud slipped through a line of low shrubs that separated the Presidential Villa from villa 4. Lights were on in both villa 4 and the villa next to it. Daud took a step forward and then froze. A small moving light appeared at the front corner of villa 4. A figure dressed in black emerged holding a tiny flashlight.

Not long after Hana returned from having lunch with Jakob and his new client, the law firm receptionist buzzed her.

"Abdul Erakat is on the phone. He says it's personal."

"I'll take it."

Since getting married, Hana and Daud

had been sharing her car. While he was out of the country, she'd secretly been trying to locate a vehicle for him to drive. When she first met Daud in Jerusalem, he drove a rugged green Land Rover that he loved but didn't own and had to turn in when he stopped working for the Israeli government. Abdul Erakat was a car dealer Hana had encountered at a local deli frequented by Arabs in the city. She'd asked him to be on the lookout for a similar used vehicle.

"Give me some good luck and throw me in the sea," the man said, quoting a familiar Middle Eastern proverb. "I've found a Land Rover for you, but you'll need to act fast. It's not going to last long on the market. It's a true off-road version, not something a soccer mom would drive."

Hana listened as Abdul described a five-year-old Land Rover with all the features Daud would want. There were only 40,000 miles on the odometer.

"That checks all his boxes," Hana replied. "What about the price?"

Abdul mentioned a figure that was more than Hana wanted to pay but didn't cause her to reject the deal.

"Would you want to finance it?"

"No. I'd pay cash."

"That's what I figured. I never have been

able to understand the love affair Americans have with paying finance charges on loans. If you're interested, I'll arrange for a mechanic to check it out."

Hana didn't like to make snap decisions but realized she didn't have the luxury of waiting.

"Go ahead. I'm not an expert and will need to trust you and your mechanic." Hana paused. "One other important thing I forgot to ask. The Land Rover that Daud drove before was green."

"This vehicle is white with black accents."

Hana hesitated.

"Mrs. Hasan," the car dealer said after a moment passed. "Color matters much more to women than to men. You can trust me on that too."

Thirty minutes later an email from Abdul arrived in Hana's inbox with photos of the vehicle. It was clearly in better shape than the one Daud drove in Israel, which made Hana more comfortable with the price. Her excitement began to build. Plotting to buy the car also gave her something positive to focus on as a way to relieve stress. The phone buzzed. It was Gladys Applewhite, Mr. Lowenstein's administrative assistant.

"Mr. Lowenstein would like to see you," Gladys said in her silky southern accent.

Hana closed her computer screen. "On my way," she replied.

The executive offices for the three named partners were in a row on the south side of the building and featured panoramic views of the north side of Atlanta. Mr. Lowenstein was sitting behind a large desk with his necktie loosened and a file folder in hand. Stocky and gray-haired, the Jewish lawyer was an admiralty law expert who collected miniature antique sailing ships that he displayed under glass covers. Some of the rigging for the ships seemed so fragile that it looked in danger of dissolving if exposed to the atmosphere.

"How is Jim Collins treating you?" Mr. Lowenstein asked.

Because Hana worked on international transactions, she spent the majority of her time under Mr. Collins's supervision. Collaborating with Leon Lowenstein in the Neumann case had given her the opportunity to interact with one of the other senior partners.

"He's keeping me busy."

"Good. Jim tells me your skill in the nuances of American transactional law has really increased. You're catching problems that other young attorneys, even those who graduated from US law schools, might miss."

"Translating documents forces me to consider what the words really mean."

"I can see that," Mr. Lowenstein said. "Are you ready to work with me again?"

Hana was puzzled. Mr. Lowenstein was also her boss, and assignment of work at the law firm wasn't usually on a volunteer basis.

"What kind of work?" she asked.

"I'm part of a civic group that is organizing community events to bring together people from different ethnic and religious backgrounds for dialogue and education about controversial topics. I think it would be wonderful if you, as a Christian Arab and Israeli citizen, participated in an interfaith forum about Israel."

Hana's perspective about life in Israel was shared by more Arabs than many people in America realized, but she nevertheless spoke for a minority.

"Who else would be speaking?"

"The planning committee is still lining up the participants, but there will likely be a couple of Jews with divergent views, an Arab Muslim professor, another Christian who believes differently than you do. We'll see how it shapes up."

Hana instantly imagined chaos on a stage.

"It won't be a free-for-all," Mr. Lowenstein continued as if reading her thoughts. "There will be ground rules with a format similar to a political debate."

"Political debates in Israel can be very contentious," Hana replied. "Candidates interrupt and yell insults at each other."

"That's happening more and more here too. But we'll figure out a way to make it civil without being too formal. The event is still in the planning stage, but I wanted to mention it to you now. We'll hold it at a neutral site able to accommodate the number of people expected to attend."

"Would you expect a couple hundred people?"

Mr. Lowenstein shook his head. "No, more like two to three thousand. This will be heavily promoted, and I anticipate a huge response from the Jewish community. It will be a nonprofit fund-raiser for some humanitarian organizations, which will increase participation."

"Three thousand people," Hana repeated.

Hana had been a skilled debater in high school, but she'd never spoken before such a large crowd.

"If you think I'm qualified," she continued slowly.

"I think you'll be fabulous," Mr. Lowenstein said. "So, you'll do it?"

Hana couldn't come up with a legitimate reason to turn him down. It would be an opportunity to share her views about not only geopolitics but also her Christian faith. She nodded. "Yes."

"Great!" Mr. Lowenstein clapped his hands together. "I can't wait to hear what you have to say myself."

CHAPTER 5

Creeping forward, Daud moved in a semi-circle until he was slightly behind the dark-clothed figure at the rear corner of the Kolisnyks' villa. He dashed across the open space and leaned against a privacy wall where he paused to calm his breathing. He inched along and quickly glanced around a corner before pulling back. There was no one in sight. The other person had either entered the villa or moved on.

At the rear of the villa were French doors in the middle of a long glass wall. Two pairs of sandals were neatly positioned in front of the doors. A multicolored beach towel was draped over a lounge chair. The French doors were unlocked and slightly open.

Daud entered the villa. There was a large kitchen and a dining room area with a glass-topped table. Two half-empty glasses of wine remained on the table. One of the chairs was turned over onto the floor. Daud listened for the sound of voices but heard nothing. A faint light came from a hallway to the left. Carefully making his way down the hallway, he checked three bedrooms, all empty. Retracing his steps, he moved to the front of the house and entered the foyer that was brightly lit by a large chandelier. A staircase directly across from the front door led to the second floor. Suspecting the master bedroom was upstairs, Daud quietly climbed the steps and moved silently down the hall. Reaching a pair of double doors, he listened again. He heard a man's voice but couldn't understand the words, which were followed by a muffled moan.

Bursting through the door, Daud saw a medium-size dark figure standing over Artem Kolisnyk and his wife, both of whom were lying facedown on the floor. There was a gun in the intruder's left hand. A ski mask concealed his face. The man spun around to confront Daud, who struck the intruder's left hand so that the gun skidded across the floor. Like most skilled military or law enforcement professionals, Daud had a favorite move for taking an opponent to the ground and immobilizing him. However, the intruder effectively countered Daud, and both of them fell to the hard floor where they rolled over and over several times until coming into contact with a large bed. The intruder pulled a small knife from a sheath on his leg and tried to slash Daud's throat. Daud parried the blow but suffered a cut to his right forearm. As the intruder's left arm moved forward, Daud grabbed it and twisted the man's hand, and the knife fell to the floor. Daud knocked it away and with his larger body weight and strength flipped the intruder so that he ended up face-first against the stone floor with Daud on top of him.

"Kill him!" Artem shouted to Daud in Russian. "He was going to stab Esma and then shoot me!"

Kolisnyk had managed to stand. His wife remained on the floor sobbing.

The intruder squirmed and Daud tightened his grip, causing the man to grunt in pain and curse in Arabic.

"Did he speak to you in Russian?" Daud asked Kolisnyk in Russian.

"No," Artem answered. "Only Arabic."

The man suddenly twisted his body and swung one of his feet toward Daud's head. It was an expert martial arts maneuver. The man's shoe hit Daud's left cheek, causing his grip to weaken on the man's left arm. The intruder wiggled free and punched Daud in the chin. The man scrambled away and lunged for the gun, but Artem Kolisnyk kicked it farther away. Daud jumped up and tackled the man, striking him in the back of the neck with the full force of his left forearm. The man collapsed onto the floor. Daud delivered a second blow to the man's temple, and the attacker slumped to the floor, unconscious. Artem picked up the gun and with a shaking hand pointed it at the immobile form. Before he could pull the trigger, Daud snatched the gun from the Ukrainian's hand.

"You don't want to do that," he said in Russian. "Explaining a dead body is much harder than reporting a burglar on your way out of the city."

"What do you mean?" Artem asked.

"Do you want the publicity that will come if you're interviewed by the police after you kill someone?"

Artem looked at his wife, who was staring at Daud.

"You should have listened to me at the restaurant!" she shouted at her husband in Arabic.

"I couldn't reach anyone in Cairo to find out if they sent him, and Uri didn't answer his phone," Artem replied in the same language. "I don't know who he is or why he's here."

"He kept that man from killing us!" his wife yelled as she pointed at the motionless figure on the floor.

Artem turned to Daud. "Who do you work for?"

"All I can tell you is that my job is to safely take you to a boat slip at the marina. Uri and the Americans are there waiting for you."

"We've got to get out of here," Esma said to her husband in a desperate voice. "For a genius, you're acting like a fool."

Artem Kolisnyk hesitated. The man on the floor groaned.

"Quick, give me two of your belts," Daud said to Artem.

The Ukrainian stepped into a large walk-in closet. While he was gone, his wife looked at Daud and silently pleaded for help. Daud secured the assailant's hands and feet before checking the unconscious attacker for identifying information. The man's pockets were empty. Removing the would-be assassin's mask, Daud took a photo of the man's face. He was in his mid- to late twenties with a dark complexion, military-style haircut, and thin mustache. Daud slipped the man's weapon into his coat pocket.

"I need another belt," Daud said.

Artem stood to remove the belt from his

trousers.

"I'll get one," his wife said.

Esma returned with a slender pink belt embedded with sequins. Daud used it to cinch together the other belts binding the intruder's hands and feet so that he was lying in a curved position.

"We should leave now," Daud said.

"What can we bring?" Esma asked.

"Only what you can easily carry. We're going to walk out the back of the villa toward the beach and circle around to the street and take a taxi to the marina. As soon as we're there, you can call the resort and report the break-in."

Without saying anything to her husband, Esma Kolisnyk grabbed a carry-on bag with a fake leopard-skin cover and began to throw things into it. Moving much slower, Artem opened a small dark suitcase. Daud breathed a sigh of relief. The man sent to kill the Kolisnyks had done a better job of convincing the Ukrainian and his wife to trust Daud than any reasons he could have come up with.

Hana reopened the email from Abdul Erakat several times during the afternoon. Looking at the photos of the Land Rover took her to a happy place, and she hoped

73

the mechanic didn't uncover a problem that would nix the deal. She closed the email and quickly checked one of the news outlets she followed in Israel. It was a mistake. Every mention of terrorist activity in the Middle East caused her heart to leap into her throat as she wondered if the events might impact Daud. There was a knock on her door, and Janet entered. She paused when she saw Hana's face.

"Is everything okay?" Janet asked. "You look glum."

Hana managed a slight smile. "I'm worried about Daud," she replied. "The longer he's gone, the harder it is to remain calm."

Even though Hana and Janet had a close relationship, the assistant didn't know the full extent of Daud's prior activities and the ongoing threats hanging over him and Hana.

"That's lesson number twenty-eight in marriage," Janet continued in a light tone of voice. "I'm glad to have the house to myself and the kids during the first day Donnie's out of town because I don't have to pick up his dirty socks. After that, I begin missing both Donnie and his socks."

"Daud washes and folds his own clothes."

"Don't make me jealous." Janet put her hands over her ears. "I came in to remind you about the conference call you have with

Mr. Collins and the new client from Israel in forty-five minutes. Mr. Collins is logging in remotely from his house at the beach. For some reason it's not on your calendar."

"I thought it was for later this afternoon and didn't know it changed." Hana tapped her forehead in frustration. "I thought the client was in California."

"That's one reason you have me in your life. I'm sending you the information you need to look over before the call."

There was a lot more to review than Hana anticipated, and she was able to push her concern for Daud to the edge of her mind as she concentrated on reading the Hebrew and English memos and emails already exchanged between the parties.

The bound man moaned and strained against the belts.

"Ready to go?" Daud asked the Kolisnyks in Russian.

"Almost," Esma replied. "Should I take my jewelry?"

"Valuables only," her husband replied. "And we can buy new clothes wherever we're going."

Daud led the way down the stairs and to the kitchen area at the rear of the villa.

"We were drinking a glass of wine when

he surprised us," Esma said. "The wine wasn't as good as the bottle you ordered for us at the restaurant."

"Quiet," her husband said.

"Yes, it's better not to talk," Daud said. "I'm going to call a taxi before we go outside."

Daud phoned the young driver. "I'm leaving the Four Seasons with two friends, but don't come to the front of the resort. Meet us in ten minutes at the corner of El-Shaikh Zayed Street and the access road for the resort. Don't be late."

"I'll be early, sir," the driver replied.

Daud slipped the phone into the pocket of his jacket next to the gun. "Stay here while I check outside. I want to make sure it's safe."

As he stepped onto the patio, a full moon was rising in the sky. A shadow to the right of the villa seemed to move and Daud froze. A moment later he felt a slight breeze on his cheek and realized the shadow came from a small palm tree. Returning inside the villa, neither Artem nor Esma was waiting where he'd left them. He heard a door open. It was Esma coming out of a half bath.

"Artem went upstairs," she said when she saw Daud. "We both needed to go to the bathroom."

"Upstairs?" Daud replied.

"The master bedroom. He also forgot something that he wants to take with him."

"Stay here."

Daud dashed into the foyer and ascended the stairs two at a time. He paused at the door and peered through the opening. Artem was standing several feet from the intruder. In the scientist's hand was a small book.

"You will not escape the sword of judgment," the man on the floor said in Arabic. "Wherever you go we will find you and your wife."

"Who sent you and why?" Artem asked.

Daud stepped into the room and spoke to the Ukrainian in Russian. "Let's go! There's no point in talking to him."

"I want to know why he came here to kill us," Artem answered in the same language.

"And you, too, will suffer wrath," the man on the floor said, trying to move his head so that it faced toward Daud.

Daud picked up on a Lebanese accent.

"I still say you should kill him if he's not going to tell us anything useful," Artem continued to Daud in Arabic.

"That's what he wants," Daud answered in Russian. "He believes a martyr's death guarantees his entrance into paradise. He's not a threat now, and I'm not an executioner."

"I don't know what you said, but you're a coward!" the man shouted in the direction of Daud.

Daud motioned to Artem, and they left the room. The man on the floor continued to yell at them as they descended the stairs. Esma was still sitting in the chair where Daud had left her.

"Is there a chance that man will get free and come after us?" she asked Daud anxiously.

"No," he replied.

"I still want to know who he is," Artem repeated. "I saw you take a picture of his face with your phone. Will you tell me what you learn?"

Daud didn't answer. As soon as they reached the soft sand, Esma took off her shoes and stuffed them in the top of her bag. The moon was shining and its light reflected off the water. After a couple hundred meters, they turned away from the sea into an undeveloped area between hotels.

"Ouch!" Esma cried out and stopped. "I've hurt my foot."

"Put your shoes on," her husband replied.

Esma tried to take another step and cried

out louder. She remained rooted where she was and began to cry.

"I can't put any weight on it," she said, sobbing.

Daud stepped closer and knelt down. "Let me see," he said.

Esma held out her right foot. Daud ran his palm across the sole and felt a large sandbur. He pulled it out and tossed it to the side.

"It's not much farther," he said.

As they neared the road, he saw the taxi pulled onto the shoulder.

"That's our ride," Daud said. "Let me do the talking."

Hana left the office following the conference call with Mr. Collins and the new client. Several times during the conversation she was able to head off a misunderstanding because of the client's limited knowledge of English. By the end of the conversation, the CEO had decided to move forward with the law firm's representation of the Israeli company.

Hana was able to leave the office early enough to pick up Leon at the usual time. The dog cheerfully woofed in greeting.

"What was his report card for the day?"

Hana asked the worker who brought him to her.

"B-minus," the young female worker answered.

Hana had trouble believing her dog was capable of anything less than perfect behavior.

"What was it this time?" she asked. "Failure to share toys with others or disrupting mealtime for the other dogs in his group?"

"Neither. Leon tried to bite a new dog we introduced this afternoon. There were several seconds of serious aggression before we separated them."

"Whose fault was it?" Hana asked, her eyes wide. "Leon has never shown that kind of behavior around me."

"That's because you're not a male threatening his position. Leon is a teenager beginning to assert himself in the pack. The new dog, a German shepherd mix, is about the same age and pumping out similar hormones. We'll back off and reintroduce them in a controlled environment as a first step."

Once in the car, Leon licked Hana's hand as she shifted the car into reverse.

"That's not the same as asking for forgiveness," she said.

Her phone vibrated, and Sadie Neumann's face appeared with her father's phone number beneath it. Hana put the car in park and answered.

"It's Sadie," the eight-year-old girl said.

"How was school today?" Hana asked in Hebrew.

Sadie attended a Jewish day school where she was learning conversational Hebrew. She was a precise mimic with an excellent accent.

"Fine," she answered, also in Hebrew. "We studied math, English, Hebrew, science, and learned how to make red pepper hummus."

"I love red pepper hummus," Hana responded, noting the introduction of the new word "pepper."

"That's why I'm calling you," Sadie said, switching to English. "Daddy said I could invite you over for dinner if it's not too late."

Hana didn't have any plans. "How do you say 'dinner' in Hebrew?" she asked.

Sadie repeated the words for the evening meal in Hebrew and added the terms for breakfast and lunch.

"I have Leon in the car," Hana said.

"Oh, he's invited. I'm going to make way more hummus than Daddy and I can eat. We need help."

"Let me speak with him, please."

"This invitation is Daddy-approved," Ben said when he came on the phone. "Jakob

Brodsky told me Daud is out of town, but if it's not convenient on such short notice —"

"No, it's a great idea. I'd love to come. What are we going to eat besides red pepper hummus? I'll be glad to pick up something."

"I'm going to throw together a salad," Ben answered. "Sadie is learning to eat salads if I fix them exactly the way she wants."

"With chicken and cucumbers on it," Hana heard Sadie call out. "And that red dressing."

"Russian dressing," Ben said. "And garlic croutons."

"Garlic?" Hana asked.

"The stronger the better."

Hana enjoyed hearing this kind of detail about Sadie's life. "So what can I bring?" she asked again.

"A rotisserie chicken from the grocery store would save me a trip," Ben said.

"Done. And I'll buy an extra bag of garlic croutons."

"See you in a bit," Ben said.

"Yes! She's coming," Hana heard Sadie squeal in the background.

Hana pulled out of the parking lot. Looking at Leon, who was resting his face on the seat, she knew one other item she needed to buy at the store: a small bag of dog food.

Sadie might be venturing into new culinary fields, but salads weren't on Leon's menu.

Sadie might be venturing into the ordinary fields, but salads weren't on Leon's menu

CHAPTER 6

The young taxi driver opened the trunk. He glanced curiously at Artem and Esma as he placed their small bags inside.

"Is there more luggage?" he asked.

"No," Daud answered. "Take us to the marina."

Daud sat up front with the driver after Artem and Esma climbed into the backseat. The driver kept glancing at them in the rearview mirror.

"Where are you from?" the driver asked, directing his question to the occupants in the rear seat.

"Privacy, please," Daud replied, placing a fifty-dollar bill on the seat so the driver could see it.

The young man glanced down and shrugged. Everyone in the taxi remained silent during the ten-minute drive to the marina. Daud sent a text message to Charlie.

En route to marina with both A and B. Sending photo of intruder apprehended at their villa. Identity unknown.

"Park there," Daud said, pointing to a space near the west-side entrance to the marina.

"I can take you closer," the driver answered. "Taxis are allowed inside. I can drive you to the end of the pier where your boat is tied up."

"This is far enough," Daud replied.

Daud's phone vibrated. It was a response from Charlie.

Proceed to rendezvous.

The driver unloaded the bags and placed them on a wooden boardwalk. Daud gave him two fifty-dollar bills. The young man's eyes widened.

"Will you need any more rides?" he asked.

"Stay here," Daud replied. "I'll return shortly."

Once they were about twenty meters from the taxi, Daud spoke to Artem. "Time to call the police and report the burglary at the villa."

"I don't know the phone number."

Daud had the contact information for the

local police saved on his phone as part of his preparation for the mission. He pulled up the number so Artem could see it.

"Why don't you call them?" the Ukrainian asked.

"Quit being stubborn," Esma interjected. "Do you want the police to arrest the man who tried to kill us or not? If you don't want to make the call, I'll do it!"

"Okay, okay," Artem replied grumpily.

"Keep it short," Daud said. "Speak in Arabic. Identify yourself and report a break-in at villa 4. Don't let them know you're no longer there. It's good if they consider it an emergency."

Artem stared at Daud for a moment. As was the case at the restaurant, something in the Ukrainian's countenance made Daud doubt the level of the scientist's cooperation.

"Put the phone on speaker," Daud added.

Artem punched in the numbers. Daud tensed. A male voice answered.

"Police Department."

"This is Artem Kolisnyk. My wife and I are staying at the Four Seasons Resort and want to report a burglary."

"Spell your last name."

Artem froze. "Uh, the villa is registered under the name Artem Bakaj."

Daud grabbed the phone from the scientist's hand. "Villa 4!" he said. "Come as soon as possible. It's an emergency!"

He ended the call and returned the phone to Artem.

"I was going to say it," Artem said.

"Follow me," Daud said, turning away.

"Will you carry my bag?" Esma complained. "My arm hurts."

Daud grabbed the small suitcase, which was surprisingly heavy. They walked about fifty meters along a sandy access road. To the right was a long, low building that contained offices for charter services based at the marina. The moonlight made it easy to see. They reached a boardwalk. Wooden piers extended from the boardwalk out into the sea. Boats owned by the charter companies filled the first two piers. Their destination was the final pier where the largest private yachts docked.

"We're going to one of those?" Esma asked when they stopped at the pier entrance that was blocked by a locked metal gate. "We saw some of those yachts when we took our excursion to Tiran Island."

"Be quiet," her husband barked. "Let me do the talking."

Daud entered the code that unlocked the gate. Artem lagged behind. As they approached the third yacht, a man dressed in dark clothes came down the gangway to the pier. Esma, who was walking beside Daud, stepped back.

"He's dressed like the man at the villa," she said anxiously.

"He works with me," Daud answered. "His name is Joe, and he speaks Arabic."

They reached the gangway. Joe, a clean-shaven man in his late thirties, greeted them in Arabic with an American accent.

"This way," he said.

"I'm not going on board without talking to Uri," Artem said to Daud in Russian.

"Bring Uri Bondar," Daud said to Joe in Arabic.

Joe hesitated. "I'll check," he said and went on board the vessel.

They waited on the pier. A minute passed. Then two minutes. It would take only a short time to drop off the Kolisnyks. After that, Daud's job was complete. He could swing by his hotel and head straight to the airport where he would book a seat on the next flight to Amman, Jordan. From there, he would return to the US.

"Why is it taking so long?" Artem asked in Russian. "If Uri is here of his own free will, he should be able to come and talk to me."

"I don't know," Daud replied. "My job

was to bring you here safely and translate anything into Russian if needed. But that may not be necessary because your Arabic is decent, and I assume you also speak English."

"Not so well," Artem answered in Hebrew.

Daud glanced sideways.

"You speak Hebrew, don't you?" Artem continued in the same language. "And surely you know I'm Jewish."

Daud didn't answer. Kolisnyk was not a name normally associated with Jews from the former Soviet Union.

"Are you working for the Mossad?" Artem persisted.

"Don't do that," Esma cut in in Arabic. "Can't you tell that he doesn't understand you? I hate it when you talk in Hebrew."

"We can talk in Arabic, Russian, or English," Daud said in Arabic.

Daud was getting uneasy about the delay. At that moment three figures appeared at the top of the gangway: Joe, a woman named Lynn — a CIA bureaucrat who had been present at the final planning meeting held in Washington, DC — and a third man who was bald, short, and overweight. Daud assumed it was Uri Bondar, whom he'd not met. Joe held a flashlight that he pointed at the gangway.

"Uri? Is it you?" Artem called out in Russian.

"Yes, yes, it's me," the shorter man answered in the same language.

The three people from the yacht reached the pier. Uri was older than Artem. He and the Ukrainian briefly embraced.

"Why didn't you come onto the boat?" Uri asked.

"I needed to see you," Artem replied. "What's going on? I thought I was going to see you next week in Cairo."

"I'm not going to Egypt. The Americans are going to relocate me to California with a new name and a job that pays three times what we were going to earn working for the Egyptians. The first year's salary has been paid in advance and is already in my offshore bank account."

"California?" Esma asked. "I've always wanted to go to California."

"How do you know they're going to follow through with their promises?" Artem asked, ignoring his wife.

"I have it in writing," Uri answered, tilting his head toward Lynn. "And do you really believe the situation in Egypt is going to be stable? A regime change or promotion of a general who didn't like us could end our freedom or our lives."

"Mr. Kolisnyk. We're prepared to extend the same relocation offer to you we made to Mr. Bondar," Lynn said in Russian. "And include your wife. You would be working for an American company with a guaranteed salary for five years."

"It will be enough to set us up for the rest of our lives," Uri added.

"Let's do it," Esma jumped in. "My family in Alexandria won't have anything to do with me because I married outside Islam. I'm ready to start over in America."

Artem hesitated. "I'd like to talk to Uri in private," he said.

"Step over there," Lynn said, pointing to a slip where a yacht lay at anchor.

Esma started to follow, but Artem stopped her. "This needs to be man-to-man," he said.

"Why can't I listen to what —" she protested, but her husband turned his back on her and put his hand on Uri's shoulder. Esma remained beside Daud, Lynn, and Joe.

"This is not a good idea," Daud whispered to Lynn in English. "They should be in a secure location. We ran into serious problems at their villa."

"This is a secure area," Lynn replied.

In the circle of yellow cast by a light on

91

the pier, Daud could see Uri and Artem gesturing animatedly as they talked. Esma gave Daud a pouty look. Suddenly, there was a loud pop, and Uri Bondar's arms flew up in the air. He fell off the pier into the water. Artem spun around, stared at Esma and Daud for a split second, and then dived into the water in the opposite direction.

Leon lifted his nose with interest when Hana placed the rotisserie chicken and a bag of garlic croutons on the rear seat of the car. She gently shook a bag of dog food in front of the dog's face before putting it on the floorboard in front of him.

"They only had the expensive kind, which should make you happy," she said as she started the car's engine.

Leon opened his jaws in a big yawn and rested his head on the seat. It was a fifteen-minute drive to the gated neighborhood where Ben and Sadie lived in a modern townhome.

Ben worked as a manager at a men's clothing store, but instead of spending the money he received from the lawsuit filed after his wife's death to purchase a bigger house or a nicer car, he had invested it for Sadie's future.

"It's what Gloria would have wanted," he

said to Hana when she asked about his plans.

The metal security gate at the entrance to the neighborhood slowly swung open. After making a couple of turns, Hana parked half a block from the townhome. Leon looked out the window and woofed.

"You know where you are," Hana said as she attached a leash to the dog's collar.

Grabbing the groceries from the rear seat and the dog food from the front floorboard, Hana let Leon lead her down the sidewalk to the correct townhome. The door flung open before Hana rang the doorbell.

"Hey!" Sadie flung her arms around Hana's waist.

In the almost two years since they'd first met, Sadie had undergone a significant growth spurt and transitioned from a compact child to a gangly girl with legs that seemed to lengthen by the month. Her wavy black hair flowed down her back. She had dark, bright eyes, and a smile that started out exuberantly on the left side of her face and fizzled when it reached the right side. Damage from a knife wound inflicted by the terrorist who killed her mother kept Sadie's lips from naturally curving upward. Additional plastic surgery would have to wait until she was older. Sadie released her grip on Hana and grabbed Leon's head with both hands so she could vigorously rub the fur behind the dog's ears.

"He loves that," Hana said.

"I know," Sadie said as she leaned over and let Leon lick the end of her nose. "Can I let him play in the backyard while we make the hummus? I bought him a new chew toy."

"Sure."

Hana followed Sadie through the open living and dining room to the kitchen at the rear of the house. Ben stood at the sink rinsing lettuce. Sadie's father was five feet ten with wavy dark hair similar in color to his daughter's except that his was increasingly streaked with gray. In the five years since his wife's death, Ben hadn't remarried or seriously dated.

"More salads are on the menu for me," Ben said after he greeted Hana. "Sadie poked my stomach the other night when I was wearing pajamas and asked me why it was so soft and fluffy."

Hana laughed. She glanced through the door and saw Sadie throwing a yellow tennis ball for Leon to retrieve.

"Leon perked up when he saw Sadie," Hana said. "He was tired after a long day at the kennel."

"Thanks for coming over on the spur of

the moment," Ben replied. "Sadie loves anything spontaneous."

"With Daud out of town, my little house feels lonely, so it was perfect timing."

As soon as she said the words, Hana realized that Ben might compare Daud's temporary absence with Gloria's permanent one. Thankfully, Ben didn't seem to make the connection as he placed two ripe tomatoes on a cutting board.

"Do you think we should keep the chicken warm in the oven?" he asked.

"Yes. And do you still have a bowl for Leon's food?"

"It's in there," Ben said and pointed to a lower cabinet.

Hana retrieved a pink bowl Sadie had insisted on buying for Leon and filled it with food. Ben diced the tomatoes. A long, narrow cucumber lay untouched on the counter.

"I'll slice the cucumber," Hana said, sliding the cutting board toward her.

"Thanks," Ben answered. "Besides having a soft belly, there is another reason I want to eat healthier and lose weight."

Hana cut three perfectly uniform thin pieces of cucumber.

"Why?" she asked.

Ben glanced over his shoulder at the

kitchen door that remained closed. "I've met someone."

Hana stopped in mid-slice. "To date?" she asked.

"Yes. And I'd like to talk to you about it."

Esma Kolisnyk screamed.

"Go after Bondar!" Daud yelled at Joe. "I'll get Kolisnyk!"

There was another loud pop, and a bullet splintered a board on the dock at their feet.

Daud pushed Esma Kolisnyk toward Lynn. "Get her on the yacht!" Daud said.

Lynn remained frozen in place.

"Now!" Daud commanded.

Without waiting to see if Lynn obeyed, Daud sprinted to the spot where Artem had dived into the water and followed him into the sea. Daud came up about ten feet from the pier. The water was warm and heavy with salt, which made it easy to tread. He heard the splash of someone else entering the water and assumed it was Joe on the opposite side of the dock. There was another loud pop. Daud tried to listen for the sound of Artem moving through the water but heard nothing.

He swam a few strong strokes parallel to the pier and toward the shore. The shadows cast by the yachts and the pier made visibility poor even with the brightness of the moon. He grabbed a large bolt that connected the pier to a post and strained to see in the darkness.

"Over here!" he heard Joe call out. "I have Bondar."

The whole marina would soon be in an uproar. A sick feeling rose in Daud's stomach. With all the gunfire and commotion, the police or Egyptian military would arrive soon, and Daud would have no chance of avoiding capture. He released his grip on the bolt and slipped quietly through the water to the next piling. He wasn't even sure Artem Kolisnyk could swim. The size of the yachts in this section of the marina meant the water had to be at least ten meters deep, and a poor swimmer wearing shoes and clothes would have trouble staying afloat. Daud had to locate Artem soon.

He moved around the piling so he could push off with his feet. As he reached the dock side of the piling, his right hand encountered something wet and bony. It was Artem's hand wrapped around a wooden crossbar. Daud grabbed the Ukrainian, who tried to pull away, but he was no match for Daud's strength.

"Let me go!" Artem sputtered in Russian. "You have no right to keep me here!"

Daud called out in English, "I have Kolis-nyk!"

Daud could hear voices calling out from other boats in the marina, but there were no more gunshots. Artem tried to kick him from beneath the water, but it was a feeble effort. Daud repositioned his grip on the Ukrainian.

"Were you going to abandon your wife?" he asked the scientist in Russian.

Kolisnyk didn't answer. Daud could see a ladder several meters away and tried to calculate whether he could successfully drag Artem there. He heard footsteps overhead. A voice called out above them in English.

"Daud, where are you?"

It was Joe. A flashlight played across the water.

"Here!" Daud answered. "I'm holding on to a crossbeam for one of the pilings. I have Kolisnyk."

The flashlight came closer, and Joe's face appeared. He was lying on his stomach on the dock. His hair was wet, and he shone the light on Daud and Artem. The glare from the flashlight forced Daud to shut his eyes. The sound of sirens blared in the distance.

"We've got to get going," Joe said. "The police are on their way."

"I demand you turn me over to the police!" Artem said in Russian.

"Hand him to me," Joe said.

Daud dislodged Artem from the wooden beam so that Joe could get a firm grip on the Ukrainian's shirt.

"Push," Joe said to Daud.

"Stop!" Artem called out.

Joe was a strong man, and he pulled Kolisnyk upward. Daud put his hand on the Ukrainian's lower back and pushed. When he did, one of Artem's feet flew out and hit Daud in the nose so hard that it stunned him. Joe dragged the scientist out of the water and onto the pier.

"You're hurting me!" Artem protested.

Shaking his head to clear it, Daud pulled himself onto the pier. Joe was half guiding, half dragging Artem toward the Americans' yacht. Daud could hear the Ukrainian yelling for help in Arabic. A spotlight from another boat shone directly on them. There was no place to hide.

Daud glanced over his shoulder behind him. If someone wanted to shoot him, now was a prime opportunity. He sprinted up to Joe and Artem so he could help Joe drag the Ukrainian onto the American yacht. As soon as they were aboard, the gangway began to rise in the air and the yacht moved away from the pier. In the distance, Daud could see the lights of emergency and police vehicles arriving at the spot where the taxi waited. The young taxi driver would soon be interrogated.

"Where is Bondar?" Daud asked Joe in English.

"Below deck receiving medical attention. He was shot, but I was able to pull him out of the water before he drowned."

"How badly is he hurt?"

"I'm not sure. He was bleeding from a wound to the upper body."

Artem ran his hand through his hair. Wet and disheveled, he looked exhausted and frail.

"You could have been shot too," Daud said to him in Russian.

"Maybe, maybe not." Artem shrugged.

The yacht quickly picked up speed, the lights of Sharm el-Sheikh spreading across the nighttime horizon.

"I'll take Kolisnyk below," Joe said to Daud in English. "Lynn's orders are for you to stay topside."

"Topside?"

"Your job is finished. Remember, you were supposed to drop them off and head to the airport. We'll take it from here."

"What am I supposed to do now?"

"That's above my pay grade," Joe said, lifting one shoulder.

An American soldier came on deck with an assault rifle in his hands and stood near Daud.

CHAPTER 7

"I'm listening," Hana said to Ben as she slid a few thin pieces of cucumber into the salad bowl.

"I need your perspective," Ben said. "We both know that Sadie believes you hung the moon and stars."

It took Hana a moment to grasp the meaning of the comparison. "I love Sadie," she replied simply.

"And you've helped keep her emotional tank full when there were plenty of reasons for it to run dry."

Hana had spent a lot of time over the past eighteen months with Sadie — reading, listening, playing, and, importantly, singing over the young girl in Arabic and Hebrew. Hana believed some of the words she sang swirled upward as intercession to the God who perfectly loved the motherless girl.

"I'm willing to back away when another woman enters her life," Hana said slowly.

"I'll be thrilled if you meet and marry someone who can be a real mother to Sadie. I don't want to be a roadblock to your happiness."

"No, it's not that at all," Ben said. "You've never crossed any boundaries. I want your help in easing Sadie into a new transition."

Hana sliced a few more pieces of cucumber. "What can you tell me about the woman you're dating?"

"It's moving fast," Ben replied. "Which is exciting and scary. Laura and I met ten weeks ago through a mutual friend, and we've talked almost every day since. She works as a custom designer at a jewelry boutique not far from the clothing store I manage. She's eight years younger than I am and never married. We've gone out to dinner several times when Sadie was spending the evening with Gloria's parents."

"Has Sadie met her?"

Ben shook his head. "Not yet. I never wanted to introduce a woman into Sadie's life unless I believed the relationship might last."

As she listened, Hana's internal alarm bells sounded. "The practical side of me says you're moving too fast," she said.

"Didn't you decide that you wanted to marry Daud by the second date?"

"True," Hana admitted. "Is Laura Jewish?"

"Yes," Ben answered. "She used to go to synagogue when she was a kid but hasn't connected with organized religion as an adult."

Hana and Ben had never seriously discussed matters of faith. She knew Ben occasionally attended synagogue, but beyond sending Sadie to a Jewish day school, Hana didn't know what he believed. She decided it was a good time to ask, but before she could speak, he continued.

"Laura is fine with me continuing to raise Sadie in the same way Gloria wanted until she's old enough to make choices for herself. What's rocked my world is the chemistry between Laura and me. It's incredible."

"What do you mean by chemistry?"

"The enjoyment we have in being together. We never feel bored, and I've been able to talk to Laura in a way I've not experienced with another person since Gloria died."

Hana's concern for Sadie morphed into protectiveness. The door to the backyard opened, and Sadie entered. She gave Hana another quick hug.

"You wear the most awesome perfume," Sadie said. "Last week Daddy let me buy some perfume with my own money, but I can't use it; I only take the top off the bottle and sniff it. It's not the same. Katelin says perfume changes when it mixes with the oils on your skin."

"Katelin is the new expert on everything in Sadie's life," Ben said.

"Let's make the hummus," Sadie said. "I have the recipe memorized."

"You're in charge," Hana said. "I'll be your helper."

"That's called a sous-chef," Sadie added.

After washing her hands at the kitchen sink, Sadie opened the cupboard and took out a can of chickpeas that she placed on the counter along with a lemon, a clove of roasted garlic, a bottle of olive oil, salt, and a small container of cumin.

"Chickpeas don't come from chickens," Sadie said. "They are a bean. People have been eating them for seventy-five hundred years. Nathan argued with Mrs. Rosenstein about them coming from chickens until she told him to be quiet."

"I've seen the plants they grow on," Hana said.

"You can cook dried chickpeas," Sadie continued. "But that takes a long time, so we're going to use some from a can."

Hana remembered large pots of chickpeas

cooking on the stove at her grandmother's house. Over the next few minutes, Sadie gave a precise commentary as they mixed together the ingredients for the hummus.

"We don't want it to get runny," she said.

Hana took a picture of the little girl standing on her toes as she worked. After a final scrape with the spatula, Sadie announced that the hummus was finished. Hana lifted out the food processor blade, and Sadie carefully spread the hummus on a white plate.

"The way food looks is art, just like a painting," she said.

Hana glanced at Ben, who mouthed, "She got this from her mother."

"Ready for the red peppers," Sadie said. "We roasted a bunch of them at school and took off the skins."

Sadie retrieved a plastic bag from the refrigerator and picked out pieces of diced pepper and placed them on top of the hummus.

"The little black parts are okay to eat," she said. "It doesn't taste burned."

"Do you want to top it off with more olive oil?" Hana asked.

"Yes, yes, I forgot. Will you pour it into the tablespoon so I can drizzle it?"

Hana's English vocabulary was extensive,

but "drizzle" was a new word for her. The golden oil glistened in tiny pools.

"Beautiful," Hana said. "It almost looks too good to eat."

"Nothing is too good to eat if it tastes good," Sadie answered. "I like it on a pita chip."

"Let's all take a bite at the same time," Ben suggested.

They each dipped a chip into the hummus.

"This is very creamy and fresh tasting," Hana said.

"Because we just made it. Mrs. Rosenstein said the ingredients have to be added in the right order so the hummus doesn't get messed up."

"That's true about a lot of things," Hana said with a glance at Ben. "If you want something to turn out perfectly, it's important to keep that in mind."

It took the yacht twenty minutes to reach its destination, a US Navy vessel. The yacht slowed when it was about five hundred meters from the ship, a modified Ticonderoga cruiser. Joe, Lynn, and several other people Daud didn't recognize came up on deck. The Kolisnyks and Uri Bondar weren't with them. Lynn came over to Daud.

"I guess you're wondering how you're going to be extracted?" she asked.

"Yes, and a ride to a safe harbor on that naval vessel suits me fine."

"Not happening," Lynn replied bluntly. "This is an entirely US operation at this point. Joe is going to be on the yacht and coordinate dropping you off anywhere you like along the coast within a reasonable distance of Sharm el-Sheikh. You can exit the country per your previous plan."

"That won't work," Daud responded sharply. "There will be descriptions of me circulated by the police, most likely with photographs taken at the restaurant where I made contact with the Kolisnyks. Egyptian law enforcement and military personnel will be looking for me all over town, including the airport."

He quickly explained what happened at the restaurant and in villa 4.

"That doesn't change anything on our end," Lynn replied. "We prepared a second set of identity papers if you'd like to use them. Joe has some extra clothes you can change into. The two of you look about the same size."

"I want to talk to Charlie," Daud said, trying to stay calm.

"Not now," Lynn said flatly. "Charlie will

be in touch with you later. If you want to avoid the airport, you can freelance an alternate exit strategy. You're a contractor, so at this point you can act on your own initiative without prior authorization."

She handed Daud an envelope. Inside was a new passport using the same photo as the one for Rasheed Sayyid. His new name was Ibrahim Abadi, a Jordanian citizen. Also included was a credit card and a Jordanian driver's license.

Daud squared his shoulders and pointed across the water. "I want to board the cruiser," he said. "Wherever it's going, I can get off and make my way to the States."

"No, Mr. Hasan. And that's final."

Lynn turned and left Daud. Joe came up to him.

"Our orders are to wait in the cockpit," he said to Daud.

Fuming, Daud followed Joe to the bridge where the captain of the yacht manned the wheel. The skipper was a small, wiry Frenchman whom Daud had briefly met at the last planning meeting for the mission. The captain and his two French-speaking African crew members were also independent contractors hired for the mission. The captain greeted Daud in French. Daud responded in the same language.

"That was scary back there," the captain said, shaking his head. "In case the Egyptians are on the lookout for this vessel, I'm going to find a quiet spot and anchor up for four or five days before going through the Suez Canal for the return voyage to Marseilles."

"Can I go with you?" Daud asked, keeping the conversation in French.

"No, no," the captain answered, shaking his head. "The head woman told me no passengers allowed except Joe. I think he's here to make sure we follow orders."

"Where should I go ashore near Sharm el-Sheikh?"

"There's a cove between El Tor and Sharm el-Sheikh. Nearby is the Suef fishing resort where you can rent a car in the morning."

"Speak English so I know what you're talking about," Joe cut in.

"I was explaining how to make the perfect crepe," the captain answered with a wink toward Daud.

"Cut the comedy," Joe said.

From the bridge, Daud could see the entire front deck of the yacht. The launch from the cruiser arrived, and several sailors came on board. Bright lights illuminated both ships. Artem and Esma appeared with guards on either side of them. One man had

110

a firm grip on Artem's right arm.

"I don't think Kolisnyk will jump off the boat into the ocean," Daud said.

"We didn't think he would dive into the water at the marina," Joe replied.

"True," Daud admitted.

A few moments later two men bearing Uri Bondar on a stretcher made their way across the deck. Bondar's eyes were closed. Bandages covered the right side of his neck and face.

"He got nicked in the neck," Joe said. "A fraction of an inch closer in and he'd be in a body bag."

"Any idea who fired the shots at the marina?" Daud asked.

"No, and I heard Kolisnyk telling Lynn about the attack at their villa. Close call. Good work. This mission was much dicier than they led us to believe in the briefing sessions."

Hana, Ben, and Sadie ate at the small table in the breakfast nook. Sadie insisted on sitting so she could watch Leon in the backyard and kept up a running description of the dog's antics throughout the meal.

"A squirrel that steals the food from our bird feeder hopped up on the fence, but it ran away when it saw Leon."

"He would be more likely to lick it than bite it," Hana said.

After they finished the meal, Sadie disappeared into her room. Ben and Hana cleaned the kitchen.

"Laura loves to cook," Ben said. "She really wants to come over and prepare a nice dinner for me. I'd like to do it, but there's no one to babysit Sadie this week, and I'm not —"

"She could spend an evening with me," Hana said. "She's begged to do that for months. It's been tough to schedule since the wedding, but with Daud out of town, this would be a perfect time."

"Could she spend the night? If Laura fixes a fancy meal, we'll be eating late. I could come to your house early the next morning to pick up Sadie for school."

Hana hesitated, but she'd already committed to the idea of an evening with Sadie. "Okay," she said. "I could do it either tomorrow night or the following night."

Ben grabbed his phone. "Let me text Laura first and find out what works best for her," he said.

Hana scooped a small portion of hummus into a plastic container to take home. Ben's phone buzzed, and he left the kitchen to accept the call. He returned with a broad

112

smile on his face.

"We're set for tomorrow night. That's the only time Laura could squeeze it into her schedule. Could you pick up Sadie at school? I'll arrange for her to be at the extended day program."

Hana checked her phone to make sure she didn't have a late-afternoon commitment at the office. "I can be at the school by the regular time."

"Great. I'll email the office and let them know you're still on the list of people authorized to pick her up."

Ben stopped and glanced back at the living room where he'd just been. "Do you think I should take down the photos of Gloria hanging on the wall before Laura gets here?"

They went into the living room, and Hana tried to put herself in Laura's shoes. There was one photo of Ben, Gloria, and Sadie taken at the beach when Sadie was a baby in her mother's arms. In another picture Ben and Gloria were wearing jackets and standing on a mountain in Maine.

"Laura needs to see the photos," Hana answered. "She already knows Gloria was a huge part of your life, but seeing the pictures tells her you're a man who's continued to care and didn't try to forget his wife after her death."

"I'll never forget," Ben said slowly. "But I do want to move on. It's been five years. That's a long time."

"Hana!" Sadie called out. "I've finished in my room! You can come in now!"

Hana and Sadie spent forty-five minutes reading together.

"Time for bed," Hana said.

"Can you stay and tuck me in?"

"No, but would you like to come to my house tomorrow after school and spend the night with me?"

Sadie's face exploded with excitement. "Yes! Did Daddy say I could?"

"It was his idea."

Sadie jumped up and opened the door of her closet. She pushed aside some clothes and pulled out a small suitcase on rollers. The suitcase was navy with white flowers.

"I'd better pack now," she said. "I'll be too sleepy in the morning and might forget something."

It seemed like a logical plan, and Hana helped load the suitcase. Sadie wore uniforms to school, so deciding on an outfit for the following morning was easy. Picking what she wanted to wear after school with Hana and the right pajamas took much longer.

"Will we play outside with Leon?" Sadie asked.

"Maybe."

"And because I'm going to your house, I want to bring Fabia," Sadie said. "I have to be careful with her now. Her head is kind of loose."

Sadie opened the small drawer in the nightstand beside her bed and took out the brown-skinned doll she'd named after one of Hana's cousins. Fabia's bedraggled condition was the result of overuse through love, not neglect. Sadie gave the doll a quick kiss and laid her in the suitcase.

"That's it," she announced. "I'll carry my pillow. Do you still have the toothbrush you bought the last time I stayed with you?"

"Yes."

"And I love your shampoo. It smells way better than what Daddy buys me."

Sadie gave Hana a final tight hug. "I love you," Sadie said when she released her.

"I love you too."

CHAPTER 8

Daud placed his hands on the side railing of the yacht. The moon was below the horizon and stars covered the sky. It had been half an hour since they left the navy vessel. The French captain came up to him and pointed to a dinghy strapped to the deck.

"You'll use that so you can make it all the way to shore. There's a beach about a kilometer west from the resort. I suggest you go ashore and enter the resort from land."

"Without a car or luggage?" Daud asked.

The captain shrugged. "We'll lower the dinghy in a few minutes."

Fifteen minutes later Daud climbed down a chrome ladder and into the dinghy. It bobbed up and down in low waves that didn't bother the larger boat. The captain tossed him a bottle of water.

"Bon chance!" he called out.

Daud pressed the start button for the motor. The engine coughed twice and sputtered to life. He opened the throttle, and the little boat shot through the water with unexpected power. He pointed the bow toward a faint line of lights the captain had identified as his target. The dinghy bounced up and down across the water.

A few minutes later the inflatable craft crested a gentle wave and scraped against the sand. Daud hopped out and dragged the boat out of the water. He then made his way through the grass and bushes to the coastal highway. The shoulder of the road was a mix of ground-up shells that crunched against the soles of Daud's shoes. He saw the lights of an approaching vehicle and moved back into the shadows. After passing by, the car stopped and backed up. Daud could either dart back into the darkness toward the beach and raise suspicion or engage in a conversation that he hoped would appear normal. The driver lowered his window.

"Do you need a ride?" a young man asked.

"I'm on my way to the Suef resort," Daud replied. "I was out for a walk and came up from the beach."

"Get in," the man offered. "They shut the gates after midnight, but I know the guard on duty and can get you in."

Daud hesitated. In addition to the driver, there was a sleepy-looking boy of about ten in the passenger seat. The presence of the boy caused Daud to relax.

"Thanks," he said. Daud opened the door and got in the backseat.

"I'm Mohammed Nadir and this is my little brother, Adil," the man said. "We live in the old town of Sharm el-Sheikh."

"Ibrahim Abadi," Daud said.

"We're on our way home after visiting our sister in Dahab."

It turned out that Daud was farther from the fishing resort than he'd thought. During the short drive, he learned that Mohammed and his brother came from a Bedouin family who left their nomadic lifestyle and settled in the village of Sharm el-Sheikh a hundred years previously. Since then, they'd become successful traders and merchants, first with camels and livestock and more recently with locally produced crafts that they sold to shops in Sharm el-Sheikh and exported to Europe. The business generated enough income that Mohammed and all his brothers owned cars. Adil piped up and said his greatest desire was to own a guitar, not a car. He'd already written five songs.

"We're about to sign a deal to ship some

of our products to America," Mohammed announced proudly. "Our wholesaler lives in a city called Atlanta. I looked it up on the internet. It's very lush and green. Have you ever been to America?"

"Yes, and Atlanta is in a beautiful part of the country."

"You know it?" Mohammed exclaimed and punched his little brother in the arm. "See, I knew we were supposed to pick him up! It will bring us good luck in America!"

Mohammed turned off the roadway in front of a sign announcing the entrance to the Suef fishing resort. They came to a gate that consisted of a single metal bar across the road. There was a tiny guard shack with no lights showing.

"No one is here," the driver said. "I'll take you to the hotel."

It was several hundred meters to the low-slung hotel for the fishing resort. Daud's American money was soaked, but he handed Mohammed a slightly soggy fifty-dollar bill.

"No," the young man said as he held up his hand in refusal. "Your presence is a sign of blessing on our business in America."

Suddenly, Daud had another idea. "Adil, how much does a good guitar cost?" he asked the boy.

"Four hundred American dollars, sir," the

boy answered. "I've saved eighty-seven dollars so far."

Daud peeled off $350 and showed it to Mohammed. "May I give him the money to buy the guitar?"

Mohammed's eyes widened. "Why would you do that? Are you a *malak*?"

"No, just a man who believes in the dreams of a child."

"Thank you, Mr. Abadi," Mohammed said, taking the money and passing it to his little brother, who was staring wide-eyed at Daud.

"Receive it," Daud said with a smile. "Along with my blessing to all in your family. My prayers go with you from this day forward."

"I will write a song about you," Adil replied excitedly. "I can already hear the sound in my head."

Unable to shake her concern for Daud, Hana stayed awake later than normal before finally falling asleep. When she awoke it was almost 5:00 a.m. Her time with the Lord in the night was an invitation, not a command, and since she usually woke up around 6:00 a.m., she rolled over in bed to grab another hour of sleep.

When she got up, she brewed a pot of

strong Arabic coffee flavored with cardamom. The coffee was served boiling hot, and Hana poured just enough of the dark liquid to cover the bottom of a small handleless cup. Once the coffee cooled, she drank all of it in one sip. The custom in her home when guests were present was to refill the cups with small amounts multiple times as an ongoing affirmation of hospitality. It was a beautiful custom that produced a friendly rhythm to a visit. Hana stopped at three modest portions. The potent caffeine was eye-popping.

Curling her feet beneath her on the sofa, Hana read from Psalms, Jeremiah, and Ephesians. She was a Bible grazer and didn't follow a systematic reading plan. However, she often followed themes that opened up to her. Writing in her journal, she made a few notes about a passage in Ephesians that affirmed the vastness of God's love and then reread the prayers she'd offered two nights before. The journal entries tethered her to a place of continuing communion, and her life-long study of the Scriptures enabled her to draw from an inexhaustible library. After she prayed for Daud, her heart was drawn to pray for Ben and Sadie. She did so, then added a new name — Laura.

Arriving at work, Hana stopped at Janet's desk on her way to her office. The assistant lifted her fingers from the keyboard and removed her earbuds.

"Did they have summer clerks at the law firm where you worked in Israel?" she asked.

"Occasionally, but it's not as common as it is here."

"Jimmy Duncan is old-school," Janet replied, shaking her head. "I'm used to clerks typing their own research memos, but Jimmy is dictating like he was Mr. Collins or Mr. Lowenstein."

For many US law firms, hiring a student prior to the final year of law school provided an opportunity for a three-month job interview. Jimmy Duncan, an eager young law student with red hair and freckles from the University of Georgia Law School, had been assigned to Janet, who was already at maximum capacity.

"What is the memo about?" Hana asked.

"Conflict of law issues related to a dispute between a company based in New York and our client here in Georgia. In that Deep South accent of his, Jimmy sounds like he's fighting the Civil War all over again."

"Is the research good?"

"Yes," Janet sighed. "I believe we'll see him in his own tiny office after he graduates and passes the bar exam next year. If our office manager tries to assign him to me on a permanent basis, I'll need you to go to war to protect me."

Hana laughed. "Do you have time to hear about my time with Sadie last night?" she asked.

"Always," Janet answered, turning her chair away from her computer. "Jimmy isn't a partner yet."

Hana told Janet about preparing and eating Sadie's hummus.

"Adding the red peppers sounds like something I'd like," Janet said. "Most of the hummus I've tried reminded me of a cross between the white paste we used to glue papers together when we were kids and watered-down cement."

"Where have you eaten hummus? That sounds terrible."

"Actually, that's only true about my mother-in-law's hummus," the assistant answered with a grin. "Donnie's mother can cook lobster thirty different ways, but when she tried to go Middle Eastern, she fell off the boat somewhere between Maine and the Mediterranean. Her hummus sticks to the roof of your mouth, and you have to pry it off."

Hana laughed. "I'll bring you some of

Sadie's tomorrow," she offered. "Unless she and I eat it all when she spends the night with me."

"A sleepover!" Janet exclaimed. "What's the occasion?"

Hana told her briefly about Ben and Laura.

"How did you feel when he broke the news to you? I mean, even though Sadie isn't your child, you've taken her into your heart in a huge way."

"True," Hana replied slowly. "I wasn't jealous, just concerned that Ben makes the right choice. I can't imagine what it would be like to try to create a new marriage after your spouse died so young."

"And the trauma of a murder."

Hana remembered the tears she'd cried the last time she visited Jerusalem's Hurva Square, the site of the terrorist attack that killed Gloria. On that day, she'd not shed tears of grief but wept with rage directed toward the evil that took the young mother's life and scarred Sadie inside and out.

"Take it moment by moment and realize that you're not in control," Janet continued. "Not wanting Sadie and Ben to suffer anymore is completely understandable."

Hana nodded.

"What's on your calendar for today?"

Janet asked.

"Working on a few projects for Mr. Collins and not sending you any dictation so you can finish what you need to do for Jimmy."

"I like that plan," Janet said and put the earbuds back in place.

"Mustafa is dead and in the company of martyrs," Khalil said soberly.

Rahal, who had just come in from a business meeting with a member of the Qatari royal family, stared in shock at his favored assistant.

"How?" he managed.

"I'm not sure. The Egyptian police found his body at the resort where Kolisnyk was staying. He'd been tied up and shot in the head."

Rahal eyed Khalil, who seemed surprisingly stoic in light of the horrifying news. As a Hafiz, Khalil must have resources to draw from at a moment of profound grief unknown to Rahal.

"Mustafa's last message came after he left the restaurant where an Arab man accosted Kolisnyk and his wife while they were eating dinner," Khalil continued. "He told me he was going to wait for them at their villa."

"Did the Egyptian police mention Kolisnyk in their report about Mustafa?"

"I'm trying to obtain that information. There is a lawyer in Sharm el-Sheikh who claims he can provide us with a copy of the police file. I've wired him the money needed for baksheesh."

Bribery was a common part of business dealings in the Middle East.

"I've also asked him to obtain the security camera footage from the resort and the restaurant."

"What about from inside the villa?"

"Not likely," Khalil said and shook his head. "Mustafa would have disabled any cameras, but I will check."

The two men stood in silence for several moments.

"This is even more reason to avenge ourselves against Kolisnyk," Rahal said.

"Yes. And with the help of Allah, I will track him down wherever he hides."

Toward the end of the day, Hana received a phone call from Abdul Erekat about the Land Rover.

"I just talked to the mechanic," the car dealer said. "Except for needing new brakes, the vehicle is in good shape."

Hana was excited about surprising Daud but also nervous in case he wouldn't like the huge gift.

126

"You think I should buy it?" she asked, more to herself than to Erekat.

"If that's what you want, you should snatch it up. A Land Rover set up like this is common in South Africa but not so much in America."

"Okay," Hana said decisively. "I'll take it. What's next?"

"I can deliver it to you tomorrow either at your office or your home. All I'll need from you is a cashier's check for the purchase price and associated fees. I can break that down in an email."

"Could you bring it to my house tomorrow evening around six o'clock?"

"Send me your address. Will your husband be at home? I know you want to surprise him."

"Probably not. He's out of the country, and I don't know when he'll be back." Hana instantly regretted the last part of her comment.

"See you tomorrow evening."

Five minutes later Hana received an email from Abdul. Everything looked in order, and she went downstairs to a branch bank in the building to get a cashier's check. She worked on multimillion-dollar deals for clients all the time, but this was the largest monetary transaction she'd ever done on her own. The withdrawal didn't leave much in her savings account. Hana slipped the large check into her purse.

"You never told me about the new case Jakob Brodsky wanted to talk to you about," Janet said when Hana returned to her office.

Hana quickly summarized the conversation with Jakob and Vladimir Ivanov.

"That only sounds a little bit safer than tracking down terrorists so you can sue them."

"Don't worry. I'm not getting involved beyond helping Jakob locate an expert who can advise them about ancient artifacts. Mr. Collins is keeping me plenty busy."

CHAPTER 9

The following morning Daud rented a vehicle at the fishing resort. The only car available for lease all the way to Amman was a BMW sports car. Daud bought a pair of dark sunglasses in the gift shop at the fishing resort along with a few souvenirs that would support his story as a business-man who purchased a few trinkets. He put on the sunglasses and was careful to obey the speed limit. Stopping at a red light in the center of Sharm el-Sheikh, he glanced sideways as a taxi pulled up beside him. It was owned by the same company as the cab driven by the young man who'd taken him and the Kolisnyks to the marina. The taxi driver looked very young. When the light changed, Daud pulled forward, and the taxi driver honked his horn. Daud flinched as the vehicle sped by him, but then realized the driver was impatient with another driver who hadn't responded fast enough to the changing light. Daud approached the hotel where he'd stayed. A police vehicle was parked in front of the lobby. Only upon reaching the edge of Sharm el-Sheikh did Daud begin to relax.

It was a three-hour drive to the Taba crossing into Israel. From there, Daud could drive across the desert to the Jordanian border. When he reached Taba, he slowed to a stop. There were fifteen or sixteen vehicles in front of him, including four tour buses. Three Egyptian border guards surrounded the first car in line. Beyond the guards was the passport control office where Daud would pay an exit fee in order to leave the country. His greatest concern was that photographs of his face from the restaurant had fallen into the hands of the police in Sharm el-Sheikh and been sent to the border guards.

The car at the front of the line was cleared to move forward. Next came a bus, and Daud watched as the people on board slowly got off. He checked his watch and eyed the border patrol office where any information about him would be received. Fences extended on either side of the road. It could easily be over an hour before he reached the front of the line.

A slender young border patrol officer with

the wispy beginnings of a mustache on his upper lip began walking down the row of vehicles with a piece of paper in his hand. He stopped at each car and looked at the driver and passengers. He reached the BMW, and Daud lowered the driver's-side window.

"Because of the number of cars waiting to cross, we're going to open another line," the young man said.

Daud couldn't see what was in the young man's hand.

"I've always wanted to ride in one of these," the young man continued. "The richest man in the village where I grew up drove a BMW. He used to pay me to wash it."

"This is a rental," Daud replied. "I'm on my way to Amman."

The guard walked around the back of the car to the passenger seat. Without warning he suddenly opened the door and got in. Daud jumped. The guard then placed the paper in his hand on the dashboard. Daud could barely make out a grainy photo of a man, but he didn't remove his sunglasses to get a better look. The guard rubbed his hand across the leather seat.

"Nice," the young man said. "Drive over there."

Daud pulled out of line and drove forward to the designated spot. The Israeli border was less than ten meters away.

"May I see your passport and registration for the vehicle?" the guard asked.

Daud handed him the passport. "The registration is in the glove box," he said.

The young man looked at the passport. It contained a forged entry stamp from Jordan to Egypt. "You've not been traveling very much," he observed.

"It's a new passport."

The guard nodded and opened the glove box to study the registration paperwork.

"This is a good year," he said as he read. "The next model wasn't as fast. I think the company was trying to sell them to rich young girls to drive in the city."

Daud strained to get a better view of the sheet of paper. He was able to make out the name Rasheed Sayyid printed beneath the photo. He immediately adjusted his sunglasses so they were even closer to his eyes. Through the windshield he could see three additional border officers who had left the terminal building and were walking in their direction. The young man returned the registration to the glove box.

"Go to the passport office," the guard said. "Are you transporting anything?"

"Just a few souvenirs from a fishing resort where I stayed near Sharm el-Sheikh."

Daud handed the guard the plastic bag of items he'd purchased that morning at the gift shop. Inside the passport office, a bored-looking clerk gave Daud a receipt for the exit fee and stamped his passport. Outside, all four of the border guards were now circling the BMW. As he drew closer, Daud could see a captain's insignia on the shoulder of one of the men.

"What were you doing in Sharm el-Sheikh?" the officer asked.

"Business meeting."

"You didn't drive this vehicle to get there?"

"No, I flew in from Amman. This is a rental."

The captain pulled the other men aside. They huddled and talked. After a few moments the young guard who'd helped Daud glanced over at him and then touched the weapon on his hip. The captain and the young guard came over to him. The captain asked to see the exit document Daud had received in the passport office. He read it and handed it back to him.

"Have a pleasant trip," the officer said.

The guard raised a metal bar blocking the road in front of the BMW. Daud waved to the young man as he passed by. Normally, border patrol officers smiled as frequently as guards at Buckingham Palace, but the young man grinned and waved in return.

Daud crossed the invisible line that separated Egypt from Israel and breathed a huge sigh of relief. A sign in Hebrew, Arabic, and English welcomed him to Israel. Never had he felt so welcomed.

Hana left the office to pick up Sadie.

"Have fun," Janet said.

"Sadie is a great houseguest if you don't mind answering a lot of questions. I think she'll make an awesome trial lawyer when she grows up."

"She loves everything that has to do with you."

"And Leon."

"Take pictures of the two of you doing something fun and send them to me."

It took forty-five minutes to drive to Sadie's school that was adjacent to one of the larger synagogues in the city. Two security guards patrolled the line of cars that snaked their way to the main building. Teachers on duty connected the right child with the right vehicle. Hana saw Sadie talking to several of her friends. She looked up and waved excitedly. Hana pulled to the curb, and a teacher came over to the car. Hana lowered the window and introduced herself.

"Mr. Neumann notified the office that you would be picking up Sadie," the woman replied with a smile. "Have a good evening."

In spite of a recent growth spurt, Sadie still wasn't tall enough to sit in the front passenger seat of a car. She deposited her backpack and overnight suitcase on the rear floorboard.

"Are we going to pick up Leon?" she asked.

"Yes. Will you tell me about your day?"

It took only one question to launch Sadie into a fifteen-minute summary of her life at school. The little girl was extremely observant and remembered with precise detail what people said and did.

"But I didn't let Jasmine ignoring me and sitting at the table with Emily and Shakira make me mad," she said. "I just went over and sat with Katelin and Morgan. That was way more fun because Morgan just got back from a trip to Spain with her parents and older sister. She said the Spanish we've been learning at school really works. She talked to people who understood what she was saying. You and Daud went to Spain on your honeymoon, didn't you?"

"Yes."

"Where did you go?"

Hana told her about Seville, Grenada, and Cordoba.

"I think Morgan went to Grenada, but I'm not sure." Sadie paused and looked out the car window for a moment. "If I visited Israel, would I be able to talk to people in Hebrew like Morgan did in Spain?"

Hana answered in Hebrew, and Sadie replied in the same language. The conversation continued for a few more simple sentences.

"That answers your question," Hana concluded in Hebrew. "Your Hebrew is clear and easy to understand."

They reached the dog day care center. Hana parked near the front door.

"Come inside with me to get Leon," she said.

The dog greeted them with several loud barks and trembled with excitement. Sadie knelt down and rubbed the sides of his head with her hands. The dog jumped into the rear seat with her. Sadie spent the rest of the drive talking to Leon. They reached Hana's house and pulled into the driveway.

"Can I walk him to the corner and back?" Sadie asked.

"I'll go with you."

Hana lived on an infrequently traveled dead-end street in a quiet neighborhood, but she wasn't going to let Sadie out of her sight. On the way to the corner, Leon stopped repeatedly to investigate an interesting smell.

"I wonder what he's smelling," Sadie said. "Did you know a dog can smell forty times better than a person?"

When Hana worked as a security officer at Ben Gurion Airport near Tel Aviv, they regularly used bomb- and drug-sniffing dogs. The animals demonstrated remarkable speed and accuracy. Leon halted for the fourth time at the base of an electric company power pole. When they reached the corner and turned around, Leon began to pull harder on the leash. The only thing that interested Leon more than smells at the end of his nose was the prospect of food in his mouth. Sadie held the leash with both hands.

"Heel!" Hana commanded.

Leon quickly dropped back to Sadie's side. Sadie patted him on the head.

"Good boy," she said.

"He wants his supper," Hana said.

After they'd returned to Hana's house, Sadie used a bright red cup to scoop three generous helpings of food into Leon's metal bowl. Hana gave the dog fresh water.

"That will keep him happy for a few minutes while we prepare our dinner. We'll start with the rest of the hummus you made the other night. I saved it for us to share."

There was only enough hummus for each of them to eat two pita squares.

"It still tastes good," Sadie said, "but I can tell it's not fresh. It makes me more hungry."

"Shouldn't you say hungrier?" Hana asked.

Navigating Anglo-Saxon words and their illogical forms was one of the hardest aspects of English for both Hana and Sadie. The girl wrinkled her forehead for a moment and silently mouthed the options.

"Either one is okay, but when I haven't eaten for a long time, I feel more hungrier," Sadie answered.

"When did you go a long time without food?"

"On Yom Kippur. My grandparents didn't eat anything for the whole day. I tried to do it too."

"That's called fasting."

"There wasn't anything fast about it. It seemed like the day would never end. I drank a glass of milk. I'm not sure if that's cheating, but it tasted yummy."

"You're not fasting tonight. I thought we could make some homemade pizzas."

A big smile creased Sadie's face. "Will this be like the last time when I could put anything I wanted on my pizza?" she asked.

"Of course."

Hana had already prepared the dough. Taking the two lumps from the refrigerator, she let Sadie flatten one of them with a rolling pin while the tan-colored baking stone heated up to 500 degrees in the oven. Sadie liked thin-crust pizza. She was beginning to branch out from generic cheese pizza, and Hana had purchased a variety of toppings. She laid them out on the kitchen counter.

"Here are artichoke hearts, cooked ground beef, diced sun-dried tomatoes, sliced onion, spinach, two kinds of mushrooms, peppers, three varieties of olives —"

"The olives are for you," Sadie interrupted. "I bet you'll eat all three."

"You are correct," Hana replied, popping a green one into her mouth. "I eat olives any way I can get them."

There was also Swiss chard, roasted corn, mozzarella, and goat cheese.

"Goat cheese?" Sadie wrinkled her nose.

"I grew up eating it all the time. Ours came from goats in the town where we lived."

Sadie took a tiny piece of goat cheese and put it in her mouth. Her negative expression didn't change.

"At least you tried it," Hana said.

"What will you do with the stuff we don't put on the pizzas?" Sadie asked.

"Toss it into salads. Nothing will be wasted."

Sadie carefully spread marinara sauce to the edges of her pizza, sprinkled on mozzarella cheese, and added beef, tomatoes, mushrooms, and corn. She picked up an artichoke heart and nibbled it.

"This is good," she said before strategically adding one to each quadrant of her pie.

Hana piled on everything except Swiss chard, onions, and spinach. Once the cooking stone was thoroughly heated, Hana slid Sadie's pizza onto the sizzling rock. Leon had finished eating and stood at the counter with his nose in the air, sniffing the ingredients.

"He smells the goat cheese," Sadie said. "May I give him a bite?"

Hana rarely offered Leon table scraps. "Yes."

Sadie held a piece in her open palm. Leon immediately licked it up with his broad tongue. When the edges of the pizza started

140

turning brown, Hana removed it and put hers into the oven.

"It looks yummy," Sadie said, staring at the bubbling cheese.

Hana took a photo of Sadie and her pizza to show Ben and Janet.

"Help me set the table," Hana said.

Sadie didn't yet know where everything went on a table. It was the sort of thing a mother would teach a daughter.

"You sure are quiet," Sadie said. "What are you thinking about?"

"Sorry," Hana replied, dodging the question. "If you're serving dessert at a fancy party, the fork goes on the left side of the plate, and if the dessert is eaten with a spoon, it's placed on the right side. For regular meals like ours, the dessert utensil is placed above the plate like this."

Hana placed a spoon in a horizontal position.

"What are we having for dessert?" Sadie asked.

"Ice cream."

"Chocolate?"

"Double chocolate."

The timer sounded and Hana took her pizza from the oven. Sadie's pizza had cooled enough that she could eat it. They sat down, and Sadie held out her hand so

Hana could hold it while she prayed a blessing in Hebrew.

"I love the way you make the words sound," Sadie said when she opened her eyes. "But I didn't understand everything you said."

"I didn't just thank God for the food; I also prayed a special blessing for you and your daddy."

"Will you teach me a Hebrew prayer?"

"I'm sure you've been learning them in school."

"Yeah, but I want to know one that no one else says."

Hana thought for a moment. "Okay," she said. "I'll start with the blessing I just prayed for you and your daddy. I asked God to be close to you all the time and reveal himself to you in a way that you can really know it."

Sadie was a quick learner, and before they finished a second slice of pizza, she could repeat the prayer without mistakes.

"Can I tell it to my daddy?" she asked. "He's not that interested in talking Hebrew."

"Yes, he'll love it coming from you."

Sadie was hungry and left only one narrow piece of pizza.

"Homemade pizza is like the hummus,"

she said, daintily wiping her mouth with a napkin. "It tastes so much better when you make it yourself. Maybe I'll be a chef when I grow up."

After they ate ice cream, Hana let Sadie take a shower and wash her hair with Hana's shampoo. The little girl came out of the bathroom wearing her pajamas and insisted that Hana smell her hair.

"I hope the smell lasts until I go to school tomorrow," Sadie said, holding a thick strand of black hair to her nose.

They spent the rest of the evening working on a puzzle and reading to each other. Sadie yawned twice but tried to stifle it.

"You can't hide that you're tired," Hana said. "Brush your teeth, and I'll tuck you in."

"And sing a song?"

"Of course."

While Sadie brushed her teeth, Hana positioned Sadie's pillow with Fabia propped up on it. After Sadie climbed into bed, Hana tucked the sheet under her chin.

"Fabia is going to sleep between us," Sadie said, moving the doll to her left.

"Perfect."

Sadie wiggled into position. "Do you ever sing to Daud?" she asked.

"He's heard me sing," Hana replied

slowly. "But he's never asked me to sing a song for him like I do for you."

"You should," Sadie said. "He'll like it, and it won't make me jealous. I'm ready for my song."

"Close your eyes."

Hana began to hum. It always took a while for a spontaneous song to grow and build. Tonight, the words rose up from the deepest part of her heart. When that happened she always sang in Arabic. She began with a prayer for inspiration that transitioned into declarations of the will of God over Sadie Neumann's life. Hana had a rich, mellow alto voice. It was the perfect sound for releasing a song with substance, a musical foundation upon which to build life. Even after Sadie was asleep, Hana continued to sing in a soft voice until fully releasing the pleasant burden of her heart. Finishing with the rise and fall of a final hum, she leaned over and kissed Sadie on the forehead.

CHAPTER 10

A young woman wearing the olive-green uniform of the Israeli border patrol began asking Daud the standard entry questions in Arabic. Daud showed his passport and replied in the same language. She searched the vehicle and told him he could proceed into the Israeli terminal to complete the process for entry into Israel and approved passage to the Jordanian border. Daud bought a cup of coffee to drink and filled out the necessary paperwork. After completing the forms, he returned to the parking lot and checked his watch. It was another six and a half hours to the capital of Jordan, home to over four million people. Daud placed his right hand on the driver's-side door handle.

"Ibrahim Abadi?" a male voice called out in Israeli-accented Arabic.

Daud turned around. Three male and one female Israeli border patrol officers approached him.

"Yes," he replied.

"Come with us," one of the men said.

The green-clad Israeli officers escorted Daud back to the terminal and led him through a security door to a holding room that contained only four plastic chairs. No one spoke to him until they were in the room. Daud suspected he'd been singled out as an object lesson for training purposes.

"Stand against the wall with your hands to your sides," a male officer said in broken Arabic.

Daud submitted to the search that revealed nothing except his passport, the exit permit stamped on the Egyptian side of the border, and a wallet containing a single credit card and driver's license. The officer in charge, a man in his thirties with "M. Abelman" embossed on a plastic name tag, opened the other compartments of the wallet and carefully examined it.

"Nothing else?" he asked Daud.

"No, except a cell phone that's in my vehicle. Why am I being questioned?"

"Tell us about your activities since you arrived in Egypt, Mr. Abadi," the officer responded. "Begin with your entry from Jordan."

As part of the mission, Daud had a pre-

146

pared response that meshed with his alias as Rasheed Sayyid and included details an interrogator could verify without uncovering the real reason Daud had traveled to Sharm el-Sheikh. Nothing like that existed for Ibrahim Abadi.

"I spent four days in the Sharm el-Sheikh area, and I'm on my way back to Amman." Daud stopped.

"Where did you stay?"

Daud gave the name of the Suef fishing resort since it was the only place where the registration would match the name on his new passport. Abelman motioned to the young woman, who immediately left the room. Daud knew that in a few minutes he would be asked where else he'd stayed in Sharm el-Sheikh.

"Does the name Rasheed Sayyid mean anything to you?" the officer asked.

Daud's eyes widened. He now knew what had happened. His photo hadn't stayed on the Egyptian side of the border. Anyone suspected of a crime in Egypt wouldn't be welcome in Israel either. He paused before answering. The officer turned to one of the other guards, who handed him the wanted poster. Seeing it up close, Daud recognized it as an image taken when he'd subdued the security guard at the restaurant. The officer continued.

"I don't want to upset our Egyptian neighbors by letting you avoid prosecution for crimes committed by Rasheed Sayyid in Sharm el-Sheikh. You're going to have to convince me why I shouldn't turn you over to them."

Daud glanced around at the other personnel in the room. The young men were attempting to look relaxed and nonchalant, but he could sense their tension. The officer was also on edge.

"Who on duty today has the highest level Israeli security clearance?" Daud asked in Hebrew.

"That would be me," Abelman responded in the same language with a surprised expression on his face.

"I'm going to give you a phone number for a government office in Tel Aviv," Daud continued. "Someone there will tell you what to do with me but will want to limit the number of people who know about it."

"What kind of government office?" Abelman asked.

"Make the call and you'll find out," Daud replied.

The young soldiers glanced at each other and stared at Daud. Abelman turned to the young man who'd searched Daud.

"He was clean?"

"Yes, sir."

Abelman hesitated.

"Would you feel better if I were in restraints?" Daud asked, holding out his hands. "If so, put on a set of handcuffs."

"Do it," the officer in charge said.

The young man who'd frisked Daud gingerly secured handcuffs on Daud's wrists.

The door opened and the young woman returned. "Mr. Abadi only stayed at the resort for one night."

An hour later and as the result of communication with Aaron Levy, Daud's old boss with the Shin Bet, the senior border patrol officer escorted Daud back to the BMW.

"Thank you," Daud said, extending his hand to the border patrol officer.

"You're welcome," Abelman replied and then offered Daud a folded copy of the wanted poster. "Would you like a souvenir?"

"No, I'd rather not have to explain it when I cross the Jordanian border."

Hana woke up to the sound of Sadie mumbling something in her sleep. Lying still, she tried to discern if it was the sound of a nightmare emerging from the trauma of the girl's past.

"No, Katelin," Sadie said distinctly. "That's my seat."

Hana relaxed. Sorting through conflicts common to eight-year-old girls was a twenty-four-hour-a-day job. The muttering ceased, and Sadie's breathing became steady. Hana slipped out of bed and went into the living room, where the most prominent sound was Leon snoring in his cage in the kitchen. The dog might moan and groan in his sleep, but he lived a carefree life, and Hana didn't worry about his emotional health.

Hana curled up on the sofa with her legs beneath her and opened her Bible. The time she'd spent singing over Sadie before the girl fell asleep was fresh in her mind, and she wrote down some of the words and phrases that had bubbled up from her spirit during the spontaneous worship and intercession. She also wrote the prayer she'd taught her young guest at the dinner table. At the bottom of the page she wrote Sadie's full name and the date. She then went back to the top and reread what she'd written. Revelation and insight have multiple layers for those willing to search for new facets of truth. A particular phrase about Sadie encountering God's jealous love caught

Hana's attention. She closed her eyes to rest there for a while.

"Hana."

The tiny voice interrupted Hana's thoughts and caused her to jump. Sadie had quietly crept into the living room.

"I'm thirsty and I want some juice, but I don't want to wake up Leon by going into the kitchen."

Hana's thumping heart slowed. "Wait here," she said.

Hana poured a small cup of juice. Leon opened a single eye when she closed the door of the refrigerator but didn't react to her presence. She took the cup to Sadie, who was sitting on the couch looking at Hana's prayer journal.

"You write in three languages?" Sadie asked, turning the pages. "English, Hebrew, and what's this one?"

Hana resisted the urge to grab the private journal from Sadie's hands. Even Daud knew not to peek at the pages. If Hana wrote something she wanted him to read, she showed him where to start and stop.

"Arabic too. And yes, it depends on who and what I'm thinking and praying about."

"God knows how to speak and read all languages," Sadie said. "A boy in my class says God only speaks and reads Hebrew

151

because that's the language of the Torah. I think he's wrong, and I'm going to tell him about you."

"Do you think that will change his mind?"

"No." Sadie sniffed. "But he should know how smart and close to God you are. I always get goose bumps when you sing and pray."

"Goose bumps?"

"I feel tingly," Sadie said, rubbing her arms. "It happened last night when you thought I was asleep."

Hana nodded. "I get it. And you were asleep."

"Really? Then why do I remember you kissing me on the forehead?"

"Okay, you fooled me."

"That's not why I faked sleep. I didn't want you to stop if you thought the song wasn't making me sleepy. It worked. I was so relaxed."

Sadie glanced down at Hana's most recent entry written in Arabic.

"Can you tell me what this says? Arabic writing is so pretty. It looks like lines swimming across the paper."

"Let me read it out loud. Then I'll tell you what part of it says."

"Why not all of it? Is it about me?"

"Be glad I'm not sending you straight

back to bed."

Sadie nestled in close and listened as Hana read the prayers and declarations. When she finished, Sadie sighed.

"I heard my name, but you pronounced it differently," she said.

"That's right. And I wrote it in Arabic letters at the bottom of the page."

Sadie carefully studied the forms and shapes that made up her name. "I want to learn how to do that," she said. "Will you teach me?"

"Yes, but not at three fifteen in the morning. You need to get back in bed and sleep."

"What about you?"

"I won't be long."

Sadie hugged Hana and returned to the bedroom. Hana flipped to an earlier entry in the prayer journal where she'd written prayers in English for Ben and Sadie asking God to bring the right person into their lives, not to replace Gloria, but to fulfill her own unique role. Hana wrote Laura's name in the margin with a big question mark beside it, then repeated the prayer. When she finished, her phone, which she'd placed on an end table beside the sofa, buzzed twice to signal a text message. It wasn't unusual for Hana to receive a message in the middle of the night from her family in

Israel since it was morning in the Middle East. She didn't recognize the phone number of the sender. Opening the text, she gasped and raised her hand to her mouth.

Just boarded a flight to New York. Will see you this evening. All is well. I carry you always in the center of my heart. Daud.

Tears of relief and gratitude gushed from Hana's eyes at the release of pent-up worry and fear. When her eyes cleared, she read the text over and over so she could savor every word. She decided it was worth recording in her journal with the date and time of receipt. When she finished, she prepared to return to bed. Suddenly, she realized that she hadn't responded to Daud's text.

Hallelujah and much love forever and ever. I can't wait to see you and hold you in my arms. Hana.

She found Sadie asleep. Hana didn't bother to close her eyes. Instead, she liberated her imagination to think about Daud's return. Sometimes it was better to be excited than rested.

Hana heard Sadie stirring around 6:00 a.m. The girl rolled over, and her eyes blinked open. She stretched her arms above her head. Hana turned on her side so she faced her.

"I'm so happy," Sadie said.

"Why?"

"I sleep the best at your house than anyplace else. I love my room, but it's so refreshing here."

Hana smiled at Sadie's description. "I'm glad it makes you feel that way. What do you want for breakfast?"

"Surprise me."

Sadie flopped onto her back and splayed out her arms on top of the cream-colored duvet.

"Would you like it served in bed?" Hana asked.

Sadie came fully awake at the question and stared at Hana. "Are you serious?"

"No. Let's fix it together."

"Okay, I guess so. Can I take Leon outside?"

"Yes."

Leon circled Sadie excitedly in the kitchen while she tried to attach his leash. When she opened the door, he dragged her into the yard. Hana watched from the window. Once he was on the grass, the dog settled down. He trotted to the edge of the yard and continued a couple of feet into a wild, wooded area. Sadie brought him back into the house where he loudly lapped up water before eating his breakfast. Hana poured Sadie a glass of orange juice and a cup of black coffee for herself. Sadie scratched Leon's ears.

"If you ask my daddy, do you think he'll buy me a puppy for my birthday?"

A dog had been on Sadie's wish list for Hanukkah and her birthday as long as Hana had known her.

"What does he say when you ask him?"

"To stop asking."

"Then I don't think I can help. Would you like a Middle Eastern breakfast?"

"I don't want any of those little fish," Sadie replied. "I tried them once with my grammy and I didn't like them."

"Sardines."

"Yeah. Do you have any of the granola you make yourself? I like that with milk and cut-up pieces of banana on top."

Hana had purchased the ingredients to fix shakshuka, a North African–style poached egg and tomato dish that was popular in Israel for breakfast, but she could save the ingredients and prepare it for Daud, who loved it.

"Okay."

They sat at a table at the end of the living/

dining room nearest the kitchen. The granola included rolled oats, multiple kinds of chopped nuts, coconut flakes, apricots, raisins, dried pineapple, and diced dried dates as a sweetener. Dates were Hana's childhood candy. She ate her granola mixed with plain organic yogurt.

"I never went back to sleep after we got up in the night," Hana said.

"Aren't you tired?"

"No, excited." Hana smiled. "Daud texted me. He's going to be home this evening."

"Yay! I wish I could see him."

Sadie liked to squeeze Daud's arms and feel his muscles. He'd grown up with a brother and no sisters, so relating to a little girl was new territory for him.

"We'll do that soon. I have a surprise for him."

Hana told Sadie about the Land Rover. The girl's eyes widened. "That is a big gift. And it's not his birthday?"

"Not for a couple of months."

Sadie ate thoughtfully for a few moments. "If you buy him a car, he should buy you something big too."

"What would you suggest?"

Sadie touched the diamond ring on Hana's left hand. "You already have a nice ring."

She pointed to Leon, who was munching on a large bowl of dry food. "And you have a dog."

Sadie continued to eat. "I know!" she exclaimed. "And it's something I bet you want! Do you want to guess?"

Hana had no idea what might be in Sadie's head. "No, tell me, please."

Sadie leaned closer across the table. "Daud should buy you a house of your own. You can make it all pretty with the things you especially like."

A home of her own was a desire so deep in the shadows of possibility that Hana hadn't let herself glance in that direction. Sadie's words brought it abruptly into the open.

"Where did that idea come from?" she managed.

"Maybe it's like what you write in your book when you wake up in the night," Sadie replied matter-of-factly as she took another bite of granola with a thick slice of banana on top. "If you write it down, make sure you do it in English and say that it was my idea."

CHAPTER 11

Rahal Abaza was used to getting his way and succeeding in everything he attempted. Mustafa's death was a failure. During the past three years, Rahal, Khalil, Mustafa, and a small cadre of followers had helped arm Shiite guerrilla fighters in Yemen and murdered two Koreans who came to Qatar under the pretext of being foreign workers but who were secretly working for a Christian organization seeking to convert Muslims. Most recently they'd torched the home of a Sunni professor living in Kuwait who promoted interfaith reconciliation within Islam. The professor's teenage daughter died in the fire.

The plan to kill Artem Kolisnyk was an ambitious objective. The Ukrainian scientist had defrauded them of over a million dollars after furnishing hundreds of pages of worthless documents supposedly regarding short-range missile technology. Rahal had hoped to sell the information for a profit to Iran and give it for free to Hezbollah, the Shiite terrorist organization in Lebanon. He'd been humiliated when he learned Kolisnyk had omitted key technical data.

A sandstorm was moving across the desert north of Doha. Rahal and Khalil were sitting together on an outside terrace beneath a large umbrella that shielded them from the late-afternoon sun. Khalil was on the phone with the lawyer in Sharm el-Sheikh. He mostly listened. When the call ended, Khalil turned to Rahal, who could see a tear in his assistant's right eye.

"The lawyer says the Egyptians buried Mustafa in a pauper's grave with no marker."

The two men sat in silence for several moments.

"But his name is honored and glorious," Rahal said.

Khalil wiped his eyes and cleared his throat. "Kolisnyk didn't kill Mustafa. The report filed by the Egyptian police says a foreign agent named Rasheed Sayyid killed Mustafa and kidnapped Kolisnyk and his wife. The Egyptians believe the agent was working for the Americans or Israelis. He took the Kolisnyks to the marina in Sharm el-Sheikh where there was a gun battle. The police don't know whether Kolisnyk and his wife survived or not. They were last seen near a large private yacht registered to a Frenchman. The yacht left the marina during the fight. The Egyptians don't know who was on it, but they did not find any bodies at the scene."

Rahal thought for a moment. "The Egyptians would manufacture a story about a kidnapping as a ruse to throw off anyone who is after Kolisnyk. Remember, I thought the Egyptians were going to take him to Cairo so he could work for them."

"Maybe, but the lawyer believes Kolisnyk was kidnapped. He claims the high-level official he spoke with at the police department would tell him otherwise."

Rahal twirled the fringe of the white robe that covered his arms. "Sayyid may be the man Mustafa saw approach Kolisnyk at the restaurant earlier that evening," he said.

"Yes. Our solicitor is going to send me a link to a video posted on social media involving an argument between Kolisnyk and the man at the restaurant. He says a security guard also got involved. The Egyptian police used the video to somehow link Sayyid to the Kolisnyks and Mustafa. The lawyer says it's going to take more money to find out why."

Rahal set his jaw. "The lawyer in Sharm el-Sheikh is robbing us. He already knows the answer."

"Should I pay him?"

The rapidly moving sandstorm was now receding across the horizon. Doha would be spared a messy cleanup. Rahal stood up. "Yes, but tell him this time we want everything."

Exhausted, Daud slept during the flight from Amman to New York. It was early in the evening when he arrived in Atlanta and called Hana to let her know he was on the ground.

"I'm inside the airport," she said in Arabic and told him the location of the coffee shop where she was waiting.

"That wasn't necessary. I could have met you at the curb."

"Trust me," Hana said.

"Habibi, ya nour el ein," Daud replied, which meant, "My love, you are the light of my eye."

"I wish I'd said it first."

"It's better coming from the man."

Even though he was tired, there was anticipation in Daud's step as he made his way through the crowded airport. He saw Hana before she saw him. She was wearing a casual blue dress that he liked. Without a doubt, Hana was the most beautiful woman on earth. She saw him, and a joyous welcome radiated from her smile. Daud jogged toward her and wrapped his arms around her as tightly as he could without hurting her. It was several seconds before he lessened his grip and kissed her on the lips.

"I missed you," they both said simultaneously and then repeated it together again.

Hana laughed and kissed Daud. They walked arm in arm. Hana chatted away about some of the things that had happened while he'd been away. He didn't care what she said as long as he could listen to her voice. Suddenly, she stopped as they approached a row of exit doors.

"Were you ever in danger?" she asked, turning toward him. "I tried not to worry too much, but you know it was impossible not to."

"There were some moments —" Daud began, thinking about the cut on his arm that he would have to explain to her later. "But I'm here with you."

They continued out of the airport.

"Did you receive any extra attention from airport security?" Hana asked.

"No, I breezed through passport control, even though —" Daud stopped.

"What?" Hana asked, glancing sideways. "Can you tell me?"

"I was traveling with false documents given to me as part of the mission."

Hana nodded. "Did they show that you were married?"

Daud realized that his wedding ring was still in his pocket. He pulled it out and quickly slipped it on his finger. "No, I'm listed as single to avoid more questions that would require backup data. I'll turn the documents in when I travel to Washington in a few days for a debriefing."

One of the things Daud had worked on in his mind during the ninety-minute flight from New York to Atlanta was a bluntly honest report for Charlie.

"How long will that last?" Hana asked.

"Only a day. As a contractor, I'm more on the periphery than when I worked for the Shin Bet in Israel."

Hana stopped. "Close your eyes and take me by the hand," she said.

"Why?"

"Just do it."

Daud shut his eyes and let Hana guide him a few steps forward and then around a corner.

"You can let go now," she said.

He smiled. "But I don't want to."

"Open your eyes."

Daud opened his eyes. There was a row of vehicles in front of him. To the right was a blue minivan and to the left a brown pickup truck. Directly in front of him was a white Land Rover. Except for the color, it could have been a twin to the vehicle he drove when he lived in Jerusalem. Daud shook his head and blinked his eyes.

"What?"

"I bought it for you," Hana announced, speaking rapidly. "Do you like it? We've been talking about you needing a car, and I know how much you loved the Land Rover you drove when we first met."

Daud looked it over and thought about the tense moments he'd spent in the rented vehicle as he tried to escape from Egypt.

"What do you think?" Hana continued anxiously as Daud remained silent. "Is the color okay? I know it's not green like your other one, but the dealer who helped me find it said that wouldn't be important to a man."

"I, uh, it's great," Daud managed.

"Oh." Hana's face fell.

"No, no, no!" Daud gathered himself. "It looks like it's in great shape. The color is fine. And I'm really glad you didn't buy me a BMW."

"A BMW?"

Daud laughed. He felt the tension and stress lurking in his soul draining out. Hana looked totally confused. Daud put his arm around her.

"This is the best gift anyone has ever given me."

Hana awoke in the night and a split second later realized that Daud was sleeping soundly beside her. She sank back with relief into her pillow. Daud's right arm was hidden beneath the covers. All he'd told her when he showed her the angry gash was that he'd had to unexpectedly defend himself, which caused panic to rise up inside Hana like an ocean wave. Daud promised to make an appointment with a doctor if it showed any signs of infection.

Seated on the sofa, Hana took out her journal and began to record not her fears about Daud's arm being infected but her thanks that Daud was alive. She quickly filled several lines with words of gratitude. Daud's work had always been dangerous, yet necessary to save the lives of others. But now she was ready for the perilous times to end. Wanting to focus on something positive, she made an entry in her journal expressing appreciation to the Lord for bringing them together and followed this with a list of dreams for their future.

Hana had wondered if marriage would diminish her sense of intimacy with the Lord because she now shared her love so deeply with another human being. The opposite had occurred. Daud's love for her and hers for him had expanded her capacity to receive divine love. More love opened the door for more love that opened the door for more love in a beautiful paradox. Hana closed her eyes as a wave of deep peace washed over her. Even anxiety with a reason evaporated in the presence of all-encompassing grace and shalom.

When she returned to bed Daud hadn't moved an inch, and he remained asleep when Hana woke in the morning. She tiptoed into the kitchen to prepare the shakshuka she'd offered Sadie. Thirty minutes later a sleepy-eyed Daud appeared. He had a serious case of bed head, and his black hair stuck up at odd angles.

"Do you want me to take out Leon?" he asked between yawns.

"No, I'll do it in a minute. Take a shower and comb your hair so I can recognize you."

Daud disappeared. He took long showers and loved standing motionless beneath hot water. By the time he returned wearing a blue cotton shirt and white shorts, breakfast was almost ready.

"That's much better," Hana said, pointing to Daud's head.

He came over and kissed her. "You look beautiful no matter the time of day or night," he said. "How do you do that?"

Hana pointed to the coffeepot. "Fix a cup of coffee the way I like it while I decide whether to answer that question."

They ate at the small round table where Hana and Sadie had enjoyed pizza. She'd positioned the table in front of a large window so they could see the backyard.

"Tell me every detail about buying the Land Rover," Daud said. "I was in shock last night and didn't react as I should have. I can't remember seeing a true off-road vehicle like that since I came to America."

Hana told him about meeting Abdul Erakat at the Lebanese deli and how quickly the car dealer was able to put together a deal.

"How did you pay for it?" Daud asked.

"With my own money that I saved before we were married," Hana answered with an edge in her voice.

"I would have been glad to help pay for it too."

"But then it wouldn't have been a present."

Daud reached across and touched Hana's hand. "And like I said last night at the airport, it's the best present I've ever received. I'm going to find a mountain road where a regular vehicle can't go and take you all the way to the top."

Hana didn't relish the thought of bouncing up and down on a rough road but generated a halfhearted smile. "We can have a picnic," she said.

They ate in silence for a few moments.

"I've been thinking about another way to spend money," Hana said. "What do you think about looking at houses?"

"Now?" Daud asked, raising his eyebrows.

Hana told him about her conversation with Sadie.

"Where would you want to look?" Daud asked.

Daud's question was completely practical, but it touched a place of deep sadness in Hana's heart. In Arab culture, family bonds were greater than all other allegiances, and clustering together communally was common. Hana's large family believed strongly in this principle. However, because of Daud's previous work for the Shin Bet, a place for the young couple in Israel was out

169

of the question. The threats related to his undercover activities, particularly caused by his work in the Neumann case, were too great.

"I don't know," she sighed.

"Would it have to be in Atlanta?"

"What do you mean? This is our home now."

Daud didn't immediately respond. "You're right," he said. "This is the place to begin, but we need to save more money toward a down payment. I'm not comfortable with the America way of borrowing all the money for a home and then paying so much interest on the debt. I'm glad you didn't borrow any money to buy the Land Rover and should have made that clear. But can we buy a vacant lot and build a house over an eight- or nine-year period like your father did?"

"Most places wouldn't allow that kind of delay," Hana said doubtfully. "American construction laws are different. I'm just so glad you're home that I don't want to think about anything else."

She took her plate into the kitchen. Daud followed with his.

"Do you want to leave Leon with me?" he asked. "I don't have any plans except to go for a run."

170

"No, he's already on the schedule for the kennel, and you need a day to relax. How does your arm feel?"

Daud glanced down at the cut. It was red and somewhat inflamed, perhaps because of the time he'd spent in the water searching for Artem Kolisnyk. "I think it will be fine."

"Remember your promise to call the doctor if it gets infected."

CHAPTER 12

After Hana left for work, Daud logged in to his business email account. There were inquiries from two US companies interested in his services. One was from a company in South Carolina marketing solar energy technology to Israel and Jordan. He sent a reply requesting more details. He then sent Charlie a secure email notifying him of his return to Atlanta. Thirty minutes later the CIA officer responded with the time and place for a meeting two days later in Washington to debrief about the Sharm el-Sheikh mission. Daud looked up the address for the building and pulled it up on Google Earth. It was in a nondescript office park several miles from the center of the city. Not surprising. Covert operations weren't always based at the CIA's headquarters in Langley, Virginia. Daud booked a flight.

Putting on his running shorts, shirt, and shoes, Daud drove the Land Rover to the access point for a series of trails that paralleled the Chattahoochee River, a broad waterway that flowed through the metropolitan area. Daud was a strong, muscular man, and his running style was thunderous, not light-footed. He could wear out a pair of running shoes in three months or less. One thing he'd enjoyed since moving to Atlanta was running through deciduous forests that didn't exist in the Middle East. The canopy of leaves overhead created a kaleidoscope of sunny patterns on the ground. The physical exertion quieted competing thoughts and enabled him to focus. He returned to his brief conversation with Hana about buying a house.

The possibility of living in Israel was taboo to Hana because Daud couldn't guarantee her that the people who wanted him dead were out of the picture. But America still felt like a temporary way station, not a long-term destination. Jerusalem was the place on earth that owned his heart. Financially, it would be difficult for them to have a place of their own in Jerusalem. The Holy City's popularity with diaspora Jews from all over the world made it a very expensive place to live. A house was out of the question, but an apartment in a large building could be an option. They would need to avoid Beit

Hanina, the Arab neighborhood where Daud lived when he worked as a private investigator and undercover agent for the Shin Bet. Not many Jerusalem neighborhoods had a significant mix of Jews and Arabs, but there were a few exceptions, including the French Hill area where Hana had lived when she attended Hebrew University. A modest apartment for two in French Hill, while extremely pricey by Atlanta standards, would be reasonable in Israel.

Five miles into the run, Daud reached a turnaround spot at the edge of the river. It was a place where weekend rafters would take out boats and inner tubes after floating in the slow-moving current. Today there were a couple of pickup trucks in the parking lot but no sign of people. Daud paused to look across the broad expanse of the river. He felt his cell phone vibrate. It was the number for Hana's law firm. Usually she called him directly from her cell phone.

"Did you lose your phone?" he asked in Arabic.

"Excuse me," a man replied in English. "This is Leon Lowenstein."

"Hello," Daud said in English. "I thought it was Hana calling."

"Sure. I understand you've been out of

174

town for a couple of weeks. Welcome back."

"Thanks."

"Did Hana mention the interfaith forum we're sponsoring about Israel?"

"No."

Daud listened as Mr. Lowenstein described the purpose of the gathering and Hana's role in it. Even though he'd just been thinking about living in Israel, Daud was immediately concerned about her safety.

"With her unique perspective, the attendees will hear vital insights," Mr. Lowenstein continued. "And I was wondering if you'd be interested in organizing security. Hana told me that's what you've been doing for the past few months. We'd pay you market rate."

Event security wasn't really Daud's area of expertise.

"I mostly work with companies setting up offices in the Middle East," he replied and then pulled out an English phrase he'd recently added to his professional lexicon. "I create long-term protocols for businesses."

"This would be easy compared to that. Everything would be local. Talk it over with Hana and let me know. I'd like to give you the business."

The call ended. During the rest of the run, Daud didn't think about apartments in Jerusalem. He thought about the significant security needs for a crowd of two to three thousand people. In Israel such a large gathering would mandate sophisticated metal detectors and screening stations for everyone wanting to enter the venue. Suspicious persons would be profiled and subjected to closer scrutiny. Even with the changes implemented since 9/11, America remained an open and vulnerable society. And for Hana to speak publicly about Israel and the relationship between Arabs and Jews was inviting serious trouble.

"How does it feel to have your man back in the nest?" Janet asked.

"It's a small nest, and he's a big bird," Hana answered with a smile. "But because it's Daud, I don't mind being crowded."

"You should seriously think about finding a larger home. That tiny place is barely bigger than a backyard playhouse."

"It's fine for now."

"Not if Leon gets any bigger or you do too." Janet patted her stomach.

Hana's eyes widened.

"I know it's none of my business," Janet quickly continued. "But I've told you before what a great mother you'll be when you decide it's time to take that step."

Hana laughed. "How do you expect me to work after this conversation? All I'll be able to think about is a bigger house and how to decorate the nursery."

Inside her office, Hana hummed a melody from her childhood. It was a song her mother sang to her. The simple lyrics focused on familial love and joy. Having a baby and buying a new house were much bigger decisions than purchasing a used Land Rover.

Shortly before noon, Hana received a phone call from Jakob Brodsky. The first thing he did was ask about Daud.

"It's great that he's home safe and sound," Jakob said. "I know you're relieved."

"Yes."

"I wanted to give you a quick update on our case for Vladimir Ivanov."

"When did it become our case?"

"Anytime two people share lamb seasoned with curry sauce, there's an instant bond."

"I'm not sure I agree, but I'm listening."

"Vladimir's aunt in Haifa found an inventory of the great-grandfather's collection. It was prepared as collateral for a loan and certified by a Russian bank officer on May 14, 1910. The first page lists the more important items, like the coins minted during the Bar Kokhba revolt and a clay olive oil lamp. The ceramic head appears directly beneath the coins and is described in Russian as 'decorated head of ancient high-ranking female.' I've seen a copy and should have the original document by the end of the week."

Hana didn't want to squelch Jakob's enthusiasm, but she had to tell him the truth.

"A Russian bank officer doesn't qualify as an archaeological expert," she said. "How would he know it was ancient or a high-ranking female?"

"He wouldn't, but the document establishes the existence of the head in a private collection long before the time when fraud in these types of ancient artifacts really took off. And it syncs up perfectly with the old photographs. I did some research after our lunch, and the big market in fakes didn't develop until after the Dead Sea Scrolls were discovered in 1948. Before that, bogus items surfaced occasionally, but it wasn't a booming business, and never an option for a poor Russian immigrant working on a collective farm in northern Israel. Vladimir's great-grandfather didn't have the cash to buy anything, whether genuine or fake."

Jakob was making a few good points, but they supported only the fact that whatever Vladimir's ancestor took with him from Palestine to Belarus was at least a hundred years old.

"Okay, but that doesn't help you locate the supposed queen's head now. That's what you really need to know."

"Which is where you and Daud come in."

Hana realized she'd fallen into Jakob's trap. She couldn't suppress a smile.

"What do you have in mind?" she asked.

"You and Daud speak multiple languages and have extensive personal contacts within Israel, the West Bank, and elsewhere in the Middle East that I can't touch. He's worked as a private investigator, and you're a lawyer licensed in Israel. What I'd like to do is develop an action plan and go over it with both of you to see what makes sense. I'm setting up a dummy company to act as Vladimir's agent. That keeps his family's name out of the picture and will make inquiries businesslike. Of course, if we locate any of the stolen items, there will likely be a lawsuit to recover them, and the Russian bank inventory will be powerful evidence. Mr. Lowenstein might not let you help me file a lawsuit, but you could direct us to lawyers who could help in Israel or one of the surrounding countries if it becomes necessary."

"Several of those countries don't have a reliably functioning legal system."

"But some do. Since the Gulf War, there seems to be a lot of traffic in antiquities passing through the Persian Gulf states like Bahrain, Qatar, the United Arab Emirates, and Iraq. Publicity about the discovery of the king's head near Metula might flush out whoever has possession of the queen because her value would skyrocket, through a sale to either a museum or a private collector. Most of the items like the coins and pottery are generic, so they will be hard to identify unless chain of custody can be established linking them to the Russian colonel. The queen is the crown jewel."

Hana was impressed with Jakob's creativity. "Daud is keeping a low profile and can't travel all over the place meeting people and asking questions."

"And he knows how to do things discreetly. I don't want to put him in danger, but I bet he'd love to sink his teeth into a project like this."

"I'll mention it to him," she said noncommittally.

"I'd rather make the pitch directly —"

"No. I want to do it."

Jakob paused for a moment. "Then promise you'll do it with the same enthusiasm I have."

Daud picked up Leon from the dog day care center. He'd never owned a pet and was still getting used to the idea of sharing his home with an animal, especially one as big and hungry and hairy as Leon. But Hana loved the furry black-and-white creature. Daud led Leon away from the kennel toward the Land Rover. The dog resisted when they neared the vehicle.

"If you don't want to ride, it's going to be a long walk home," Daud said in Arabic.

Leon sniffed an area near the rear tires. After his run, Daud had driven through a marshy patch not far from the river and collected mud in the rear wheel wells. Apparently Leon's nose picked up an interesting scent in the dried residue. Daud let Leon sniff until the dog seemed satisfied.

"Maybe you could be trained to sniff out contraband," Daud continued in Arabic to Leon. "That way you would have a job to go to every day and contribute to the household income."

Leon looked at Daud with soulful brown eyes before jumping into the passenger seat of the vehicle. An hour later Hana walked through the door, and Leon leapt up from his spot on the kitchen floor and bolted to the door to greet her. She grabbed the dog's head with her hands and planted a quick kiss on the top of his head. She then turned to Daud and extended her arms for an embrace.

"Shouldn't you kiss me before you kiss the dog?" Daud asked.

"There's plenty of love to go around. Help me with the groceries. I'm going to fix you a nice supper."

Daud grabbed all six plastic bags and brought them into the kitchen. Hana was pouring dry dog food into Leon's metal bowl.

"He's already eaten," Daud said, placing the bags on the kitchen counter.

"But that doesn't mean he isn't hungry. I've seen your appetite roar back within an hour of finishing a meal."

"True," Daud admitted.

"Tell me about your day," Hana asked cheerily as she began to unpack the grocery bags.

Daud told her about driving the Land Rover to the trailhead near the river.

"Did you go into any rough areas?" Hana asked.

"Just a little bit of mud that I washed off

after I picked up Leon. He seemed to like exploring a new smell."

"Yes, he's always had a curious nose," Hana said as she rinsed fresh green and red peppers in the sink. "And by the way, I called the vet and scheduled an appointment for him to be neutered."

"Have you ever thought about training him to do something?" Daud asked.

Hana gave Daud a puzzled look. "He's passed all the levels of obedience training at the kennel," she said. "He failed some lessons the first time and had to take them over, but eventually he made it all the way through. I have a certificate to prove it."

"I was thinking about something more financially beneficial."

Daud carefully laid out his idea about training Leon as a detection dog. Hana let him talk as she continued to prepare the food.

"Dogs in the canine unit were invaluable," Daud concluded. "Leon is still just a big puppy, and we could have him checked out by a training facility to determine his aptitude."

"Were any of the IDF dogs ever killed or injured?"

"Uh, not that I recall."

Hana dumped cut-up peppers and onions

into a saucepan of olive oil and faced him. "Leon's most important aptitude is the thing you mentioned when I walked through the door a few minutes ago," she said.

Puzzled, Daud asked, "He can eat all the time?"

"No, his ability to love. That's all I expect or want from him."

As if on cue, Leon walked over to Daud and licked his hand.

"See," Hana observed. "He loves you too."

Hana waited until the last minute to add the thinly cut pieces of Kobe steak to the onions and peppers sizzling in the pan. She didn't want to overcook the expensive steak strips.

"The rice is ready," Daud said.

When they sat down to eat, Daud prayed a blessing. "And God bless Leon," he said in conclusion.

"Even if he doesn't become an income generator for our household," Hana added.

Daud grinned. "Training Leon to work in security at the airport may not be the best idea I've had since we married," he said.

"It was entertaining," Hana replied. "Most of the dogs we used at the airport were German shepherds or Belgian Malinois, although another breed would occasionally be thrown in. I don't ever remember seeing a dog similar to Leon."

At the mention of his name, Leon left the kitchen and trotted into the eating area with his nose in the air.

"No, you're not eating table scraps," Hana said to him in English. "Lie down on your bed."

Daud reloaded his plate with food. "Mr. Lowenstein called me this morning," he said. "He told me about the interfaith forum he's putting together and asked me if I could oversee security for the event."

"What did you say?"

"I didn't commit. My bigger concern was about you participating as a speaker. Are you sure it's a good idea?"

Hana paused before taking another bite. "It came up while you were gone. There might be risks, but it seemed too good to pass up. How else am I going to get a chance to speak to that many people at once about what we both believe? And with you in charge of security, I'll feel safe."

They ate in silence for several moments.

Hana's casual response didn't really reflect how she felt. She knew Daud was right. It was hypocritical for her to be worried about him and tell him he couldn't worry about her.

"Do you want me to tell Mr. Lowenstein

I can't do it?" she asked.

"Maybe," Daud replied.

"Are you serious?" Hana laid her fork beside her plate.

"Did you think I'd just say okay?" Daud asked. "I don't want to keep you from doing something you believe in and want to do, but I need more time to think about it."

Hana tilted her head to the side. "Out of courtesy to Mr. Lowenstein, I need to get back to him soon," she said.

"Sure, that makes sense. I do too."

Hana finished the meal with mixed emotions swirling around inside her. She was glad Daud placed such a high value on her safety but chafed at any restrictions. When she and Jakob were held hostage in Jerusalem, Daud had been forced to act as if he were cooperating with the terrorists. He'd even slapped Hana as part of an interrogation. Afterward, Hana learned Daud's actions were strategic and ultimately led to their rescue, but the incident still troubled her. After dinner she fixed hot tea, and they sat together in the living room.

"Oh, there's something else I needed to tell you that came up while you were gone," she said when they sat down. "It has to do with Jakob Brodsky and a new case."

Daud was immediately interested in Vladimir Ivanov's story. "I'd like to see the photos," he said. "And I'm already thinking about some people in Israel I can recommend to him."

"That's what he's looking for. But with Jakob it might not end there. There's no way the law firm will allow me to get involved as co-counsel, so it will be totally different from the Neumann case."

"I understand. I'll give him a call after I get back from Washington."

CHAPTER 13

Daud left Reagan International Airport and
took an Uber to the meeting with Charlie.
It would be his first time to actually meet
the person in charge of the Sharm el-Sheikh
mission. Daud had some words of construc-
tive criticism for him. The driver stopped in
front of a small two-story building that
looked identical to ten other buildings in
the business complex. The windows were
opaque, and there was no signage on the
exterior except a number — 6035. The front
door was locked, and Daud pushed a button beneath a small speaker. After he identified himself, the door clicked open.

Inside, he encountered a burly young
guard who asked him to empty his pockets
and then waved a wand over him. It clicked
when it reached Daud's right calf. The
young man looked up with raised eyebrows.

"Surgery?" the man asked.

"No, shrapnel fragment from an old land mine."

When he was on active duty with the IDF, Daud and some friends had been hiking in the Golan Heights when a cow in a nearby field stepped on an old Syrian land mine and blew it up. Three tiny jagged pieces of metal flying six inches off the ground shot twenty meters through the air and into Daud's right leg. He pulled up his pant leg and showed the guard the jagged scar.

"Okay," the man said. "The conference room is upstairs to the left."

The meeting room was empty. There were several bottles of water on the table. Daud sat down to wait. A few minutes later a tall, lanky man in his fifties with closely cut gray hair entered.

"Mr. Hasan," the man said with a clipped accent. "Pleased to meet you. I'm Charlie."

Charlie sat across from him. The place at the head of the table remained empty.

"Is anyone else coming?" Daud asked.

"No, but everything we say is being recorded."

"I understand," Daud replied.

Charlie's manner immediately reminded Daud of Aaron Levy. The similarity helped him relax.

"Did you prepare a written report?"

"No," Daud replied, raising his eyebrows. "That wasn't in my orders."

"Good. I don't want there to be a written report. Did you take any notes or prepare any memos about the mission on your computer, phone, or by hand?"

"No. I treated it as a covert operation."

"That's correct," Charlie said as he opened a bottle of water and pushed it across the table to Daud. "I've already met with all others involved in the extraction of Mr. Kolisnyk and Mr. Bondar from Sharm el-Sheikh. Tell me what took place from the time you identified the Kolisnyks at the restaurant and received my message to proceed."

Daud was used to giving verbal accounts of his activities, but not in English. He normally had an excellent ability to communicate details and in a clear, chronological order, but doing it in a language that was his fourth best after Arabic, Hebrew, and Russian was a challenge. Charlie listened without interruption all the way to Daud's arrival at the Newark International Airport. He then spent the next hour and a half asking questions that Daud recognized as having two primary purposes: extracting more information if it existed and probing to see if Daud's story remained credible upon closer scrutiny.

"Talking this long in English is difficult for me," Daud said, taking a sip of water.

"Certainly," Charlie said, leaning back in his chair. "It's clear you didn't approve of the way Lynn supervised the operation."

"Correct. Placing members of the team, along with the Kolisnyks and Uri Bondar, in danger on the dock could have been a disaster. And I should not have been dumped off at the beach and left to find my own way back to the US. I was provided a second passport but nothing else. There was a lack of planning about my exit strategy. It made me believe I was considered . . ." Daud paused as he searched for the right word.

"Expendable?" Charlie suggested. "I understand why you might feel that way, but we also put out a false story about you trying to leave the area through Egypt. That meant the assets searching for you were divided. Your safe return from the mission was a high priority."

Daud wasn't convinced. Charlie continued. "Subsequently, there have been inquiries to our Department of State from the Egyptian government about what happened at Sharm el-Sheikh. The photographs and video taken of you by patrons at the restaurant appeared on social media, and the Egyptians sent them to us for assistance in identification. There is one significant difference between the information they provided and what you just told me."

Daud couldn't recall omitting anything important.

"What is it?"

"The Egyptians now claim you killed the man you encountered at the Kolisnyks' villa."

Daud's mouth went dry. "That's not true."

"You would have been justified in killing him. We're still working on finding out who he was and how he died. Did the wanted poster at the Taba border list any crimes?"

"No, all it said was that I should be arrested so that the police in Sharm el-Sheikh could question me."

"With the video and photos from the restaurant, there's a strong likelihood the Egyptians will identify you. In today's world it's almost impossible to remain invisible."

This wasn't a shock, but it was tough being confronted with the fact that his identity would be compromised.

"What do you think the Egyptians will do?" Daud asked.

"Nothing," Charlie replied. "Because I suspect they killed the intruder after they interrogated him and extracted all the information they could from him. We may or may not receive confirmation of my theory or identify the man who died. Also, I don't know if there was a connection between the intruder and whoever fired the shots at the marina. The situation was much more volatile than anticipated. Lynn was focused on removing the Kolisnyks and Uri Bondar from the area and didn't consult with me about your status."

"I'd like to know more, both about the assassin at the villa and what happened at the marina."

Charlie screwed the top back onto his bottle of water. "We accomplished our goals when we extracted Artem Kolisnyk and Uri Bondar, so answering those questions has a low priority. If you want to find out more, it will be up to you. In the meantime, I agree with your criticism of the way Lynn handled your exit strategy."

Daud knew it was as close to an apology as he was likely to receive.

"One other matter," Charlie added. "I'd like to discuss another mission with you. I think you'll find it —"

"No, thanks," Daud said.

Since Daud was out of town, Hana borrowed his Land Rover and drove it to work. Sitting in traffic elevated above ordinary cars gave her a heady feeling of superiority, but navigating congested streets in a bigger, bulkier vehicle gave her a headache. She was glad when she finally pulled into a space in the parking deck. Before going inside, she took a photo of the Land Rover on her phone to show Janet. The secretary was furiously typing away when Hana approached and interrupted her. Janet placed her earbuds on the desk beside her keyboard.

"Jackson talks so fast he sounds like one of those disclaimers at the end of a drug commercial on TV warning you that taking the pill they're advertising might make your great-grandchildren sick."

Jackson Culpepper was one of the other associates who fed work to Janet. He specialized in employment law for big corporations. When Jackson had a project, it usually involved a lot of paperwork.

"I'll try not to give you much to do until you're finished," Hana said.

"No, I need a break from the motormouth."

"Motormouth" was a term new to Hana.

"Let me show you a photo of Daud's new vehicle," she said. "I drove it to work because he's out of town for the day."

"That's a serious ride," the legal assistant said, looking closely at the phone. "It looks like it could rumble over a big tree trunk if it fell in the middle of a road."

"Except for the color and a few scratches, it's almost exactly like the one he was driving when we first met in Jerusalem."

"Donnie picked me up in a white pickup for our first date. It had more scratches than paint, but he'd done his best to clean it up. That told me a lot about him. Where is Daud traveling this time, or is that a secret?"

"It's not a secret. He's in Washington, DC, but I don't know exactly where he was going for his meeting or who will be there."

Janet shook her head. "Before I met you, I thought being married to someone like Daud would be exciting, but now I know the stress outweighs the adventure. Do you want me to ask the senior partners to give you a big raise so that Daud can stay home and bake cookies?"

Hana smiled. "Daud would eat all the cookies."

"I could use a cookie even though it's early in the morning," Janet said, picking up the earbuds. "A sugar rush would help me keep up with Jackson."

Hana spent the first half of the morning working alone in her office, followed by a long conference call with Mr. Collins and a big client. After the conference call, she checked her cell phone and saw that she'd received two text messages from Ben Neumann wanting to talk to her. Hana immediately called him.

"Sadie is struggling," Ben said. "She met Laura last night. I set everything up perfectly. We ate at a chicken restaurant in the shopping mall near the townhome. Sadie loves that place."

"Where she goes with her poppy," Hana said, referring to Sadie's maternal grandfather.

"Yes. Sadie was rude and pouty."

"Did you try to talk to her about it afterward?"

"Several times, before she ordered me to leave her room so she could go to sleep. I was so anxious and upset that I pressed her too hard, which didn't help. This morning she came out of her room at the last minute and was all business getting ready for school. On my drive to work I thought about you because the two of you have such a special relationship."

Hana could hear the stress in Ben's voice. "You want me to talk to her?"

"Yes, and I'd prefer sooner rather than later, but —"

"I'll pick her up from school this afternoon," Hana said before Ben could finish.

"What are you going to say?"

Hana opened her mouth but then shut it. "I'm not sure," she said. "What do you want me to say?"

"Whatever it takes to get her unstuck. I know it will fall on Laura and me to make this work for Sadie in the long run, but we need reinforcements now. The evening Laura came over and fixed dinner at the townhome, we had a serious conversation about the future and want to get married soon. There's no need for delaying the wedding except for the time it takes to bring Sadie around to accepting the change."

Hana knew that was a pretty big "except." A knot formed in the pit of her stomach. It wasn't her job to manage Ben's life, and she'd never met Laura, but she couldn't shake her reservations about what was happening.

"Daud is out of town and won't be back until late tonight. I'll figure out something fun to do with Sadie and ease into a conversation about what she's feeling and why."

"That's exactly what she needs," Ben replied. "Like any guy, I immediately launched into fix-it mode instead of listening and letting Sadie unpack her emotions."

"What time should I bring her home?"

"No curfew. If she doesn't finish her homework, I'll write an excuse for her teacher. Just do what you think is right. And thank you."

The call ended. Hana pushed away from her desk. Her appetite evaporated. Instead of going out for lunch, she decided to skip eating and pray.

Hana waited in the line of cars. When she crept closer to the pickup point, she saw Sadie standing on the curb looking in her direction. Sadie didn't recognize the Land Rover, so it wasn't until she saw Hana's face that a big smile creased her face and she waved excitedly. Seeing the smile instantly made Hana feel more optimistic. She'd imagined Sadie crying all day at her desk. It took a few more minutes for Hana to reach a spot where one of the teachers on duty released Sadie, who climbed into the rear seat and fastened her seat belt.

"Wow, I feel like I'm on a safari," she said. "Is this Daud's new car?"

"Yes."

"And he let you drive it?"

Hana smiled. "Actually, he's out of town, and I didn't ask him."

"It's okay," Sadie replied. "He loves you

bunches."

"Where would you like to go?" Hana asked.

"You're leaving it up to me?"

"Yes. Anyplace you choose."

"Let's get ice cream."

The ice cream parlor had been a recurring destination during their relationship. The first visit didn't end well when Sadie mentioned that she'd shared an ice cream treat with her mother moments before Gloria was murdered. Follow-up trips had been much more benign. While she drove, Hana prayed that this visit would have a positive outcome. From the rear seat, Sadie jabbered about her day at school without any mention of her dad or Laura.

"What did you do today?" Sadie asked, suddenly switching gears.

"I worked in my office for a while and then participated in a conference call. I translated from English to Hebrew and Hebrew to English for the people on the phone."

"One day we should agree to only talk in Hebrew no matter how hard it is," Sadie said. "They call that submersion."

"Immersion," Hana corrected her. "But it's the same idea."

"Let's don't do it today," Sadie added.

"My brain is already tired from school."

There were only a couple of cars parked in front of the ice cream parlor. Sadie hopped out and waited for Hana at the front door.

"Can I get anything I want?" Sadie asked.

The menu included massive sundaes that cost as much as a meal in a nice restaurant. Hana hesitated.

"What I really want is one scoop of pistachio in a waffle cone," Sadie continued. "Maxie, a new girl at school, told me it's her favorite."

"Do you want a sample to make sure you like it?" Hana asked.

Sadie sampled a tiny spoonful of the light green ice cream with olive-colored nut particles mixed in. "Yes, I like it," Sadie said and nodded.

Hana went traditional with a scoop of natural vanilla bean ice cream in a cup. They sat at a small square table. Sadie licked the ice cream and nibbled a piece of her waffle cone.

"I'm glad you picked me up from school," she said. "I didn't want to see my daddy. I'm mad at him right now."

Hana resisted the urge to ask a question to which she already knew the answer.

"Do you know about Laura?" Sadie continued with a forlorn expression on her face. "I guess she's his girlfriend."

"Yes. Your daddy told me about her the evening I came over and we made homemade hummus. And I know they had dinner together the night you stayed at my house."

"Why didn't you tell me about her?"

"That was for your daddy to decide."

"He should have said something to me before taking me to a restaurant to meet her for the first time. She walked up and kissed him on the lips! I didn't know who she was."

Hana didn't have a good defense for Ben. "I'm sure he did what he thought was best."

"He was wrong! I have to say I'm sorry when I make a mistake. Don't you think he should too?"

Hana knew she had to proceed delicately. "Did you tell him that?" she asked.

"No, it will just make him madder. He didn't yell at me, but I could tell he was mad." The words tumbled fast from the little girl. "I didn't want Laura to hug me. She tried to grab me when we finished eating, but I didn't let her and walked away. When I looked over my shoulder, I saw her give my daddy a mean look. I don't ever want to see her again!"

Hana's ice cream remained untouched while she listened. Sadie had gone much deeper in her analysis and rejection of Laura than Hana would have imagined.

"Would you be willing to give them a second chance to do things better?" she asked tentatively.

It was a risky question, because a negative answer would reinforce and harden Sadie's position.

"I don't know," Sadie answered with a shrug. "Maybe."

"Would it help if I talked to your daddy about how you feel?"

"I guess so."

"What would you want me to say to him?"

Sadie was silent for several moments. Then she brightened up and smiled. "Tell my daddy that I want him to meet someone just like you!"

CHAPTER 14

Daud rode a MARTA train from the airport to a station not far from their house and caught an Uber ride. Once home, he saw Hana's car parked in her spot and smiled at the thought of her navigating Atlanta traffic in the Land Rover. She was a good driver, but the large, heavy vehicle required extra space to maneuver. Daud started a load of laundry. Checking his watch, he sent Hana a text asking her if she wanted him to pick up Leon. She quickly replied.

No. I have him.

A few minutes later Hana came through the door with Leon on a leash. She was trying to control the dog while holding her cell phone to her ear. She thrust the leash toward Daud.

"Can you take him for a quick walk?" she asked, slightly breathless. "I need to finish this call with Ben Neumann."

Daud took Leon outside. He could see Hana walking back and forth and talking in an animated fashion. When he reentered the house, Hana had gone into their bedroom. Daud fed and watered Leon.

"Are you okay?" he asked when Hana returned.

Barefoot, she'd changed into workout clothes. "No," she replied, flopping down in a chair at the table where they ate.

Daud listened as she explained what was going on with Ben and Sadie.

"I shouldn't have told Ben that I had questions about his relationship with Laura, but one comment led to another, and when he began defending himself, I felt trapped. It took me almost half an hour to back away from the hole I dug. I never told him what Sadie said about wanting him to meet someone like me. If that ever comes out, he might totally cut off my relationship with her."

"Maybe you should end it voluntarily."

"What!" Hana exclaimed.

"There was a season for you to be involved with Sadie," Daud replied in a level tone of voice. "But it's clear she's connected with you in a way that's going to make it hard for her to develop a healthy relationship with any potential stepmother."

Hana stared wild-eyed at him for a moment before bolting from the table to the bedroom and slamming the door behind her. Daud started to get up and follow her but stopped. Leon was barking at the loud noises. Grabbing the dog's leash, Daud wrote a brief note on a whiteboard stuck to the refrigerator.

I'm taking Leon for a walk.

It was early evening, and as the sun dipped below the tree line the temperature cooled quickly. The night's first crickets were tuning up their songs. Daud's agitation caused him to walk rapidly, which suited Leon, who trotted to keep up.

"I was very calm and didn't raise my voice," Daud said to the dog when they reached the corner at the end of their street and turned right on the sidewalk. "And anyone who heard the facts would agree that what I told her was true."

His tongue hanging out of his mouth, Leon kept looking straight ahead.

"Should I have forced my way into the bedroom to continue the conversation?" Daud asked.

Leon glanced sideways at Daud but continued walking.

"No." Daud stared down the sidewalk toward a large oak tree. "Hana needed space, and you and I needed a walk."

Hana lay sobbing on the bed with her face buried in a pillow. What made the pain worse was a nagging thought in the back of her mind that there was a sliver of truth in what Daud had said to her. Her relationship with Sadie, as beautiful and sweet as it had been, might have a jagged, negative edge. She crammed that thought back into her subconscious by reminding herself that she wasn't opposed to Ben remarrying. She'd be thrilled if the right woman joined him in loving Sadie. All Hana did was voice a reasonable reservation about Laura, a woman she hadn't met. That admission caused another wave of sobs that included a mixture of embarrassment and personal frustration. Hana flipped over onto her back, grabbed a wad of tissues from a box on the nightstand, and wiped her eyes. She breathed in and out several times to regain her composure.

Getting off the bed, she cracked open the door. Daud was gone. She saw his note on the refrigerator. Seeing his handwriting reminded her that he'd picked a terrible

206

time to coldly suggest that Hana cut Sadie out of her life. Another tear coursed down Hana's cheek.

She began to prepare supper, which was a salad topped with smoked salmon. The longer it took Daud and Leon to return, the more anxious she became. She put the finishing touches on the salad and put it in the refrigerator. Ten minutes later Daud opened the door. He gave her an apprehensive look that caused her to burst into tears again.

"Should I leave?" he asked. "I tried to give you space."

"No, no," Hana said, holding up her hands. "I'm a mess and I know it."

Daud released the dog's leash. Leon immediately pattered over to Hana and pressed against her leg.

"He knows you're upset and wants to comfort you," Daud said.

Hana rubbed Leon's head. It actually did help soothe her.

"There was truth in what you told me," she said to Daud, keeping her head down. "But it's hard for me to hear it right now."

"And the last thing I want to do is hurt you."

Hana's lips trembled again, but she pressed them tightly together. "Let's eat."

Dinner together was an act of normalcy that helped Hana more than she suspected.

"Tell me what you can about your trip to Washington," she said.

"There's not much I can say because the details are classified," Daud replied. "The man in charge of the mission reminded me of Aaron Levy and agreed with my assessment of the operation."

A knot formed in Hana's stomach. "Did he mention working with them in the future?"

"Yes, but I told him I wasn't interested."

Hana looked at him with surprise. "Are you serious?"

"Yes."

Hana quickly wiped away another tear. "That's a happy one," she said. "I'm so relieved. But I don't want to change who you are."

"It's too late for that," Daud said, smiling. "Marriage is changing both of us."

They were able to relax for the rest of the evening. Shortly after the time Sadie normally went to bed, Hana asked Daud whether he thought she should call Ben and apologize. He paused for a few moments before shaking his head.

"I think you should allow time for him to talk to Sadie and think about things himself.

Calling so soon makes you look pushy."

Even though she wanted to clear things up, Hana knew it might be best to hold off, for both her and Ben.

"Okay, I'll wait a day or two."

When she slipped out of bed in the middle of the night and returned to the living room, Hana was thankful that she and Daud had resolved the tension between them. One of the lessons drilled into her by her mother was not to let the sun go down on anger. Now that her emotions had calmed, Hana was able to pray for Ben and Sadie. And Laura.

In the morning she had an email from Jakob wanting to discuss Vladimir Ivanov's case. She mentioned it to Daud. "He really wants to talk to both of us," she said.

"Let's meet him either at your office or for lunch."

"I'll suggest the office," Hana said.

"Should I wear my dark-blue suit and yellow power tie?"

Hana shook her head. "No. A yellow tie isn't going to make you any stronger."

After Hana left for work, Daud dropped off Leon at the vet's office and went to a local park to exercise. It was going to be a hot day, and by the time he finished, the sun had risen in the sky, taking the temperature up with it. On his way home, he received a text from Hana.

Meet with Jakob at 1:30 p.m. and Mr. L at 3:00 p.m.

With several hours to fill, Daud completed two proposals for American companies about setting up security protocols for branch offices in the Middle East. One was in Egypt and the other in Lebanon. For the latter, Daud included a scenario in which he would travel to Beirut to provide direct assistance. He didn't include a similar option for the Egyptian project, even though the company's office was in a nice area of Cairo, nowhere near Sharm el-Sheikh or the Taba border crossing. Daud didn't want Egyptian border guards or security police to see his photo at any time in the near future.

He parked the Land Rover in a space reserved for visitors to the law firm. He'd been to the office several times and recognized the young receptionist on duty. While he waited, Daud flipped through an American magazine that focused on economic issues. The door to the office suites opened. It was Hana's assistant.

"It's good to see you," Janet said with a

big smile. "Hana isn't back from a lunch meeting with an out-of-town client and wants you to wait in one of our conference rooms."

Daud followed Janet to a large conference room. It contained a long table with seating for at least thirty people.

"This is where Hana and Mr. Lowenstein first met Jakob Brodsky," Janet said when they entered. "Did she ever tell you about it?"

"No," Daud replied.

"Oh, it was dramatic. And I'm not just talking about seeing the surveillance video of the attack in Jerusalem. That's the day Hana's heart went out to Sadie Neumann."

"Yes, they have a close relationship."

"The closest. Would you like something to drink?"

"Water, please."

Daud sat down and waited. He knew Hana talked to Janet about personal as well as business matters and wondered if she'd asked the assistant what she thought about the latest developments with Ben, Sadie, and Laura. When Janet returned, Jakob was with her.

"Hana should be back shortly," Janet said. "I'll leave you two to talk."

Jakob placed his leather bag and a cup of

coffee on the table. The two men shook hands. Jakob sat beside Daud.

"What did Hana tell you about Mr. Ivanov and the ancient artifacts owned by his great-grandfather?"

Daud summarized what he remembered. While he talked, Jakob removed a laptop from the bag and turned it on. He showed Daud the old photographs and the information given by the Russian bank.

"This time we're not dealing with terrorists," Jakob concluded. "If there are any bad guys, they're probably wearing thick glasses and sitting behind the counter of an antiquities shop in Israel, Riyadh, or Doha. Do you think you can help?"

"Maybe. There are people I can call who may know other people."

"Excellent. Since I last talked to Hana, I used the shell company I created for Vladimir to post inquiries on the Russian web about purchasing biblical artifacts with Bitcoins. If the stuff is still in Russia, that might generate a response. I also provided links to several of the news articles about the king's head discovered in Metula and to websites and forums followed by people interested in that sort of thing. The oligarchs and billionaires created by Putin are looking for things to spend their money on."

"If one of them bought the queen's head, how would you get it away from them?" Daud asked. "They're not wearing thick glasses and sitting in an antiquities shop in Israel. This sort of person would not give up anything he wanted without a fight, and they don't fight by any kind of civilized rules."

"I'll figure that out later," Jakob answered. "The first step is to see if we can locate anything on the list. Along with you making some personal contacts, I'd like your help in setting up a similar search program in Arabic and Hebrew. That way I can cast a much wider net. Hopefully, you and Hana would be willing to read and translate the responses that come in. Because I'm being so specific, it wouldn't take a lot of time, and I think it would be interesting work."

Jakob placed his laptop on the table and took Daud on a tour of the Russian web. Daud was impressed by Jakob's efforts. There were multiple responses to his inquiries. Daud could speak Russian fluently, but his reading wasn't very good. Jakob translated.

"None of these are good leads," Daud said.

"Yet." Jakob raised his right index finger and continued. "But each interaction increases visibility. I'm not discouraged."

Daud thought about the two proposals he'd worked on earlier in the day. By turning down the CIA project, he certainly had time to help Jakob if he liked.

"Could I work on this whenever I wanted to?" he asked.

"Sure. Vladimir has been waiting for decades, but the discovery of the king's head gives us a unique opportunity to act. You could identify yourself with a pseudonym as an employee of Vladimir's corporation."

"Pseudonym?"

"Fake name."

"At first I would only contact individuals I can trust to keep my involvement confidential."

"Sure. I know you were recently out of the country for a while. Are you still working on a project?"

"Only business consulting jobs. It's slow, but I get a few inquiries based on referrals from people I help."

Jakob lowered the laptop's screen. "I don't know when or if I'll be paid by Mr. Ivanov," he said. "I've taken the case on a contingency basis, but I can pay you out of my firm —"

"No, no," Daud said, holding up his hand.

"You are a friend. I won't charge you to talk on the phone and translate a few lines of text on the computer. If you want to put me on a plane, that's a different matter."

"Understood," Jakob said. "And Hana already warned me not to jeopardize your security. You'll decide when or if you want to use your real name. I won't mention you to Vladimir or anyone else. All he knows is that I have multilingual friends with Middle Eastern connections who may help."

"Okay."

Jakob checked his watch. "I guess we're finished here," he said. "Thanks much."

CHAPTER 15

Rahal parked his charcoal-gray Bentley in the climate-controlled underground parking deck. When sandstorms swept in from the Arabian Desert and blanketed Doha with light brown dirt, Rahal's fleet of seven cars remained pristine clean. He had a full-time chauffeur, but often drove himself, especially when he wanted to drive fast. High speeds accentuated the luxury car's smooth ride. Rahal took his tablet from the passenger seat and tossed the keys to his chauffeur.

"How was the car, sir?" the driver asked with a slight bow.

"Perfect," Rahal replied. "I could tell a difference with the new tires."

"Yes, sir. I'm glad you liked them."

Rahal paused. "Your son, Yanis, is he doing well?"

"Excellent. He's been studying hard and looks forward to his next meeting with you."

While he waited for an elevator in the marble-floored lobby of the building, Rahal checked his tablet. There was a message from one of his managers requesting a phone call. Rahal called the young man before entering the ornate front door for the floor that contained the family's living quarters. Inside the residential area a servant pointed toward a salon where Khalil was sitting. Rahal raised his finger to signal the need to wait and called the manager.

"Is there still a problem with the steel shipments?" Rahal asked the supervisor.

There had been a frustrating delay in importing steel beams one of his subsidiaries sold to construction companies that were building the skyscrapers popping up all across Doha.

"No, sir. The Korean cargo ship docked earlier this morning, and x-ray examination of the sample beams is complete. They meet our standards and cost forty percent less than what we have paid for German or American steel."

This would have a significant impact on Rahal's profit margin and provide another example of Allah's blessing.

"Good," he said. "Place an order for more so we can have more on hand."

Rahal ended the call and Khalil stood.

"May we speak in private?" the younger man asked.

Rahal led the way to his private office that overlooked the water. Khalil began to speak as soon as he closed the door. "We have more information about the man who killed Mustafa. He entered Egypt using the name Rasheed Sayyid; however, he left the country with a Jordanian passport identifying him as Ibrahim Abadi. That's the name he used when he entered Israel at the Taba crossing. I doubt either one of these is his real name."

"Israel?" Rahal interjected. "So he was Mossad."

"Maybe," Khalil replied. "The Egyptian authorities let the killer slip through their fingers at the border. After he reached Israel, they lost his trail."

"The Egyptians are lazy dogs."

"Not too lazy," Khalil said. "In addition to the images from the cell phone videos taken at the restaurant in Sharm el-Sheikh, the Egyptians found surveillance recordings of Sayyid/Abadi taken at a local hotel where he stayed for several days, along with video from the exit office at the Taba crossing."

Khalil pressed a button on his tablet and handed it to Rahal. There were six video clips, each no more than thirty seconds in length. In two of them a muscular Arab man walked through the hotel lobby, then entered the hotel restaurant. In the others he continued across the lobby, past the registration desk, and through sliding glass front doors. The quality was much clearer than the cell phone images taken in the dark restaurant. The images from the border clearly showed the same man wearing dark sunglasses. Rahal watched the sequence twice and then returned the tablet to Khalil.

"What is the value of these?" he asked. "I can see his face better, but he's not doing anything."

"It's his face that may help us. With your permission, I would like to circulate these images and find out if anyone sympathetic to the cause of jihad can identify him. Whether he works for Mossad or the Americans or both, someone knows his name."

Rahal hesitated. Thus far, they had kept such a low profile that risk of their own identification was minimal. It had been a great relief that the Egyptians were unable to identify Mustafa and trace him back to Khalil and Rahal.

"I have great concern for your anonymity," Khalil continued.

Rahal nodded. "You know my thoughts. Let me see the videos again."

This time Rahal noticed something else. On every occasion Sayyid/Abadi carried himself with an arrogant confidence that caused righteous rage to rise up in Rahal's heart.

"This man does not deserve to live," he said, returning the tablet to Khalil. "He killed Mustafa and sabotaged our revenge against Kolisnyk."

"May I try to track him down?"

Rahal stared out the window for several seconds. Over the years he'd learned to trust his instincts in making difficult decisions.

"Yes," he answered. "And perhaps he can lead us to Kolisnyk as well. The key to triumph in jihad is perseverance."

"Until death." Khalil rose to his feet.

Hana rushed into the conference room. "Sorry I'm late," she said. "Where's Jakob?"

"Already left," Daud answered. "He told me what he's doing and asked for my help. I agreed."

"I'm sure that made him happy." Hana sat in the chair Jakob had recently vacated. "He was concerned I wouldn't be enthusiastic enough in convincing you to get involved."

Daud gave Hana a summary of the conversation.

220

"You can do a better job of controlling Jakob's demands on your time than I can," she said when he finished. "But explain again how your identity is going to remain hidden when you're communicating with someone you don't trust."

Daud held his finger along his upper lip to mimic a mustache. "I have many disguises even you don't know about."

Hana rolled her eyes. "Can you entertain yourself in here until it's time for us to meet with Mr. Lowenstein?" she asked.

"Yes." Daud took out his phone. "I'm going to start working on my list of contacts for Jakob. The first person I thought about is an art dealer who hired me several years ago to find out which of his employees was stealing from him. He's someone I trust completely."

"Did you find the thief?"

"Yes, it turned out to be his son."

Hana left the conference room to tie up several loose ends that remained from the luncheon with the client. The time passed quickly, and she looked up in surprise when Janet tapped on her door before opening it.

"You have an appointment with Daud and Mr. Lowenstein on your calendar in two minutes," the assistant said.

Hana walked rapidly to the conference

room, but Daud wasn't there. Not wanting to keep Mr. Lowenstein waiting, she continued to his office, where she found Daud and the senior partner sitting across from each other and laughing.

"Come in," Mr. Lowenstein said, motioning with his hand. "I saw your husband sitting in the conference room. He's been entertaining me with stories from his boyhood growing up in the desert."

"Did he mention removing the stingers from scorpions and letting them crawl all over his body?" Hana asked.

"No," Daud answered. "I was telling him about the time a friend and I tried to tame a wild donkey so we could sell it to a Bedouin family. We ended up with bruises instead of shekels."

"Daud agreed to help with security for the interfaith forum," Mr. Lowenstein added. "He says waving a metal-detecting wand over people on their way into the room will not be sufficient. I also remembered that you worked in security at the Tel Aviv airport, so it would be good to hear from both of you at once."

"This will be Daud's area of expertise," Hana deferred.

Daud pressed his hands together in a gesture that had become familiar to Hana.

It meant her husband was about to express a strong opinion.

"I think we should handle the event as if the prime minister of Israel was going to be there," he said. "That means thoroughly checking every person, sending them through a sensitive metal detector, and conducting interviews with select individuals."

"Interviews?" Mr. Lowenstein raised his eyebrows.

"We would profile people: young males without other companions, certain ethnic groups, individuals with Middle Eastern names on their ID. Things like that."

"Americans won't go along with that," Hana interjected. "They'll be offended and say it's too much."

Mr. Lowenstein spoke before Daud could respond. "I hope they do complain," he said. "An experience is often more powerful than a lecture."

Hana gave the senior partner a puzzled look.

He continued. "If people are shown what's necessary to protect those attending public gatherings in Israel, it will underline the words spoken during the forum about the threats the Israeli public faces every day in such a deeply divided society."

Many times Hana had heard Mr. Lowenstein offer a point of view that wasn't on her radar.

"If I'm allowed to implement the level of security I'm recommending, it will make me feel a lot better about Hana participating," Daud said.

"That settles it then," Mr. Lowenstein said, rising from his chair. "Daud, you will be in charge of security for the event. As part of your written proposal, include an explanation that the attendees will experience a level of security that people in Israel, both Jews and Arabs, would encounter if the forum were held in Jerusalem."

"One other thing," Daud said. "Profiling can involve Jews as well as Arabs. Security personnel in Israel don't ignore any source of a threat. That applies to certain segments of Jewish society. Remember, it was a Jewish extremist who assassinated Yitzhak Rabin."

"Hmm," Mr. Lowenstein said. "I'd better run that past the other members of the planning committee."

After Daud left, Hana left her office door cracked open. She could hear Daud talking to Janet, but she couldn't make out what either of them said. A few minutes later there was a soft knock on her door, and

Janet entered. She had a few sheets of paper in her hands and placed them on Hana's desk.

"Daud is a dreamboat," the assistant said.

"That needs an explanation," she replied.

"Sorry. He's so obviously head over heels in love with you that any woman on the planet would want to be in your shoes."

"What makes you think that?" she asked.

"The look in his eyes when he talks about you speaks volumes. And his dreamy accent makes me think of the old movies I watched as a kid, the ones in which a handsome, dark-haired man on a camel rides up and the young heroine instantly falls in love with him."

Hana laughed. "Daud's grandfather was a camel broker. Camels are marvelous creatures for crossing a desert, but there's nothing romantic about them. If we'd met on a camel ride, I'm not sure it would have gone any further."

"Yes, it would have," Janet replied. "Your stars were meant to cross. Oh, how was the meeting with Mr. Lowenstein?"

Hana hadn't yet told her assistant about the interfaith forum.

"I'd come if it's not too expensive," Janet said. "Some of those things can be pricey."

"I'll ask Mr. Lowenstein for some free

passes. I'm sure he'll give me a few. I want at least one friendly face in the crowd."

"And it would give me an excuse to buy a new dress. What sort of things would you say?"

"I thought I would begin with my family's story. My ancestors moved to Nazareth from Lebanon around four hundred years ago and endured centuries of second-class status and discrimination as Christians in the Ottoman Empire."

"Oh, I like making it personal. What kind of discrimination are you talking about?"

"It always included paying extra taxes. Sometimes the taxes were so high that it kept the Christian people in perpetual poverty. And there were rules that restricted Christians and Jews from certain occupations. They could never openly practice their faith, and there were strict mandates against sharing their beliefs with others. They even had to wear special clothes or sew identification patches on their garments."

Janet's eyes widened. "Like the yellow stars the Nazis forced the Jews to wear?"

"That's where the Nazis got the idea."

"This is going to be dramatic," Janet said, nodding. "I know there will be tons more for you to tell, and I can't wait."

She handed Hana the papers in her hand.

"Here's the agreement you dictated before lunch. You said you wanted to review a hard copy."

Hana took the papers. Especially with English, she preferred to hold a sheet of paper in her hand and jot notes before making changes on the electronic version. Shortly after she finished, there was another knock on her door.

"Janet, you don't have to knock every time!" she called out.

The door opened. It was Mr. Lowenstein. Hana started to stand up.

"Stay seated," Mr. Lowenstein said, motioning with his hand. "It slipped my mind earlier, but I wanted to find out what Jakob Brodsky is up to. Gladys told me that Daud met with him in one of our conference rooms."

"I hope that was okay," Hana said. "I was supposed to be there but didn't make it because of an unscheduled lunch with Mr. Collins and the CEO of the Maricoma Group."

"It's not a problem," Mr. Lowenstein said. "Tell me about Brodsky."

"He's investigating a new case," Hana answered. "Jakob wanted to explain the situation to Daud and ask for his help."

"Did he ask you to assist him?"

"Just to offer advice."

"Which is what lawyers do," Mr. Lowenstein shot back. "Your employment agreement with the firm requires you to devote one hundred percent of your legal efforts to what we do here. We've invested a lot in your professional development."

Hana's mouth went dry. "And I appreciate all you've done for me."

"You can talk with Jakob on your own time, but not while you're here at the firm."

"Yes, sir."

The senior partner left. Hana stared unseeing at her computer screen for several seconds. It was fine for Mr. Lowenstein to ask her to work on a non–law firm project like the interfaith forum that wouldn't generate any billable hours, but that didn't mean she had any leeway of her own.

Daud decided his first step in helping Jakob would be to reach out to Avi Labensky, a Jerusalem art dealer. The son of Holocaust survivors from Latvia, Avi was a person with many diverse connections. It took several minutes for Daud to locate the former client's information. Pulling up his investigative report, he remembered the sadness on Avi's face when Daud presented overwhelming proof that the art dealer's son had been stealing thousands of shekels from his father for almost ten years. Avi didn't report his son to the police but terminated Yoni's employment with the family business.

Daud hadn't eaten lunch and fixed a sandwich of salami and spicy Italian ham on ciabatta bread topped with provolone cheese, hot pickled peppers, and a sauce made with lime juice, garlic, and oregano that Hana kept in the refrigerator. He settled down in front of his computer, took a big bite, and noticed that he had several new emails. One was from Avi offering to Skype with him.

"Shalom," Avi said in Hebrew when the face of the sixty-year-old Jewish man with a bushy gray beard and black-rimmed glasses came into view. "Is this my friend Daud calling from America?"

"It's me," Daud answered in the same language. "And I'm honored that you call me a friend."

"One who brings repentance to a house is the kind of friend all men need."

"What do you mean?" Daud asked.

"I should have called you two years ago," Avi began and rubbed his chin. "Yoni has been restored to my heart. After I told him he no longer had a place in the business, he moved to Tel Aviv and didn't speak to me

229

for months. Then I received a check in the mail from him making payment for some of the money he stole. It wasn't much, but it was the first of many checks since then. So far he's paid back almost half of what he owes and regularly visits in our household, which makes his mother happy. Yoni is a different man. The burden of his sin weighed him down. He doesn't know it, but once he pays half the debt, I'm going to forgive the rest. If you hadn't uncovered what he was doing, none of this would have happened. That's why I call you a friend of our house."

Yoni had been surly during the investigation, an attitude that made sense once Daud discovered what was going on.

"That's good news," Daud replied. "What is he doing in Tel Aviv?"

Avi shrugged. "Something to do with the internet that I don't understand. But I asked the son of a friend to check out the company to see if it was legitimate, and he reassured me it is on the level. Yoni has always been a quick learner. He's even met a girl from Netanya whom we like. They served in the same army unit."

Daud couldn't remember Yoni's job in the IDF, but it wasn't unusual for men and women to have similar roles.

"Tell me about you," Avi continued. "I asked a question about America and didn't give you a chance to answer."

"I'm married," Daud said and gave the art dealer a short history.

"I hope living in the US isn't a permanent move," Avi said. "We need people like you to prove the politicians wrong about Jews and Arabs not being able to dwell together in peace. I'd like to send you and your bride a wedding gift."

"Talking to you and hearing about Yoni is gift enough," Daud said with a smile. "But I would appreciate your advice. It has to do with antiquities, not art."

Without revealing any names, Daud briefly told Avi the story of Jakob's client and the stolen ceramic female head. Preferring to hear from Avi first, he didn't go into Jakob's plan of action to find and recover the stolen items.

"Stealing by the Russians was just as illegal as by the Germans," Daud said.

"True, and I know about the recent find in Metula," Avi replied. "It was in all the papers. An eighth-century BCE ceramic piece with the kind of detail and craftsmanship worthy of a king will earn it a prime spot in the Israel Museum. But it's highly unlikely the great-grandfather of the man from Belarus owned its twin."

"I realize that," Daud replied. "But Hana's colleague wants to investigate it, and I've agreed to help him. My first act was to contact you."

Avi scratched the left side of his neck. "I know many of the old-timers in the antiquities trade, both Jew and Arab. The government has tightened down a lot since the days when almost anything was available for cash at the right price. Most of my contacts have retired or moved on to something else, but there are a few I can reach out to. Someone might have information about the kind of piece you're talking about. What should I tell them? I wouldn't mention the Metula find because that would either scare them off or cause the price to go up too much."

"Mention there's a discreet collector who is interested in that type of item."

"I'm not sure that's the best approach," Avi said, leaning in closer to the camera on his computer. "I think I should make the inquiry for myself, not as a middleman. That will allay suspicions."

"You would do that?" Daud asked in surprise.

Avi rubbed his hands together in front of him. "Yes, it would be a better way."

"Then I'd better tell you what Hana's colleague is about to do in an effort to track down the items and how I fit into his plans."

Daud told Avi about the Russian internet sites and the plan to expand the same thing into Israel.

"That may produce results in Russia, but not here," Avi said when Daud finished. "I'd rather give old-fashioned word of mouth a try. I can toss a small pebble into the pond and see where the ripples lead without creating too much disturbance. Can you send me more details?"

"Yes, and I'll include an inventory of other items owned by the great-grandfather. There might be a chance some of them are still together or the discovery of one could lead to information about the others."

"Okay," Avi said. "I'll give this some more thought and let you know what I think after reviewing the inventory."

"Thanks." Daud paused. "And please keep my name confidential. I need to stay in the background."

"Understood." Avi yawned. "I'm ready for a final glass of wine and bed."

"Good night," Daud said.

"Blessings on you and your wife," Avi replied. "May you have as many children as Jacob."

Daud smiled. He and Hana wanted children eventually, but producing patriarchs for twelve tribes was a bigger job than they could take on.

CHAPTER 16

Hana had trouble shaking off the negative feeling from her conversation with Mr. Lowenstein. She tried to put it out of her mind during the drive home. As she pulled into the short driveway for the house, her phone vibrated. It was Ben's number. Saying a quick prayer, she parked the car but didn't get out.

"Hello," she said, trying not to sound too cheerful or too serious.

"It's Ben. Is now a good time to talk?"

"Yes. I wanted to call you the other night and apologize, but —"

"No apology necessary," Ben cut in. "But I'm glad you waited because some other things have happened."

Leon scratched the passenger door panel with his left paw. Hana leaned over and opened the door. Leon ran to the house and yelped. Daud opened the door and peered out curiously at Hana, who pointed to her cell phone.

"Hold on," Ben said. "Sadie is supposed to be reading in her room, but I hear her in the hallway and need to see what's going on."

Hana could hear muffled talking.

"Sadie was hungry and made a run to the refrigerator," Ben said when he returned. "We made a strawberry gelato last night. I've never been much of a cook, but if this keeps up, she's going to end up opening a restaurant and hiring me as her assistant."

"You're a good dad," Hana replied.

"Who wants to be the best father I can be," Ben answered. "I've decided to cool things down with Laura for a while and told Sadie when she came home from school this afternoon. You would have been proud of the way she responded. She listened without interrupting, and when I finished she gave me a long hug followed by a kiss on the cheek. It may work out with Laura, but I want to be sure the relationship has what it takes to last."

Hana felt a weight lift from her shoulders. "Is there anything you want me to do? I want to help, but I'm not sure how."

"Let's wait on that."

"Whatever you say," Hana quickly replied. She wanted to ask Ben if she could speak to Sadie for a few seconds and tell her good night, but Daud's counsel from the previous day held her back.

"And thanks so much for getting in touch with me," she concluded.

The call ended. She slipped her phone into her purse.

A subdued Leon was standing over his metal feeding bowl while Daud poured the food.

"That was Ben Neumann," Hana said. "We had a good talk, and I think things are okay between us. I can't say the same thing about Mr. Lowenstein."

Hana told Daud what the senior partner had said to her about working with Jakob Brodsky.

"I wouldn't make too big a deal out of it," he said when she finished. "He's just being a boss."

"Yeah, but it still stung."

Hana saw a large bowl of salad fixings on the kitchen counter. Daud followed her gaze.

"I fixed salad for supper," he said.

"Did you eat a sandwich when you came home from the office?" Hana asked.

"What makes you say that?"

"Because you don't eat like a rabbit unless you've gorged like a lion."

Daud gave a soft roar.

"I was going to fix something with protein," Hana continued. "But if you're not hungry —"

"No, that sounds great."

While they ate, Daud told her about his Skype session with Avi Labensky.

"I think he's right about how to begin the investigation in Israel," he said. "It should be focused, not general. And there's nothing for you to do at this point that will upset Mr. Lowenstein. I can talk to Jakob directly."

CHAPTER 17

Over the next month and a half, Daud spent a lot of time working on two new consulting projects, including the one that would require a short trip to Lebanon. The day he'd closed the deal, he scheduled a flight leaving two weeks later.

The day he was scheduled to depart for Beirut, Daud jerked awake when Hana suddenly jumped out of bed and rushed into the bathroom. It was several minutes before she returned. By then the sun was up, and light beams illuminated the bedroom. Daud could tell from the expression on Hana's face that she didn't feel well.

"What's wrong?" he asked.

"Upset stomach," she replied. "I added too much baharat to the chicken and rice last night."

For supper Hana had transformed what would in most cultures be a bland dish into a fiery concoction by throwing in a blend of

239

Arabic spices known as baharat, a seasoning loaded with Aleppo peppers and two other types of chiles.

"I loved it," Daud said.

"Me too, at the time, but not this morning."

Hana stayed in bed while Daud took a shower.

"Should you stay home from work today?" he asked when he came out of the bathroom. "I can take care of you until I leave for the airport at ten thirty."

"No, I don't have a fever, and there's an important meeting on my schedule."

"That someone else could handle."

"Not really. Mr. Collins wants me to translate as well as offer legal advice. Janet's Hebrew and Arabic need a lot of work."

Hana's attempt at humor eased Daud's concern.

"Do you want me to fix you a cup of coffee?" he offered.

"No, I'll drink tea instead."

Daud heated a cup of water in the microwave. He dropped in a tea bag to steep and took Leon out for a walk around the yard. When he returned, Hana was still in bed with her eyes closed.

"Now I'm worried all over again," he said.

"Don't be. Is the tea ready?"

"Yes. Do you want me to bring it to you?"

"No, thanks," Hana answered, propping herself against the headboard. "And I haven't been in the bed this whole time. I went to the bathroom again."

"Did you get sick?"

"My stomach is upset, but not because of the baharat."

"What is it then?"

"Come, sit beside me." Hana scooted over slightly and patted the sheet.

Daud joined her. Hana reached out for his left hand and held it. "Come home safely from Lebanon."

"I will," he replied, puzzled. "It's a quick trip into a good part of Beirut where problems are rare. That's why I'm recommending the area to the client. What's wrong with you?"

"Nothing is wrong," Hana said as a small smile creased her lips. "You're going to be a father. I had my suspicions, and while you were fixing the tea, I took a home pregnancy test that I bought a couple of days ago. The results are in the bathroom."

Daud's jaw dropped open. "I'm going to be a *babai*," he said, using the Egyptian term for daddy. "Are you sure? I mean, I hope you're right —"

"I'll go to the doctor, of course, but you

can see the results for yourself. Two lines equals positive; one line is negative."

Daud went into the small bathroom and saw a plastic object that looked like a chubby thermometer on the counter beside the sink. In the middle of an oval window were two very distinct lines. He returned to find Hana with her arms crossed and a satisfied expression on her face.

"I hope you're as thrilled as I am," she said.

"Yes, yes, yes!" Daud repeated before reaching the level of excitement he wanted to communicate.

Hana beamed. "Good. I know that's true, but I'm sure I'll need more reassurance as we go along."

Daud couldn't keep his eyes off Hana while she sat at the table sipping tea and eating a piece of dry toast. When she caught his eye, the sparkle he saw melted his heart. The thought that he was going to be a father drove everything else from his mind.

Hana finished her tea and went into the bedroom to get ready for work. Daud quickly researched fetal development and downloaded an app that would give him daily updates on the baby's progress. At six weeks, the unborn child was about the size of a sweet pea. There was a bag of frozen peas in the refrigerator. He opened it and placed a few samples in the palm of his hand. They varied in size, and he wondered which one most closely resembled the new life in Hana.

"What are you doing?" Hana asked when she returned from the bedroom.

"Looking at our baby," he answered.

Daud showed her the app on his phone. Hana picked up a single pea and kissed it.

"What am I supposed to do with the pea now?" Daud asked when she returned it to his hand. "It wouldn't seem right to put it in the bag and return it to the freezer."

Hana held out her hand. "I'll take it to work and put it on my desk and see if anyone notices."

Pregnancy was bringing out a quirky side of Hana that Daud hadn't seen before.

"How are you feeling now?" he asked.

"Better. The tea and toast helped. That may be my favorite breakfast for a while."

Daud held out his arms and held her close. He kissed the top of her head.

"Will you pray for me, us, our new family?" Hana asked in a quiet voice.

Daud closed his eyes and spoke of thanksgiving and protection. He ended with words of welcome to their child.

"Promise me again you'll be safe," Hana

said, patting him on the chest. "You're traveling a long way for two days on the ground."

"Two days too many," Daud replied. "But I'll be extra careful. Will you see the doctor while I'm gone?"

"I'll try to make an appointment, but it will probably take a while to get in to see her."

Daud put away the clean dishes while Hana remained at the table sipping a second cup of tea.

"You may receive a packet of information from Avi Labensky while I'm gone," he said. "I asked him to send it to your attention at the law firm."

"Why not here?"

"I didn't want to give him our home address. Avi is discreet, but I don't know who has access to his computer." Daud paused. "He said something about us having children when we talked several weeks ago. He prayed I'd be as fruitful as the patriarch Jacob."

"One sweet pea at a time," Hana said, laughing. "Should I open the package from Avi?"

"Yes, and let Jakob know when it arrives." Daud finished wiping down the kitchen counter.

Hana spoke. "Let's wait a few weeks to tell our families. Once my mother knows that I have news, she'll guess what it is."

Later Daud walked Hana and Leon to the car.

"Text me while you're away," she said.

Daud wasn't a prolific text writer, but at that moment he wasn't going to deny Hana anything she asked.

"Absolutely."

During the drive to the dog day care center, Hana talked to Leon about the baby.

"It doesn't mean I love you less," she said. "And I'm sure your heart is big enough to welcome a new member to the household."

She stopped for a red light. Leon's broad tongue was hanging partway out of his mouth. Hana didn't look forward to the dog licking the baby's face.

"Put that tongue back in your mouth," she said.

Leon looked at her with his big brown eyes, flapped his tail against the floorboard, and left his tongue out as far as possible.

Hana decided not to share her big news with anyone in Atlanta until she went to the doctor for one hundred percent confirmation. But inside she knew a massive change had occurred.

"Good morning," she said to Janet when

she reached the assistant's desk.

"You're later than usual," Janet replied. "Are you okay?"

Hana thought about the sweet pea in her purse and smiled. "Yes. Daud left this morning for a couple of days in Beirut to set up security in a new branch office for one of his clients."

"And that makes you smile?"

"No, of course not. But it's a quick trip."

"If Donnie goes on a business trip, I miss him because he's not there to help with my younger daughter's homework."

Janet had a son and two daughters. Her oldest child, a son, would be going away to college in the fall. The younger daughter was in middle school, and the older daughter was just entering high school.

"Oh, I put the early mail on your desk," Janet continued. "There was a long cardboard tube that someone mailed from Israel. The name and address for the law firm were handwritten and barely legible. It's a miracle that it arrived."

Hana took out the green pea and placed it beneath her computer monitor where she could see it all day. It would be fun bringing in an object comparable in size to the baby, at least until the unborn child reached cantaloupe size. Touching her abdomen,

Hana offered up a quick prayer that both she and the baby would have a good day.

She pried open the cardboard tube. Inside were several rolled-up sheets of paper written in Hebrew. She could quickly tell they contained information related to the art dealer's efforts to locate the ceramic figure once owned by Jakob's client. Remembering Mr. Lowenstein's warning not to work on non–law firm business, Hana slipped the sheets into the top drawer of her desk. Curious as to why the information was shipped in a cardboard tube instead of an envelope, she picked up the tube and peered into it. There was something else. Inserting her finger, she was able to pull out another rolled-up piece of thick paper.

It was a signed print by an Israeli artist whose name Hana didn't recognize but who used a bright, casual style that she instantly liked. The oil painting depicted a Jerusalem street scene from an older part of the city. A young woman with wisps of black hair flowing onto her shoulders and wearing a bright green dress and simple sandals was leaning back in a chair that rested against a limestone wall. Shafts of sunlight revealed interesting textures in the stones. At the woman's feet was a cream-colored blanket with two babies lying on it. One child was grasping the other's foot, as if about to put it in his or her mouth. Affixed to the bottom of the print was a Post-it Note from Avi Labensky. The print was a wedding gift. The title of the work was *Jacob and Esau at Play,* which answered the question about the babies' gender. Hana suddenly wondered if there might be some similarity between Avi and her uncle Anwar. If so, maybe she should have brought two peas to work instead of one.

She considered taking a photo of the painting and sending it to Daud, but she decided it would be better for him to see it in person first. Instead, she sent a group text to him and Jakob, letting them know about the arrival of the information from the art dealer. Jakob immediately responded with a request to meet with her. She answered.

Only during lunch or after work. Not at the firm.

Jakob suggested noon for lunch. Before responding, Hana contacted her doctor's office to see when she could schedule an appointment for a pregnancy test. It would be a couple of weeks before the obstetrician could see her. Hana followed up with Jakob and gave him a later time to meet for lunch because she wasn't sure how long the meeting with Mr. Collins and some clients would last.

After catching up on her emails, she left her office and walked to the break room for a cup of coffee. As the dark liquid hit the bottom of the cup, Hana realized strong coffee might not be good for her baby. She poured the coffee down the sink and returned to her office where she quickly researched the issue and read that pregnant women should limit caffeine intake to 200 milligrams a day. That equaled a single cup of coffee. Because the English tea Hana drank at home contained caffeine, she'd likely met her daily limit. Hana rubbed her temples where a headache was forming and tried to concentrate on her work. The pain in her head increased during the meeting with Mr. Collins and the clients from Ra'anana, a modern technology hub near Tel Aviv. Fortunately, she didn't have to do much translating because everyone on the conference call spoke English. She was rubbing her head when she returned to her office for a few minutes before leaving to meet Jakob.

"Headache?" Janet asked.

"Yeah, no coffee all morning."

"Why not? You always have a cup or two."

Realizing the conversation might quickly go where she didn't want to follow, Hana gave a short answer. "I drank tea with breakfast this morning."

"Which probably had as much kick as brown-colored water."

"I don't always drink coffee," she said.

"Name a day in the past month when you didn't," Janet replied. "And you're squinting your eyes like you're really in pain."

"It hurts some," Hana admitted.

Janet opened a desk drawer and took out a bottle of pain pills. "Two of these should help."

Hana reached out with her right hand but quickly pulled it back. She wasn't sure the pills would be safe.

"No, thanks," she said. "I'm off to lunch with Jakob Brodsky and should be back by two o'clock."

Hana took three steps and realized she'd left the information from Avi Labensky in her desk drawer. She returned, grabbed it, and held it up as she approached Janet's desk.

"The packet from Israel is really for Jakob," she said. "And I didn't read it here since I couldn't bill the time to a client."

Suddenly, Hana felt dizzy. She placed her

hand on the corner of Janet's desk to steady herself. She blinked her eyes until the room stabilized.

"I need to eat," she said. "Get some carbohydrates in my system."

"Are you sure you should drive?" Janet asked with concern in her voice.

"Yeah, I'm fine now."

CHAPTER 18

It was only a fifteen-minute drive to the restaurant where Hana was to meet Jakob. She'd recommended it because it featured hot sandwiches, a favorite of Jakob's, and provided booth seating for privacy. When she walked by Jakob's car, Hana saw two large boxes of documents in the rear seat. The Jewish lawyer was waiting for her near the front door of the restaurant. Vladimir Ivanov was with him. The man from Belarus stood and bowed when she approached. The lunch crowd had thinned, and there were plenty of places to sit.

"I hope you haven't been waiting long," Hana said.

"It worked out for the best. I was able to get in touch with Vladimir so he could join us. He's excited that we're making progress."

"I'm not sure if that's true. I haven't reviewed the information from Daud's contact in Jerusalem yet."

They stepped to the counter to place their orders. Ivanov spoke to Jakob.

"Vladimir wants to order the same thing as you. He really enjoyed the lamb curry at the Indian restaurant."

"You first," she said to Jakob.

He ordered a large Italian sub with double meat. Hana eyed the menu posted on the wall and stepped up to place her order.

"I'd like a side of sauerkraut, two dill pickles, and several pieces of salami. No bread."

The young woman taking orders stared at her for a second.

"And I'll pay whatever it costs since it's not a menu item," Hana added.

The clerk called over the middle-aged manager and told her about the order. The matronly woman glanced at Hana and nodded. Meanwhile, Jakob spoke to Ivanov, who gave Hana a puzzled look. The two men talked back and forth in Russian. Jakob ordered another large Italian sub.

"Vladimir is wisely following my culinary guidance today," Jakob said to Hana. "Are you on some kind of weird low-carb diet?"

"No."

They sat in a booth. Hana placed the papers she'd received from Avi Labensky on the table. Jakob thumbed through them. Ivanov picked up one of the sheets and nodded.

"That's a copy of the inventory for the Russian bank loan," Jakob said. "Daud sent that to Avi for me. He didn't have to return it. Everything else is in Hebrew."

Hana quickly began translating. There was a list of people Avi had contacted about the item he described as a "ceramic figurine." Beside each name, the art dealer provided a short description of the person and what he'd learned from his initial communication with them. Their food arrived. After a few bites, Hana continued translating. It was a varied group with less than half of the people identified as "antiquity dealer." There were three archaeologists on the list.

"That's interesting," Jakob said. "I hadn't thought about contacting a professional archaeologist, but it makes sense. There's a chance someone might ask an archaeologist to evaluate the queen's head."

Hana swallowed a bite of salami wrapped around a pickle. Her head still hurt, but her stomach felt better. She flipped to the next page.

"The third archaeologist is an Israeli woman who agreed to meet with Avi in person and offer suggestions."

"What's her name?"

Hana referred to an earlier sheet of paper. "Daniella Rubin. She's been digging in the Negev for the past few years searching for more relics related to the Essenes who lived at Qumran and wrote the Dead Sea Scrolls. She's also an expert in Bar Kokhba coins, so Avi must have mentioned those to her." The color-coded spreadsheet included Avi's remarks about the inventory presented to the Russian banker and the range of value for some of the items on the list. Hana explained what the art dealer wrote and Jakob translated for Ivanov, who smiled and nodded his head appreciatively.

"There's more about the Bar Kokhba coins," Hana continued. "Avi says the coins could range in value from a few hundred dollars to tens of thousands depending on the date of minting and value. The coins from the first year of the revolt are worth a lot more than those from years two and three. Your client's great-grandfather had several first-year coins, and Avi says that even though the old photographs Daud sent him aren't the best quality, the earliest coins could be extremely valuable. He recommends that you have the photographs digitally enhanced so the peculiarities of each coin can be analyzed. They're as unique as a human fingerprint."

"The enhanced photographs are already done," Jakob replied. "And they are amazing. I can send them to Avi immediately. I knew that might be important and wanted to be proactive."

Hana kept reading. "Avi didn't share the photos with anyone yet."

"Daud and I talked about that," Jakob said, leaning forward. "We decided to keep things generic, especially with the queen's head, until it makes sense to share more details. Even then, I don't want the photos loose on the internet. The trick is to attract interest and obtain information without giving too much away ourselves."

"I have no idea how that works," Hana replied, pausing to eat another bite of sauerkraut.

Jakob took a drink of water. "What else does Avi have to say? I'm liking this guy more and more."

The art dealer had done a lot of work, considering there was no promise of payment. To her, it indicated how much he must respect and like Daud. Avi had included a summary of the current state of the law in Israel about buying and selling antiquities and the penalties for violating the law.

"But those provisions wouldn't apply because Vladimir's great-grandfather acquired everything when the Ottomans were still ruling Palestine," Jakob said.

"True, but it might take a court proceeding to establish the chain of title prior to 1978 when Israel passed a law regulating antiquities."

"That's where you come in," Jakob began.

"Not so fast," Hana replied. She told him about her conversation with Mr. Lowenstein.

"Maybe if I call him —"

"That would make it worse," Hana interjected. "Let's keep things between us informal."

Jakob chewed thoughtfully. "The odds aren't that great that any part of the collection is in Israel. Most likely everything is somewhere in the former Soviet Union."

Hana reorganized the papers. "If you'd like, I'll take these home and translate from Hebrew to English while Daud is out of town."

"That would be great."

When they were ready to leave, Ivanov reached into his pocket and tried to hand Hana a wad of money. She could see a collection of wrinkled five- and ten-dollar bills.

"That's not necessary," she said.

"Let him pay you," Jakob suggested. "It will make him feel better."

"But that's exactly the sort of thing that violates my employment contract at the firm."

Jakob shook his head. "You teach me something almost every time we get together. Find out the name of one of Mr. Lowenstein's favorite charities, and I'll recommend Vladimir make a donation in your honor."

Hana thought about the interfaith forum and told Jakob about it. "There will be charities linked to the event," she said.

"Sounds good. And I want to come hear what you have to say."

"Only if you sit near the front of the room and make silly faces to get me to laugh."

"Would I do that?" Jakob grinned.

While he waited for his flight from New York to Beirut, Daud clicked open an email from Hana that contained a link to the information sent by Avi Labensky. He read the information before boarding his Air France flight.

It was midmorning when the plane landed at the Beirut airport. Daud took a taxi to Le Gray Beirut, a local hotel. Even though Lebanon was under the de facto control of

Hezbollah, the Shiite-based "Army of God," the business and cultural center of Beirut retained its classic French-inspired beauty and cosmopolitan feel. Daud's client was located in a district where international businesses clustered together. When he arrived at the office, Daud was greeted by a young woman dressed in European clothes.

His local contact was a Lebanese man named Youssef who came from a Maronite Christian family. The Maronites were an ancient Christian sect that traced their roots to the disciples in Antioch and had lived in Lebanon for over a thousand years. Youssef, a slender young man with a thin black mustache, picked up Daud at the hotel.

"Welcome to Beirut," Youssef said with an upper-class Lebanese accent. "Would you like some coffee?"

They stopped at a fancy coffee shop where Daud learned that Youssef had spent time studying at the Sorbonne in France and turned down an opportunity to immigrate to France upon graduation.

"Many of my Lebanese classmates saw the degree as a way to escape Lebanon," he said. "But Beirut is my home, and when the opportunity to work with an American tech company came up, I took it."

"Were the Americans looking for someone

like you with extensive local connections?"

"Yes," Youssef answered, nodding. "One phone call can lead to many others. What do the Americans call it? The domino effect?"

"Maybe. My wife is the one who knows the American idioms."

They spent the rest of the day inspecting and evaluating Youssef's implementation of the security protocols included in Daud's plan. The American company wanted to develop local business but also bring in clients from other Middle Eastern countries for presentations. Daud wasn't an expert in cybersecurity, but he knew how to protect the physical location of the office and the people working there, and how to set up safe ingress to and egress from the city for wealthy clients at risk of kidnapping for ransom. During short breaks he kept checking his phone for news from Hana, but nothing came through. True to his promise, he sent her several texts.

"I agree with the hotel you selected," Youssef said. "It's close by, and the owners want to protect their reputation with foreigners. One of the managers at Le Gray is a distant relative on my mother's side. I wasn't familiar with the transportation company you recommended. It's small."

The transportation service was owned by two brothers who had a secret relationship with Israeli defense officials. Daud knew they'd provided intelligence information about local terrorist activity. Their drivers were skilled operators of armor-plated vehicles and performed double duty as bodyguards.

"They can handle any situation," Daud said.

Toward the end of the day, Youssef invited Daud to join him for dinner.

"My wife and parents will be there," he said. "I think you will enjoy meeting my father."

"Thanks, but I'm tired from the flight," Daud replied.

Back at the hotel, he ordered room service for dinner. There was no word from Hana. Finally, he received multiple text messages sent throughout the day. His favorite was the one that read:

All is well with our sweet pea and me.

Daud sent a long response to Hana. Before going to bed, he checked his phone one last time. There was an email from Avi Labensky.

261

Received a nice email from your wife. Have you thought about moving back to Israel? If so, I know about a bungalow in Abu Tor. It's not on the market, but the owner is willing to sell.

Abu Tor, meaning "the father of the bull," was a neighborhood south of the Old City of Jerusalem. It was named after one of Saladin's generals, a man who in legend rode a bull into battle against the Crusaders. Abu Tor had a long history of joint residence by both Arabs and Jews, and the predominantly Jewish section was one of the staging grounds for the Israeli army before it captured the Old City during the Six-Day War in 1967. Currently, the entire neighborhood was an example of coexistence between the different groups.

Daud read the email several times. With each reading his interest increased. He knew what Hana's reaction would be. But Daud felt unrooted in America. Except for Jakob and his girlfriend, Emily, Daud and Hana hadn't developed any close friendships. Hana's social world still revolved around her family in Reineh. Daud had joined a local soccer club, but once the season was over everyone had drifted their own way. He and Hana had visited multiple churches but never settled on a spiritual home. The only real benefits to living in America were that being in a foreign country brought him and Hana closer because they spent so much time together, and they were safer. Daud's enemies were six thousand miles away.

He sent Avi a quick thank-you and told him he was in Beirut on business for a couple of days. The art dealer replied immediately.

Come to Jerusalem when you finish.

Daud had a dilemma. A side trip to Jerusalem would require him to change his return flight to America by at least one day, possibly two, which would upset Hana, both because of the delay and because he would be returning to Israel. But the pull of the ancient city on his soul was great. He paced back and forth in his room for several minutes before answering Avi.

I'll be there tomorrow evening.

CHAPTER 19

Throughout the evening Hana checked her phone for more messages from Daud. She'd finally received his texts, but he hadn't replied to her responses. She suspected a problem with internet service in Beirut. Hana had spent time in the city, especially when she was in high school, and knew it well.

Some of the emotional feelings and physical sensations Hana had experienced over the past couple of weeks now made sense. After eating a light supper, she spent the evening studying fetal development and nutritional recommendations for pregnant women. There were innumerable opinions and blogs. Some were clearly off the wall; others raised issues that seemed legitimate.

In an ideal world, Hana's relatives would play a huge role during her pregnancy and immerse her in so much love her emotional tank wouldn't run dry. But for Hana and

Daud, safety issues trumped everything. At least she would soon be able to talk long-distance to her mother, Farah, and Fabia about all things related to childbearing.

Before going to bed, she checked a website she followed about local real estate. For several months she'd sporadically read about new houses coming onto the market. Pregnancy created a new dynamic. Even though she was still in her first trimester, her mother-to-be status kicked into gear. A cute older home about fifteen minutes from where they currently lived caught her eye, and she entered the address in her phone so she could drive by the following day to check out the neighborhood. The listing price for the house was high, but finding the perfect property would justify flexibility.

When she awoke in the night, Hana expected her time with the Lord to focus on prayers for the baby. After all, the tiny child had been secretly living and growing for several weeks without a single prayer uttered on his or her behalf. But after thanking the Lord for the new life, Hana's thoughts turned toward Daud. That prompted another round of the all-too-familiar fight with anxiety and fear. Agitated, Hana rose from the couch and paced back and forth across the room for several minutes. She hated the disruption but felt powerless to banish it.

Sitting down with her journal, she flipped back to some of the prayers she'd written while Daud was on the mission for the CIA. Repeating them brought small comfort. Before returning to bed, she sent him a text, asking how he was doing and telling him how much she looked forward to seeing him. It was midmorning in Beirut, and he should be awake. The message did not show delivery, and she followed up with a phone call that went to voice mail. Nevertheless, hearing the sound of his voice in his away message calmed her. Daud never sounded anxious or afraid. He was a rock from which calming water could always flow to her.

Nausea forced Hana out of bed the following morning and into the bathroom. She'd increased her fluid intake, but that didn't seem to help. After taking a shower she ate a cracker, but her body was craving hot tea. Knowing it would eliminate a later cup of coffee, she reluctantly gave in and brewed a cup of tea. The tea calmed her stomach so much that she concluded it was smart to surrender to what her changing body demanded. Leon leaned against her leg, and she scratched the dog's ears.

"With the money we save on coffee, I can

buy you more treats," she said, taking another sip of tea. "But there are going to be other expenses that will eat up those savings."

Leon panted quietly in satisfaction, and Hana daydreamed about the future. After dropping him off at the dog day care center, she didn't drive directly to the office but took a detour so she could see the house she'd read about the previous evening. Near the entrance to the neighborhood was a small commercial area that had a grocery store, a drugstore, and a couple of restaurants, including one that served Greek food. At the moment no food seemed appealing to Hana, but a gyro with extra onions, fresh tomato, and tangy tzatziki sauce might be welcome someday.

She came to a four-way stop and turned into a neighborhood of homes that looked around fifty or sixty years old. Built on small lots, many of the houses had been renovated and updated. Hana instantly liked the feel of the area. She passed a young woman pushing a double stroller with twins on board. Hana thought again about the painting from Avi Labensky and smiled.

She slowed to a stop in front of the home recently listed for sale. Painted a creamy tan, the house sat on a lot that gently sloped to the street. There were two pop-out dormers on the second level. From the description she'd read, Hana knew all three bedrooms and the two full baths were upstairs. The most attractive exterior feature of the house was a small sunroom to the right of the front door. The dwelling was surrounded by carefully maintained flower beds and azaleas with a pair of red maples in the front yard. A wooden privacy fence peeked out from either end of the house. Having an enclosed area where Leon could roam free would be wonderful. There was a single garage with a white door. Cars were parked alongside the curb up and down the street. Hana remembered her uncle Anwar's word about a promised land. This might be it for her, Daud, and their family. She took her phone from her purse and began to take pictures.

Daud ate breakfast at the hotel. He'd already changed his flight plans. Instead of traveling from Beirut to New York, he would go to Athens, Greece, and then take a short flight to Ben Gurion Airport. He would arrive by early evening, spend the night in Jerusalem, and return to the US twenty-four hours later than planned. He sent his schedule to Avi, who agreed to pick him up at the airport. An email to Hana was much briefer and left out any details of the side trip to Israel so she wouldn't worry. Daud simply let her know he would be returning to Atlanta a day later than originally planned.

It was a thirty-minute taxi ride to the airport. Outside the terminal, Daud reached for his wallet so he could pay the fare. Glancing up, he saw a young Arab man raise his hand to attract the driver's attention. The man looked vaguely familiar, but Daud couldn't place him. He didn't know anyone in Beirut except Youssef and the brothers who ran the transportation service. Daud handed the driver enough money to pay the fare, adding a generous tip.

"Thank you, sir," the driver said, grinning in appreciation.

Daud's suitcase and a leather satchel were on the seat beside him. He opened the door as the man who'd hailed the cab reached the passenger window and spoke to the driver. Now that the man was closer, he reminded Daud of the assassin from Sharm el-Sheikh. There was a remarkable resemblance. The man didn't pay attention to Daud. "Phoenicia Hotel," he said with a Lebanese accent.

Daud exited the cab. The man slipped past

him into the backseat. As he made his way into the terminal, Daud wondered if the report of the assassin's death was erroneous. However, it couldn't be the same man he encountered at the Kolisnyks' villa. If so, the recognition would have been mutual and violent. Daud didn't completely relax until he'd safely boarded his flight to Athens.

Hana wasn't surprised when she received the text from Daud letting her know he'd be arriving home a day later than planned. It was an ambitious goal to think he could accomplish everything he needed to do quickly in Beirut given the deterioration of infrastructure in many parts of the city.

She spent the rest of the evening translating and typing a summary of Avi Labensky's report for Jakob. The concentration required got her mind off the news from Daud. As she worked, she thought about how amazing it would be if any of the stolen items could be recovered by Jakob's client. It was late when she finished and sent the summary to Jakob and crawled into bed. She didn't pray in the night and slept past her usual time to get up in the morning. After a quick breakfast of tea and crackers, she dropped off Leon and drove to the office.

When she had finished checking her emails, Hana invited Janet into her office.

"I looked at a cute house yesterday," Hana said. "Would you like to see some pictures?"

"You bet."

Hana pulled up the listing photos and also showed Janet the pictures she'd taken on her phone.

"It's adorable," Janet said. "Are you going to make an offer?"

"Daud doesn't know anything about it. Remember, he's out of the country for a few days and won't be back until the end of the week."

"That didn't keep you from buying his dream vehicle. It's only fair that you could take the first steps toward your dream house."

Hana eyed Janet skeptically. "Are you serious?" she asked.

Janet grinned. "No, but I feel empowered giving you advice that I wouldn't take myself. Look, you don't have to wait until Daud gets back to contact the Realtor and set a time to see the inside. The outside is cute, but there might be something funky about the interior that's a deal breaker."

"Funky?"

"Odd or so bad that it knocks it off the list. Usually it has to do with the kitchen or

271

the layout of the bedrooms."

Hana hesitated. "I guess there's nothing wrong with calling the Realtor."

"Absolutely not, and you might get a feeling about the place that's either good or bad, which means a lot to a woman but is incomprehensible to a man."

"Okay." Hana nodded. "I'll do that."

"Do it soon. A house like that might not last long on the market."

Hana called the listing agent and scheduled a viewing of the house later in the day. After she talked to the agent, her excitement began to build. She even kept thinking about the house while she was working on a complex purchase/sale agreement for one of Mr. Collins's clients. Shortly before leaving for the appointment with the real estate agent, she received a call from Ben.

"Sadie was talking about you on the way to school this morning," Ben said. "She suggested the five of us get together for dinner."

"Five of us?"

"You, Daud, Sadie, Laura, and me," Ben answered.

"Did she explain what she had in mind?"

"You know Sadie. Sometimes you only see the tip of the iceberg, and there's a lot more hidden beneath. The question popped out of her mouth as I was pulling into the school, and I didn't have a chance to ask her reasons. Would you be open to the idea?"

"Yes, if you think it's a good idea, but I'd still like to understand Sadie's goal, at least in a general way."

"Yeah," Ben replied. "But Laura jumped on it and suggested I call you."

Hana was apprehensive. "Would you talk again with Sadie and let me know?"

"Sure."

The call ended, and Hana left her office.

"Are you going out for lunch?" Janet asked, looking up from her computer.

"No, I scheduled an appointment to look at the house I showed you."

"That's exciting!" Janet beamed. "Take tons of pictures of the inside."

"I'll take a few, but I'm more interested in how it feels."

"Oh, that will hit you within a few seconds of entering the front door."

"Do you want me to pick up something for you to eat on my way back to the office?" Hana asked. "I may stop off for a salad."

"No, thanks. I have leftover spaghetti in the refrigerator in the break room."

Hana had eaten Janet's spaghetti in the

past. The assistant made it with thick noodles and a spicy meat sauce. It was better than any spaghetti Hana had ordered in an Italian restaurant since moving to America.

"That sounds delicious."

"Would you like some? I brought more than I should eat. It's a good batch. Donnie ate three servings before I made him stop."

"Are you sure?"

"That will give us a chance to talk more about the house."

Daud had an uneventful flight from Athens to Israel. Once at Ben Gurion Airport, he called Avi Labensky.

"Sorry I'm not able to pick you up," the art dealer said.

"I can catch a cab. Should I tell the driver to drop me off at your home or the art shop?"

"Neither. We're having a nice dinner. There's someone I want you to meet."

"Who?"

"Daniella Rubin, the archaeologist I mentioned in my report to you and Jakob Brodsky."

"I skimmed the report, but I don't remember her name." Daud paused. "And remember, I don't want my name associated with

274

the search."

"Which I've mostly honored, but Daniella is a professional who understands the need to be discreet. We can fill you in on what she thinks at dinner."

Daud was irritated with Avi for not maintaining confidentiality but didn't complain. The art dealer was doing a lot of work without any demand for payment.

"Let's meet at the Jerusalem Overlook?" Avi suggested. "I've not been there for a while."

The Overlook was an excellent restaurant, more popular with Arabs than Jews. But it wasn't a good place for Daud. He could easily run into someone who knew him, and even a friendly face could create a problem.

"Not there," Daud replied and suggested a kosher restaurant in western Jerusalem.

"Great!" Avi exclaimed. "You're still the best investigator on the planet. How else would you know that's one of my favorite places? The Argentinian beef there is very good, and because it's passed kashruth, I can order it rare. I'll make a reservation."

After talking to Avi, Daud gave the name of the restaurant to a young Jewish taxi driver who nodded his head. "I know it."

During the forty-minute drive, Daud checked his emails and sent a text to Hana confirming his return flight. She immediately responded.

Great! Hope you're getting everything finished. I'm having a wonderful day! Can't wait to tell you about it. Much love.

Relieved that Hana sounded upbeat, Daud relaxed as the vehicle sped toward Jerusalem on Highway 1. When they arrived at the restaurant, the parking lot was full of expensive cars.

"I hope you have a reservation," the driver said when Daud paid the fare.

Inside, Daud glanced around but didn't see Avi. The maître d' gave him a long look, most likely due to Daud's Arab ethnicity.

"Daud!" a loud voice called out.

He turned and saw the rotund art dealer, a drink in his hand, hurrying toward him from the bar. Beside him was an attractive, deeply tanned Israeli woman in her mid- to late thirties. She was wearing dark slacks and a white blouse, with a thick gold chain around her neck. Avi shook Daud's hand and spoke in Hebrew.

"I'd hug you, but I don't want to baptize you with my scotch and water," Avi said. "This is Daniella Rubin."

The archaeologist shook Daud's hand

with a strong grip and gave him a formal greeting in Arabic spoken with a British accent.

"Hebrew is fine with me," Daud replied. "Especially in this place."

"Of course." Avi patted Daud on the back with his free hand. "It is so good to see you. A lot has happened in your life since we last met. There is a table reserved for us."

"Avi tells me you served in the IDF," Daniella said as they followed the maître d'.

"Yes."

Daud was again miffed at the art dealer for sharing this sort of background information.

"What unit?" the archaeologist continued.

"I can't discuss it," Daud replied.

"Intelligence unit would be my guess," Daniella said and touched her finger to her lips. "I'm an inquisitive person, but I know when to stop asking questions. I worked as an archaeologist in the army. They called me in when the military uncovered something that might be of historical importance."

They reached a table in the rear corner of the restaurant. Daud instinctively sat with his back to the wall so he could see the entire room.

"Does everyone want beef?" Avi asked. "If

so, let me order for the table."

Both Daud and Daniella nodded. Avi selected entrées, appetizers, and wine.

"I'll leave the sweets to you," he said after the waiter left. "Let's get right to it. Daniella, please tell Daud why you may be able to help his American friend."

"What have you told her?" Daud asked before the archaeologist could answer.

"Not as much as she figured out on her own."

Daniella reached into her purse and took out the photos of the Bar Kokhba coins Jakob had sent Avi.

"My expertise lies with the Bar Kokhba coins," she said. "The number of specimens in this collection from the first year of the revolt caught my attention. Even from these old pictures it's clear some of them were in outstanding condition. We're talking about museum pieces, not badly worn slugs stuck in a collector's drawer. The rebels used Roman silver and bronze coins as blanks and filed off the pagan Roman images so they could restamp them with Jewish symbols, even though doing so to Roman money was punishable by death. The new script inscribed on the coins was ancient Hebrew from the time of the Davidic dynasty, most likely a way to identify with the Jews' glorious past."

Daud glanced at the photos, none of which he'd seen. There was a surprising amount of variety. The symbols on the front or back included a lyre, a vine leaf, a palm tree, a cluster of grapes, two trumpets, the ark of the covenant, and a stylized impression of Herod's magnificent temple destroyed during the first revolt in AD 70. He could make out the words "Freedom" and "Jerusalem."

"The vast majority of coins from the revolt contain the name Shim'on, for Simon bar Kokhba," Daniella continued, "but a few of the earliest coins in Year One are inscribed with the name of 'Eleazar the Priest.' There are three of those in this collection. One in particular caught my attention."

She pointed to a photograph. Daud could barely make out the name Eleazar.

"I may have seen that coin," Daniella said. "It's owned by a private collector who asked me to confirm its authenticity before she bought it."

Daud perked up. "Tell me more," he said.

The archaeologist began turning the photo in different directions as she pointed out things Daud didn't know were significant.

"The lyre is rare," she said. "And the clarity of the impression is extremely sharp."

The next few minutes were a crash course in Bar Kokhba coinage. When the archaeologist paused, Daud pointed to the photo of the coin featuring a lyre and the name Eleazar the Priest.

"Who owns the coin in that picture?"

"I'm not prepared to provide that information yet," she answered. "The owner is a client, and I have an obligation to her. She paid a lot of money for her piece, and I'm aware of the possible consequences if it was stolen."

"How much would it be worth?" Daud asked.

Daniella shook her head.

Avi spoke. "I recommended in my report that your American friend have the photos digitally enhanced," Avi said. "That will make additional details easier to see."

"I'm sure he'll do it," Daud replied.

Their steaks arrived. Avi hadn't exaggerated. Beef served in the Middle East rarely met the standards for top-rated steak restaurants in the US, but Argentinian beef came close. The juicy steak restored Daud's energy.

"What about the other items on the list?" he asked Daniella. "Did any of them catch your attention?"

"As soon as I saw the reference to the ceramic head, I suspected what was going on," she answered. "Everyone knows about the recent discovery of the ceramic king's head at Metula, and it makes sense that anyone who believes they have a comparable piece might see this as a good time to come forward and test the market. The government would certainly be in on the bidding."

"I told you she was smart," Avi said, pointing his fork at Daniella. "She has that investigative gene, just like you."

"Do you believe a piece similar to the king's head might exist?" Daud asked the archaeologist.

"Asked that way, I'd say yes. But the quality of the piece found at Metula was so exceptional that it's unlikely a twin is out there. Even one of lesser quality would still be a very important discovery, though."

"How do you suggest we find it?"

Daniella carefully cut another piece of steak before looking up at Daud. "The best way is for it to find you."

CHAPTER 20

While they ate the warmed-up spaghetti, Hana scrolled through the photos of the house. Janet peppered her with questions about the residence, which was originally built in 1949 and had been updated within the past five years.

"That's an amazing kitchen," Janet said. "I love the way light comes in from the backyard and illuminates the little island. The white cabinets and light gray countertops really go well together. Are the countertops granite?"

"No, the real estate agent said they were made from something called engineered stone."

"Oh, that's better than granite in my book. Not as finicky as granite."

"Finicky?"

"Hard to take care of. Show me the sunroom. Is it next to the kitchen?"

"Yes."

The bright, airy room contained a wicker sofa, two wicker chairs, a low table, and a wide array of plants.

"You should try to get them to include the furniture in the sale. It goes perfectly in that room."

"The agent said that was an option. I didn't ask how much it would increase the price."

"I bet not a lot," Janet said. "Specialty items like those don't have big value on the used furniture market."

The virtual tour of the house continued upstairs to the bedrooms.

"The master bedroom isn't very big," Hana said. "It's fine by our standards, but I know Americans like larger bedrooms."

Janet agreed. "Yeah, and the bathroom is tiny. They didn't build big walk-in bathrooms in 1949. Where does that door lead?"

"Another bedroom."

Hana pulled up the next photo. It was a small bedroom painted pale yellow with a dormer window.

"Perfect for a nursery," Janet said. "The twins can share a bedroom until they're ready for middle school."

"Twins?" Hana asked.

"I'm kidding. But any woman as focused on a new nest as you are is getting ready for something."

Hana ate a bite of spaghetti to conceal the expression on her face. They finished with photos of the well-manicured backyard.

"Will you want to maintain all those plants and weed the grass?" Janet asked skeptically. "You already have a full-time job."

"I'm not sure. Daud grew up in the desert with nothing to look after except potted plants. There were only a few flowering bushes at my parents' home with nothing as fancy as this house."

"What's next?" Janet asked when Hana put down her phone.

"I wait for Daud to return from his business trip so I can show him."

"Like I said earlier, you probably need to act fast."

"I know," Hana said, trying to suppress her anxiety. "Another woman arrived to look at the house when I was leaving."

"That could signal a bidding war. But don't worry. You just bought Daud the car of his dreams, which means a lot of credit stored up in the marital influence account. This may be the time to cash it in."

Rahal was eating dinner with his wife in a small dining room with large windows on two sides. The sunset over the desert was an explosion of red and orange. There were three cooks on their staff, and it wasn't unusual for the couple to eat something different. She preferred chicken; he liked lamb. But they both ate fish, and tonight the chef had prepared a delicately seasoned white fish with a creamy sauce and a dash of spicy heat. The chief steward placed the main course on the table with a flourish. He returned less than a minute later. Averting his eyes from Rahal's wife, who had lowered her veil to eat, the servant bowed before Rahal.

"Please forgive me, sir, but Mr. Khalil wants to speak to you. He says it's urgent."

Rahal eyed the fish that would be flavorful for only a few more minutes before it cooled. Ignoring the conversation, Rahal's wife continued to eat.

"Send him in," Rahal grunted.

"He needs to speak to you privately."

Rahal turned to his wife. "Leave," he said.

Without a word of protest, she raised her veil and left the room. Rahal knew his wife wouldn't hesitate to voice her displeasure later, though.

Khalil entered. "My apologies, sir," he said. "But while I was in Beirut we received a response to our posting of the hotel

285

surveillance videos and restaurant photos from Sharm el-Sheikh. A man who looks similar to Sayeed/Abadi was involved in the arrest of a group of Sunni jihadists last year in Jerusalem. The leaders of the group were Chechens, including a man named Anzor Varayev, who is currently in an Israeli prison. The remaining members of the group placed a bounty on the man who betrayed them. This is the man."

Khalil pressed a button on his tablet and a picture of an Arab man in his early thirties came into view. Taken from the side, the image wasn't much better than the ones from the Sharm el-Sheikh restaurant.

"I can't tell if it is the same person," Rahal said.

"I'm having it analyzed," Khalil replied. "If this is the man, then his name isn't Ibrahim Abadi or Rasheed Sayyid."

"What is it?" Rahal asked.

"Daud Hasan."

Avi insisted that Daud spend the night as a guest at his home in the Yemin Moshe neighborhood just outside the walls of the Old City. As he lay in bed, Daud listened to the night sounds from the open second-story window. Unlike Tel Aviv, which never slept, even on Shabbat, Jerusalem grew

286

quiet after sunset and individual sounds were recognizable. He could hear violin music playing softly from the courtyard of an adjacent house where a group of people had gathered for a party. Laughter rose to the window along with greetings to late arrivals. Eventually Daud figured out they were celebrating the news that a young couple was expecting their first child. He missed Hana and wondered where and how they could celebrate their good news with family and friends. He turned away from the window and closed his eyes.

Daud awoke early in the morning, took a shower, and went downstairs. Avi's wife, Rachel, was a friendly woman who'd immigrated to Israel as a teenager from France. Fresh coffee and a selection of five pastries were laid out on the dining room table. Rachel was sipping coffee and reading a popular Israeli newspaper. She greeted Daud in French-accented Hebrew.

"You must try every one of the pastries before Avi gets here," she said. "Otherwise he'll grab them like a big bear."

"Did you make them?" Daud asked as he poured a cup of coffee.

"Only the one topped with orange marmalade. The others come from a shop in the neighborhood."

Daud sampled the tart treat topped with marmalade and immediately placed a second one on his plate.

"I wish I could take some of these back in my luggage to America," he said. "My wife would love this because it's not too sweet."

They sat at the table and chatted for several minutes. Rachel was an amateur artist who specialized in still-life paintings. Several pieces of her artwork hung on the walls of the dining room. Daud asked about them.

"And they're not for sale," Avi announced when he entered the room. "After we're dead and gone, they're going to be recognized as masterpieces."

Rachel shook her head.

"I see you discovered the marmalade tarts," Avi continued. "Next time you're in Jerusalem, you need to visit when she makes date bars worthy of a reception at the prime minister's office."

Daud smiled. "I'll look forward to that. When I was a teenager I worked several summers harvesting dates."

During the leisurely breakfast conversation, Daud avoided revealing too much personal information. He wanted Avi and Rachel to believe that he and Hana were living in the US solely because of her job opportunity.

"But of course you want to return to Jerusalem," Rachel said.

"We'll see," Daud replied noncommittally.

Avi popped a final bite of pastry into his mouth and checked his watch. "We'd better get going for our appointment to see the bungalow," he said. "The owner sent me a key, but I want to get there as early as possible so that we're not rushed."

Avi drove a French car. It wasn't far to the Abu Tor neighborhood. From his years living in Jerusalem, Daud was familiar with the area, which included a combination of larger homes built in the late 1800s by prosperous Christian and Muslim Arab families and smaller apartment buildings constructed for Jewish immigrants. Hebron Road was the main thoroughfare. They turned onto a side street with mostly large Arab homes, some converted into multifamily dwellings. Several of the houses had enclosed gardens and courtyards.

"If the people who built these houses had known at the time what they would be worth today, they wouldn't believe it," Avi said when they passed a meticulously restored villa. "That one has been owned by the same family for over a hundred years."

They turned onto another road and began

to climb higher.

"The 1949 armistice line went along this street," Avi continued. "Some of these homes still have bullet holes in them from those battles or the ones fought in 1967."

They passed under the shade of a row of trees. Avi pulled to the curb in front of a spacious home. An iron railing ran along the sidewalk.

"Here we are," he said. "The main house is divided into four apartments, none of which are on the market. The place I want to show you is in the rear."

It was a warm morning. Daud followed Avi down a narrow alleyway between the main house and another residence next to it. The shaded walkway was cooler than the street.

"Only a motorcycle or bicycle can navigate the alley," Avi said.

"Are there parking privileges on the street?" Daud asked.

"Yes. Each unit receives one spot."

The alley ended, and Avi opened an iron gate. To the right was an extensive garden surrounded by a two-meter-high stone wall. Directly in front of them was a small, one-story building that looked about the same size as the miniature house where Daud and Hana lived in Atlanta. Daud was immediately disappointed.

"This was the servants' quarters," Avi said. "It's bigger on the inside than it looks."

Daud wondered if he had wasted a trip. "I hope so."

Hana bought a nice frame and hung the painting from Avi Labensky on the wall in the living room. To clear a space, she took down a faded old English landscape that belonged to her landlord. The Jerusalem street scene of the woman with the two babies didn't fit with the Early American decor of the living room, but Hana remembered a spot in the new house that would be perfect — the upstairs bedroom with the dormer. Light from the dormer window would illuminate the woman and two babies, causing the figures to come to life. Hana imagined hanging the painting in the bright room.

She continued her routine of tea and crackers, then loaded Leon into the car for the ride to the dog day care center. Hana laid her hand lightly on her abdomen as she waited for a stoplight to turn from red to green. Even though it was too early for any visible evidence of changes to her body, she knew she was pouring life energy into the tiny baby hidden inside. She lovingly patted her belly.

"Good morning," she said.

As soon as she arrived at the office, Hana's stomach suddenly rose up in open rebellion. Janet glanced up wide-eyed from her computer screen when Hana put her hand to her mouth and rushed down the hall toward the restroom. It was several minutes before she returned.

"What's wrong?" Janet asked.

"Upset stomach," Hana replied.

"Do you need some medicine? I keep something in my desk in case a bad burrito gets ahold of me."

"No, thanks, I don't want to take anything. I'll be fine in a few minutes."

Janet's eyes narrowed. "Why won't you take something? And how do you know you'll be okay in a few minutes? And why did you stop drinking coffee?"

Hana felt trapped.

Janet put her hand in front of her stomach and extended it outward. "Are you?" she asked.

Hana came closer to the assistant's desk and glanced around to make sure no one was approaching.

"Please, I haven't even told my mother," she pleaded. "Daud and I are going to wait a few weeks until I'm further along."

Janet raised both hands in the air as if signaling a touchdown in a football game.

"That is wonderful news!" she exclaimed and then quickly lowered her hands and spoke in a soft voice. "But I will forget this conversation ever took place until after you talk to your family."

Grateful for Janet's sensitivity, Hana glanced at the green pea that still rested in front of her computer screen. She knew the baby was doubling in size weekly and would soon reach the walnut stage. There were no walnuts in her small pantry at home, but she could buy two, one for her and one for Daud to carry around in his pocket.

Once her nausea was gone, Hana turned on her computer. Toward the top of her in-box was a group email from Mr. Lowenstein. In it, he provided additional details about the forum where she would speak. The event now had a name — Greater Atlanta Interfaith Convocation on the Israel/Palestine Issue. Hana was not familiar with the term "convocation" and looked it up in the dictionary. The British definition stated that a convocation was often an important gathering of church officials. That immediately caught her attention.

There were sixteen other recipients of the email. Hana didn't recognize any of them but looked for clues. At least half the people were likely Jewish patrons of the event, but there were a couple of men with Arab surnames. Hana checked out the background of a man named Muhammed Tahan. Born in the ancient city of Hebron, he had been educated at Cambridge in the UK and the University of California at Berkeley. Tahan currently worked as a history and philosophy teacher at an exclusive prep school in Massachusetts.

A man like Tahan would have heard every argument on the Israel/Palestinian issue and have a response prepared for each one. But Hana knew her personal story would speak louder than an argument. She could then add her belief as a Christian that the promises of God in the Bible, not human-centered agendas, were the keys to a correct understanding of the region and its people. Before working on a file for Mr. Collins, she spent thirty minutes jotting down notes and thoughts about what she might want to say.

Chapter 21

The former servants' quarters had been built with meleke limestone, the same material used to construct the Western Wall and other famous Jerusalem structures. The stones sparkled when illuminated by the rays of the sun. Avi unlocked the door. Cool air from the stone pavers on the floor and the surprisingly high ceiling welcomed them as they entered a small foyer with openings to the right and left. There was a silk Persian rug on the floor.

"The servants were paid well," Daud observed, pointing at the rug.

"That's a modern addition," Avi said with a smile. "I sold it to the owner along with a painting that you'll see in the salon."

The salon, or living room, was to the left of the foyer. The smooth stone floor continued into the salon, which featured a rarity in Jerusalem houses: a fireplace positioned between the two windows.

"Does the fireplace work?" Daud asked.

"Yes, and there are three in the main house. Both buildings were designed by a British architect who was thinking more about English winters than Middle Eastern heat. The fireplace is great for the one or two days of snow we have a year in Jerusalem."

"It makes the room seem —" He stopped.

"Cozy?" Avi suggested.

"Or welcoming."

The furniture was comfortable and didn't detract from the basic beauty of the room. There were three different paintings on the walls.

"Which painting did you sell the owner?" Daud asked.

"The landscape from the Negev."

The artist had skillfully captured the desert terrain where Daud grew up. The starkness of the brown and reddish rocks, scraggly plants clinging to the soil, and sharp-edged wadis invited the human eye to examine detail. Daud stepped closer. When he did, he saw a tiny white flower tucked away in the corner. It was a Negev lily.

"The lily is out of place," he said. "If there's one lily there should be many more. They store up water in their bulbs and blossom all at once in the fall."

"That's intentional," Avi replied. "The artist told me he included it to remind the viewer that beauty can emerge at any time in the harshest environment."

"Even out of season?"

"Especially out of season. The longer I live, the more I understand what he meant."

Daud followed Avi into a small dining room that connected to a kitchen at the rear of the house. The rectangular kitchen was surprisingly large. Several windows offered a nice view of the garden. There was ample space for an eating area at one end of the room. The stone floors were softened by area rugs.

"The kitchen was updated five years ago," Avi said.

Daud could see himself fixing coffee in the morning and helping Hana cut up the ingredients for supper in the evening. He smiled at the thought of a baby in a high chair with Leon curled up nearby on the cool stone floor.

"What about the bedrooms?"

"That's why the house is bigger than it looks," Avi said. "The original bedroom was incorporated into the kitchen. Let's see the addition."

Daud followed Avi into a hallway. To the right was a spacious master bedroom with an expansive view of the garden through large plate-glass windows. The bathroom had both a freestanding tub and a shower. The fixtures were top-quality.

"This is very fancy," Daud observed. "Maybe too fancy."

"For you, but not for your wife. Every woman likes to think there's a place in the world where she can be pampered."

To balance the master suite, there was a smaller bedroom with its own tiny bath. At the end of the hall was a room currently set up as an office. It also had a nice view of the garden and the wall surrounding it.

"Okay," Daud said to Avi. "I'm impressed, but with the location and all the upgrades, this is going to be out of our price range."

"We've not seen everything. Come outside."

"Let me take some photos first," he replied. "I should have been doing that earlier."

Daud quickly retraced their steps with his phone in his hand. He included a short video of the kitchen. They exited through a rear door and stepped into a garden lined with shrubs and flower beds. Cascading over the walls in two corners were large bougainvillea bushes covered in red blossoms. Avi led the way to the side of the house closest to the boundary wall. Set into the wall near the chimney were iron steps ascending to the flat roof. Daud followed the art dealer up fourteen stairs. A waist-high wall surrounded the rooftop patio. The owners had turned the large area into a place for social gatherings. There were comfortable all-weather chairs, couches, and several glass-topped tables.

"A lot of people can fit up here," Avi said. "I've been to parties with forty or more."

Daud wasn't interested in throwing large parties in Jerusalem. What caught his attention was that the increased elevation on the rooftop opened a vista beyond the garden wall. Daud snapped more photos and then took in the view. Avi pointed with his right hand in the direction Daud was looking.

"That's the demarcation line that existed between the two areas in 1949," Avi said. "In fact, it zigzagged around this house, which was in the Jordanian section until 1967."

Standing in a place that once marked the physical division in the land between the groups who'd fought to possess and control it, Daud felt a seriousness come over him. He was astride history, in a place with past, present, and future significance. He didn't normally think in these terms, but the impression was as vivid as the colors of the flowers in the garden below. He glanced at Avi. The art dealer seemed casual and relaxed.

"What's the asking price?" Daud asked.

"It's not officially on the market," Avi answered, "but the owner is interested in selling. I can pass along the range he mentioned to me."

Avi gave a bracket of figures that caused Daud to inhale sharply.

"There's no way I could come close to the lower end of —" Daud started.

"Don't let that discourage you. If you're interested, I can act on your behalf. Remember, people have been haggling over prices around here since the first time a man took a clay pot to the center of a village to sell it."

Hana drank an entire glass of water in a few gulps. Drinking multiple glasses of water throughout the day forced frequent trips to the restroom. Shortly before noon, she was returning to her office from her fourth break of the day when Janet, who was on the phone, raised her finger to slow her down. Her assistant placed one hand over the receiver.

"It's Jakob Brodsky. Do you want to talk

to him?"

"Yes."

Hana shut her door and accepted the call.

"How are you doing?" Jakob asked.

"What do you mean?" Hana asked sharply.

"I didn't mean anything. It's just an expression of speech. You know, another way to say hello."

"Sorry," Hana replied. "I've had a rough morning."

"Would it help if I bought your lunch? I don't mind paying, and I know it's a good way to avoid breaking the rules laid down by Mr. Lowenstein."

"This is about Mr. Ivanov's case?"

"Yes."

Hana had brought a light lunch from home, but getting away from the office for an hour would be a welcome break. "Okay, but nothing heavy or spicy."

"I thought you were on a sauerkraut, pickle, and salami diet."

"Not today."

"That cuts out Indian or Italian, but I was thinking about Mediterranean. What about that Lebanese deli near your office? I know you like it."

It had been a while since Hana had seen Mr. Akbar, the owner, but the deli was small and didn't have a lot of seating. She often stood and ate at a counter.

"They only have a few tables. Will Mr. Ivanov be joining us?"

"No, and I bet the owner will save us a spot if we call ahead. Would you like me to do that?"

"Okay."

"I'm on my way. Wait about fifteen minutes before leaving."

When it was time to leave for lunch, Hana decided to walk the five blocks to the restaurant. Halfway there, she regretted her decision. It was hot outside. Fortunately, Mr. Akbar had the air conditioner running on high, and a blast of cold air greeted her when she entered the restaurant. The owner saw her and pointed to the back corner, where Jakob was sitting at a small table for two. Hana grabbed a paper napkin from a container and wiped her forehead.

"Did you walk?" Jakob asked. "It's over ninety degrees outside."

"Which sounds hotter than thirty-two degrees Celsius but isn't," Hana answered as she sat down.

"I'll drive you back to the office. Are you ready to order?"

"Yes."

They went to the counter.

"I'll have the sfiha," Hana said to the

young man taking orders.

"Me too," Jakob said, then added, "even though I have no idea what that is."

"It's a pie made with spicy lamb, onions, and tomatoes," Hana said. "The spices vary, but usually include chili pepper, pomegranate concentrate, and cumin."

"I thought you didn't want spicy," Jakob said, perplexed.

"That was thirty minutes ago."

Hana realized she needed another restroom break. By the time she returned, the food was on the table.

"Daud likes sfiha a lot," she said when she sat down. "I bet he ate some while he was in Beirut."

"Is it also popular in Jerusalem?"

"Yes, but not always easy to find."

They each took a couple of bites.

"This is good," Hana said. "If you ever eat sfiha again, compare it to this."

Jakob took a long drink of water. "Avi Labensky sent me an email this morning about the conversation he and Daud had with Daniella Rubin, the archaeologist. As an expert in Bar Kokhba coins, she told them that some of the ones in the collection are so unique that —"

Hana had been eating while she listened. She was about to take another bite but stopped as her heart seemed to skip a beat.

"What conversation?" she demanded.

"In Jerusalem. I guess it was yesterday, although I may be off because of the time difference. Rubin wants the enhanced photos of the items in the collection, especially the coins, before agreeing to do anything else, so I'm glad I have that in process. The fact that a legitimate archaeologist is willing to get involved is huge. I didn't know about the differences between the coins minted during the three years of the revolt, but apparently that is a big deal."

"Yes, yes, but Daud isn't in Jerusalem," Hana said. "He had to spend an extra day in Beirut. They must have talked on the phone."

"That's not the impression I got," Jakob replied, taking a drink of water. "Anyway, whether in person or not, I'm encouraged."

Jakob continued tossing out ideas about how to recover the Ivanov collection. Hana only half listened. She took her phone from her purse and checked to see if she'd missed a text or email from Daud announcing a change in plans.

Jakob paused. "Is there something you need to take care of?" he asked.

"Not right now," Hana said, returning her phone to her purse. "I just know Daud wouldn't take a spontaneous trip to Jerusalem. The risk for him in Israel, especially Jerusalem, is still too great."

"Has anything happened recently?"

"No," Hana replied and then quickly amended, "At least, I don't think so."

Jakob was silent for a moment before he spoke. "Are you sure Daud would tell you?" he asked.

Instead of quickly saying yes, Hana paused.

"I don't know," she answered, trying to keep her voice from trembling. "He might keep information secret as a way to protect me. That's the way he's lived his life for years. His family never knew much about his work. But for something this important . . ."

Jakob continued to eat. Hana abandoned her food as she wrestled with her thoughts and emotions.

"Shouldn't you eat?" Jakob asked softly. "You said it was good."

"It is," Hana sighed. "And I should eat."

She took another bite of sfiha. The flavorful dish no longer held her interest. Anxiety rose up within her. She glanced around the busy restaurant.

"I'm sure everything is okay," Jakob said. "Daud is one of the most capable people

I've ever met."

"He wasn't very capable the night we were held hostage at his apartment in Beit Hanina."

Hana had forgiven Daud for putting her in mortal danger before she married him, but there was still a corner of her heart that didn't completely trust his judgment.

"True," Jakob said. "I've just tried to focus on the fact that we survived."

They finished the meal in uneasy silence.

"Was there anything else you wanted to tell me?" Hana asked as Jakob finished his meal.

"I like sfiha," he said and paused. "And I was excited about the recent developments in the Ivanov case and wanted to bounce my ideas off you. I'm sorry I upset you."

"You didn't do anything wrong."

"It's hard for me to believe that when I see the look in your eyes."

"I guess it's getting harder for me to hide my feelings," Hana said with a sigh.

"I'll give you a ride back to your office."

CHAPTER 22

Khalil handed Rahal a report about Daud Hasan. They were meeting in a cozy study where Rahal liked to read and pray.

"Daud Hasan is the man who was in Sharm el-Sheikh," Khalil said, not trying to hide his excitement. "Photo analysis confirms it one hundred percent!"

Rahal maintained a calm exterior. He motioned for his assistant to sit down. Khalil sat on the edge of a small straight-backed chair while Rahal read the report.

"He's a Christian," Rahal said. "Which probably explains some of his actions. Find out more about his family and religious connections."

"Yes, sir," Khalil replied, making a note on his tablet.

Rahal was impressed with the details Khalil had been able to pull together in such a short time. It included dates for Hasan's military service in the IDF and information about his work as a private investigator. There were photos from his website and testimonials from representative clients.

"So the private investigator job was a front for his government work on behalf of the Jews," he said, glancing up.

"Only in part. He ran a business from his base in the Beit Hanina district of Al-Quds," Khalil replied, using the Arabic name for Jerusalem. "But he shut it down after the Chechen operation and went underground. Someone else rents the apartment in Beit Hanina where he lived."

There were multiple photos of Daud. In one taken near the Sea of Galilee, he was carrying a backpack.

"Where did you find these photos?" Rahal asked.

"Mostly from the website of his previous business, and by searching the accounts of his friends on social media. He worked for American and EU companies doing background checks on potential employees in Palestine as well as investigations for lawsuits."

"And played football."

"Correct."

Rahal turned the page. There was a photo of a young Arab woman wearing Western clothes with a little boy sitting in her lap.

"Who is this?" Rahal asked, holding up the report.

"A Christian Arab woman named Fabia Yamout who lives in Reineh, a town near Nazareth. Last year she posted a photo on social media of Hasan with another woman who may be his girlfriend or wife. That post is on the next page."

A smiling Daud Hasan stood next to an attractive Arab woman in a white dress. They were standing beneath an arbor covered in bright flowers. The decadent images made Rahal sick to his stomach.

"This is part of a wedding celebration," he said.

"Probably, but we need to confirm it," Khalil said.

"Great work!" Rahal exclaimed, returning the tablet.

"Do you want me to initiate communication with the Chechens?" Khalil asked. "At least one of the members of their cell was killed at Hasan's apartment and almost a dozen were arrested by the Israelis. That's why they placed a bounty on Hasan. I'm sure they possess addition information, but they are also well-known to both the Jews and the Americans. It's likely the Mossad and CIA monitor their communications."

Rahal hesitated. "Look into the connections between Hasan and the town you mentioned near Nazareth."

"Reineh."

"Yes, and hire a private investigator of our own. Pull a page from Hasan's protocol and tell the investigator it has to do with a background check for a potential employer in the US."

Daud and Avi reached the bottom of the steps.

"You saw the quality of the modification to the kitchen and the addition of the two bedrooms to the house," Avi said. "It increased the value of the property by at least thirty percent. And I forgot to tell you that it's fee simple land."

Over ninety percent of the real estate in Israel was owned by the government or quasi-government entities that leased the property to residents for a ninety-nine-year term. The Israelis believed this reflected the ultimate reality that only God could "own" land in perpetuity. The remaining ten percent of the land, mostly in urban areas and often the property of orthodox or Catholic churches or well-established Arab families, was outside the system. The land could therefore be transferred and sold without restrictions or time limits, just as real estate in the US and Britain. In an older Arab area like Abu Tor, it made sense that there would be property available for outright purchase.

"Okay," Daud replied with a nod. "It would be nice to say the property was truly ours."

They retraced their steps down the alley to the main street. By the time they reached the car, Daud already wanted to turn around and walk through the house again. The pull of the bungalow on his soul was intense. He stared at the small part of it that remained visible from the street until Avi pulled away from the curb.

"Thanks for taking me there," he said as they drove away. "You were right. It is a special property."

"Which is another reason I'd better handle the negotiation for you. Once the seller sees your eyes, he'll know you want it badly."

"Thanks, but you can't handle what will be the hardest part of the negotiations," Daud replied.

"Why not?"

"It will be with my wife."

Back at Avi's home, they went to the art dealer's office. It was a chaotic room filled with paintings leaning against the walls, small statues and busts, and folders filled with papers randomly stacked on the floor.

"How do you find anything in here?" Daud asked.

"It can be a challenge," Avi replied as he sat down in front of an ancient desktop computer. "I clean it once a year when I have to pay my taxes."

Daud touched a small ornamental chair that looked like an antique. "Can I sit on this?" he asked.

"Yes, it's a fake," Avi replied. "The real ones are worth fifteen thousand shekels. I rescued that one from circulation so no one could be duped."

Daud sat beside Avi while the art dealer logged on to the computer and initiated the Skype call to the owner of the Abu Tor house, a man who lived in Marseilles.

"Keep clear of the camera," Avi said. "Remember, I don't want Louis to see your eager face."

Fifteen minutes later Avi rolled away from the computer.

"That went well," he said.

Daud shook his head. "I don't know. He seemed set on his price."

"Oh, that's the first step of the dance. I'll let Louis think about things for a few days, then contact him again."

"Don't spend too much time on this until I talk to Hana."

"This is fun for me. And even if you're not ultimately interested in buying the house, I'll probably sell him a painting or two."

Hana finished supper and took Leon outside. She checked her phone for the status of Daud's flight from New York to Atlanta and estimated that he should be on the ground at Hartsfield Airport within an hour. Sitting on the living room sofa, Hana ran through scenarios of how to address her husband's deception in failing to tell her that he went to Israel from Beirut. She couldn't decide whether to pretend she didn't know the truth and see if he volunteered it, ask questions that might result in evasive answers, or confront him directly. Listening to lies would be the most painful option, but if a deep flaw in their relationship needed to be revealed, that was the best course. Unable to sit still, she began to clean the kitchen counters that were already spotless. Leon whimpered and nuzzled her leg. She patted the dog on the head and scratched behind his ears.

"You know I'm upset," she said. "If only people could be so perceptive."

It turned out that Daud's flight from New York to Atlanta was delayed. It was after midnight when the lights of a vehicle finally shone through the window. Hana brought herself fully awake. Leon woofed when Daud opened the door. Wagging his tail, the dog pattered over to him. Daud scratched him on the head and looked up at Hana.

"How are you feeling?" he asked. "Sorry I'm late."

"Okay," Hana replied. "How was Beirut?"

"Fine. I liked the young man who is going to run the office."

While Daud unpacked his suitcase, he told Hana about Youssef.

"What kind of problems did you run into?"

"None, but I communicated with Avi while I was there and flew from Beirut to Athens and then on to Jerusalem. It was a spur-of-the-moment thing. That's why I stayed over an extra day. I knew it would worry you, so I didn't send a text or email."

The fact that Daud wasn't planning to lie to her unleashed the built-up tension and anxiety inside Hana. Tears sprang to her eyes.

"I already knew you went to Israel," she said, her voice trembling. "And I couldn't believe you didn't tell me."

Daud stepped across the room and wrapped his arms around her. Hana buried her head against his shoulder.

"I'm sorry," he said after several moments passed. "I should have let you know."

Hana lifted her head. "Jakob found out you had a meeting in Jerusalem with Avi and an archaeologist. He told me about it at lunch without realizing I was in the dark. It set off all kinds of alarm bells for me."

Daud didn't say anything but continued to hold her. When he released her, she looked up into his eyes.

"I have to think differently," he said. "It's not like the past when my family never knew what I was doing. I was wrong."

Hana nodded. Daud rubbed his temples.

"Would you like some tea?" she asked.

"It's late —"

"No, I want to stay up for a few minutes."

While Hana was putting a pot of water on the stove, Daud called out to her from the living room. "Where did you find that painting?"

"Avi Labensky sent it to us as a wedding gift along with the information he collected for Jakob. If I'd known you were going to Jerusalem, you could have thanked him in person."

Hana joined him.

"Do you like it?" Daud asked.

"Yes. Avi has great taste. I'd be interested

in learning more about the artist."

They sat on the sofa to wait for the water to boil.

"A lot has happened here while you were gone," Hana continued.

"I have more news too."

"I found a house," Hana said slowly. "And it's just about perfect."

Taking out her phone, she showed Daud the photos from the viewing and gave him a running commentary of her opinion about every feature. Partway through, the water pot whistled and she went to the kitchen to prepare the tea.

"I should let you ask questions," she said when she returned. "I'm talking way too much."

"No, go ahead."

Hana didn't reveal the listing price until the very end. She felt Daud stiffen when she told him how much the owners wanted.

"But it's worth every dollar," she said. "And it's not out of line for the neighborhood. I did some checking, and property values in that area are continuing to climb. Janet says we might end up in a bidding war that drives the price even higher. There's no question a bank will approve us for the purchase. Our financial guidelines are much more conservative than most Americans'."

"We're not Americans."

"True, but at least have an open mind about it, okay?" Hana said.

"Okay." Daud stretched his arms out in front of him and yawned.

Hana yawned too. "I think we both need to get some sleep," he said.

"But you have more news."

"It really is late and can wait."

The following morning Hana Skyped with her mother and cousins while Daud finished eating breakfast.

"We would love to have you visit America whenever you want to," she said to her mother. "We may even be in a new house."

"Really? That's exciting."

Daud listened again to the information about the house in Atlanta. He'd woken up early in the morning, partly due to time differences with the Middle East but also because he wasn't sure what to say to Hana about the house in Abu Tor. He'd promised to be more open with her, but he couldn't figure out how to mention returning to Israel and living in Jerusalem.

"My family is finally realizing that we're going to live in America," Hana said to him when the call ended.

"That may change when your mother

finds out about the baby. She won't like the idea of a grandchild across the ocean where she can't hold it as often as she likes."

"That's why having a house where they can stay with us is important. If they came now, we'd have to put them up in a hotel. The house I looked at is set up great for guests."

Daud managed a weak smile but wasn't sure it was very convincing.

"Do you think it would be okay to tell people at work that I'm pregnant even though we haven't told our families?" Hana continued. "I'm so excited that I'm about to pop."

"Uh, that's up to you."

Hana took a final drink of tea. "I'm going to do it. It fits so nicely with the news about the house."

Daud didn't point out that the same rationale applied to the conversation Hana had just completed with her family. "Okay," he said.

Thirty minutes later Hana left for work. Daud was relieved that she didn't ask him about his other news from the trip. Going for a run, he spent five miles thinking about the issue without reaching a conclusion.

Hana's face beamed as she approached

Janet's desk. "Daud said I can officially tell you," she announced.

"About what?" Janet asked innocently.

"I'm pregnant!" Hana exclaimed.

"Awesome! May I share the good tidings of great joy?"

"Yes, with anyone at the office except Mr. Collins and Mr. Lowenstein. I'd like to do that myself."

Janet leaned over and pressed a button on her keyboard. "I have an announcement queued up to send to the people I know would want to celebrate with you."

"Mr. Collins is out of town in New York, so I'll email him," Hana said. "What about Mr. Lowenstein's status?"

Janet picked up the phone, pressed a few buttons, spoke, then listened. "Gladys says he's on his way and should be here in a few minutes. He doesn't have anything on his calendar for the next thirty minutes."

Hana was staring out the window at the expansive view from Mr. Lowenstein's office when he arrived.

"You needed to see me first thing?" he asked. "Is there a problem?"

"No, sir," Hana replied. "I'm pregnant and wanted you to hear it from me."

"Congratulations," Mr. Lowenstein said as a broad smile creased his face. "How far along are you?"

Hana provided her best guess and answered several follow-up questions. The older lawyer was about the same age as her father, and talking to him made Hana miss her dad. She suddenly became teary.

"Are you okay?" Mr. Lowenstein asked. "There are tissues on the table."

"Yes, it's just that talking to you makes me miss my father. I Skyped with my family this morning, but we're not telling them about the baby until I see the doctor. I really miss them and want them to come for a visit."

"Are you still in that tiny rental house off Piedmont Road?"

"Yes, but I looked at a three-bedroom house that just came on the market. I think it would be a great place to start a family."

As soon as she spoke, Hana felt she'd overstepped a professional boundary, but Mr. Lowenstein had raised the subject.

"Do you have any pictures?" he asked.

"Yes."

The senior partner sat beside her. When Hana tried to scroll quickly through the photos, he made her slow down so he could ask questions.

"I'm taking up too much of your time," Hana said.

"No, I need moments like these more than you do," Mr. Lowenstein said. "If we bill an hour less today, it won't make a difference by the end of the year."

Hana's eyes widened.

"But if you ever quote me, I'll deny it," the lawyer continued.

Hana smiled. "Agreed."

Finally, Mr. Lowenstein returned to his place behind his desk. "Did you read the email about the forum on Israel?" he asked.

"Yes, sir. I've started organizing my thoughts."

"Excellent. Have you decided how you're going to conclude your opening remarks?"

It was an unexpected question.

"No, I've focused more on the beginning," Hana responded slowly.

"Which is fine, but make sure you lay the foundation for where you want to take the audience."

Hana was silent for a moment. An idea bubbled to the surface.

"I'd like to end with a message of hope, not based on a political solution but on a change in the minds and hearts of the people."

"That's ambitious."

"And I'd relate it to the next generation," she continued. "There are no three-year-old children in Tel Aviv, Ramallah, or Nazareth filled with prejudice and hate."

"I like it," Mr. Lowenstein answered. "It's the kind of challenge that is practical as well as inspirational."

Later that morning Hana took a call from Jakob.

"Is Daud back in town?" he asked.

"Yes, he got in last night."

"It's none of my business, but is he in hot water for not telling you about his side trip to Israel?"

"No, he immediately told me about the detour to Jerusalem."

"That's a relief," Jakob said. "As a fellow male, I was rooting for him and hoping he would come clean without having to be cross-examined first."

"Remember, I'm not a courtroom lawyer."

"It doesn't matter. Any woman wanting to uncover the truth can grill a guy better than a first-rate trial attorney."

Hana chuckled. "Daud and I had some other things to talk about too. We have big news."

"You're leaving Collins, Lowenstein, and Capella to open your own law office?"

"No. Why would I want to do that?"

"To be free like me."

"I like it here, and the only kind of leave in my future is maternity leave."

"You're pregnant?"

"Yes. That's a requirement to be off work for the birth of a baby."

"Congratulations! Maybe you should stay at the law firm and keep your insurance coverage," Jakob replied with a smile in his voice. "I'll call Daud to congratulate him, and there are new developments in the Ivanov claim. Daud's detour to Jerusalem may have been stressful for you, but it was good for me."

CHAPTER 23

Returning from his run, Daud turned on his laptop. Fifteen minutes later his eyes grew heavy and he lay down on the sofa where he fell asleep. He was in a semiconscious state when Jakob called.

"Hello," Daud said groggily.

"Were you asleep? Hana told me you might be jet-lagged."

"Just waking up from a nap," Daud said.

"If you want me to call back later, just let me know —"

"It's okay," Daud said as he sat up on the sofa.

"First, sorry I blew your cover with Hana about the trip to Jerusalem. She told me a few minutes ago that she wasn't mad at you."

"That's good to hear. I thought we worked through it okay last night."

"You can be my counselor when I ask Emily to marry me. Anyway, I've been communicating fast and furious with Avi and Daniella."

Daud was surprised that Jakob was now on a first-name basis with both the art dealer and the archaeologist.

"I sent Avi the digitally enhanced photographs of the Bar Kokhba coins along with the one of the ceramic queen's head," Jakob continued. "The next thing I know, I'm on Skype with both of them from Avi's art shop in Jerusalem. Daniella believes she knows who has possession of one or more of the coins."

"She mentioned that as a possibility at our dinner in Jerusalem but wouldn't tell me."

"The enhanced photographs changed her mind. They removed her doubts about the coins and convinced her it was her duty to notify the woman who has them that they may have been stolen from the rightful owner. Daniella promised to contact her and let me know what she says."

"Where does this woman live?"

"In an area of Jerusalem I've never heard of that sounded like Tabitha."

"Talbiya," Daud said.

"Yeah, that's it," Jakob replied.

Daud sat up on the sofa. "The president of Israel has his official residence in Talbiya," he said. "The area has old mansions built by rich Arab Christians who purchased land from the Greek Orthodox Church a hundred years ago. It's not far from the Old City. Anything else about the woman? Do you know her name?"

"No, but if she's rich, she might fight to keep the coins. Mr. Ivanov may end up being more interested in recovering the coins than locating the queen's head."

If he had a base of operations in Jerusalem, Daud could be in the middle of the investigation. Jakob's case had captured his interest.

"I'm shutting down everything else I've been doing on the Russian internet to focus on this," Jakob continued. "The postings on Russian social media have dwindled to nothing except ads from people trying to sell me something that has nothing to do with ancient artifacts. Do you agree working with Avi is more efficient than starting up a similar program in the Middle East?"

"Yes. As long as he's willing to help, you should ask him to do so."

"Most of me believes that's true, but even with the input from Daniella, I may send up a trial balloon by posting a request for information on a couple of websites I've already located. Would you have time to compose the text if I send it over to you? It shouldn't take very long."

Daud hesitated. He didn't want to waste his time, but one lesson he'd learned as a private investigator was not to limit his efforts to one course of action. "Not until I finish a report for the client who sent me to Beirut."

"Great." Jakob paused. "And congratulations on your news."

"Did Avi Labensky tell you about the house in Abu Tor?" Daud asked in surprise.

"I have no idea about a house in Abu-anything," Jakob answered. "I'm talking about the fact that you're going to be a father."

"Yes, yes," Daud replied, shaking his head at his own stupidity. "We're excited. And don't mention anything about Abu Tor to Hana. We've not discussed it."

"I've learned my lesson. I'm not talking to Hana about anything unless she brings it up. Then I'm going to listen, nothing else."

Rahal enjoyed spending time alone in a sauna. The hot room gave him an opportunity to retreat into his thoughts as impurities escaped through his pores. The steam room was well equipped with cold drinks, multiple places to sit, and piped-in music. An intercom connected him to the outside. He was sitting on a marble bench sipping a drink when a voice came over the intercom. It was Khalil.

"Sir, I'm here for our appointment and will be waiting for you in the lounge."

Rahal checked a digital clock on the wall. He'd forgotten about the meeting with his assistant. He took a final dip into a pool of icy water in one corner of the room. Invigorated, he put on a luxurious white robe with gold piping and entered the lounge adjacent to the sauna.

"Do you have the financial reports for last week?" Rahal asked.

"Yes, sir."

Khalil handed him a thin folder that Rahal quickly flipped through. Oil revenues had been on a steep downward slope for over a year. The depressing financial figures ruined in a matter of seconds the beneficial effects of his hour spent in the steam room. Rahal tossed the folder onto a side table. Sitting down in a small chair, he crossed his legs.

"There is good news," Khalil continued.

Rahal pointed to the folder. "An increase in income of two percent from our services to the American military base hardly qualifies as good news."

"It has to do with Daud Hasan."

Rahal perked up. "I'm listening."

"We hired a private investigator with an office in Al-Quds. As soon as I mentioned that I worked for an American company interested in hiring a man named Daud Hasan, the investigator told me that he'd known Hasan for years."

"That's risky," Rahal cut in. "He might notify Hasan that someone is making inquiries about him."

"We don't care if he does," Khalil replied. "The investigator told me Hasan is living and working in America, so it's natural that a company would be conducting a background search before contacting him."

"Good point," Rahal said.

"Because of his existing knowledge of Hasan, the investigator said he would be able to respond quickly. I promised a bonus payment if he did so."

Khalil held up his tablet. "I already have his report and can summarize it for you."

"Go ahead."

Khalil hit a few buttons. "Hasan left Palestine because he married an Arab woman who is working for an American law firm in Atlanta, Georgia. Her name is Hana Abboud. She's from Reineh, and I confirmed it's the same woman in the photo I showed you the other day."

"Excellent," Rahal said. "Did he find out their address?"

"No, but he gave me the name of the law firm where the wife works. I went on their website and confirmed that she's still there. She mostly uses the name Abboud, not Hasan. I'm sure their personal information and location can be obtained easily."

"One option would be to inform the Chechens where Hasan is living and find out if they are serious about exacting revenge," Rahal said.

"I mentioned that in my report. And I would like to target his wife as well. It should be possible to do so easily, especially if we offer to fund the operation for the Chechens."

Rahal thought for a moment before responding. "I agree."

Now that her pregnancy was public knowledge in Atlanta, there was one person Hana wanted to share the good news with as soon as possible. It was 3:00 p.m. before she could carve out the time to make the phone call. She reached Ben Neumann at work.

"I have some personal news that I'd like to share with you and Sadie," she said.

"Are you pregnant?"

"How did you guess?"

330

"It wasn't that hard," Ben said, laughing. "Congratulations to you and Daud."

"Thanks."

"And I totally understand why you want to tell Sadie in person. Would you have time to swing by the house today for a few minutes on your way home from work?"

Hana had been working hard all day and could afford to leave a few minutes early.

"Yes, but I can't stay for dinner. I want to get home to Daud. He's been out of town for a few days and just returned last night."

"I'll let the visit be a surprise," Ben said. "Are you going to bring Leon?"

"If it's okay with you."

"That will double Sadie's joy."

Hana sent Daud a text telling him what she was going to do. He responded immediately.

Will bring home Chinese food

Hana sent a smiley face in reply. One of their first meals together had been at a tiny Chinese restaurant in Jerusalem where Daud arranged for them to have the whole place to themselves.

"I'm going over to Ben Neumann's townhome to tell Sadie about the baby," Hana said to Janet as she left her office.

"How do you think she'll take the news?"

"She'll be happy."

"I hope you're right," Janet said slowly. "There's a chance she might feel jealous, if not immediately, then after she has time to think about it. Sadie knows you've given her your heart, and it will hurt when she realizes she'll have to share you with someone else besides Daud, even if it's your own child."

It was a possibility Hana hadn't considered. During the drive she prayed about what Janet said.

Leon woofed in greeting as Sadie threw open the door.

"I was in the living room and saw you walking down the sidewalk," she said.

Sadie knelt down, buried her face in Leon's fur, and ran her fingers over his back. The dog tried to turn his head to the side so he could lick her, which he did when she faced him. Ben appeared in the doorway.

"Come in," he said. "Letting a dog lick a child's face in public may violate the rules of the homeowners' association."

"I'll take Leon to the backyard," Sadie said, trotting off with the dog in tow.

Hana could smell something baking in the kitchen. "What are you cooking?" she asked.

"Sadie is making homemade cookies. As

you've seen, the culinary class she's taking as part of the science curriculum has had a huge impact on her. She doesn't just learn what to put into a cookie; she learns how the ingredients interact at the molecular level."

"She's so smart."

"Speaking of cooking, would you and Daud be available one night this week for dinner with Laura and me? After taking a break, we've been spending more time together, and things are better than ever."

"Probably," Hana replied casually. She knew the meeting would have to take place eventually. "I'll talk it over with him and let you know."

Through the double glass doors, they could see Sadie and Leon playing in the backyard.

"Sadie has new-dog fever in the worst way," Ben continued. "I've told her it's not a good idea to leave a dog alone all day while I'm at work and she's at school, but she's not buying my argument. Also, Laura is highly allergic to any form of animal dander. Her eyes start itching if she comes too close to dogs in a public park. It would be cruel to introduce a puppy into Sadie's life and then have to give it away."

"There are hypoallergenic breeds. I know

someone who has a —" Hana started but stopped when Sadie burst into the kitchen.

"He's playing with the ball I bought with my own money," the little girl announced. "It has batteries and squeaks and rolls on its own."

Leon leapt into the air and pounced on the live-action toy as it scooted away.

"Can you stay for supper?" Sadie asked. "We're going to eat pasta cooked in the microwave. I can share with you."

"No, I just stopped by for a few minutes, but I'd love to try your cookies and take one to Daud."

"Can you help me with my homework?" Sadie begged. "I have to explain to someone what goes on inside a cookie while it bakes."

Ben moved toward the kitchen door. "I'll let you ladies have a cookie talk for a few minutes."

Sadie checked the timer on the oven. "They still need to bake for five minutes, but I can tell you what's happening while we wait."

They sat at the kitchen counter as Sadie rattled off the chemical changes taking place in the cookie dough. Hana was impressed. The beeper sounded. Sadie jumped up and slipped an oven mitt over her hand, then took the hot cookie sheet from the oven. It was an act that she couldn't have done when they first met. She placed the sheet on a metal trivet, reset the timer, and returned to the counter.

"They need to cool for a few minutes before we eat them. I call these 'extra-special cookies' because they have all the stuff I like in them."

"They smell delicious."

"You need to sign this sheet of paper that says I explained everything so I can give it to Mrs. Rosenstein."

Hana signed the sheet of paper and added a sentence about Sadie's excellent job.

"Thanks," Sadie said. "Would you like milk with your cookies?"

"Yes."

Sadie opened the freezer and took out two frosted glasses. "Milk tastes better in a cold glass."

She carefully poured milk into the glasses and placed one in front of Hana, who took a sip.

"It's whole milk," Sadie continued. "Do you believe that skim milk is whole milk with water added?"

"I've never thought about it, but that makes sense."

"No, we learned that they put whole milk in a machine that spins it around really

335

fast." Sadie paused. "It's called a center-fudge and makes some of the fat go down a tube."

"Centrifuge," Hana corrected, thinking about the more ominous use of the spinning devices to prepare uranium for nuclear weapons.

"Yes, I have trouble getting that right. Mrs. Rosenstein brought in some raw cow's milk for us to try. I was scared at first, but when I took a sip it tasted like melted vanilla ice cream. I told Daddy we should buy some. He could put it in his coffee."

"I drank raw goat's milk every day when I was a girl," Hana said. "We even poured it on our cereal."

The beeper sounded again. Sadie dislodged the cookies from the metal sheet with a plastic turner. The cookies were speckled with chocolate chips, crushed pecans, and flakes of coconut. Sadie put one on a plate and presented it to Hana, who inhaled the fragrance before taking a sample bite.

"This is delicious," she said immediately. "I can see why you call them extra special."

Sadie beamed. They each ate a cookie, then another.

"Wait," Hana said. "You haven't eaten supper yet."

"It's okay," Sadie said dismissively. "I'm with you."

Hana took a drink of milk. "It's because you're so extra special to me that I stopped by," she said. "I wanted to share some exciting news with you. Daud and I are going to have a baby."

Sadie's eyes widened. She immediately glanced at Hana's abdomen.

"I just found out a few days ago, so you can't tell by looking at me. But it won't be long before the baby will grow bigger and bigger."

Hana took out her phone and showed Sadie the approximate size of the unborn child. Sadie's half-eaten cookie remained untouched as she stared at the images.

"What do you think?" Hana asked.

Sadie took in a deep breath. Her eyes were serious. She looked directly into Hana's face. "I'm kind of excited, but are you and the baby going to be okay?"

Hana instantly realized Sadie's response was an unexpected consequence of the death of the little girl's own mother. For Sadie, the connection between mother and child was not a safe one. Hana reached out and pulled Sadie in close for a long hug.

"Everything is going to be fine," she said, stroking the girl's dark hair.

Sadie buried her head into Hana's shoulder. It had been a while since she'd held Sadie like this. Hana realized how much she missed it and how deeply she loved the girl. After a minute passed, she kissed the top of Sadie's head and released her.

"I love you," Sadie said. "And I hope you have a girl. If you do, you can name her Sadie. I don't mind sharing my name."

Hana embraced Sadie again. "That is one of the most giving, unselfish things I've ever heard."

"Not really. But if you do it, you may want to use a nickname so you don't mix us up."

"I'd never let that happen." Hana took another bite of cookie and patted her stomach. "Whatever his or her name, my baby loves your cookies. I'd like to take a couple of them home for Daud, but I can't promise I won't eat them in the car on the way."

CHAPTER 24

The fragrance of fresh-baked cookies caused Leon's nose to twitch. Hana wasn't tempted to eat the treats during the drive home from the Neumanns'. Her heart was heavy with the still-fresh layer of trauma that the news of her pregnancy had revealed in Sadie. The death of the child's mother was a wound requiring many healings.

"I'm home," she announced as she stepped through the door.

Daud was rubbing his eyes as he stood in his socks beside the sofa. "Sorry, did I wake you up?" Hana asked.

"No, but Leon did." Daud yawned. "Supper is in the oven."

"And Sadie baked dessert." Hana held up the plate of cookies.

Hana brewed tea. When they sat down to eat, the only sound at the table was the clicking of chopsticks.

"Would you ever like to go back to the

Chinese restaurant where we ate in East Jerusalem?" Daud asked, expertly scooping up some rice and delicately seasoned chicken.

"That was a wonderful meal," Hana answered. "And even more so because you reserved the whole restaurant just for us."

"They only had a few tables, and it was around four thirty in the afternoon. They wouldn't have had many customers anyway."

"Don't cheapen the memory."

"That's not possible, because you were with me."

Hana smiled and pointed a chopstick at Daud's face. "Well said. Tell me about your day."

"Except for going out to pick up the food, I was here all day writing reports and resting."

"Didn't you talk to Jakob Brodsky? He told me he was going to call you."

"Yeah, we talked twice."

"He said there was new information about the Ivanov matter."

"Yes."

Hana listened to Daud describe the status of the investigation. "You'd like to be in the middle of it, wouldn't you?" she asked. "I can hear it in your voice."

"I'm an investigator," Daud said and shrugged. "That's what I've done for years. Even before I was a professional, I spent a lot of time as a kid roaming about the desert investigating things."

Daud got up to fill his bowl with more food.

"You must be hungry," she commented.

"Yes, and I don't want to snack later. You know how Chinese food doesn't stay with you."

"Oh. Ben invited us out for dinner with him and Laura, his girlfriend."

"Without Sadie?"

"Right. He believes it would make things more complicated if Sadie was there. I remembered what you told me about letting Ben set the agenda, so I didn't argue."

"And you think dinner with them is a good idea?"

"It has to happen eventually. I'd rather start collecting information now rather than later."

"Collecting information?" Daud replied. "I'm supposed to be the investigator."

"This is an investigation of the heart."

Hana told him about her time with Sadie at the townhome. She became teary when she told him about the girl's reaction to the news that Hana was pregnant. "Isn't it sad that Sadie immediately made a connection between my being a mother and danger?"

"Yes, but it's sweet that she wants to share her name. How about Miriam Sadie Hasan?" Daud offered.

"That might work."

They finished their meal.

"Ready for a cookie?" Hana asked.

"Or cookies."

While Hana warmed them in the microwave, Daud sent a text to Ben about dinner. He immediately replied.

"Tomorrow night for dinner with Ben and Laura," he called out to Hana.

Hana returned with the cookies. "Before meeting with them, would you like to see the new house? I can't wait to show it to you in person."

"I guess so."

"Don't you agree that we'll need more space for us and a baby?" Hana asked. "With only one bedroom and bath, this house isn't going to work for us."

"I'm willing to consider a move. To the right house in the right place."

Something about the way Daud spoke didn't sound like a yes, but Hana wasn't sure exactly why.

"Okay," Hana said. "Oh, do you want some milk?"

"No, thanks."

Deciding to change the subject, Hana told Daud about her milk conversation with Sadie.

"It brought back memories of the goat's milk I drank as a girl. Is that what your mother gave you?"

"Yes, and I also drank camel's milk since my grandfather was a camel broker."

"How did that taste?"

"Salty — and it can have strange flavors depending on what the camel has been eating. My grandfather loved it warm and straight out of the camel. I remember him taking big gulps that caused it to run down the corners of his mouth. If we give it to our baby when she's little, she'll like it her whole life."

Hana stayed up later than usual reading and listening to music. Daud went to bed early. When she awoke in the night, Hana slipped out of bed and returned to the living room. The first matter on her heart was Sadie. She meditated on God's promises to the orphan and the fatherless, substituting *mother* for *father.* The tenderness and zeal of the Lord's affection toward those who had suffered great loss never failed to touch Hana deeply. She prayed from Psalm 142 that the Lord would watch over Sadie's way.

Turning to Psalm 37, she asked that he take note of the motherless girl's grief and hold her hand. Hana prayed that the next time she held Sadie's hand it would reflect the spiritual reality.

She then shifted to her desire for a home. Daud could be either methodical or decisive, which presented a challenge. They'd had minor disagreements but not yet faced a major life decision. The move to America from Israel was dictated by circumstances beyond their control. The possibility that Daud might not go along with her desire for a new house caused a knot to form in Hana's stomach. She quickly turned to a familiar verse in Proverbs and softly read it out loud: " 'By wisdom a house is built, and through understanding it is established.' "

Bowing her head, she prayed that Daud would have both wisdom and understanding. She then turned to Psalm 127 and read it in a slightly louder voice: " 'Unless the Lord builds the house, the builders labor in vain. Unless the Lord watches over the city, the guards stand watch in vain.' "

Her eyes closed, Hana raised her head upward as if hoping an extra few inches would propel her prayers toward heaven.

"That's a good prayer," said a male voice, causing Hana to jump.

Daud stood directly behind the sofa.

"Now you can pray that my heart won't fall out of my chest," Hana answered. "How long have you been standing there?"

"Long enough to listen to you read and pray scriptures about a house. I think wisdom and understanding are important for both of us, not just me."

Hana realized she'd made the mistake of applying the truth to someone else while ignoring its relevance for her. "Should I start over?"

"No, no, but as I listened I thought there was something that goes along with the wisdom and understanding both of us need."

"What?"

"Faith," Daud said, putting his right hand on her shoulder. "Faith makes wisdom and understanding practical. Otherwise they're just ideas in our heads."

Hana reached up and placed her hand on top of Daud's. "Okay," she said, closing her eyes. "We ask the Lord to build our house with wisdom and understanding and faith."

"Amen," Daud said. He returned to the bedroom.

Once alone, Hana quickly wrote what they'd prayed in her journal.

■ ■ ■ ■

The following morning Daud talked again with Jakob. Their discussions about the Russian internet had triggered an idea unrelated to Vladimir Ivanov.

"Would you be interested in researching something for me in Russia?" Daud asked.

"How could I turn you down after the help you've already given me? What's it about?" Jakob quickly responded.

"The background of a Ukrainian scientist named Artem Kolisnyk. He's an expert in missile technology."

"Whoa," Jakob answered. "This sounds like something for the CIA or the Mossad to check out."

"They're not available."

"And I'm a poor substitute. Why are you interested in him?"

Daud had to be careful. He didn't want to breach governmental security protocols surrounding the Sharm el-Sheikh mission. He remembered a few general facts from the briefing dossier.

"He's in his midfifties and lived for a while in Kharkiv."

"Along with a million and a half other people."

"And worked for several years at Khartron Corporation, a company that sold military equipment and technology on the black market to anyone who would pay for it," Daud added.

"A rogue scientist," Jakob responded. "Guys like that are much more dangerous than an ordinary terrorist with a bomb strapped around his chest because their knowledge could kill thousands of people."

"It's his past history I'm interested in, especially anybody he's made mad and why. I don't care about his current status."

"Have you already researched Kolisnyk on Russian websites?"

"No, I don't want anyone to track anything back to me."

"How does that not create a problem for me?" Jakob asked.

"If you don't want to do it, I'll understand and —"

"No, no. I get why you need a buffer between you and anything on the internet. As a Russian American sitting in his basement surfing the internet, I'm not likely to attract attention."

"You don't have a basement at your apartment."

"It's a figure of speech. That's helpful background on the Ukrainian. Let me go

347

back to my original question. Why are you interested in this guy? You're not going to build a rocket in the woods next to your house, are you?"

"No. And I'd rather leave the why out of it."

Before they met Ben and Laura for dinner, Daud was going to join Hana to view the new house. Just as he was walking out the door, his phone vibrated. Jakob. He answered as he slipped behind the steering wheel of the Land Rover.

"Did you receive my email?" Jakob asked.

"I saw it in my queue but haven't read it," Daud answered as he started the Land Rover's engine.

"You were right," Jakob said. "Artem Kolisnyk is as much entrepreneur as he is scientist. He's been peddling his services for years through this Khartron outfit. Most of the items they sold were Russian, but they included a mix of Chinese equipment as well. I'm sure they bribed the Ukrainian authorities so they could stay in business. Kolisnyk provided knowledge and expertise. I had to dig, but I found links to dissatisfied customers who called him out by name as a crook. It was like reading an online rant by someone who buys an electric motor that looks good on the outside but doesn't work when hooked up to a machine."

"Anything specific?"

"Sometimes the plans he supplied didn't enable the customers to do what he promised, which made them mad. He blamed them for not following directions."

The picture became clearer for Daud. "If Kolisnyk and his group didn't deliver what was ordered, how did they get paid?" he asked.

"It wasn't a total train wreck. They often provided valuable information and material but not always up to the expectations of their customers. The purchasers weren't necessarily sophisticated; they just had money and wanted guns and rockets. And they were deceptive themselves. The deals required them to sign an agreement that they were acquiring the technology for commercial, not military, purposes, although I doubt anyone took the restrictions seriously."

Daud himself had used the promise of sophisticated computer software to lure and trap criminals and terrorists. It was a commonly used strategy because the bait was so enticing.

"Khartron is defunct," Jakob continued. "My guess is the negative results and feedback drove Kolisnyk and his buddies out of business and into your world. Am I right?"

Daud ignored the question. "What about the identity of anyone who might be very mad at him?"

"I didn't get into any of that yet."

"Would you do that?"

"I can try," Jakob responded.

Hana and the real estate agent were standing in the yellow nursery room attached to the master bedroom when they heard the door knocker.

"That must be your husband," the agent said.

"Please wait up here," Hana said. "I want to see the expression on his face when he walks through the house for the first time."

The young woman nodded. "Watch his body language. That can be more revealing than a person's words."

Hana was confident that she could discern Daud's thoughts without needing words to do so.

"And please don't think we're being rude if we speak Arabic," Hana added. "My husband understands English, but we usually communicate in Arabic, especially about important matters."

"No problem," the woman said with a

wave of her hand. "My husband is from the mountains of north Georgia, and my parents in Boston think he speaks a different language from the rest of us."

Downstairs, Hana stopped for a moment to run her fingers through her hair before flinging open the front door.

"Welcome home!" she said, using an Arabic word for "home" that signified a fancy dwelling where a wealthy family lived.

"And where are these rich people?" Daud asked, glancing around.

Hana grabbed his hand and quickly kissed him on the lips. "They just kissed," she answered. "The real estate agent is upstairs. I'm going to give you a tour of the first floor myself."

Hana tried to speak extra slowly. She didn't want her enthusiasm to elicit a counterbalancing negative reaction from Daud.

"Why are you talking like that?" Daud asked after she explained the superiority of engineered stone to natural granite.

"What do you mean? I'm just trying to make myself clear."

"You're dragging out your words. It sounds odd."

"I never criticize the way you talk," Hana said.

Daud stopped walking. "Is there something wrong with the way I talk that you've not told me? Most people think my Egyptian accent sounds classy."

"Is that what they told you in Beirut?" Hana said. "Everyone knows the Lebanese accent is the most beautiful."

"Excuse me," a female voice interrupted them.

It was the real estate agent. "I really enjoyed listening to you talk in Arabic," she continued. "It sounds like such a passionate language."

"It can be," Hana answered in English, eyeing Daud. "I was about to show my husband the sunroom."

After the testy exchange in the kitchen, it was impossible for Hana to discern much from Daud's body language. His obvious stiffness could be a result of their linguistic spat, not his opinion of the house. She tried to relax as they climbed the stairs to the second level. They went into the master bedroom, followed by the big reveal of the adjacent yellow bedroom.

"This would make one of the cutest nurseries in Atlanta," the agent gushed. "I wish my baby could have greeted the morning every day from a room like this one."

Hana held her breath as Daud slowly

glanced around and then peered out the dormer window. He returned to her side but didn't look at her.

"It's very nice," he said to the agent. "A good-size room and close to the main bedroom."

Hana felt tears suddenly fill her eyes. She leaned over and squeezed Daud's hand. He responded slightly before releasing her hand.

"And there's room for a family to grow," the agent announced as she stepped into the hallway. "The other bedroom is large enough that two children could share it. It has an adjacent bath with double sinks. The layout is perfect for boys or girls who are close in age."

After they finished viewing the inside of the house, they went downstairs and into the backyard. The agent was a plant enthusiast and effortlessly rattled off the names of the bushes and trees.

"Where are the date palms?" Daud asked when the young woman paused to catch her breath.

"Date palms?" she asked with a puzzled look on her face.

"He's joking," Hana cut in. "There is so much variety with the plants that almost nothing is missing."

"Right," the young woman said. "I'm not used to Middle Eastern humor."

A light breeze caused a few strands of Hana's black hair to brush across her face before she pushed them back.

The agent spoke. "I believe I already know the answer, but what did you think of the house?" she asked.

Hana restrained herself in deference to Daud. "Go ahead," she said.

Ignoring the agent, Daud looked at Hana. "I understand why you like it so much," he said.

Hana appreciated being understood, but she wanted more encouragement on the ultimate issue. "But do you like it enough to make an offer?"

Daud hesitated.

"It's a hot property," the agent cut in. "The woman in our office who represents the seller is a go-getter who will have a sold sign in the yard before you know it. Are you preapproved for a loan of up to ninety percent of the asking price?"

Hana had taken that step without letting Daud know. "Yes," she said. "And we can pay a ten percent down payment."

Daud cut his eyes toward Hana and raised his eyebrows but didn't speak.

"Let's do this," the agent said, patting the

laptop computer she carried in an over-the-shoulder satchel. "I know you like to negotiate, but you'll risk losing the house if you do. In my opinion, you should submit an offer for the asking price so we can close the deal before a bidding war begins."

"How do you know we like to negotiate?" Daud asked before Hana could respond.

"I mean, this isn't like those Arab markets you see on TV," the agent started, then awkwardly paused. "You know, where people bargain over the price of shoes, oranges, tomatoes."

Daud looked at Hana. "When was the last time you saw your mother bargain for a pair of shoes?"

"We'll get back to you as soon as possible," Hana said to the agent. "We've not had a chance to talk it over. Remember, this was Daud's first chance to see the house."

"Okay," the agent said, shaking her head. "But it would be a crying shame if you miss out on this property."

"That's why they sell tissues," Daud answered. "To wipe away tears."

The agent gave Hana a horrified look.

"We'll talk," Hana replied, pressing her lips together. "Thanks again for meeting us on short notice."

CHAPTER 25

Hana followed Daud down the driveway to his vehicle and sat in the passenger seat.

"What's the address for the restaurant?" Daud asked, taking his cell phone from his pocket. "I'll enter it so I won't have to worry about following you."

"That real estate agent thinks I'm married to a tyrant who doesn't care if his wife cries or not," Hana said. "She probably believes you like it when I cry."

"That's not true."

"Then why did you say that about buying tissues?"

"She came across as a racist trying to pressure us into making an offer to buy the house without having a chance to talk privately."

"Yeah," Hana sighed. "And I'm sorry I snapped at you in the kitchen about your accent. You sound like an Egyptian aristocrat. I've always enjoyed listening to you."

"I should have let it go."

"That makes me feel better," Hana said, giving him a hopeful look. "Are you ready to talk about the house?"

"Let's eat dinner first."

It was after 9:00 p.m. when Daud and Hana left the restaurant and waved good-bye to Ben and Laura. Daud reached out and took Hana's hand as they walked to their cars.

"You were quiet during the meal," Hana said, her face illuminated by a security light on a high pole. "What were you thinking about?"

"I was thinking about our first dinner in Jerusalem and how excited I was," Daud replied. "I didn't have any questions for Ben and Laura."

"Did I ask too many?" Hana glanced up anxiously.

"I bet you didn't ask half the questions you wanted to."

"You already know me too well," she said. "But what about Ben and Laura? Do you see them together in a marriage?"

"They seemed to get along fine."

Hana released Daud's hand and leaned against her car. "Did you see the way Laura cut her eyes toward Ben when I asked where Sadie will go to school after the sixth grade?

Laura was making sure he answered the way she wanted him to."

"Maybe, but it's not a bad thing that they're talking about it now so they can agree rather than disagree later. And re-member —"

"It's none of my business," Hana replied. "I felt you nudge me with your foot under the table."

"It was a friendly nudge."

"Actually, I found myself liking Laura more than I thought I would. She has a good sense of humor and loves to cook, both of which will be great for Sadie, and the story about her sister who married a man with two children shows that she has some experience with stepparent issues. She's close to her family. That's a positive sign. And her job schedule is flexible, so she can be there for Sadie when Ben can't."

"You know who she reminded me of?" Daud asked.

"Who?"

Daud pointed his finger at Hana's nose. "You."

He could see Hana start to protest.

"Not in every way," Daud continued. "But there were similarities. You're both passion-ate people in a way that's not so obvious at first, but you can feel it bubbling beneath the surface. And when Laura talked about Sadie's needs, it made me believe she already loves her. This relationship is not just about her and Ben."

"It sounds to me like you were thinking about more than our first dinner date in Jerusalem."

"A little bit." Daud smiled.

"Let's go home," she said with a yawn. "We still need to talk about the new house."

Daud didn't reply. Hana unlocked the door of her car and prepared to get in. She stopped and turned around.

"Do you want me to dye my hair blond so I'll be even more like Laura?" she asked.

"No!"

Although local residents complained about aggressive drivers, Daud found navigating the well-marked streets of Atlanta easier than anyplace he'd driven in the Middle East. He never had to worry about motorcyclists zipping between cars when traffic slowed or multiple vehicles disregarding lane lines like a herd of irritable goats. It was easy to keep up with Hana. When they arrived at home, Hana yawned three times in quick succession.

"This has been an emotional day," she said. "We'll talk about the house in the morning. Our baby is telling me to go to bed and sleep."

"I'm going to read for a while."

Hana yawned a final time. Daud kissed her before she plodded off to the bedroom. A few minutes later when he peeked into the bedroom she was sound asleep, her hair splayed across her pillow. Even in the faint light, her dark hair glistened. Daud crept forward and held a few strands in his fingers. There was no way she could ever change that color.

Settling onto the sofa, Daud opened his computer and looked at photos of the house in Abu Tor that he'd transferred to his laptop. He'd genuinely liked the Atlanta house and understood why Hana loved it. And as he listened to her talk and saw the property through her eyes, he began to wonder if the possibility of living in Jerusalem was more imagination than reality. If passion lay at the center of Hana's heart, Daud knew his core was practical. And keeping Hana and the new life within her safe and secure would be his number one priority for as long as he had breath in his body. He lowered the top of his laptop, but it didn't click shut.

When she awoke in the middle of the night, Hana was groggy. Although she usually got out of bed, she occasionally slept through the night. This seemed like one of those nights. She rolled onto her side to return to sleep, but minutes later she was still awake.

After making a cup of tea, she sat on the sofa with her legs curled up beneath her. She reached over to move Daud's laptop. When she did, her thumb slipped beneath the lid and opened it farther. The welcome screen appeared. It was a photo from their honeymoon in Spain. Hana was standing at the edge of the Mediterranean on a sunny day with several multicolored sailboats as a backdrop. She typed in Daud's password so she could look at other pictures from the trip. When she opened his general photo file, she noticed there was a batch of recent pictures taken within the past week. The first one was a street scene from Jerusalem. Curious, she clicked on another photo, then another and another. The same older Jewish man appeared in several of them, along with the exterior of a small house built with Jerusalem stone. Suddenly, she pushed the laptop away.

Hana glanced over her shoulder at the bedroom to make sure Daud wasn't spying on her and stared at the laptop as if it were alive and threatening her. She looked over her shoulder again. There was no doubt in her mind that Daud had looked at a place to buy or rent when he was in Jerusalem. That thought called into question the whole reason for his detour from Beirut in the first place. Anger at his dishonesty rose up inside her. His promise to be open with her had proved hollow. She stood up rapidly so she could storm into the bedroom, jerk him awake, and demand an explanation.

Once on her feet, she felt the room begin to spin and plopped back down on the sofa. She'd read that she might experience unsteadiness during pregnancy. As she waited a couple of seconds for her head to clear, she looked again at the laptop. The photo on the screen showed the exterior of a stone cottage that didn't look much bigger than the house where they lived now. She was appalled that Daud would consider dragging her into danger to hide in a tiny stone cave.

Repositioning the laptop, she flipped through the photos. Once she viewed the pictures from inside the Jerusalem house, she was surprised by its size but unimpressed by the style and layout. Additional bedrooms had been stuck haphazardly onto the central core with a narrow, elongated kitchen. The rear of the property revealed a nice walled garden and a much larger house adjacent to the smaller one. Hana still didn't know where the buildings might be in the city, but the additional pictures answered one question.

"It was the servants' quarters," she muttered.

She followed Daud and the Jewish man up the stairs to the flat rooftop. The first image from the roof provided the clue she was looking for. In one corner of the frame was a small section of the stone wall surrounding the Old City of Jerusalem. From the angle of the photo, Hana guessed Daud was facing north, which meant he was near either Talbiya or Abu Tor. Both were areas with a long history of Arab presence. The rooftop was surrounded by a low wall, but Hana doubted it would be safe for a small child. She immediately stopped her train of thought. The only issue was how to best communicate her rejection of the idea to Daud. Where they were going to live was a question she'd assumed they settled when he joined her in America.

Hana closed the photo file and turned off the laptop. Opening her Bible to the Psalms, she read for a few minutes, but the words on the page didn't penetrate past her eyes into her mind. Then she suddenly closed the book. There were many verses in the

Psalms about Jerusalem, and she didn't want to stumble across one that by co-incidence challenged her opinion. Reopen-ing the Bible, she turned to much safer ground in the New Testament.

In the morning Hana fixed Daud a full breakfast even though her stomach wouldn't allow her to eat it.

"That wasn't necessary," he said when he came into the kitchen and discovered what she'd done.

"I can still cook something nice for you," she said.

She handed Daud a miniature cup filled with thick, jet-black coffee flavored with cardamom and saffron.

"Can't you have a sip?" he asked, smack-ing his lips. "This is fabulous."

"No, it's tea for me."

Hana sat at the table and nibbled on crackers and drank tea while Daud ate. He liked eggs over easy with the yoke spilling onto the plate when pierced. Along with the eggs, she'd toasted an English muffin and topped it with orange marmalade. It was a breakfast of mixed cultures.

"How was your time in the night with the Lord?" he asked, his mouth still partly full.

"Fine," Hana replied.

"I woke up once when you were awake,"

Daud continued.

"You didn't sneak into the living room and spy on me, did you?"

"No," Daud replied, giving her a puzzled look. "If I had, what would I have seen you doing?"

Hana's morning nausea rushed to the surface, and she ran from the table to the bathroom. After getting sick, she splashed water on her face, but it didn't really refresh her. She returned to the table and took a tentative sip of tea.

"Are you better?" Daud asked with concern in his eyes.

"A little, but I won't feel right until I find out why you lied to me. I saw the pictures of the tiny house in Jerusalem. Where is it? In Talbiya or Abu Tor? I couldn't tell for sure from the portion of the Old City wall in the background. Daud, you can't hide something important from me and pretend that we are communicating the way we should. It really hurt my feelings."

Daud looked stunned as the torrent of words spilled forth from Hana. "I probably would have showed you the photos of the house eventually," he said when she finally paused. "And one of your two guesses was right. It's in Abu Tor. Avi Labensky knows the owner, a Frenchman in Marseilles who's interested in selling to the right buyer."

Daud was speaking in such a matter-of-fact tone of voice that Hana wasn't sure how to respond.

"Is that an apology? Why didn't you tell me the reason you went to Jerusalem?"

"Because I wasn't sure about it myself. I liked the house but didn't mention it when I returned home because you were so excited about the house here in Atlanta."

"I thought we agreed that living in Israel was out of the question."

"For now. I wasn't trying to deceive you. I didn't see the point in telling you because there's no way I'd force you to move someplace you don't want to live."

Daud's last statement drained the fight out of Hana, who still felt lousy. She felt tears pool in her eyes. She wiped them away with a napkin.

"So can we make an offer on the house here in Atlanta?" she asked.

"Yes." Daud nodded. "I'll call the real estate agent myself."

CHAPTER 26

The US government paid twice as much for food and cleaning services as the going rate in the rest of Qatar. Large, well-placed bribes with key members of the ruling family routinely guaranteed that Rahal was the successful bidder. He was relaxing over coffee with the two men who supervised the operation at the Al Udeid base when Khalil entered the room and bowed respectfully.

"Join us," Rahal said to his favorite assistant.

The other two men exchanged a surprised look. As a Shiite underling, Khalil was never included in Sunni social gatherings.

"We're still talking business," Rahal continued as he glanced at the other two managers.

"Thank you, sir," Khalil replied, "but I don't want to intrude and will wait outside until you finish."

"Very well," Rahal said with a wave of his hand.

After Khalil left, Rahal spoke to one of the remaining men. "Khalil is very valuable to me. I want you to hire some Shiite workers to assist here in the office. They can be very good employees."

"Are you sure?" the man asked. "And not just to be janitors?"

"Do as I ask," Rahal replied smoothly.

"Yes, sir," the man replied.

Thirty minutes later Rahal and Khalil were alone, and he told his assistant what he'd done.

"That is gracious and pleases the Almighty," Khalil said. "But do you think your action might cause them to question whether there has been a change in your beliefs?"

"They make too much money to complain about anything."

"I trust your wisdom," Khalil replied, glancing over Rahal's shoulder at the closed door. "And I have an update for you about Hasan."

"I'm listening."

Khalil turned on his tablet as he spoke. "We hired a private detective in the US and told him that we needed a background check on Daud Hasan and his wife. He

368

confirmed what we had already learned from the private investigator in Al-Quds and supplied some additional information. They are indeed living in Atlanta, where the wife works at a law firm with the name of Collins, Lowenstein, and Capella. One of her bosses, a man named Leon Lowenstein, is a Jew."

"This woman has no shame," Rahal said.

"It was harder to find out what Hasan is doing, but since leaving Palestine, he hires himself out as a consultant for businesses wanting to open offices in Arab countries. And based on what happened in Sharm el-Sheikh, we know he is also working for the CIA and the Mossad."

Khalil handed the tablet to Rahal. "This is a photo of where Hasan and his wife live. If you scroll over, you can see their vehicles and the outside of the office building where Abboud works."

"This is a tiny house," Rahal said in surprise. "I would think they would live in a nicer place."

"Who knows what they do with their money?" Khalil shrugged. "But there is no security at the house. It is in a residential neighborhood with multiple points of entry and exit."

"No gates or guards?"

"None," answered Khalil.

"They are either careless or stupid."

"Perhaps," Khalil said, raising one shoulder. "But this is America, where people feel safe. I also obtained a copy of a lawsuit Abboud's law firm filed to recover money from a US company linked to a martyr who killed an American Jewish woman several years ago in Al-Quds. Abboud worked on the case along with a Jewish lawyer named Jakob Brodsky. They traveled together to Al-Quds."

Rahal nodded. "This is good work."

"It is easy to find information in America. Their army has powerful weapons, but the people are weak and unprotected."

"What else?"

Khalil scooted his chair closer. "I contacted the Chechen group that issued the bounty on Hasan's head directly."

"Was that wise?" Rahal asked sharply. "We know the Americans and Jews are probably watching them."

"I set up a false online identity in the UAE. I even flew to Dubai to do it. Any investigation will lead to Dubai and no further. The Chechens are aware that we've located Hasan, and I sent word that there is specific information available to them if they furnish a plan of action."

"Did you offer them money?"

"No, but we can use cryptocurrency if needed."

Rahal put his fingers together in front of him. "What if the Chechens can't act within the US?"

Khalil stared directly at Rahal. "I would go."

Daud left a message for the listing agent about the Atlanta house. As a lawyer, Hana was better suited to handle the discussion, but Daud wanted to show her how serious he was about following through on his commitment to make an offer on the house. A few minutes later Jakob called.

"Fresh news gets attention," he said when Daud answered.

"What do you mean?"

"The posts you set up for me on the Israeli forums have drawn lots of responses. The problem is, I don't have any idea what the people are saying," Jakob explained.

"I'll log on to my computer and let you know if there's anything important."

"Great. I'm also supposed to hear from Daniella Rubin before the end of the day. She's meeting with the rich woman who may have some of the Bar Kokhba coins. My gut tells me this could be a breakthrough, but my mind warns me not to get my hopes up."

"Is Avi going with her to the meeting?"

"I'm not sure. I communicated directly with her. Daniella's English is great, and she seems very interested in what I'm trying to do."

"I hope Avi will be there. I trust him. I'm not sure about the archaeologist," Daud said.

"Avi seems to trust her."

"In his business he can't trust anyone but has to work with everyone. I'll call him. I need to talk to him about something else."

"And I'm still working on your Ukrainian scientist. It's clear that most of the customers for their consulting firm were located in the Middle East, Mexico, or South America," Jakob added.

"I understand the Middle East, but why Mexico or South America?"

"Most likely drug cartels looking for advanced weaponry to use in their private wars and against government troops. I don't speak Spanish, but a woman who works for another lawyer in our building translated the information for me."

"Does she know what you are doing?"

"Nothing beyond research for a client. Everyone is aware that I'm always getting involved in something outside the normal scope of law practice. Anyway, there wasn't anything specifically written about Kolisnyk in Spanish. I'm still trying to track down the sources for the negative comments about him that I found the other day. That will be hard to do since the entries were on the Khartron website and didn't reveal the email address of the sender. I may be able to peek behind the curtain since the consulting firm is defunct and not maintaining a current firewall."

"You know how to do that?" Daud was impressed.

"Not at a sophisticated level, but I recognized the platform used to create the website and downloaded a manual that explains how to access it. The Russian internet has always been more like the Wild West than what we have in the US and Europe."

"Wild West?"

"It's a reference to the frontier days of American expansion before the government was in control of a region."

After his conversation with Jakob, Daud logged on to the Middle Eastern forums. The comments and responses, in both Arabic and Hebrew, were all from people wanting to sell items, not replies to the specific requests for information. It was late afternoon in Jerusalem, and Avi would likely be at his shop.

"Daud?" the familiar voice asked when he answered the phone. "Good timing. I'm meeting tomorrow with Louis. He's flying in from Marseilles to buy two paintings from me. What should I tell him about your interest in the bungalow in Abu Tor?"

"Hana has found a house that she loves here in Atlanta."

"Atlanta? Is it built with Jerusalem stone?"

"No, but there's no use talking with Louis about Abu Tor."

"That won't stop me," Avi said.

"Maybe you should buy it."

"Only to rent it to you."

Daud smiled, but he also felt a twinge of regret.

"Listen," Avi continued, "you and Hana should come to Jerusalem and see the house before you decide what to do. Often a person can't figure out if they like a painting until they see it in person. Photos don't do it justice. It's the same with a house."

"I'm not sure she'd make the trip for security reasons."

"Security reasons? Are you running from the police?"

Daud regretted his honesty. "No, but there are complicating factors for me in Israel from my previous work."

Avi was silent for a moment. "Okay, I respect your decision."

Instead of feeling joy at Daud's agreement about the house, Hana was unsettled. A dark cloud surrounded her thoughts as she made her way to her office.

"Good morning," Janet said cheerily. "I put the information you need for the conference call with Mr. Collins on your desk."

"Thanks." Hana continued past the assistant and closed the door of her office.

When she turned on her computer, Hana saw the now shriveled-up green pea she'd brought from home after first learning she was pregnant. The pea was no longer an accurate representation of the tiny child, and she gently placed it in the trash can. There was a knock on her door.

"Come in!" she barked.

The door opened and Leon Lowenstein entered.

"Mr. Lowenstein," Hana said.

"Yes," the senior partner replied with a puzzled expression on his face. "And I intend to stay that way for the rest of the day. Are you in the middle of something important?"

Remembering Mr. Lowenstein's kind offer to be a paternal sounding board if she ever needed one, Hana started to speak but stopped. "Sorry. I do have a conference call scheduled to begin in the next half hour."

"Okay, I'll be brief."

"Actually, I'm confused about something that doesn't have anything to do with the office," she blurted out. "Except that it does because it has to do with whether Daud and I buy a house in Atlanta or consider moving back to Israel. We're about to make an offer on a house that I really like on Berkdale Drive here in Atlanta. Mr. Collins once mentioned the possibility that I could continue working for the firm from Israel, but I wouldn't want to presume that without the partners deciding it made sense —" Hana stopped her stream-of-consciousness dam break midsentence.

"And you're worried whether it would be safe for you and Daud to live in Israel, not only for yourselves, but even more so now that you're pregnant."

Hana half expected to burst into tears, but none came. "Yes," she replied simply. "Like I mentioned, I've found a perfect house about twenty minutes from the office, but without telling me, Daud checked out a place in Jerusalem when he was there last week. All this came out at the breakfast table this morning, and I'm not sure I handled it very well."

"My wife isn't a morning person so we avoid serious conversations before noon," Mr. Lowenstein said.

"It wasn't a question of timing to talk; it has to do with figuring out God's will for our future."

Mr. Lowenstein smiled. "I'm not a rabbi."

"I know, and it's unfair to dump this on you."

"But I can still offer advice if you want to hear it," Mr. Lowenstein continued.

"Okay, I'm listening."

Mr. Lowenstein leaned forward slightly in his chair. "Don't make an important decision until you're both confident it's the right thing to do. That may not sound profound, but it's true."

"Daud doesn't even know about my doubts," Hana said with a sigh. "And if we don't make an offer on the Berkdale Drive house, we'll lose it."

"I obviously know you a lot better than I do Daud, but he seems like an honest, sincere man. Otherwise you wouldn't have married him. It's important where you and Daud live, but it's more important how working through this decision impacts your relationship with each other. Neither one of you wants to look back with regret or blame."

Mr. Lowenstein's words pulled Hana out of the pit she'd fallen into.

"That helps a lot. Thanks."

"My desire would be for you and Daud to buy a house and settle down here in the US," the senior partner replied with a smile.

"I value your opinion."

"Here's my opinion," Mr. Lowenstein responded. "You are a unique, remarkable woman who doesn't realize the impact you have on everybody who comes in contact with you for more than five minutes."

The tears Hana suspected were lurking behind her eyelids gushed to the surface. She grabbed a tissue from a box near her computer.

"And I'm not going to apologize for making you cry. It's probably good for you."

Hana simply nodded. "Why did you stop by to see me?" she asked after she wiped her eyes and blew her nose.

"So we could have this talk," Mr. Lowenstein replied as he stood up. "Anything else on my mind can wait."

After the conversation with Mr. Lowenstein, Hana sent Daud a short text:

Don't make an offer on the house yet

The message showed delivery, but Daud didn't immediately answer. Hana began reviewing the documents for the conference call, which ultimately lasted almost two hours. Shortly after she returned, the receptionist buzzed her.

"Your husband is here," the young woman said.

"What?" Hana blurted out. "I'll be right there."

Wearing a sport coat, Daud was chatting with the receptionist, who was staring at him with big eyes.

"I could listen to him talk all day," the young woman said to Hana. "His accent reminds me of someone in a movie."

Daud stepped forward and kissed Hana on the lips. "I want to see my lawyer," he said.

Hana entered the security code for entry to the office suites. Daud followed her into the hallway.

"What's going on?" Hana whispered intently as they passed cubicles where people were working. Several stared at them.

"I have legal business to discuss with my lawyer," Daud said.

"I heard that."

She led the way into her office and closed the door. Daud sat in the solitary chair across from Hana's desk.

"I have a document I want my lawyer to look over," Daud said as he reached into the inner pocket of his jacket and took out some papers. "My English is getting better every day, but I don't trust myself to understand legal words."

He slid the papers across the desk to Hana, who soon recognized the standard-form residential real estate contract. She saw the name of the Realtor who had shown them the house and recognized the address of the property.

"No," she said. "Didn't you get my text telling you to hold off making an offer?"

Daud leaned forward in the chair. "I paid more attention to the words of my wife, whom I love and cherish."

Hana glanced at the opening paragraph of the contract. "You made a full-price offer," she said. "Didn't you want to negotiate?"

"Not if it means we run the risk of losing it. The listing agent confirmed what we heard the other day. A house like that isn't going to sit on the market and could end up in a bidding war. The smartest way to move would be to accept the asking price."

Hana knew she should act grateful and elated. "We both know we really weren't in agreement this morning," she said slowly.

"Are we in agreement now?"

"Do you still want the house?" Daud replied.

Hana remembered Mr. Lowenstein's advice. "Yes, but only if you do too. I don't want either one of us to look back with blame or regret."

"No regrets and no blame," Daud answered. "Sign below my signature so we can scan the contract and send it to the listing agent. I told her to be on the lookout for it before the end of the day."

"Let me read it more closely."

Hana began reading the standard real estate contract approved by the Realtor association. She knew the process involved filling in the blanks with any special restrictions clearly identified. Daud hadn't included any conditions beyond the normal requirements related to clear title and home inspection. He'd even included more earnest money than typically required. If the owners wanted to sell at the asking price, the offer would likely be accepted.

"The listing agent said increasing the earnest money deposit would help convince the sellers to pick us if a competing full-price offer came in," Daud said as if reading her mind.

"And we're not asking them to leave the

furniture in the sunroom."

"The agent said we can bring that up later but not to include it in the offer."

Hana forced herself to read the contract again.

"Is there a problem?" Daud asked after several minutes passed.

"Yes." Hana dropped the document on her desk and stared at her husband. "I'm not satisfied with the process."

"Process? I tried to simplify it as much as I could."

"I'm talking about the process between you and me," Hana said and pointed her finger at Daud. "I heard what you said about no regrets or blame, but I feel like you're caving in to emotional pressure from me and agreeing to something that you're not convinced is the right decision for us as a couple and a family."

"Are you saying we didn't argue enough?"

"No," Hana replied with frustration. "It's just that —" She stopped.

Daud spoke. "Look, I knew before we married that we were going to live in the US, and I moved here with a clear under-standing of our immediate future."

"We agreed on that."

"Yes, and even though I'd like us to consider moving back to Israel, nothing has changed about the genuine concerns you have about our security and safety. In six or seven months we're going to have a child to think about. Maybe it's a matter of timing, and it's too early to consider a place like the house in Abu Tor. Someday that might be possible, but not now."

"That helps me a lot," Hana said slowly.

Daud pointed to the contract on her desk. "Sign it, and I'll deliver the agreement to the real estate office in person."

After a moment's hesitation, Hana picked up her pen and turned to the final page. Daud always signed his name with a bold flourish that communicated a confident man who wasn't ashamed or apologetic about who he was or what he thought. It had always been an accurate representation of the real person. Until now. The signature on the contract was emphatic, but his act of signing it didn't match the Daud Hasan she'd married.

"Let's give it another night," Hana said, lowering her pen.

"Why?" Daud asked.

"Because I can't sign it, at least not yet." Hana's voice trembled.

"You realize we might lose —"

"Yes!" Hana cut in. "Yes! There's no point in repeating the obvious!"

Daud pressed his lips together tightly. He slowly picked up the contract and returned it to the inner pocket of his jacket. They sat in silence for a few seconds. Hana didn't trust herself to speak and was apprehensive about what Daud might say.

"Would you like me to pick up Leon so you don't have to do it later?" he asked calmly.

"No, I'll do it." Hana sighed. "Go home, but don't eat a big lunch. I want to fix dinner for us. It's the least I can do after jerking you around about the new house."

CHAPTER 27

Rahal and Khalil sat beside each other in comfortable chairs. It was early evening, and the lights of Doha were beginning to twinkle. They were high above the city, a perfect vantage point for perspective on the world below. Khalil was reciting a long section of the Qur'an. Rahal closed his eyes as he listened to the unparalleled beauty of the flowing Arabic.

Khalil stopped at the device alert sound that interrupted his narration. Rahal opened his eyes and turned toward his assistant. "Continue."

"It could be the Chechens," Khalil said, picking up one of two tablets he'd brought with him. "This tablet is dedicated to the account in Dubai."

Rahal wanted to close his eyes and return to the inner place he'd been before, but it was impossible to do so. Instead, he sipped dark coffee from a small cup. Khalil finished reading.

"They are prepared to act against Hasan if he returns to Palestine. People loyal to their cause remain in the vicinity of Al-Quds, and the reward for his death will attract interest from others."

"Who knows when that might happen? What about eliminating him in America? We can finance any operation and provide sufficient details about Hasan's activities and habits to make an operation much easier."

"I told them all of that. Perhaps they don't have the logistical ability to act in the US."

"How hard can it be? All it takes is someone willing to sacrifice himself for jihad. Nothing is going to come from reaching out to these Salafis."

Rahal took another drink of the bitter liquid in the cup. He could tell Khalil was waiting for additional instructions. Rahal lowered the cup to the table. "Develop our own plan," he advised.

"It's in process," Khalil said and touched his tablet.

"Good. Who will be in charge of the operation?"

"I will."

"You'd go to America?" Rahal asked, sitting up straighter in his chair. "We can recruit others to act on our behalf and supervise from here. The three cousins from Yemen would be perfect. They can obtain refugee status in the US and are zealous for our cause."

"I must avenge Mustafa."

"No!" Rahal shook his head. "I forbid it. You are too valuable to me here."

Khalil bowed his head and left the room. Rahal stared unseeing through the windows as the sky darkened. To risk losing Khalil was too great a sacrifice. Even for jihad.

The advice Daud received before marriage about the unfathomable mysteries of the feminine psyche was true, especially when a woman was pregnant. But because of Hana's deep spirituality, he'd not had serious concerns. The events of the past weeks had shaken his confidence. He tightly gripped the steering wheel of the Land Rover as he maneuvered through traffic. Not that his commitment to the marriage was weakening. On the contrary, he'd felt surprisingly empowered by his decision to yield to Hana's desires about living in America. His own decision was a paradox he still needed to figure out — how giving up his rights was an act of strength, not weakness. His phone vibrated. It was Hana's law firm, which meant she was calling from her office phone. He offered up a quick prayer before answering.

"Did you change your mind about me picking up Leon?" he asked in anticipation of her likely request.

"Excuse me," a male voice responded. "This is Leon Lowenstein."

"Mr. Lowenstein." Daud swerved slightly and then made a quick correction to stay in the correct lane. "I thought it was Hana calling from the law firm."

"Who is Leon?" the senior partner asked.

"Hana's dog. He wandered out of the woods a couple of years ago, and she took him in."

"And she named him Leon?"

"Yes."

"After me?"

Daud suddenly realized Hana had never told Mr. Lowenstein that she'd borrowed his first name and given it to her pet. He felt trapped.

"Yes, and he's a fine animal."

Mr. Lowenstein was silent for a moment and then burst out laughing. Daud slowed to a stop as a traffic signal turned red.

"Promise me that you'll send me a picture of my namesake," the lawyer said, regaining his composure. "I can't wait to tell my wife about this. She's a huge animal lover and will think it's hilarious."

Not always sure about the twists and turns of American humor, Daud was relieved by Mr. Lowenstein's response.

"I'll take a photo this evening. Hana and I usually board him during the day while we work. That's why I mentioned picking him up."

"Leon," Mr. Lowenstein repeated and chuckled into the phone. "Is he a purebred or a mutt?"

It took Daud a few seconds to decipher the question. "He has mixed parents," he replied, hoping that made sense.

Mr. Lowenstein laughed again. "I have a checkered history myself," he said. "But I didn't call to talk about dogs. I'm sitting here with Amanda Fletchall, the event planner for the interfaith convocation. She's giving me a strange look, so we need to move this conversation forward. I'm putting you on speakerphone."

"Mr. Hasan, it's nice to meet you," a high-pitched female voice said. "Mr. Lowenstein has been telling me a bit about your professional qualifications. You're from Israel and worked as a private investigator?"

"Yes."

"Tell me about your experience handling

security for events."

"My time was mostly spent questioning people pulled out of line at a checkpoint since Arabic is my first language."

"Arabic. That's odd for an Israeli, isn't it?"

"Daud is an Arab," Mr. Lowenstein cut in. "I thought that would be clear from his name."

"I'm not familiar with Middle Eastern names," Amanda replied.

The phone was silent for several seconds.

"Hello?" Daud asked. "Are you still there?"

"Yes," Mr. Lowenstein replied. "Amanda had a question for me off-line."

Daud suspected he knew the topic. "Is it about an Arab supervising security at an event where there will be a lot of Jewish people present?"

"Yes," the lawyer answered. "And that's not going to be an issue."

Daud wasn't so sure but didn't voice his doubts.

Amanda spoke. "Given the anticipated attendance, we've reserved a large ballroom at a local hotel not far from the law firm's office. I'll send you the name and address of the hotel along with the name of the assistant manager who has been assigned to us."

Daud turned left behind a FedEx truck. "Hotels can be difficult to secure because they are set up for convenience of service with multiple entry and exit points," he said. "Also, people would be coming and going for reasons unrelated to the event. Does the hotel manager know we will require extra security measures? A controversial topic like this will attract negative attention."

"Our goal is to make it welcoming and safe for everyone," the event planner replied cheerily.

Daud doubted that was entirely possible.

"You can work out the details directly with the hotel staff," she continued. "They'll provide the schematics of the layout. I've already sent Mr. Lowenstein an email with all the pertinent information. He'll forward it to you later today."

"And identify their head of security?"

"Yes, his name and contact information are also included in the email. I've worked with him before. He's a retired Atlanta police officer."

"That's it for now," Mr. Lowenstein said. "Communicate directly with the hotel, but copy me on anything you send Amanda."

"Okay," Daud said.

"And pat Leon on the head for me," the senior lawyer added. "Don't forget to send me a photo."

Arriving home, Daud dropped the real estate contract beside a stack of papers next to his computer. His stomach growled, and he warmed up a bowl of yellow rice and grilled chicken they'd eaten earlier in the week. There was no danger of a small snack ruining his appetite. Logging on to his laptop, he saw an email from Jakob with the subject line "Artem Kolisnyk." Daud cringed when he saw that Jakob had showcased the scientist's name.

Jakob had successfully gained access to the website for Khartron Corporation, the defunct Ukrainian consulting firm, and downloaded a long list of email contacts originating from all over the world. Seeing the unusual IP addresses, Daud wished he still had the ability to forward this type of information to Aaron Levy and the IT experts with the Shin Bet security service. They would be able to analyze it quickly. But Daud and Jakob were on their own.

Jakob had parsed out emails sent directly to Kolisnyk's account with the company. Surprisingly, there were fewer than a hundred of these. Daud focused on the ones written in Arabic, which accounted for about thirty percent. Most of them were simple inquiries. Future discussions likely would be in person, on the phone, or via other more secure internet links that wouldn't create an easy trail for someone else to follow. It wasn't possible for Daud to determine the country of origin. As he kept reading, he found three emails from different sources registering specific complaints about Kolisnyk's nonresponsiveness. It wasn't much, but Daud created a separate file for the three sources. The front door opened. Hana entered with Leon close behind her.

"There are groceries in the car," she said to Daud, who was sitting in front of his laptop. "Unless you're in the middle of something important."

"I'm finishing up."

Hana placed two bags of groceries on the kitchen counter and poured a heaping cupful of dry dog food into Leon's metal bowl. Daud headed out to the car and soon returned with the remaining plastic bags.

"You could have ordered takeout," he said as Hana unpacked the groceries.

"We're not eating all of this tonight," she replied. "I'm going to stir-fry steak with onions and peppers. We can warm up the yellow rice left over from the other night."

"I'll do that," Daud immediately offered.

"Not yet," Hana replied. "That will only take a minute or two."

Daud took out his cell phone and took several photos of Leon with his muzzle buried in his food dish.

"Why are you doing that?" Hana asked as she sliced the steak into thin strips.

"Mr. Lowenstein asked me to do it," Daud replied. "He called me about the interfaith debate. There was a woman in his office who is helping coordinate the event. Did you meet her? She's going to send me —"

"Mr. Lowenstein doesn't even know I have a dog," Hana said. "Why would he want a picture of Leon?"

Hana stopped with her knife in midair.

Daud gave her a sheepish grin. "Lower your knife," he said. "He knows that the dog's name is Leon."

Hana swallowed. "How did he react?"

"When he mentioned how much his wife would enjoy the story, I relaxed," Daud said.

"Then let's send him a good one that he can show Mrs. Lowenstein, not a picture of Leon with his nose in a bowl. Mr. Lowenstein might get the idea that I think he eats too much."

"He could lose more than a few pounds,

especially if he went running with me," Daud responded.

Hana laughed as she pointed the knife at Daud. "Don't criticize his weight. A man Mr. Lowenstein's age doesn't have your metabolism."

Leon finished his meal, and Hana positioned the dog, Daud, and herself on the couch for a group selfie. Leon licked Hana's cheek on the first attempt. Five tries later she was satisfied and showed the picture to Daud.

"Leon is looking straight at the camera, and that's a decent photo of us."

Daud tilted his head to the side. "You're always beautiful. I look like I just woke up from a long nap."

Hana stood in front of the stove while she composed a message to send with the picture. Once satisfied, she showed it to Daud.

"That's perfect," he said.

While she finished stir-frying the food, Hana turned to Daud, who was still sitting on the sofa scratching behind Leon's ears.

"I'm ready for you to warm up the rice," she said.

Daud put the bowl in the microwave. "I'll let you have most of it," he said as the food rotated on a frosted glass carousel. "I'm going to focus on the meat."

"There's plenty of rice for both of us."

The microwave beeped. Hana divided the stir-fry, giving Daud twice as much.

"I'd better take it easy with the onions and peppers," she said when Daud started to protest. "I would enjoy them now and regret it in the morning."

"Then take more rice," Daud replied as he scooped most of the yellow kernels onto Hana's plate.

Hana watched him. "You ate rice earlier today," she said matter-of-factly.

"Yes, but I promise to clean my plate because I'm in the mood for butter pecan ice cream for dessert. That's one of the things I like about America."

They sat across from each other at the small table. Daud prayed a simple blessing and dug into his food. Hana picked at the items on her plate.

Daud looked up. "It really is good, especially when it's hot."

Hana ate a tiny piece of meat and a forkful of rice. "Before I can eat, I need to talk to you some more about making an offer on the new house," she said.

"Okay," Daud said as he placed his fork beside his plate.

"But you keep eating," Hana said.

Daud hesitated, but Hana refused to continue until he ate a bite of steak and onion.

"I thought about the situation while shopping at the grocery store," she continued. "When you dropped the contract on my desk, I couldn't force myself to sign it."

"I know, but I don't understand."

"It has to do with you and me more than the house. I really want us to be one."

"That's what I was trying to do."

"And I appreciate it a lot."

Neither one of them was eating.

"But until I'm sure, I don't want to do anything," Hana continued.

"Okay," Daud responded slowly. "But what do you want me to tell the real estate agent? She was expecting an offer from us already."

"I'll get in touch with her," Hana said, but something in Daud's expression changed her mind. "No, better yet, you tell her that we've not made up our minds, because that's the truth. If we lose the house —"

The logical resolve Hana had felt moments before evaporated. She couldn't fight off the tears that filled her eyes. She wiped them with a napkin.

"Ignore these," she said, blinking her eyes.

"That's impossible."

"But you have to," Hana pressed on. "Because I know the only way we can know God's will for our future is to go to Jerusalem and look at the house in Abu Tor."

Once the words passed her lips, Hana felt a release in her soul. She took a deep breath and exhaled. "There. I said it," she finished.

Daud stared at her and didn't speak. Hana stabbed a large piece of steak with her fork and stuck it in her mouth. Not having to talk because of the amount of food between her teeth, she met Daud's gaze until he looked down at his plate. He ate another bite. They each continued the meal without speaking. Hana was content to be silent. She had nothing to say and knew the next words must come from Daud. The last pepper on his plate made its way into her husband's mouth.

"All right," Daud said, placing his fork in the center of his empty plate. "How quickly can you take a few days away from the office to go home?" he asked, then quickly corrected himself. "I mean to Israel."

Hana regained her composure. "I know exactly what you mean. And if we leave on a Wednesday or Thursday and come back on a Monday, that shouldn't be a problem with work. There's even an in-person meeting with a client I can schedule in Tel Aviv. I'll talk to Mr. Collins about it tomorrow."

Daud stood, came over to her, and kissed her. "You are an amazing woman," he said when their lips parted. "And I hope that kiss didn't come with too much onions and peppers."

"It's okay." Hana smiled. "You know how much I love you and them."

"Agreeing to go to Israel doesn't commit us to anything," Daud said as he stepped back. "Think of it as an exploratory mission."

Hana's face burst into a broad smile. "And announcement celebrations with our families!"

CHAPTER 28

Daud awoke from a troubling, confusing, and ultimately terrifying dream in which he became lost in a familiar area of Jerusalem and couldn't find either Hana or their vehicle. Streets didn't intersect correctly, and usually reliable landmarks were as jumbled as puzzle pieces dumped on a table. In the nightmare he grew more and more frantic as the scene disintegrated into total chaos. He ended up standing beside a sign that read "Ben Yehuda Street" and trying to call out for help, but no sounds came from his lips. Clawing his way to consciousness, Daud carried the panic with him for a few seconds until he was able to confirm the difference between nightmare and reality. He glanced over at a still-sleeping Hana. He must not have made any noise. He dozed off until Hana suddenly rolled out of the bed and dashed into the bathroom. Daud sat up in bed and stared after her. He'd do anything to help her feel better.

Hoping a cup of tea might be welcome, he brewed a pot of her favorite and lined up several saltine crackers in a neat line on a plate. He could hear Hana taking a shower. When she emerged dressed for work, he had breakfast waiting for her.

"Thanks," she said when she saw what he'd done. "Our little walnut woke up in a bad mood this morning."

"Is that how big he is?"

"And well on her way to becoming a plum."

Hana sat down and took a sip of tea and closed her eyes. "Best tea ever," she said, opening her eyes. "You know exactly how much milk and sugar to put in it."

Daud rarely asked Hana about her middle-of-the-night time with the Lord, but after suffering through his terrifying dream, he couldn't resist.

"How was your time with the Lord in the night?" he asked.

Hana took another drink of tea before answering. "I prayed some for us and what we talked about last night, but Sadie, Ben, and Laura were really on my heart too. Even though I've cut back my direct involvement in Sadie's life, I can still pray for her."

As Daud listened, he was once again impressed with the level of unselfishness that characterized his wife's life. He wasn't sure whether to mention his nightmare. The only interpretation he'd been able to come up with was that danger and confusion awaited them in Jerusalem. Hana didn't need that kind of input.

"Then I prayed for Jerusalem," Hana continued. "I meditated on Psalm 122:6: 'Pray for the peace of Jerusalem: May those who love you be secure.' I read it over and over. I'm not even sure I understand how to love a city, but it must be possible because God says so and connects it to a promise."

Hana then quoted the verse in Hebrew, which brought out alliteration lost in the English and Arabic translations. As he listened to the ancient words, the agitation Daud had felt since the nightmare lifted.

"That's good," he said.

"Yes, I felt the same way. But it didn't change my mind about what we discussed last night. Call the real estate agent, and I'll see about fitting a quick trip to Israel into my work schedule."

"Once you know, I'll book the flight."

"One other thing," Hana said. "We should pray that if we're supposed to buy the house here in Atlanta, it won't sell."

"Absolutely," Daud replied.

Hana pointed her index finger at him. "No, you pray."

Daud's mouth suddenly felt dry. Closing his eyes, he stumbled through a few words that seemed as prayerful as ordering lunch at a fast-food restaurant. But then he felt a shift and began to speak not only from his mind but also from his spirit. The words linked him with Hana in a new way. A couple of minutes passed before he finished. He looked across the table at Hana, whose eyes were shining.

"That was different," he said.

Hana rolled her eyes. "That's a very male way of describing it."

"Okay, it felt like we were both praying even though I was the one speaking," Daud continued.

"That's much better," Hana said, smiling. "For me, it was heaven touching earth. I really liked it."

Because Hana was running a few minutes late, Daud took Leon to the dog day care center. During the drive, he phoned the real estate agent and left a voice mail that he and Hana would not be making an offer on the house at this time.

Hana arrived at the office and went directly

into a conference call with Mr. Collins and a corporate client in Ra'anana. The modern city was a technology hub not far from Tel Aviv, and a place where a lot of American immigrants lived. Everyone on the call spoke English, so there wasn't much for her to contribute.

"That went well," the senior partner said when he and Hana were alone. "Except for the questions the CFO had about how to attract the right kind of managers. That's more of a business question than a legal one."

"I could connect him with a couple of Israeli firms who may have suitable candidates."

"Why didn't you mention that during the conversation?" Mr. Collins asked.

"I wasn't sure if you wanted me to bring it up."

"It would have been fine. Be more assertive."

"What would you think about me making a quick trip to meet with the CFO in Ra'anana and the other company in Herzliya that is thinking about hiring us to handle their expansion in the US? I believe a personal visit from the law firm could go a long way in both situations."

Jim Collins eyed her curiously. "Now

that's very assertive. How long have you been thinking about this?"

"Since breakfast with Daud this morning," Hana replied with a smile. "Part of the reason is personal, but I told him I'd see if there could be a joint purpose for business. If it's okay with you, Daud could join me in Herzliya. He helps US corporations establish a presence in the Middle East, but he could assist with a company going the other way."

Unlike Mr. Lowenstein, who usually made decisions quickly, Mr. Collins was much more deliberate. Hana didn't expect an immediate answer.

The senior partner cleared his throat. "Put together a proposal and send it to me later today," he said. "I've never considered that Daud might be an asset."

Hana smiled.

"Except to you, of course," the senior partner amended. "Let me mull it over."

"Thanks."

They stood. Mr. Collins turned to leave but stopped in the doorway.

"Tell me this much now," he said. "When would you want to leave and how long would you be gone?"

"Leave as soon as possible and stay for four or five days. I'm sure we'd take one of those days to visit with my family near Nazareth so we could tell them in person that I'm pregnant."

"Right." Mr. Collins grunted and then walked the opposite way from Hana down the hallway.

Checking her email in-box, Hana was surprised to see an email directly to her from Avi Labensky inviting her and Daud to stay with him the next time they were in Jerusalem. She was about to move on to something else, but the art dealer's phone number at the bottom of the email captured her attention. It was late afternoon in Israel.

"Shalom," answered a male voice in Hebrew.

Hana introduced herself and continued in the same language. "I wanted to thank you again for the beautiful painting and for inviting Daud and me to stay with you."

"You're welcome," Avi answered. "But Daud told me the other day that personal reasons prevent you from making a trip to Israel in the near future. If things change —"

"They have," Hana said and then briefly told the art dealer about their possible trip.

"Excellent. If it works out, let me know. Our house is always open. One other thing. You can save me a phone call to Daud or

Jakob. Are you aware that there were first-year Bar Kokhba coins in the collection stolen by the Soviet military officer from Jakob's client?"

"Yes," Hana answered. "What's the next step?"

"Someone is going to have to negotiate with the current owner to determine if the coins can be recovered without the need for litigation."

Jakob was certainly capable of negotiation, but Hana knew her presence would be a big help.

"Maybe Daud and I could fit that into the trip I mentioned."

"That's one reason I brought it up. The woman is a widow from a wealthy Arab family that's lived in the Talbiya area for generations. Her last name is Zarkawi."

Zarkawi was a name often associated with Arabs originally from Jordan. Hana jotted it down.

Avi continued. "I don't know how Mrs. Zarkawi acquired the coins, but it makes me wonder whether she has more items on the list we're looking for."

Hana's interest increased. "I'll talk it over with Daud and Jakob."

"Just let me know. The house in Abu Tor

is the perfect place for the painting I gave you."

"The painting will be special wherever we live," Hana replied with a smile.

"Well said," the art dealer parried, laughter evident in his voice. "But there's no place on earth like Jerusalem."

The call ended. Hana stared out the single window of her office at a sliver of the north Atlanta skyline. Jerusalem spoke to Daud. The concrete-and-steel spires of the two nearby office buildings in the center of her line of sight were silent.

Daud went for a long run along the Chattahoochee River. Returning home, he logged on to his computer and noticed an inquiry from a potential client with an email address in the United Arab Emirates. The company manufactured plastic bottles for soft drinks and household products and wanted to open a plant near the West Bank city of Ramallah. Hana's family made plastic irrigation pipes, which was a similar but not competing business. Her father and uncles would be sources of information and might be potential customers due to their use of recycled materials. Daud checked out the business, which was five years old and had plants currently operating in Pakistan and Qatar. Expanding westward made sense. Hosni Chatti, the author of the email, was listed on the firm website as the director of development. He had learned about Daud from Youssef in Lebanon. The owners of the company had links to the Al-Qasimi family that ruled two of the seven emirates making up the UAE.

Daud sent a standard response outlining his services and costs. He spent the next hour working on a proposal for another company. Standing up to stretch and take a break, he received a call from Hana.

"Did you go for a run?" she asked.

"Yes. I wanted to get one in before it got too hot. I'm still not used to the humidity."

"I talked to Avi Labensky."

Daud listened to Hana's summary of the conversation with the art dealer. The enthusiasm in her voice encouraged him.

"I should also be there when you talk to the woman in Talbiya," he said.

Hana was silent for a moment.

"I won't intimidate her," Daud continued. "She's going to have a lawyer or family member or both with her. I'll pour the coffee for everyone and call you Ms. Abboud."

"Okay, okay." Hana chuckled. "Anyway, I have good news. I spoke with Mr. Collins this morning about taking a trip to Israel.

He requested a proposal and responded much more quickly than I expected. He approved it. Collins, Lowenstein, and Capella will pay my expenses as long as I'm able to set up a couple of business meetings, one in Herzliya and another in Ra'anana. I asked Mr. Collins if you could join me for the client meeting in Herzliya, but he turned down that part of the request."

"When would we leave?"

"As soon as I schedule the meetings with the clients. I'm waiting to hear from them now. I'm aiming for Thursday through Tuesday in Israel, with a travel day on either side. We'll squeeze in everything we need to do in Jerusalem after I finish the law firm business. Maybe we can see your mother and brothers before driving to Reineh."

Hana's initial appointment with an obstetrician was scheduled for the following week. The accelerated schedule would mean an early reveal of the pregnancy to their families.

"Have you talked to Jakob about the trip?" Daud asked.

"Not yet. If he can't go on short notice, he'll have to decide if he wants us to meet with Mrs. Zarkawi."

"Jakob will insist on being there," Daud said. "After I dropped off Leon, I called the real estate agent about the house here and left a voice mail that we're not ready to move forward with an offer."

"I checked the listing a few minutes ago, and it's still active."

"We prayed; now we'll see what happens."

Daud could hear Hana talking to someone else.

"I have to go," she said. "Janet says Mr. Lowenstein wants to see me as soon as possible. Bye."

Daud lowered the phone and returned to his computer. There was a prompt reply from Mr. Chatti in the UAE expressing further interest in hiring Daud as a consultant. The businessman had a number of questions. Daud started working on a response. Working for corporate clients could bring in a steady flow of income and be a lot safer than working as an independent contractor for the CIA in places like Sharm el-Sheikh.

CHAPTER 29

"Leon is a magnificent dog," Mr. Lowenstein said to Hana as he held up the photo on his cell phone. "I appreciate the picture including you and Daud, but I'd like one with just Leon. Better yet, bring him to the law firm and we can take a photo here in my office."

"Are you serious?" Hana asked.

"Absolutely. My wife laughed so hard she cried."

"Maybe I can pick him up early from the dog day care where he stays and bring him by."

"Is it a nice place?"

"Yes. I can monitor him via video during the day."

"Show me."

Hana opened the app on her phone. Leon was lying beside a metal water bowl with his tongue hanging out of his mouth. She handed the phone to Mr. Lowenstein. "He plays hard when he first gets there, so he's taking a break."

Mr. Lowenstein smiled and shook his head. "That's how I look in the clubhouse after walking eighteen holes on the golf course."

He watched a few more seconds before returning the phone to Hana. "Jim Collins told me about your upcoming trip to Israel," the senior partner said. "That would set up a prime opportunity for a representative of the law firm to meet with one of our shipping company clients in Rome. Book a flight that includes a day in Rome so you can meet with an executive of the company's risk management group. He's originally from Beirut but moved to Italy twenty years ago to get away from all the political problems in Lebanon."

It was a familiar tale. Every time she heard about the turmoil in Lebanon, Hana felt sad. "That should be easy to include."

"Akeem speaks passable English," Mr. Lowenstein continued. "But he's more comfortable in Arabic, and a personal visit from you would be a boost to client relations. He was excited to find out that you work here. I'll prep you thoroughly on the substantive ideas to pass along. It's a PowerPoint presentation I often give to clients."

"Okay," Hana replied. "I'm just concerned about the follow-up questions."

"One beauty of the program is that additional questions are funneled back to the firm and generate billable hours. You'll see."

Back in her office, Hana followed up with the companies in Herzliya and Ra'anana. Both wanted to meet with her on Friday. It would be a tight schedule. She found a flight that allowed a layover in Rome on the return trip and sent the itinerary to Mr. Lowenstein, who approved it. Jakob called immediately after she forwarded it to him.

"I can't make the trip," the young Jewish lawyer said. "I have a trial on the calendar, and if that doesn't go forward, I have to cram in three depositions in another case. Are you and Daud willing to meet with the rich Arab woman in Jerusalem?"

Hana knew all along that she and Daud would likely end up in the middle of Jakob's case. "Yes, so long as we do it during our personal time. That shouldn't be hard, because I'm going to conduct all my business for the firm on Friday."

"Make sure you tell Mrs. Zarkawi the story of Vladimir's family. That's our strongest argument."

"I'll work it in."

"I have one hundred percent confidence

in your ability to handle this better than anyone on the planet, even me. Even if I was there, the language barriers would make me a wallflower. Find out what you can, and we'll patch in Vladimir so the three of us can determine the best way to proceed from there."

Rahal had a headache that forced him to cancel his morning meetings and lie still in a darkened room. It was midafternoon before strong medication beat back the pain enough that he could go to his office located on the thirty-second floor.

"Are you feeling better, sir?" Khalil asked.

Rahal rubbed the area of his right temple that was most affected by the pain. He could tell that the headache still waited at the gate to storm his mind.

"For now," he replied. "I'm only going to take care of any pressing matters before going back to bed."

Khalil went over several business issues and offered suggestions.

"Those are matters you can take care of," Rahal said with a wave of his hand. "There's no need to do anything except prepare a place for me to sign and authorize your recommendations."

Khalil placed several sheets of paper on

the glass-topped table in the corner of the office where they sat. Rahal quickly scribbled his signature without reading them.

Khalil gathered them up. "Thank you," he said. "There's one other piece of news."

"Make it quick," Rahal grunted.

"We've initiated direct contact with Daud Hasan and are working on a meeting with him in Ramallah."

"You did what?" Rahal forced his half-shut eyes open wider.

"Our investigator was able to locate a recent client of Hasan, and I used his name to gain access. Using the internet presence we created in the UAE, I formed a dummy company that is going to hire him as a consultant to assist in opening a plastics manufacturing business in Palestine. I've already exchanged multiple emails with him. He's planning a trip from America to Al-Quds in the near future and may be able to include us in his itinerary. My plan is to notify the Chechens of Hasan's location and let them eliminate him."

Rahal clapped his hands together and then winced at the resulting pain. "Well done," he said.

"It's not done yet," Khalil responded. "Should we leave this up to the Chechens, or should I travel to Palestine myself? Hasan

416

has friends in the Zionist government who may have infiltrated the Chechen network."

Rahal's head was pounding again, and his stomach felt queasy. "Use the Chechens," he responded. "They are highly motivated and have people on the ground in Palestine."

Daud recommended the Jericho Agro-Industrial Park as the best place for his new client to locate its plastics business. Partially funded by the Japanese government, the industrial zone was close to Jordan with good access to the rest of the West Bank and Israel. Mr. Chatti proved to be an active client with lots of questions.

Arab chicken stew was one of the few meals Daud had perfected as a bachelor. He would prepare a large quantity, then eat it for days afterward. The stew contained both white-meat and dark-meat chicken with the skin removed. Daud moved about the kitchen. He boiled the chicken and added tomatoes, zucchini, onion, diced potato, and diced carrots, along with cloves, coriander, tomato paste, cumin, black pepper, cardamom, cinnamon, and salt. After boiling it for an hour, he let it simmer the rest of the afternoon. The smells teased his stomach and he repeatedly lifted the lid from the pot to enjoy the aroma. He sampled the broth to make sure he'd properly balanced the spices. The door opened, and Hana entered with Leon.

"That smells amazing," she said.

"And I believe it will taste good too."

Hana lifted the lid from the pot. "That looks and smells better than the chicken stew my mother makes," she said. "Sorry I'm late. I went back to the office after I picked up Leon."

"Why?"

"So Mr. Lowenstein could meet him in person."

Hana took out her phone and showed Daud a photo of Leon sitting in the senior partner's chair. In a second picture, Leon and Mr. Lowenstein were in front of the lawyer's collection of antique sailing-ship models.

"That one made me nervous," Hana said. "One swipe of Leon's tail could have wrecked an entire fleet of the ships."

"Maybe he can dog-sit while we're in Israel," Daud said with a smile.

Hana shook her head. "No. And we're not just going to Israel. There will be a stopover in Rome on the way back."

While they finished preparing the food, Hana explained the reason for the extension of the trip to Rome. She ate three bites of the stew without commenting. Daud thought it tasted good, but he'd not been shy in the use of spices and might have overdone it. After the fourth bite, he couldn't wait any longer.

"What do you think about it?" he asked. "Is there too much cardamom? I know it's potent, but if I'm going to use some, I want to taste it."

Hana held up a piece of chicken on the end of her fork. "In a few seconds this is going to be one of the best bites of chicken stew that's ever crossed my lips," she said.

Daud grinned. While they ate, Hana summarized more about her day, including the conversation with Jakob.

"That doesn't surprise me," Daud said. "I may also squeeze in some business for a new client."

He told Hana about the plastics manufacturer based in the UAE.

"Chatti originally mentioned Ramallah as a location but quickly shifted to the business park near Jericho."

"That makes sense. The development at Jericho is an island of stability."

"Do you think there might be a possibility that this company can work with your family?" Daud asked. "I especially thought about recycled materials."

"Maybe," Hana said with a slow nod. "My father already brings in a lot of that sort of stuff from the West Bank."

After the meal, they cleaned up the kitchen and loaded the dishwasher.

"Did you hear from anyone at the hotel about the interfaith convocation?" Hana asked as she scrubbed the pot used for cooking the stew. "Several emails came to me this afternoon."

"No, I'm still waiting to receive the layout and specifications from one of the assistant managers. It's going to be more complicated than the event planner hired by Mr. Lowenstein believes, and I'd like to get started before we leave on our trip."

"Send her an email with a copy to Mr. Lowenstein," Hana suggested. "That will get her moving."

Once Daud's head rested on a pillow, he could fall asleep in less than a minute. Hana lay on her back staring at the ceiling. Melding two lives together was like preparing a delicious bowl of chicken stew. She thought about the simile and smiled. Both she and Daud were being tenderized and flavored.

Unable to sleep, she slipped out of bed and checked her social media accounts in

Israel. It had been several weeks since she'd allowed herself the luxury of browsing the internet postings of family and friends in the Middle East. Fabia and Farah regularly included photos and information about their children. Other family members did the same. Hana loved keeping up with her extended relatives but never posted anything about herself. Thinking about the planned surprise visit and the chance to freely communicate made her happy.

The following morning Hana called Janet into her office and told her about the upcoming trip to Israel.

"It's great that Daud can go with you," Janet replied. "Is that when you'll tell your family about the baby?"

Hana smiled and nodded.

"That will be so awesome! And even a short side trip to Rome will be fun. Will you be a little bit nervous when you're in Israel?"

"Daud and I need to be careful. Not even my parents know the full story about our adventures last year in Jerusalem."

"I hate that what happened is still hanging over you," Janet said as her face became serious. "You deserve to be happy and carefree."

Hana half expected Janet's words to

produce tears, but instead, she felt a sense of resolve rise up inside. "Thanks," she said. "I'm happy, but I don't know anyone who is carefree."

"I had a few nonstressful days like that before the kids came along, but I didn't realize it at the time." Janet sighed. "I thought I experienced anxiety when I was single and had no children, but the responsibility of a baby changed everything forever. Not that I have regrets. I'm glad they're here. It's just a change in perspective that I wish I'd had earlier in life."

Hana glanced at the burnished walnut that rested beneath her computer screen. She knew there were many unknowns waiting in her future.

"Maybe Donnie and I will have another chance at bliss once we're empty nesters."

It took Hana a second to understand the term. She was at a completely different place in her journey.

"And I'm just trying to figure out where I should build my nest," she replied.

CHAPTER 30

Daud shifted in a window seat during the short flight from Atlanta to New York. Hana knew commuter planes weren't designed for a man his size. They'd upgraded their seats on the overseas flight to give him a few extra inches of legroom. The past few days had been a rush of activity. Hana worked late at the office several nights and squeezed in the initial visit to her obstetrician, who told her everything looked normal. The big surprise was that she was at least two weeks farther along in the pregnancy than she'd thought.

Daud leaned over and spoke to Hana. "I brought the schematic diagrams of the hotel so I can work on the security layout at some point during the trip."

"I'm glad they finally sent them to you."

"I still wouldn't have the plans if Mr. Lowenstein hadn't intervened. My Arab name didn't instill confidence in the hotel management."

Hana patted his arm. "I know you're the best."

Daud was able to sleep during most of the flight from New York to Israel. Once on the ground, they stood in the immigration line designated for passengers with Israeli passports. Their Arab names prompted a couple of extra questions by a bored young woman sitting in a tiny booth.

The airport was familiar territory to Hana. When she worked there as a security officer, she'd questioned thousands of people coming into the country. Visitors to Israel came from every tribe and language. Hana's fluency in both Arabic and French determined how her supervisors used her. Some of her favorite conversations were with French speakers from West Africa. Their exuberance at being in the Holy Land knew no limits.

At their hotel, Hana collapsed on the bed without changing clothes and fell into a sound sleep. When she awoke two hours later, she thought for a moment it was the middle of the night because Daud had completely closed the blackout curtains and it was pitch-dark in the room.

"Where are you?" she mumbled.

"Over here," Daud answered.

Hana blinked a couple of times and could make out his form in a chair on the other side of the room. She picked up her phone and checked the time.

"I'd better shower and get ready," she said.

Refreshed by the nap and a change of clothes, Hana emerged back into a room with the Middle Eastern sun streaming in. Still sitting in the chair, Daud had propped open his laptop and was typing.

"What are you going to do while I'm gone?" she asked.

"Exercise, talk to Avi, and work on the project for the plastics company."

"I can't rush through these meetings," Hana said.

Before putting the finishing touches on her makeup, Hana walked over to Daud and kissed him. "I'm glad we're here," she said. "Even though we're in a hotel room, it feels right already."

Daud smiled. "I know," he said.

Hana took a taxi to the meeting in Herzliya, where she participated in a discussion with a group of twelve Jewish men and women, including a CEO in his thirties. The tone of the conversations around the beige plastic table in the corner of a large, open office space was aggressive and argumentative, but in the rough-and-tumble world of

Israeli business, that wasn't necessarily a sign of trouble. The negative give-and-take was a common decision-making model for Israeli companies influenced by people who went through universal military service. In the IDF, junior commanders routinely challenged superior officers, and enlisted personnel did the same to junior commanders. At first, Hana's suggestions were rejected by several people who eventually came around to agreement with her position. Her Arab ethnicity wasn't an issue, and she was able to engage in the rapid-fire Hebrew conversations.

She went from there to Ra'anana and a much lower-key meeting with a client who was already firmly in the Collins, Lowenstein, and Capella fold. Hana had interacted via phone, email, and Skype with everyone in the room, and the session included celebration for past successes as well as planning for the future. As she'd suspected, the leadership wanted her to join them for dinner. Transatlantic fatigue set in during the meal. When she finally arrived back at the hotel, she encountered a fresh-looking Daud coming out of the hotel restaurant.

"How did it go?" he asked.

"Good," she replied, finally able to yawn without trying to suppress it. "But I'm not going to be able to stay up and write a report for Mr. Collins. That will have to wait until tomorrow."

Hana fell quickly asleep once back in their room and didn't wake up in the middle of the night.

The following day Daud left the hotel room to go for an early morning run. Invigorated by the dry air, he ran faster and longer than normal. Afterward, he showered in the pool bathhouse and relaxed in the water with a fruit drink beside him on the sandstone deck. Returning to their room, he found Hana awake and blow-drying her hair.

"Did you pick up the rental car yesterday?" she asked when she turned off the dryer.

"Yes, and because we can write it off as a business expense, I went for the top of the line and selected a Porsche."

"No, you didn't," Hana answered. "I bet you got a white Skoda."

"They didn't have white so I settled for light blue," Daud replied. "Hearing you guess correctly makes me feel like we've been married for twenty years and don't have any surprises left for each other."

Hana kissed him on the cheek. "Don't worry. I'll keep surprising you."

Daud sat on the edge of the bed. "How do you feel?" he asked.

"The best since I started having morning sickness."

They ate a light breakfast and checked out of the hotel. The small engine in the Skoda, a compact car imported from the Czech Republic, whined in protest during the drive up to Jerusalem. Several times Daud pressed the gas pedal all the way to the floorboard. Hana spent much of the time staring out the window.

"What are you thinking?" Daud asked as they entered the western part of the city.

"Mostly praying," Hana answered. "I didn't wake up in the night."

Daud's phone vibrated. It was Avi.

"Where are you?" the art dealer asked when Daud answered.

"Fifteen minutes or so from your house," Daud replied, placing the phone on speaker so Hana could listen.

"I'm finishing up an early meeting and close to Abu Tor. Do you remember how to get to the house?"

"Yes."

"Good. Meet me there."

"Will do."

The call ended as Daud stopped for a red light.

"My heart started pounding as you talked to Avi," Hana said when the light turned green.

"Fear or excitement?" Daud asked, glancing sideways at her.

"A combination of both."

They passed the old Jerusalem railway station, then entered Abu Tor via Hebron Road and turned onto a smaller street lined with large older homes, many with enclosed gardens.

"How much do these houses cost?" she asked.

"In the millions of dollars," Daud answered. "You know how expensive it is to live in Jerusalem in an apartment. It's even more in a detached home with a garden."

They turned onto another street, and Daud pulled to the curb in front of the house with an iron railing in front and a high stone wall along the rear.

"Here we are," he said. "You can't really see the cottage from here, but it's at the end of that short alley."

Hana stared at the main house. It was as big as anything they'd passed so far in the neighborhood.

"I wonder who built it," she said.

"I should have asked but didn't," Daud

replied. "Now it's divided into four apartments. Avi is probably waiting for us at the house."

Daud and Hana held hands as they walked down the narrow alley to an iron gate. Hana caught her first glimpse of the house and mentally clicked a photograph of the image to save in her memory.

"It's pretty," she said.

"And it's bigger than it looks from this angle," Daud said. "At first I thought it was the same size as where we live in Atlanta, but it's not."

"Daud!" a male voice called out.

A Jewish man in his sixties came up and introduced himself to Hana. Avi Labensky, with his colorful open-collar shirt and European-style pants and shoes, fit the image of an art dealer. He took a pressed white handkerchief from his pocket and wiped his forehead.

"It's a delight to meet you," he said to Hana in Hebrew. "Has Daud told you how much I like him?"

"It's been obvious from your kindness," Hana replied in the same language. "Thanks again for the beautiful painting you gave us. It greets me every morning."

"And there's a perfect spot for it in this house," Avi said. "I was enjoying the garden, but I'm ready to go inside and get out of the heat. It's going to be a hot day."

Before entering, Avi showed them a section of stone that looked slightly different from the rest.

"I've been told there was a row of holes left by machine-gun fire in 1948 that ran from here to the corner of the house."

Hana cringed at the reminder of deadly violence. The Jews called the conflict the War of Independence; the Arabs who had battled them called it the Nakba, or "Disaster."

"Any idea who fired the shots?" Hana asked.

"No," Avi answered. "Once a bullet leaves the barrel of a gun, it knows no owner."

Hana remained silent as Avi gave them a tour of the interior. Daud kept looking at her, clearly waiting for her to speak, but a strong inner restraint kept her mouth closed.

"What do you think so far?" Daud finally asked after they'd passed through the remodeled kitchen into the addition that contained the two extra bedrooms.

Hana shrugged and remained mute. She could read the disappointment on Daud's face. They went outside and climbed the steps to the rooftop. One corner of the wall around the Old City was visible in the distance. Avi pointed out where the armistice line fell following the battles in 1948 and an area of the main house damaged and repaired during the 1967 war. Hana felt tears well up in her eyes. The tears quickly spilled over and ran down her cheeks. She, Daud, and Avi were standing next to one another. Neither of the men noticed. Avi was the first to turn toward Hana and see her tears.

"What's wrong?" he asked in a kind voice. "Did I say something that hurt you?"

"I'm not sure," Hana said as she fought back the desire to sob.

Daud faced her with a look of deep concern. "Are you afraid?" he asked.

Hana simply shook her head. As the two men continued to stare at her, she turned away and walked alone to the corner of the roof that overlooked the garden. Bullet holes in buildings could be repaired so succeeding generations weren't confronted with the violence that caused them. But that was a superficial act. The forces of war leave scars in the bodies and hearts of people and the land itself. Hana's tears flowed until she couldn't see clearly what was in front of her. The garden, the large house, the city walls in the distance — all of them disappeared behind a veil of sorrow. She felt Daud's hand lightly touch her back but didn't respond. Finally, the reservoir ran dry. She took a wad of tissues from her purse and wiped her eyes and face.

"I'm ready to leave now," she said to Daud.

"Avi is waiting on the street. Is there anything you want to tell me while we're here?"

"No," Hana managed and paused for a few seconds. "Except that I felt the pain of the land and the people in a way I didn't know possible."

"In what way?"

"Not now," Hana answered. "That's more than I thought I could say."

Making sure her vision was now clear, Hana descended the steps to the ground. She again took Daud's hand in hers to reassure him as they retraced their steps down the alley to the street. Avi was standing by his car and didn't try to make eye contact with her as they approached. Hana felt herself returning to a place of normalcy.

"Thanks for showing us the house," she said.

"I'm sorry it upset you," Avi began. "If I'd known, I wouldn't have suggested you come here."

"Don't apologize. I had no idea it would

affect me so deeply. And it wasn't because I'm pregnant," Hana said with a slight smile. "Something else was going on that I'll need to talk to Daud about as soon as I understand it better myself."

"Should I contact Louis?" Avi asked Daud.

"Not yet," Daud replied. "Like Hana said, we need to talk first."

"Okay. Are we still on for the meeting with Mrs. Zarkawi in the morning?"

"Yes," Hana answered. "And I'll be fine by then."

"Are you going to be there?" Daud asked Avi. "It's already going to be crowded with Mrs. Zarkawi's son, their lawyer, the archaeologist, and us."

"Daniella wants me present. Most likely to safeguard her professional reputation regarding her interaction with Mrs. Zarkawi and the Bar Kokhba coins."

"That makes sense," Hana said.

"Would you like me to pick you up at your hotel?" Avi asked.

"Yes," Hana answered. "We'll be watching for you at the entrance."

Once Daud and Hana were in their rental car, she felt the same sense of silence descend on her that she'd felt inside the house. She knew it was unfair to Daud to clam up, especially since she'd promised to talk to him, but no suitable words formed in her mind, and she was incapable of small talk. They rode in silence to the boutique hotel in the German Colony where Hana and Jakob had stayed when they came to Jerusalem to investigate the Neumann case.

CHAPTER 31

Daud woke in the middle of the night. A sliver of light that made its way between a crack in the curtain revealed Hana sitting in a chair with her legs propped up so she could rest her chin on her knees. She was facing away from him toward the window. While he watched, she lifted her hands into the air and held them over her head with her palms open for over a minute before lowering them.

Before going to sleep, Hana had tried to explain to him what she'd felt standing on the rooftop of the house in Abu Tor. To Daud, it seemed his wife experienced something similar to his response when visiting the property, only deeper and more powerful. Listening to Hana, his own sense of the spiritual responsibility attached to the house increased. But what that meant for them individually and as a couple remained indistinct and unformed. They'd ended the conversation by agreeing on one thing: they needed to talk to Hana's uncle Anwar.

In the morning they enjoyed coffee and a traditional Israeli breakfast buffet of fruit, cheese, pastries, yogurt, and fish. Hana's appetite was good.

"Don't remind me that I ate a few bites of pickled herring the next time I'm nauseous," she said.

"Deal," Daud replied as he drank a cup of dark, strong coffee.

Daud's phone gave an alert. He furrowed his brow as he read a text message.

"What is it?" Hana asked. "Is there a problem with Avi or Mrs. Zarkawi?"

"No, Hosni Chatti, the client from the UAE, wants to meet with me today, not tomorrow. He arrived in Amman last night and doesn't want to stay over for an extra day."

"Can't you tell him you have a prior commitment?"

"He already knows my schedule. I provided it to him to avoid this type of problem."

Hana ate a piece of goat cheese. "I'd like to have you with me for the meeting with Mrs. Zarkawi, but if you can take care of your business today, then we'll have more time to drive up to Reineh, surprise my

437

family, and hopefully see Uncle Anwar."

"But I really wanted to learn more about the Bar Kokhba coins and any leads to the other items Jakob is looking for. That would be much more interesting than driving through an industrial zone in the West Bank scouting out the location for a plastics factory."

"Don't criticize plastic," Hana said with a smile. "Plastic irrigation pipe paid for everything from my baby shoes to my law degree."

Daud laughed. "Hopefully I'll be finished in time to meet you for an early dinner."

"Should I invite Avi to join us?" Hana asked.

"Sure. And you can include Daniella Rubin if you like."

Hana shook her head. "No," she answered. "I wouldn't feel comfortable discussing legal strategy around her."

Hana went upstairs to their hotel room to finish getting ready. Daud stayed behind to text back and forth with Hosni Chatti. Since the Arab businessman was coming from Amman, Daud suggested they meet at the industrial park near Jericho since it was just across the Jordan River. Chatti replied that he'd let him know where they could connect around 11:00 a.m. Daud sighed. The time for the meeting was later than he preferred and lessened the chance he would be able to make it back for an early dinner with Hana.

CHAPTER 32

Hana waited in the hotel lobby for Avi Labensky to pick her up. In a leather pouch were the digitally enhanced photos of the Bar Kokhba coins. Daud had been gone for over an hour and had probably already made his way through one of the checkpoints that existed at every significant point of entry between Israel and the West Bank. Hana didn't expect to hear from him until he'd finished his work and was on his way back to Jerusalem. The art dealer pulled into the hotel parking lot.

"Good morning," he said when she opened the front door of the vehicle. "I'm sorry Daud can't join us, but maybe it's better that he's not there to intimidate everyone in the room."

"He doesn't intimidate me." Hana smiled.

"Nor me," Avi said. "But only because he doesn't let his inner tiger loose. I've always been able to sense the beast within him."

440

The art dealer had no idea how fierce Daud could be. They merged into the late-morning traffic. It was a short drive to their destination.

"What does your insight into people tell you about me?" Hana asked.

Avi glanced sideways at her. "Your soul is a deep, deep well, and I can't see the bottom. Daud told me you were a special person."

Hana looked out the window. The appearance of large houses influenced by Renaissance or Moorish architecture signaled they'd entered Talbiya, which was slightly west of Abu Tor.

"What's it like to live here?" Hana asked as they passed a striking white villa originally owned by Constantin Salameh, a native of Beirut who first developed the area.

"Expensive in every way."

Avi turned off the street into the driveway of a home built in a Renaissance style with three date palms in the front yard. He parked behind a large older Mercedes. A stone walkway with bits of grass peeking through the cracks led to the front door that featured a brass knocker in the shape of a palm tree.

"They like palm trees," Hana observed.

"Probably because they own a lot of them."

"Daud did some research and says the family has commercial property in Israel and Marseilles."

"And probably a lot more."

The door opened, and an older Arab man wearing a white shirt and a thin black tie ushered them into a high-ceilinged foyer. The floor was covered by a very old silk rug. Avi introduced himself and Hana.

"I'll let Mrs. Zarkawi know you're here," the servant said in Arabic.

After the servant left, Avi turned over a corner of the rug and knelt down to inspect it. "This carpet is the real deal," he said in Hebrew. "Most people would hang this rug on the wall, not walk on it every day. It's not Persian. I'd say it's from the Ottoman era because whoever made it used a Turkish knot."

"You're correct," a male voice said in Hebrew.

An Arab man who looked about the same age and height as Avi entered the room. He was dressed casually in Western clothes.

"I'm Hakim Zarkawi," the man continued, extending his hand. "Welcome to my family's home."

They shook hands and made introductions. Mr. Zarkawi wore a thick gold ring on one of his fingers.

"My mother's Hebrew isn't very good, so I'll serve as translator," he said.

"That's not necessary," Avi responded in Arabic.

"Excellent," Hakim answered with a smile that revealed perfectly formed white teeth. "Follow me."

They stepped into a salon filled with antiques and ancient relics. Decorative metal latticework overlaid all the windows. The house likely had a formidable security system.

"Do you live in Jerusalem?" Avi asked Hakim.

"Not for many years. I spend most of my time in France and the UK. I flew in for this meeting."

Avi and Hana were walking slightly behind Hakim. Avi looked at her and raised his eyebrows.

"Has Mr. Barakat arrived?" Hana asked, referring to the Zarkawis' lawyer. "I met him a couple of times when I worked in Tel Aviv."

"No, once I decided to come I told him it wasn't necessary. But Ms. Rubin came early because she and my mother had other business to discuss. We'll be in the sunroom."

They entered a long hallway that led to the rear of the home.

The sunroom stretched the entire length of the back of the house. It was large enough to host a gathering of at least seventy-five people. Outside was a shady garden with a small greenhouse. Hana could see rows of flowering plants on shelves.

Mrs. Zarkawi was sitting in a wrought-iron chair covered with thick burgundy cushions. She was a small woman in her eighties with thin arms, lively eyes, and dark hair streaked with gray and pulled back in a bun. There was a walker next to her chair.

"You must be Mrs. Hasan," Mrs. Zarkawi said in Lebanese-accented Arabic. "Excuse me if I don't get up. Once I settle in a place, I don't quickly leave it."

"And I'm Daniella Rubin," said an Israeli Jewish woman in her thirties who stood to shake Hana's hand.

The two women were drinking coffee with a plate of pastries between them on a low wooden table. Daniella introduced Avi to Mrs. Zarkawi. They sat in a semicircle, with Hana and Avi in chairs facing Mrs. Zarkawi and Hakim joining Daniella on the couch. It quickly became clear that while Mrs. Zarkawi might be physically limited, she was a matriarch who controlled all conversations

444

within earshot. She peppered Avi with questions. She'd heard of his shop and had long admired a painting that a friend purchased from the art dealer.

"Paintings aren't my passion," she said. "But that one spoke to me because I remember that part of Beirut from my childhood."

"This is a beautiful home," Hana said when there was a break in the conversation. "How long have you lived here?"

The question led to a lengthy story from Mrs. Zarkawi. Her late husband's father bought the residence from another family that lived in Damascus. After the 1949 war, the Damascus family didn't want to come back to a divided Jerusalem poised on the brink of another conflict.

"My father-in-law bought it at a good price," Mrs. Zarkawi said. "He was able to see the potential for long-term value."

"I noticed the rug in the foyer," Avi said. "It's a very nice piece."

"My husband bought that for me as a gift not long after our marriage. It's a seventeenth-century Turkish Oushak rug. We both enjoyed buying items with historical value."

Hana saw Avi raise his eyebrows. The art dealer asked another question that led to a story of interest to Avi and Daniella. When there was another pause, Hakim, who'd stayed on the sidelines, cleared his throat and lightly touched his mother's left hand.

"Are you ready to talk about the Bar Kokhba coins? That's why they've come today."

"Don't rush me," Mrs. Zarkawi replied brusquely. "There will be plenty of time after lunch. I'm hungry."

Daud parked near the entrance to the Jericho industrial zone, a large, open area of land five kilometers from Ramallah. Hosni Chatti had finally agreed to meet him on-site. Designed along the same lines as similar projects in the US and Europe, the development featured a large modern sign and a futuristic welcome center. The land itself was largely empty, which meant a new company could pick where to build and receive a favorable lease rate from the Palestinian Authority. Daud checked his watch. Chatti was thirty minutes late, and the low-level government official Daud had contacted to give them a tour was waiting for them inside the welcome center. Daud's phone vibrated. It was a text message from Chatti:

Stopped in Al-Bireh due to car trouble. Can
you pick me up?

Al-Bireh was a major town in the West
Bank with a long history dating back over a
thousand years. Daud had been there several
times.

Where are you?

Chatti gave him the name and address of
a hotel near the central square. It was only
fifteen minutes from the industrial park.

Will be there shortly.

Daud entered the welcome center and
told his contact what had happened. The
man shrugged and continued to look at his
cell phone. A new message popped up on
Daud's phone.

What make and color vehicle are you driving? I'll be in front of the hotel. I'm wearing
a light blue shirt and dark pants.

Daud texted the information and pulled
out of the parking lot.

The route to Al-Bireh followed secondary
roads. The rural terrain featured the same

rolling hills as nearby Jerusalem, and it was common to encounter shepherds herding sheep or goats across the roadways. Daud drove cautiously. Insurance on the vehicle would reimburse a shepherd for the value of an animal killed by a motorist, but Daud didn't want to attract any attention. Sure enough, he rounded a sharp curve and encountered a herd of sheep in the middle of the road. A young man, his face covered with a red-checkered kaffiyeh, stood behind the sheep. Daud slowed to a stop. The young man showed no interest in hurrying the flock across the road. After waiting a few seconds, Daud honked the car's horn. The sheep skittered forward, but the shepherd stayed in the same place. Daud lowered the window of the car and stuck out his head.

"Move your sheep!" he called out.

The young man suddenly dropped to the ground. The next moment Daud heard gunshots.

The long table in Mrs. Zarkawi's dining room was covered in a delicately woven tablecloth that allowed the deep shine of the wood beneath to peek through. She placed her walker to the side and sat at the head of the table, with her son to her right.

Hana started to take a place near the other end of the table.

"No, no," the elderly lady said. "I want you beside me so we can talk."

Hana sat in an antique chair with an intricately carved back that gave it an African look. Plates on the table were filled with fresh fruit, meat pastries, and cheeses.

"Would you hand me the meat pastries?" Mrs. Zarkawi asked. "They're so much better when hot. And take a few yourself. They're not all the same, which makes it a treasure hunt finding out what's inside."

Amused at the elderly woman's attitude toward meat pastries, Hana held the plate while Mrs. Zarkawi used silver tongs to make three selections. Hana then put three on her plate as well.

"Eat that one first," Mrs. Zarkawi said, pointing to one of the pastries.

Hana bit into the best meat pastry of her life. The delicate, flaky crust concealed a seasoned lamb mix that hit all the right spice notes in perfect balance.

"This is really good," she said to Mrs. Zarkawi.

"It's a secret recipe," the older woman replied with a smile. "Now try that one."

That pastry contained chicken that was almost as good as the lamb. Without being prompted, Hana sampled the third pastry, which contained beef cut into razor-thin strips that were slightly smoky.

"They're all delicious," Hana said. "I think you already know where to find the treasure."

Mrs. Zarkawi replied, "I knew you would be able to appreciate what I have to offer. I could see it in your face when we were sitting on the veranda. Let's move to the cheese."

They followed a similar pattern with the cheeses, except the hostess described what they were eating in advance. She focused all her attention on Hana, who felt uncomfortable that no one else at the table was sharing their private conversation. When Hana turned to speak with Daniella Rubin, Mrs. Zarkawi quickly spoke up.

"The fruit doesn't need any introductions," she said. "But the dates come from trees cultivated by my husband's family for over a hundred years."

The dates were natural candy. Hana sampled one. Mrs. Zarkawi motioned to a young woman whose job was filling the guests' water glasses. The woman stepped from the room for a moment and returned with a small purple bag that she placed beside Mrs. Zarkawi.

"Now," the older woman said. "Good food is a blessing, but let's look at what you really came to see."

Hana watched as Mrs. Zarkawi's gnarled fingers loosened the top of the bag. Reaching inside, the elderly woman took out a coin and placed it on the table in front of Hana. Everyone at the table grew silent. Hana could see the image of the lyre on the tarnished silver coin that set it apart from so many other coins minted during the rebellion. Just as important was the inscription of "Eleazar the Priest."

"Pick it up," Mrs. Zarkawi suggested. "It won't break."

Hana held the lyre coin in her hand. For its size, the coin was heavy, proof of precious metal content.

"It's one of the best first-year coins I've ever seen," Daniella said. "That's what I told Mrs. Zarkawi when she asked me to evaluate it a couple of years ago."

Mrs. Zarkawi took out a second coin. Hana could quickly tell it was not in as good condition.

"If these coins could talk, what would they tell me?" Mrs. Zarkawi asked.

"I think I know," Hana responded.

Remembering her instructions from Jakob, she began with the story of Vladimir

Ivanov's great-grandfather. When she reached the part about the Soviet colonel stealing the coins from a man who'd barely survived the war, Mrs. Zarkawi shook her head sadly but didn't speak. Hana took out the digitally enhanced photos from the leather briefcase at her feet and laid them on the table. Mrs. Zarkawi moved the coins onto the photos so she could inspect them for herself. Her son also leaned in for a closer look.

"What do you think?" Mrs. Zarkawi asked Daniella.

"As soon as I saw the photos, I thought about your coins," the archaeologist replied. "May I compare them directly?"

"Yes."

The coins and photos were passed down the table to Daniella, who picked up each coin and inspected it from several different angles. She held up the inferior coin.

"This one is a possible match, but I can't say for sure."

Hana's heart fell. Daniella picked up the lyre coin and repeated the previous inspection process. While she did, Hana imagined Jakob's reaction if she had to tell him they'd failed. Nothing on the archaeologist's face revealed what she was thinking. Because she'd previously been paid by Mrs. Zarkawi,

Hana knew there was danger of bias. Finally, Daniella returned the coin to the table and looked past Hana at Mrs. Zarkawi.

"The lyre coin is the same as the photo," she said. "There are multiple points of identical markings."

Hana breathed a sigh of relief. She quickly studied Mrs. Zarkawi's face for a reaction.

"We would need more than one expert opinion," Hakim interjected. "And my mother was a good-faith purchaser for value without any prior knowledge of problems with the coins' history."

"Hakim, if I wanted to hear a lawyer talk, I would have paid Ajmal Barakat to be here," Mrs. Zarkawi said.

"She's a lawyer," Hakim said as he pointed at Hana.

"But she's different from Barakat," Mrs. Zarkawi said. "I could listen to her tell a story about anything and find it enjoyable."

"And there's more to Mr. Ivanov's story," Hana said.

"I'd like to hear it," Mrs. Zarkawi replied.

Directing every word to Mrs. Zarkawi, Hana picked up the narrative and told her about the other items on the inventory furnished to the Russian bank, including the female ceramic head. When she mentioned the head, Mrs. Zarkawi interrupted her.

"That could be a true treasure."

"Perhaps comparable to the king's head found at Metula," Daniella said. "It was in all the papers."

Mrs. Zarkawi glanced at Hakim, whose face was impassive.

"Go ahead," the older woman said to Hana.

"There's not much more. A lawyer friend of mine in the US represents Mr. Ivanov, who wants to recover the items stolen by the Soviet army officer. I agreed to help."

"What evidence do you have that the artifacts were in fact stolen from this man?" Hakim asked.

Taking out her laptop, Hana showed Hakim and Mrs. Zarkawi the newspaper article about the colonel's collection and the inventory list for the bank, both of which Jakob had translated into English. Hakim translated the information into Arabic for his mother, who listened impassively.

"This has been a very interesting meeting," Mrs. Zarkawi said to the entire table when Hakim finished. "I'm glad you came to see me. I hope you enjoyed your luncheon."

Hana didn't budge. She'd not traveled six

thousand miles to be stonewalled by an eighty-five-year-old woman, no matter how good the meat pastries on the table.

"Mrs. Zarkawi," she said. "With all respect to you and your house, this meeting isn't over yet."

CHAPTER 33

The side mirror beside Daud's left hand shattered from the impact of the first bullet. A subsequent shot came through the open window and ripped off the top of the steering wheel before destroying the glass in the windows on the passenger side of the car. Daud jerked his head back inside the vehicle and lay across the seats as he stomped the gas pedal to the floor. The car shot forward as other bullets slammed into the metal. He gripped what remained of the steering wheel, which vibrated violently as the car struck several sheep. Feeling the tires run off the pavement to the left, Daud pulled the steering wheel to the right without taking his foot from the gas. The rear window of the car was blown out by a bullet that continued through the car and pierced the front windshield as well.

Daud peeked above the dashboard and was barely able to swerve to avoid a large rock jutting up from the ground just off the roadway to the right. He crossed a ridge, and the road began to descend into a valley. He sat up in the driver's seat. Surprisingly, the rearview mirror remained intact. Daud lifted his foot from the gas and glanced behind him up the hill. He saw two men dressed in black, their faces covered with red kaffiyehs, running over the top of the ridge. Each of them had a rifle in his hands. One of the men stopped and raised his weapon to his shoulder. Daud lowered his head, pressed on the gas, and made the car zigzag down the road. He heard the sounds of several shots. A loud ping signaled that at least one bullet had struck the car.

Raising his head a second time, Daud couldn't see anyone remaining on the ridge. He floored the gas pedal again and shot down the road toward the Route 60 connector that would take him back to Jerusalem. He looked in the rearview mirror again, but no one seemed to be following him. Reaching the main highway, he entered the flow of traffic. The condition of his car unavoidably attracted attention from other motorists, and he slipped on dark sunglasses. As he neared the Qalandiya checkpoint for reentry into Israel, the temperature gauge for the engine began to move toward the danger zone. Before reaching the check-point, Daud pulled off the road into a vacant lot close to the old Atarot Airport. Opened by the British in 1920, Atarot was the first airport in the region and now served as an IDF base. Before getting out of the car, Daud checked his phone. There was a text message from Hosni Chatti:

Still waiting. Where are you?

Daud didn't reply. Instead, he phoned Aaron Levy. The phone rang six times before the Shin Bet supervisor answered.

"You're not sneaking over the border again, are you?" Aaron asked.

"I'm at Atarot." Daud told him what had happened near Al-Bireh. Partway through, Levy interrupted.

"That incident came across our intel-ligence feed a few minutes ago as a local dispute between sheepherders fighting over water rights. It mentioned that shots were fired but indicated no injuries or the pres-ence of a vehicle. There are PA investigators on the scene right now."

"It was an attempt to kill me."

"Are you hurt? Do you need medical at-tention?"

Daud wasn't wounded, but he'd been

close to death. The adrenaline that had initially insulated him from shock drained from his body. He felt himself tremble.

"No," he answered. "But I need to get back into the country. My wife is in Jerusalem and doesn't know anything about what happened."

"I'll send someone to pick you up, and we'll open an investigation without disturbing the narrative put out by the news media. We'll debrief later."

After the call ended, Daud closed his eyes for a moment before getting out of the car to inspect it. In addition to the broken side mirror and shattered windows, there were three other bullet holes in the vehicle, including one next to the engine compartment. Coolant was pooling on the asphalt beneath the front of the car. A blue minivan with Palestinian Authority license plates pulled up next to him.

"You heard my mother," Hakim said to Hana. "We've listened politely to what you have to say, and now it's time to go."

Hana glanced across the table at Avi, who didn't seem in a hurry to leave either. His body language gave her courage. She turned to Mrs. Zarkawi.

"Can you see the justice in Mr. Ivanov's

desire to recover what belonged to his family?"

"Justice has not always been the currency of this land," Mrs. Zarkawi replied soberly. "At least not for our family and maybe not for yours."

"But the opportunity to do right is the choice each of us must make during our time on earth," Hana answered.

Mrs. Zarkawi studied her for a moment. "Are you a lawyer or a priest?"

Avi spoke up. "I'd say an equal mix of both with a heavy dose of rabbi thrown in."

Mrs. Zarkawi nodded her head. She selected a plump purple grape from the plate in front of her and put it in her mouth. Everyone sat in silence while she chewed and swallowed it. She then turned to her son.

"Hakim, I know what I want to do."

"Are you sure?" he asked.

"Yes." Mrs. Zarkawi reached out and gently touched the Bar Kokhba coin with the lyre embossed on it.

"I'm going to keep the coin," she said.

Hana felt like she'd been punched. "But —" she started.

"As my fee for helping Mr. Ivanov recover what he really wants . . . ," Mrs. Zarkawi continued.

"You know where the other items are?" Hana blurted out.

"Perhaps some of them," Mrs. Zarkawi replied. "But before talking any more, I'll need a written agreement."

Hana left Mrs. Zarkawi's house with a list of terms for a contract. The Arab heiress would keep the best Bar Kokhba coin as a finder's fee in return for information leading to discovery of the queen's head. The savvy collector knew the ceramic piece was the crown jewel of the Ivanov collection and intimated she had a good idea of where it was and who had it. Hana needed to obtain the approval of Jakob and Vladimir Ivanov before drafting the final form of the agreement. Mrs. Zarkawi invited her to return the following day if Jakob and his client wanted to move forward.

"You worked Mrs. Zarkawi like a violin virtuoso," Avi observed after they said goodbye to Daniella Rubin and were inside his car.

"I wasn't trying to be manipulative."

"You didn't have to try. When you mentioned righteousness and justice, I thought I was listening to a message from a rabbi on Yom Kippur."

Avi started the engine and pulled away from the curb. Hana called Jakob. It was

461

early morning in the US, and he was at home. Hana could hear the sounds of a soccer match on TV in the background. Jakob followed the premier Russian soccer league.

"Turn down the volume on the football match and listen," she said in English.

"I like it when an American calls it football," he replied.

"I'm not American."

"And the football part of me is still Russian."

The soccer match faded into the background.

"I just left Mrs. Zarkawi's house," Hana said. "Should I start with the beginning or the end?"

"The end. I hate suspense except when it's Spartak playing CSKA Moscow."

She told him about Mrs. Zarkawi's proposal.

"My next call will be to Vladimir. What are the chances Mrs. Zarkawi will be able to deliver?" Jakob asked.

Hana relayed the question to Avi and put the phone on speaker. The art dealer slowed to a stop at a red light.

"Fifty-fifty," he said.

"If Vladimir gives me the okay, I'll want to nail this down before you leave Jerusalem. Does she know about the other items on the inventory list?"

"I can give her a copy."

"What does Daud think about her?"

"He had a business meeting in the West Bank and wasn't able to join us. Mrs. Zarkawi said she can be available tomorrow if you get back to me soon."

"Will do."

A minute later Avi's phone beeped. He passed it to Hana. "It's Daud," he said.

"Why is he calling you, not me?" she asked with a puzzled expression on her face.

The minivan contained an Arab family of six. They didn't pay attention to Daud as they piled out of the vehicle and hurried across the parking lot toward a convenience store. Daud turned the ignition key of the bullet-riddled car. The motor sputtered a couple of times and then went dead. Daud patted the dashboard. When he did, he noticed another hole, most likely from a bullet fired when he was leaning over and driving blind away from the ambush.

A couple minutes later the Arab family emerged from the store. This time the mother, who was wearing a dark-blue head covering, noticed Daud's vehicle and eyed it and him suspiciously. She motioned to her husband, who was preoccupied with a

463

little girl protesting about something. Daud didn't want to answer any questions from anyone, but there was no way to roll up a window that was no longer there. The man glanced in Daud's direction and called out to his wife.

"It's none of our business. Get in the van."

The family left the parking lot. Thirty minutes later a dark-gray sedan with Israeli license plates entered and parked beside him. A young Jewish man wearing a small brown kippah got out and showed Daud his Shin Bet identification card. His name was Gad Kopeck.

"You're not hurt or wounded?" he asked with a look of amazement in his eyes.

"No."

"A tow truck is on the way to get your car."

"It's a rental."

"Grab the paperwork so I can give it to Aaron. He'll take care of it."

Daud retrieved the rental agreement from the glove box. The paperwork was as pristine as when the agent handed it to him at the airport.

"Where do you want me to take you?" the man asked.

Daud gave him the name of the hotel in the German Colony but then wondered if it was safe. He tried to remember if he'd mentioned where he and Hana were staying to Hosni Chatti but couldn't.

"I just want to pick up my suitcase," he said. "The hotel location may be compromised."

They sailed through the Qalandiya checkpoint without being questioned when the driver showed the border patrol guard his identification.

"Call this number and give a recorded statement about what happened," Gad said, handing Daud a slip of paper with a phone number on it.

After he finished, Daud called a small hotel in the Rehavya neighborhood not far from Talbiya to see if he and Hana could stay there. There were no vacancies. Two more calls were unfruitful. They reached the German Colony hotel. Daud quickly packed his and Hana's suitcases while Gad waited outside the room. The room seemed undisturbed.

"Where now?" Gad asked once Daud checked out.

"I have a friend in Yemin Moshe. Maybe we can stay with him."

Not sure of Hana and Avi's status, Daud phoned the art dealer. "Where are you?" he asked Avi.

"Driving Hana back to your hotel. We had a good meeting with Mrs. Zarkawi —"

"Don't take her to the hotel," Daud interrupted. "Would it be all right if we meet at your house?"

"My house?"

"Yes."

Daud heard Avi relate the request to Hana.

"She wants to talk to you," Avi said to Daud.

"Not until I see her."

During the short drive to Yemin Moshe, Daud's apprehension skyrocketed as imaginary conversations with Hana ricocheted through his mind. Thankfully, they arrived before Hana and the art dealer.

"Park there," Daud said and pointed. "Once they arrive, I'll get the luggage and you can leave. Thanks for your help."

"It's my job."

As soon as he saw Avi's car, Daud walked around to the trunk that Gad had popped open. He placed the suitcases on the curb. Once he lowered the lid, Gad quickly drove away. Hana hurried over to Daud and began to pepper him with questions.

"What happened to the rental car?" she asked. "Who was that, and why did you pick up our luggage from the hotel? Is everything okay?"

"Everything is fine," Daud reassured her, glancing up and down the street. "But there's been a change in plans. I'll explain inside the house."

Daud picked up the two large suitcases, and Hana followed with her small carry-on. Avi unlocked the front door. After Hana entered, Daud leaned over and whispered to Avi, "I need to talk to Hana alone for a few minutes."

"Of course. You can use the bedroom where you stayed the last time you visited. If you need a place to spend the night, it's available."

Daud dropped off the luggage in the salon to the left of the front door and took Hana's hand. She pulled it away.

"Why won't you talk to me?" she asked, her voice shaking.

"Please, I'll explain once we're upstairs."

Daud led the way to the small bedroom with the window that overlooked the court-yard of the adjacent residence. He pushed back the curtain and peered out the window for a moment before turning toward Hana, who was still standing by the door.

"It's bad, isn't it?" she asked anxiously. "Are you injured?"

"Please, sit." Daud motioned to a single chair near the foot of the bed.

"I'd rather stand," she replied.

Daud stepped closer to her and did his best to give her a reassuring look. "There was an attack on the road near Al-Bireh," he said. "I'm okay, but the car was damaged. I called Aaron Levy, and he sent an agent to pick me up. The Shin Bet will take care of the car and deal with the rental agency. They've already opened an investigation."

Hana hid her face in her hands and began to sob. Daud waited for a moment and then sat on the edge of the bed. When Hana sniffled a couple of times, he prepared to continue his explanation, but more sobs followed. He felt tears sting the corners of his own eyes. Hana lifted her head and faced him. Her eyes were red.

"I need a tissue," she managed.

Daud found a box in the bathroom and handed it to her. She grabbed several. Her breathing continued to be interrupted by crying. Finally, she seemed to settle down.

"What happened? And don't leave anything out. I want the truth."

Daud's plan to insulate Hana from how close he'd come to death evaporated. She positioned herself in the chair. Beginning with the industrial park near Ramallah, Daud spoke in a matter-of-fact manner, as he had when he recorded the summary for Aaron Levy. When he reached the point of the first bullet that shattered the driver's-side mirror, Hana put her hands over her face again, and he stopped. Daud could see her taking big breaths in and out. She lowered her hands and put them on her belly. Daud immediately knelt in front of her.

"I'm here with you," he said. "I'm not hurt."

"But you could have been killed!"

"Yes. There's no doubt God sent his angels to protect me."

Hana blew her nose. "Go ahead."

"Are you sure?"

"Yes, and remember, the truth."

Describing what happened brought the attack vividly back to Daud. He paced back and forth as he talked. Hana stared straight ahead with her hands by her sides as she listened. He reached the detail of entering the parking lot near the old Atarot Airfield.

"That's when I called Aaron, and he sent a field agent to pick me up. I thought we should leave the hotel in the German Colony. Avi has offered for us to stay here. Would you like to do that?"

Hana looked up at him. "Couldn't that put him and his wife in danger?" she asked in a trembling voice.

Daud hesitated. "Possibly, but not likely. Since the men behind the attack failed, they'll try to disappear. That's why someone phoned in a phony report about a dispute between shepherds as an explanation for the gunshots. Aaron's men will conduct their own investigation."

"It was the Chechens," Hana said flatly.

"Maybe."

Fire flashed in her eyes. "Are there other people wanting to kill you that I don't know about?"

"No," Daud responded quickly, then paused. "Or at least I don't think so."

"Whoever did this knew you were coming and had time to plan."

"I'm almost one hundred percent sure the man who identified himself as Hosni Chatti was involved," Daud said. "He was always very insistent on knowing my specific plans. I chalked it up to his personality."

Hana rubbed her temples with her fingers. "I can't think anymore," she said. "All I want to do is go home."

"Would it help if you rested?"

"I'll shut my eyes, but I'm not going to be able to rest until I'm in my own bed in

Atlanta."

"I'll be downstairs with Avi."

CHAPTER 34

After Daud left, Hana's body began to shake. It started with her shoulders and quickly spread throughout her body. She managed to climb onto the bed and lie on top of the covers until the shaking subsided. She took several deep breaths and offered up a silent, desperate prayer that seemed to travel no farther than the ceiling.

Closing her eyes, she felt the trembling start to return. "Help!" she called out, the sound louder to her ears than it actually was.

To her surprise, the sound of her voice had a slight soothing effect.

"Yes, please help," she said in a softer tone. "I need help. We need help."

The threat of trembling retreated. Hana was able to bring to mind words and phrases that had sustained and strengthened her in the past: *Never will I leave you nor forsake you; the Lord your God is your strength and shield; the name of the Lord is a strong tower; no weapon formed against you shall prosper,* and others. The flow of divine words washed over her until she drifted off to sleep.

Hana woke suddenly and checked her watch. She'd been asleep for almost an hour. She decided she would splash some water on her face and freshen up a bit, then go downstairs to find Daud.

Daud sat at the kitchen table while Avi ground coffee beans and pressed them into the brewing basket of an old espresso machine that whistled and sputtered as it brewed the coffee. Daud's thoughts weren't in the kitchen but upstairs in the room where he'd left Hana.

"Would you like an espresso?" Avi asked. "I buy the beans from a supplier who gets them directly from Colombia and roasts them himself. I think it's the best coffee in Jerusalem."

"Uh, sure," Daud said absentmindedly.

Avi set a cup of frothy brown liquid in front of him. He'd created a tree design with the cream. Daud usually drank coffee black and unadorned but took a sip. The espresso was better than he'd expected, most likely due to the quality of the beans. Avi joined him at the table.

"Should we sit in silence, or do you want me to tell you everything that happened with Mrs. Zarkawi?" the art dealer asked. "It's your call."

"Go ahead." He listened as Avi relayed the events at the house in Talbiya. Daud tried hard to engage, but his mind wandered, and he had to ask Avi several times to repeat what he'd said.

"Are you in shock?" Avi asked after the third time Daud asked him to repeat himself.

"Everything's different when you're married," Daud replied.

"That's true."

Daud drank the final drops of his coffee. "Go ahead," he said. "I'll make myself focus."

Avi reached the part about the Bar Kokhba coins and Daniella Rubin's assessment that the lyre coin was part of the Ivanov collection.

"You would have been proud of Hana. She didn't let Mrs. Zarkawi intimidate her and somehow got behind the old woman's defenses. By that point Mrs. Zarkawi was beginning to genuinely like Hana. I mean, what's not to like? Hana called Jakob on the way over here, and he's going to check with his client before giving the go-ahead for a contract agreeing to Mrs. Zarkawi's terms. If she can deliver the queen's head, the Bar Kokhba coin will be a small price to pay."

"Yes." Daud nodded. "When I left Hana upstairs, all she wanted to do was return to America."

"But she mentioned the two of you driving up to surprise her family in Reineh."

"She doesn't want or need any more surprises in her life. And I don't have a car to drive anywhere."

"What happened to your rental? Did you have a wreck? I've totaled two cars, and Rachel is always telling me how to drive."

"No, it wasn't a wreck."

Avi opened his mouth to speak but shut it.

Daud looked directly into the art dealer's eyes. "When I told you my visits to Jerusalem had to be confidential, it was a serious request."

Avi nodded slowly. "Does it have to do with the complicating factors you mentioned when you were still in America?"

"Yes, which have become more complicated. Now my carelessness has created a very dangerous situation for everyone who gets close to me."

Avi sighed. "I'm sorry for your troubles. But my invitation for you and Hana to stay here remains open."

"I appreciate that, but you don't know the risk it could bring to you and Rachel."

Rahal stood seventy meters from the target. He took a deep breath and pulled the bow string until the arrow rested against his right ear. He exhaled and released the arrow. It arced through the air and completely missed the target. Rahal cursed under his breath. It was his third miss in a row. He'd not been able to push aside the news delivered minutes earlier by Khalil that Daud Hasan had escaped the ambush in the West Bank. Yanis, the chauffeur's son, prepared to run across the field.

"Go," Rahal said to the boy. "But only bring back the arrow that pierced the outer ring of the target."

Yanis sprinted off. Rahal turned to Khalil.

"The Chechens didn't send any of their own men," Khalil said. "They recruited locals. The Palestinian media reported it as an incident involving a dispute between shepherds."

"Once the Jews talk to Hasan they will know better."

"Certainly, but the men will blend back into their village. Unless someone talks, they should be safe."

"Who cares about them?" Rahal barked. "They failed!"

The boy reached the target and pulled out the arrow. He turned and started running back toward them.

"Where is Hasan now?"

"We don't know," Khalil answered. "He never responded to my texts after the attack."

"Of course not."

"But our communication was untraceable. Even if he enlists the help of his Jewish or American friends, the phone will lead them to the UAE and nowhere else."

Rahal flipped the string of the bow with his finger. Yanis returned with the arrow.

"Go to the car and bring me a cold drink," Rahal said to the boy. "Your father will know what I want."

"Yes, sir."

Rahal started walking forward to the fifty-meter mark.

"Eventually Hasan will show up in America," Khalil said. "I am ready to go and die there in jihad to eliminate him."

"I honor your desire," Rahal replied. "What do we know of Kolisnyk's whereabouts?"

"Nothing yet. The Americans have hidden

477

him away and likely given him a new identity."

Rahal swore again. His anger was growing.

"Hasan is a professional and is going to be hard to target," Khalil continued. "But there are other options."

"What are you saying?"

"Strike where there is weakness. I've been doing some research. Hasan's wife is going to speak at a public event in Atlanta. I've read the promotional materials. There will be hundreds of Jews and their friends present. That would be the time and place for us to act. It's likely Hasan will be there as well. Even if he's not, it would be worth it to kill his wife along with many other infidels."

"There will be security at the venue."

"Yes, but the Americans are sloppy. It's going to take place in a hotel with many entrances." Khalil paused. "Its purpose is to bring faiths together. There will be Sunnis, Jews, and Christians there to speak about religious issues in Palestine."

Rahal grunted. "If the Sunnis and Christians want to be with the Jews in this life, they can join them in the next one. But I don't want you to go. Talk to the Yemenites and develop a plan around them."

Yanis returned with a bottle of citrus-flavored beverage. Rahal removed the top and took a long drink.

"Yanis," he said, "what does the Qur'an teach about rocks, trees, and Jews?"

The boy stood up straighter. "Judgment Day will not come before the Muslims fight the Jews. The Jews will hide behind the rocks and the trees, but the rocks and the trees will say: 'Oh Muslim, oh servant of Allah, there is a Jew behind me, come and kill him.' "

Rahal looked at Khalil. "You're a Hafiz. Did he quote it correctly?"

"Yes."

Rahal spoke to Yanis. "Do you still have the gold coin I gave you for learning the names of all the prophet's bows?"

"Yes, sir. I keep it in a special place in my room."

"Have your father bring you up to my office when we return to Doha, and I will give you another one to be its friend."

Hana found Daud sitting alone in the small courtyard at the rear of the house. He had his back to her with his head bowed. She opened the door, which caused him to jump up and turn around.

"Sorry, I didn't mean to startle you," she

479

said, walking over to put her hand gently on his shoulder.

"Were you able to rest?" he asked.

"Yes."

Hana didn't tell him about the ongoing shaking that had dragged her to the brink of emotional exhaustion. Instead, she told him about the promises that flooded her soul when she cried out for help.

"That's good," Daud replied when she finished. "I tried to be calm earlier, but I'm completely tied up in knots."

"Did you talk to Avi?"

"Yes, but I only told him that something serious happened while I was in the West Bank. He wants us to stay here, but I'm not sure it's a good idea."

The door from the house opened and Avi joined them. "How do you like the guest room?" he asked Hana.

"It's nice."

"Then convince your hardheaded husband to accept my offer of hospitality to spend the night."

"I'd like that," Hana said and glanced at Daud.

"I'm not sure —" Daud started.

Avi snorted. "If you keep bringing that up, I'm going to make you explain yourself. I'm tired of hearing it. Rachel is visiting Yoni

480

in Tel Aviv for a few days, and I know she wouldn't mind. I have a state-of-the-art security system because I often bring home paintings from the shop. And no one except your buddy in the gray car knows you're here. I assume he's someone you trust."

"Yes," Daud answered. "Let me make a phone call, and I'll give you an answer."

Avi turned to leave.

"I'll come with you," Hana said to the art dealer. "I'm hungry and thirsty."

"That's an easy problem to solve. There's also a painting I want to show you. It's by the same artist who painted the one I gave you and Daud as a wedding gift."

Daud waited until the door closed before placing the call to Aaron Levy.

"What are your plans?" Aaron asked.

"I'm still in Yemin Moshe."

"I know that. I meant as far as exit strategy so I can bring my man back in."

"Return to America within the next two days. We're going to Talbiya for a meeting in the morning and then driving to Reineh to visit Hana's family. But now I'm questioning whether that's a good idea. Whoever targeted me may also be watching them."

"We're investigating the attack but don't have any hard intelligence. Our people on the ground haven't yet added anything to what you reported."

The Shin Bet had informers embedded in the Palestinian community.

"If you stay in Jerusalem an extra day or two, keep a low profile," Aaron continued.

"What about traveling to Galilee?"

"Don't go."

Daud took a deep breath. This would be hard news for Hana to receive.

Hana was snacking on cheese and crackers in the kitchen when Daud came in from the courtyard. He leaned over and kissed her on the cheek before speaking to Avi.

"We'd like to spend the night if the offer is still open," he said.

"Absolutely," the art dealer said and clapped his hands together. "And unless Hana eats a pound of cheese, I know where I want to take you for dinner. It's a place I love, but Rachel hates. They have the best meatballs on the planet. You wouldn't think a meatball would be a delicacy, but —"

"Do they have takeout?" Daud asked.

"No," Avi replied, raising his eyebrows.

"I'd rather stay here."

"Whatever!" Avi threw up his hands. "I feel like I've parachuted into a spy movie. You know, the kind where a secret agent stumbles into an innocent person's house and peeks out the window every five minutes to make sure he's not been followed."

Hana glanced toward the window. White-and-blue curtains were held back by white ties. She prepared to get up and look out. Daud touched her hand.

"It's not necessary," he said. "One of my old friends sent someone to look after us."

Hana tried to relax. She wouldn't know what to look for anyway. And the fact that Aaron Levy had authorized someone to guard them did make her feel safer. She determined to act as normal as possible.

"Avi, show me your pantry," she said, getting up from the table. "I'm in the mood for soup that will fill you up as much as a plateful of meatballs."

"That's not possible."

"You haven't eaten my makhlouta. We don't have all night to soak the cracked wheat and beans, so we'll settle for something with lentils."

Rachel had a well-stocked pantry and lacked only carrots. While Avi went to the store, Hana enlisted Daud as her sous-chef. She cut up the onions, and he ran cold water over the lentils and rice. As they worked, Daud told her about his conversation with Aaron Levy. He paused at one point.

"What is it?" she asked, glancing up from the stove.

"Aaron doesn't think we should travel to Reineh. He recommends we keep a low profile in Jerusalem."

Hana pressed her lips together tightly. "The soup needs to simmer for forty-five minutes," she said.

They worked in silence until Avi returned a few minutes later.

"Let's go back to the courtyard," the art dealer suggested. "It's pleasant this time of day when the sun goes down."

The art dealer brought along a bottle of wine and some cheese. They snacked and made small talk while waiting for the soup to simmer. For Hana, life almost seemed normal, but once when she glanced at Daud and saw him looking away in thought, she knew that nothing about their lives could ever be normal.

Later that night as they lay in bed, Hana turned so she could see out the window. Lights from houses in the neighborhood followed the contours of the Jerusalem hills.

"Are you awake?" Daud asked.

"Yes."

"Do you think we should go to Reineh?"

"I want to, but then I'm afraid to go."

Daud was silent for a few moments. "I guess we can wait to decide," he said.

Hana reached out and touched Daud's cheek. He took her hand in his and kissed it before releasing it. Hana closed her eyes. She didn't wake up until bright morning light streamed through the window.

CHAPTER 35

Daud slept fitfully as images of the attack on the road kept recycling across his subconscious. It wasn't until around 4:00 a.m. that he slipped into a level of sleep that enabled him to escape the images. After that, he didn't stir until he sensed Hana waking up. He rolled over and stared at her. Beauty in the midst of chaos. Marrying her had changed everything in Daud's life. He didn't regret the work he'd done for the Shin Bet. It saved lives. But he couldn't avoid the negative consequences that had a long shelf life. Hana sniffed and wrinkled her nose. Her eyes fluttered open. She turned her head away from the bright sunlight entering through the bedroom window and faced him.

"What time is it?" she asked, stretching her arms.

Daud checked his watch on the nightstand. "Seven forty-five," he said.

486

Hana rubbed her eyes and scooted up in the bed. "No morning sickness," she said. "That's good. And it's a beautiful day."

Daud didn't point out that it had been beautiful each morning they'd been in Israel. "What would you like for breakfast?" he asked.

"Nothing fancy. Avi has yogurt in the refrigerator. How about you?"

"Coffee is what I need," Daud said as he swung his legs over the edge of the bed.

He went downstairs in his bare feet. Avi wasn't in the kitchen, and Daud peered out the window. He saw a white car with a man sitting behind the steering wheel parked across the street. Daud knew the guard would prefer not to be openly acknowledged. The man was looking down. He glanced up, and Daud drew back from the window.

Avi had already brewed a regular pot of coffee in a simple machine next to the espresso unit. Daud poured a large cup of black coffee.

"Good morning," Avi said. "How did you sleep?"

The art dealer was dressed for the day in a casual gray shirt, dark pants, and black loafers.

"Not so well until early this morning,"

Daud replied. "Thankfully, Hana did much better. The coffee is much appreciated."

"You're welcome." Avi pointed to the window. "Is that your friend across the street?"

"I don't know him, but he's here to look out for us."

Avi poured a cup of coffee for himself and sat at the kitchen table. He motioned for Daud to join him. The art dealer looked down at the table for a moment.

"Daud, I've only known you as a private investigator, but it's obvious you are much more than that. I don't want to sound sentimental; however, I want to thank you for what you've done for our country. And I say this as a Jew to an Arab who I suspect has sacrificed more than I have to make this a safer place to live."

Not sure how to respond, Daud slowly nodded his head.

"I'm not fishing for information," Avi continued. "As much as I like to tell stories, my lips are sealed about everything that has happened here during the past twenty-four hours. But I had to say something to you this morning. It's an honor to have you and Hana in my home."

"You honor us."

"It's the least I can do," Avi said with a

wave of his hand. "And while you were awake in the night, I was tossing and turning about the house in Abu Tor. Are you sure there's nothing that can be done to make that a possibility for you and Hana? It would be a perfect place for you to live."

"No, that's settled," Daud said. "The past twenty-four hours made that decision crystal clear."

"Okay," Avi sighed. "But you have a place to stay with us anytime you want to come to Jerusalem. I also want to give the two of you a companion to the numbered print I sent as a wedding gift."

"No," Daud protested. "That's too much."

Ignoring him, Avi left the table. He returned with an unframed painting of a young couple strolling down a Jerusalem street and holding the hands of a small boy who walked between them. The artist had painted the scene from the rear so that it was impossible to tell the nationality of the couple. Man, woman, and child had dark hair and were wearing Western clothes. The setting was a brightly lit sidewalk. Daud touched the bottom of the oil painting and felt the texture of the pigments.

"This is an original," he said. "I can't accept this."

"Yes, and you will," Avi said emphatically.

"If you and Hana are forced by circumstances of your service to the country to walk away from Jerusalem, I want you to have this as a reminder that you're still moving toward a greater light for the future."

Daud felt a wave of emotion surge to the surface. "Thank you," he managed.

"You're welcome," Avi said and then smiled. "I'm not claiming to be a prophet about the gender of your child. The artist had a fifty-fifty chance of getting that right."

Checking her phone, Hana found a message from Jakob giving her permission to present a contract to Mrs. Zarkawi. Turning on her laptop, she quickly composed a simple three-paragraph agreement written in Arabic and transferred it to a flash drive. Downstairs, she found Daud and Avi sitting in the kitchen drinking coffee as if nothing terrible had happened the previous day.

"Coffee?" Avi offered.

The aroma was too much for Hana to resist. "Only a taste," she replied. "I'm really limiting my caffeine intake."

"For you, I will turn on the espresso machine," Avi said, rising from his chair.

Daud picked up the painting that was lying on a small side table. "Look what Avi gave us," he said.

"An original?" Hana's eyes widened.

"By the same artist as the other one."

She listened as Daud told her Avi's motivation behind the gift. The art dealer kept his back to her as he prepared the beans for the machine.

"Do you like it?" Avi asked when he turned around.

"I love it," Hana replied.

"Good!" Avi clapped his hands together. "For some reason this makes me more excited than if I sold the most expensive painting in my shop."

Hana stepped forward and gave the art dealer a quick hug. While they sat around the table, she told them Jakob and Vladimir Ivanov had authorized her to proceed with an agreement for Mrs. Zarkawi. Avi took the flash drive and printed out multiple copies of the two-page agreement. Both men read it.

"It's so clear even I can understand it," Daud said.

"Looks good to me," the art dealer said. "I need a lawyer like you who can put things in plain language, whether it's Hebrew, Arabic, or English."

Avi called Mrs. Zarkawi and put the call on speaker so Hana and Daud could listen. Avi greeted her formally in Arabic. She reciprocated and listened to his request for a meeting.

"Yes, I'm glad you called," the older woman said. "I have an engagement this afternoon, but if you can come this morning around eleven, we can talk then."

Both Daud and Hana nodded their heads.

"Oh, and I'd rather not have Daniella Rubin join us," Mrs. Zarkawi added.

"That's fine," Avi responded. "I wasn't planning on inviting her since this is about a legal document."

The call ended.

"Why wouldn't she want Daniella Rubin to come?" Hana asked.

"I have no idea unless Daniella is charging a consultation fee to show up," Avi replied.

Hana nodded. "That's probably it."

Avi finished his coffee and checked his watch. "I have time to run down to my shop and take care of a few things before driving to Talbiya. Help yourself to anything around the house."

After the art dealer left, Hana turned to Daud. "How did you sleep last night?"

"It was tough," he replied.

Hana reached out and put her hand on top of his. The feel of his warm skin beneath her fingers caused her to close her eyes.

"What is it?" Daud asked when she opened them after a few moments passed. "Were you praying?"

"No," Hana answered with a quick shake of her head. "Unless being grateful beyond words that you are alive and well counts."

"It counts."

Hana pulled back her hand. "Once we finish with Mrs. Zarkawi, do you want to drive to Reineh?"

Daud was silent for a moment. "Yes. I'll ask Avi if we can borrow his car."

Hana smiled. She felt the decision to see her family was a kick in the teeth to fear. "What do you want to do now?" she asked.

"I'd like to sit together in Avi's courtyard, listen to music, and read."

"Like I do in the night?" Hana asked, her eyes widening.

"Yes, only together."

Hana went upstairs to get her Bible and notebook. In the courtyard, she found Daud sitting with his feet propped up and his phone in the middle of a small wrought-iron table. Worship music was playing. He'd found a pad of paper and placed it beside the phone.

"Is that okay?" he asked, pointing to the phone. "I know it's in English."

"Yes, I listen to that a lot and sing along.

I've even translated some of the songs into Arabic."

A new chorus began.

"Do you know that one?" Daud asked.

"Only in English."

"Would you sing it?"

Hana had sung in front of Daud before, but she suddenly felt shy.

"If you don't want to —" he added.

"No, it's fine."

Hana closed her eyes. She listened to a few bars before joining in with the words. Quickly, her alto voice grew stronger. When she opened her eyes, she saw that Daud had closed his. This encouraged Hana to press in even more to worship. The song ended. The next one in the queue was also familiar to her, so she continued to sing. At the edge of her hearing she began to pick up Daud humming the melody. He didn't know the words, but his deep tone undergirded what she expressed. It was a new experience for her. When the second song ended, they joined together in another one. Daud stopped the music. His eyes were shining.

"That was glorious," Hana said. "It reminded me of the night we prayed together for a new home."

"Only better."

"Yes," Hana agreed. "We should do this

more often."

"I've never wanted to intrude," Daud replied. "The middle of the night is such a personal time for you."

Hana leaned over, took his hand, and pulled him closer. "Consider this an invitation," she said.

"Okay," Daud replied.

"Just don't sneak up behind me."

Daud smiled. "Agreed. Something else came to mind while you were singing. Hand me your Bible?"

For the next few minutes, Daud read several verses to Hana that spoke to the depths of her spirit. She sat completely still at first, not wanting to disturb the moment, but then she grabbed her journal and furiously made notes.

"That is really good," she said when Daud finished.

"Do you want to listen to another song?"

"Yes."

Three songs later they paused again. This time Hana shared a couple of verses that led them to pray together. Even though they didn't pray specifically about what had happened the previous day, Hana felt the tentacles of anxiety release their grip on her soul. She checked the time.

"Avi will be returning soon," she said.

Daud stretched. As he moved his powerful arms and stood, Hana was thankful that those arms regularly wrapped themselves around her.

"I'm glad we had a chance to do this in Jerusalem," he said.

Avi returned and insisted that Daud and Hana sit together in the rear seat of his car for the short drive to Mrs. Zarkawi's house.

"You're not a taxi driver," Daud said.

"You don't know what I did when I first moved to Israel," Avi responded.

"Did you drive a taxi?" Hana asked.

They turned left off of Avi's street.

"No, I worked in a shop in the Armenian quarter of the souk. That's where I first learned about buying and selling art."

During the rest of the time in the car, Avi told them stories about working for a man named Mr. Petrossian whose family had lived in Jerusalem for many generations. The shop mostly sold ornate ceramics and black-and-white photos of the Holy Land taken by early Armenian photographers.

"He also sold paintings and let me run that part of the business," Avi said. "I expanded it. When I went out on my own, he let me take a few items at cost to help me get started."

"Does his family still own the shop?" Hana asked.

"No, his son and daughter moved to the US after their father and mother died. I think they live in California."

They reached Mrs. Zarkawi's house.

"Did you meet Mrs. Zarkawi's security guards?" Daud asked Hana when they got out of the car.

"No."

"There's one in that building next to the garage, and I saw another peeking over the edge of the flat roof."

Hana could see a man eyeing them through an open door in the building. The same elderly servant opened the door and escorted them to the veranda where they'd met the previous morning. Mrs. Zarkawi was sitting in her chair. There was a modest spread of pastries on the table with silver carafes of tea and coffee. The elderly woman smiled when she saw Hana.

"Sit down," she said. "And this must be your husband."

Daud bowed when Hana introduced him.

"We know you have limited time," Hana said, taking the contract from her bag. "I've prepared a simple agreement for you to review and brought my laptop in case I need to make any changes."

"We'll wait until Hakim arrives to do that," Mrs. Zarkawi responded. "I want you to tell me more about your family in Reineh. I asked a friend about your father, and he was familiar with his business selling those purple recycled water pipes we see all over the country. Why did they decide to use purple? It's my favorite color."

"That was the government's requirement as a way to differentiate them from the pipes that carry drinking water and waste. My father and his brothers began the business by selling irrigation pipes, which is still a big part of their business."

As the conversation continued, Hana was comfortable focusing on her family because she didn't want to discuss Daud's background. She told Mrs. Zarkawi about Farah and Fabia and showed her photos of her nephews.

"They're sturdy boys," Mrs. Zarkawi said approvingly and then turned to Daud. "Are you like most men who want their first child to be a boy?"

Daud glanced at Hana. "I'd like a boy, but a girl would be a blessing too."

"All I had was boys," Mrs. Zarkawi said. "And here's my third son."

Hakim entered. He shook Daud's hand and took a seat beside his mother. A servant poured a cup of coffee and set it in front of Hakim.

"Now we can do business," the elderly woman said. "Hana has prepared a contract for us to read. I hope it's not too long."

Hana was glad Avi had made several copies. She passed one to Mrs. Zarkawi and another to Hakim.

"Oh, it's in Arabic," Mrs. Zarkawi said. "That's polite."

The older woman squinted as she read. Hakim frowned. Mrs. Zarkawi finished first and stared at Hakim.

"Are you still reading it?" she asked after several moments passed.

"Just checking some things."

"It doesn't have all those extra words Solicitor Barakat charges me for," Mrs. Zarkawi said. "It makes sense to me. If I help the man from Russia find the ceramic piece owned by his great-grandfather, I keep the Bar Kokhba coin."

"Very well," Hakim said resignedly. "If this is what you are determined to do."

"And even though it's not in the agreement, I wondered if there were other items in the Ivanov collection you might be willing to help us find," Hana added.

She handed Mrs. Zarkawi the list.

"Do you have a picture of the miniature

oil lamp?" Mrs. Zarkawi asked. "They've been a particular interest of mine."

Hana pulled up the photo of the lamp on her computer. Mrs. Zarkawi peered closely at the screen.

"Very nice," she said. "Because they had such a common use, not many lamps that size have extra detail on the reservoir."

There was a tiny image of an olive tree etched into the clay. Mrs. Zarkawi showed it to Hakim.

"Isn't it beautiful?" she said.

Her son leaned over. "Yes."

"Let's do our business," Mrs. Zarkawi said, turning to Hana. "May I borrow a pen? I don't carry one with me."

Mrs. Zarkawi signed the agreement with a flourish. Hana did so on behalf of Vladimir Ivanov.

"I'm authorized to act on Mr. Ivanov's behalf," Hana said, "but I'll also obtain his signature on the document and forward it to you for your records. What is your email address?"

"Hakim handles that sort of thing," Mrs. Zarkawi replied.

Hakim handed Hana a card with his contact information.

"Thanks," she said and turned to Mrs. Zarkawi. "When do you think we might hear from you?"

"Would now be too soon?" she asked with a twinkle in her eyes.

CHAPTER 36

Daud sat, a quiet observer as Mrs. Zarkawi whispered into Hakim's ear, and he left the room.

"Would you like more tea?" Mrs. Zarkawi asked Hana.

"Yes, please."

Hana had barely added milk and sugar when Hakim returned. She noted he had nothing in his hands. Mrs. Zarkawi sipped her coffee and nibbled a pastry. She then asked the servant who was hovering in the background to bring a clean hand towel. When she did, Mrs. Zarkawi carefully spread it out on the table in front of her.

"Show them," she said to her son.

Hakim reached into the side pocket of his sport coat and placed a ceramic piece of two and a half to three inches in length on the towel. The tiny statue had long hair and a band around her forehead. Streaks of pigment could still be seen on the hair. The outline of a robe was visible at the neckline.

"That's it," Hana said, wonder filling her voice. "May I pick it up?"

"Of course. It belongs to Mr. Ivanov now," Mrs. Zarkawi replied.

Hana turned the ceramic piece over in her hand and passed it to Daud. It was smooth to the touch, a testament to the firing process performed by an ancient craftsman. Daud tried to imagine how the complete statue would have looked when first created. He returned it to the towel. Hakim reached into his pocket a second time and placed a Bar Kokhba coin on the towel.

"Is that the other one we saw yesterday?" Hana asked.

"Yes," Mrs. Zarkawi answered. "Even though Daniella Rubin couldn't link it to the Ivanov collection, I bought it at the same time as the other coin and believe there is a connection. I want your client to have it."

"That is very generous," Hana said.

Daud picked up the coin. He could barely make out the marking "Eleazar the Priest" on the front. It also bore an image of the second temple destroyed by the Romans in AD 70.

"Is this a Year One coin too?" he asked.

"It is," Mrs. Zarkawi answered. "Just not

in as good condition as the one I'm keeping. I hope it will be meaningful to Mr. Ivanov."

"This is all appreciated," Hana said. "On behalf of our client —"

"There's one more thing," Mrs. Zarkawi interrupted and nodded to Hakim.

Her son reached into his pocket a third time, took out a five-inch oil lamp, and placed it on the towel beside the other two items. The lamp was in perfect condition with no significant breaks or cracks. Even from where he was sitting, Daud could see the olive tree on the side.

"And I don't need an expert to tell me about the lamp," Mrs. Zarkawi said. "I bought it at the same time as the Bar Kokhba coins."

"May I ask who sold them to you?" Daud said.

"They came from Russia," she replied. "A dealer in Istanbul who knows I collect lamps found this one. I paid quite a bit for the Bar Kokhba coin in the best condition. The second coin cost less, followed by the lamp. The ceramic head was thrown in cheaply because no one guessed how old it might be. Now we know it's the most valuable piece by far."

"And you're willing to give the other items

to Mr. Ivanov?" Hana asked.

"As long as I can keep the coin. When you talked yesterday about justice, it touched my heart, and I don't want to be part of an ongoing wrong against an innocent family. I tried to put myself in your client's position."

Daud reached over and picked up the ceramic head. It was heavier than he would have guessed.

Mrs. Zarkawi continued. "A big question for your client is what to do with the queen's head. It will take an expert to determine if it's similar to the king's head found at Metula, but I didn't want Daniella here because she might immediately notify the government and create bureaucratic problems for you."

"Understood," Hana replied.

When they stood to leave, Hana handed the ceramic head to Daud. "I don't want to be responsible for guarding this," she said.

Daud slipped the small piece into the front pocket of his shirt. Having a three-thousand-year-old treasure in his possession was extraordinary. Mrs. Zarkawi provided a small box for the lamp and a velvet bag for the coin.

Everyone stood, including Mrs. Zarkawi.

"It was an honor meeting you," Hana said.

"And you," the older woman said with a

smile. "When you return to Jerusalem, you are always welcome in this house."

Hana, Daud, and Avi walked down the stone walkway outside the house.

"Don't give the Bar Kokhba coin as a tip to a waiter," Avi said to Hana.

"It's not going anywhere," Hana answered.

"Which raises another issue," Avi said as they got in his car. "I don't share Mrs. Zarkawi's concern about the government asserting a claim. Since the items came from a private collection and were discovered before 1978, it is completely legal for you to take them out of the country if you obtain a certificate. I have a friend with an export license who can issue one. Nevertheless, in my heart I think the queen needs to be reunited with the king in a museum so people can see them together."

"That was in my mind the whole time," Hana answered.

"Why don't we leave the queen's head with Avi until Jakob and his client sort out what to do with it?" Daud suggested.

"Brilliant," Avi replied, glancing in the rearview mirror. "I go from taxi driver to depository of national treasures."

"Do you have a safe place to keep it?" Hana asked.

"Yes, yes," Avi said.

"I'll talk to Jakob about it."

"In the meantime, I'll get the certificate you'll need for the lamp and the coin."

Hana sent Jakob a note telling him what had happened at Mrs. Zarkawi's house. He replied with an email that included multiple exclamation marks, along with a promise to call as soon as he finished a deposition and was able to reach Mr. Ivanov. Daud and Hana packed their bags. Avi deposited the three items in a corner safe in his cluttered office and handed Hana a receipt.

"In case I keel over from a heart attack," he said. "I want Rachel to know who these belong to."

"Hopefully that won't happen before tomorrow," Hana said with a wry smile. Her affection for the art dealer had grown greatly since receiving the print as a wedding gift.

"I'll also put the painting in a tube and prepare the paperwork you'll need for customs," he continued.

"I wish you'd let us pay something —" Hana began.

Avi held up his hand. "Don't make me show you my mean side. It's much scarier than Daud's."

Once they'd arrived back at Avi's residence, Daud left the house and walked across the street. Hana watched from the kitchen window as he talked to the man who had been guarding them. The agent shook Daud's hand and drove away. Avi was in his office, leaving Hana still alone in the kitchen when Daud returned.

"He said they'd not picked up any chatter about me through their sources."

"Is that good or bad?"

Daud shrugged. "I'm not sure. To me, it means no one was boasting about a failed ambush. If it had been successful, multiple groups would have rushed to take credit."

Hana's phone vibrated. It was a message from Jakob. He'd taken a break from his deposition to call Vladimir Ivanov.

Ask Avi to coordinate shipment of all the items. Make sure we satisfy all legal requirements.

Hana showed the message to Daud. He brought down their luggage from the second-floor bedroom. They told Avi about Jakob's message.

The art dealer sighed. "I disagree, but I'll take care of it."

He took his car keys from a hook by the front door. "I'm not going to make a bad joke about driving safely," he said to Daud. "Have a good time, and I'll see you tomorrow."

The route from Jerusalem to Reineh was familiar to Hana. She'd made the trip many times when she attended law school at Hebrew University. Daud was a smooth, confident driver.

"Life isn't like this road," she said to Daud when they'd left Jerusalem behind. "I know every twist and turn and what's around the next corner."

"How predictable do you want life to be?"

"Probably more predictable than you'd prefer," she answered.

"My thoughts are changing about that," he replied.

Hana's mother was at home when they knocked on the door in Reineh and immediately burst into tears even before they shared their good news. They saved that until Hana's father could rush home from the office and several uncles, aunts, and cousins, including Fabia and Farah, could assemble.

"We have exciting news," Hana said, gently patting her abdomen.

The rest of her words were drowned out by cheers and applause, followed by a cacophony of thanksgiving and praise that exceeded what Daud had experienced at their wedding. An impromptu late-afternoon dinner was thrown together. The women insisted Hana sit down and watch. Daud pulled up a chair to sit beside her.

"Where's Anwar?" he asked.

"At his home in Nazareth. My mother says he's not been feeling well, and she's not sure he'll be able to join us."

"Should we go see him?"

"I don't know. Part of me says we should pay attention to what he's already told us before seeking more."

"I want more," Daud replied emphatically.

Hana patted him on the leg. "I do too, but we'll have to see."

They sat down to a dinner of tabbouleh, hummus casserole with ground beef, and lamb-stuffed zucchini with cinnamon-spiced tomato sauce. It was a totally Lebanese spread. The smile on Hana's face as she was surrounded by the love of her family was Daud's favorite part of the meal. For dessert they had nammoura, a cake made with yogurt and semolina flour, then soaked in sweet syrup and topped with almonds.

Before and after dinner, Daud took several short walks outside. He saw nothing suspicious, and as evening came he began to relax. They'd told Hana's family they were on a quick business trip.

"How is your work going?" Hana's father asked him after the plates were cleared from the tables.

"Increasing," Daud answered. "I recently helped an American company set up an office in Beirut."

That led to more questions from Mr. Abboud about Beirut, a city he knew well but hadn't visited in several years.

It was almost midnight when Daud and Hana went upstairs to a guest room in the large, rambling house.

"Thank you for bringing me here," Hana said as they climbed the steps. "It has refreshed my soul."

Daud was exhausted, and after his previous restless night, he fell asleep quickly until summoned awake by local roosters greeting the dawn.

Breakfast was a more normal affair, with Hana and Daud no longer treated like celebrities. Hana helped her mother in the kitchen. After kissing Hana on both cheeks and shaking Daud's hand, her father left early in the morning for work. Daud and Hana sat in the central courtyard of the compound and drank tea.

"My mother checked this morning on Uncle Anwar," she said. "He's sleeping most of the time, and when he's awake he often doesn't make much sense."

"That's sad."

"Yes, but we all know he wants to be with the Lord. Anyway, there's no reason not to stop by and see him. One of his great-granddaughters is sitting with him today. She's a teenager who goes to the same school I attended."

Hana and Daud said their good-byes without making definite promises about when they might return.

"Not being able to tell them when I'd see them again was tough," Hana said when they were alone in the car.

"But your mother committed to come to the US when the baby is born. That was progress."

"By then we'll have a house with a room where she can stay."

It was a very short drive from Reineh to the house in Nazareth where Anwar was staying. With Hana giving directions, Daud wound his way through the narrow alleyways until they reached an older home crammed against a row of houses.

"When he was younger, Uncle Anwar lived next to an olive grove," Hana said. "He knew every limb of each tree. I remember him talking to the trees and blessing their fruit."

"Did it work?"

"I'm not sure, but he always had money for fresh lemonade and treats for all the kids in the family."

Once inside Anwar's home, Daud could tell the great-granddaughter viewed Hana with awe as a sophisticated lawyer who lived in America. Hana asked the teenager several questions about school before they went in to see Uncle Anwar, who was in a bedroom on the main floor. He was lying down with a white sheet pulled up to his chin. His eyes were closed, and his breathing seemed shallow.

"Uncle," the young woman said, "you have visitors."

Anwar stirred and blinked as Hana and Daud came closer to the bed. His hand appeared from beneath the sheets and touched his head. His eyes opened wider. Daud could see him focus on Hana.

After a few seconds, he smiled. "Is it Hana or her angel?" he asked in a creaky voice.

"It's me, Uncle." Hana reached out and squeezed his hand. "I'm with Daud, my husband."

Anwar barely cut his eyes toward Daud

before he refocused on Hana.

"I'm going to have a baby," Hana continued.

Anwar nodded slightly.

Hana leaned in closer. "I was just telling Daud how you would bless the olive trees in your grove," she said.

"And I told you to be fruitful."

"Yes, you did," Hana replied in surprise.

"You're a good olive tree," Anwar continued. "I've been blessing you for a long time; the harvest is coming."

Daud saw Hana wipe one of her eyes.

"Thank you," she said.

Anwar slowly raised a gnarled index finger. "Give me your hand."

Hana placed her right hand in the old man's palm.

He closed his eyes and squeezed it gently. "Did you feel that?" he asked.

"Yes."

"The Lord's touch is just as real."

Anwar fell back asleep. They quietly left the room.

"That was as good as he's been for a while," the great-granddaughter said when they'd returned to the living room. "Sometimes I think he's already in heaven and comes back here for short visits."

"Has he been praying for you and speaking words about your life?" Hana asked the teenager.

"Yes," the girl replied shyly. "He wants me to be here as much as I can."

"Believe what he says," Hana responded. "From the time I was a little girl, he did the same for me. His words are still having a big impact in my life."

After saying their good-byes, Daud and Hana drove away from Nazareth toward Jerusalem.

"It sounds weird, but I feel like your uncle is in the car with us," Daud said after they'd driven a few kilometers.

Hana, who was staring out the window, turned toward him. "We're still within the area of his authority. And because we're family, there's a link in the Spirit."

Daud remembered what Anwar told him about possessing the gates of his enemies. Maybe it was the same kind of thing. If so, Daud wasn't sure his spiritual authority extended much farther than the end of his nose.

During the drive back to Jerusalem, Daud called his mother in Beersheba and arranged to have dinner with her and his brothers at a restaurant not far from Avi's house.

"Why didn't you tell me you and Hana

would be traveling to Israel?" she asked.

"The trip came up suddenly. We spent last night in Reineh, and we want to see you too."

"Are you okay?"

"Yes, of course."

There was a brief pause. "Is Hana pregnant?"

The phone was on speaker. Hana commented, "You are a better investigator than your son."

"Hallelujah! I can't wait to see you and give you a hug."

Thirty minutes later they received a phone call from Aaron Levy. Letting Aaron know in advance, Daud once again placed the call on speaker so Hana could listen.

"They captured the man who blocked your car with the flock of sheep," the Shin Bet official said. "He was a local who claims the intent was to rob you. He hasn't given any information as to the men who fired the shots. Based on the bullet fragments taken from the car, the shooters were using homemade guns most likely manufactured in a metal shop in the West Bank."

As terrible as it was, a robbery would be infinitely better than an unsuccessful assassination.

"So they could have been thieves?" Hana asked.

"Maybe," Aaron replied. "The crude weapons explain why Daud escaped. Those types of guns aren't very accurate except at close range."

Hana whispered to Daud, "I believe God's protecting angels saved your life."

"What now?" Daud asked Aaron. "We're on our way back to Jerusalem from Reineh."

"You decided to go? Any problems?"

"No."

"I'll keep you updated on our investigation. Anytime a terrorist cell raises its head, we have a chance to cut it off."

CHAPTER 37

Rahal finished his evening prayers. Sunni believers prayed five times per day with their heads touching the floor; Shia believers prayed three times a day with their heads touching a wooden plank or a clay tablet called a turbah. Covered with ornate calligraphy, Rahal's turbah was made from soil that came from Karbala, a city in central Iraq that was the place where Muhammad's grandson Husayn was beheaded in battle and buried. Rahal returned the tablet to a small cabinet and locked the drawer. There was a light tap on the prayer room door.

"Come in," he said.

"Have you finished your prayers, sir?" Khalil asked. "If not, I don't want to interrupt."

"Yes."

"I've spent much of the afternoon with Yemenites. It is three months until Hasan's wife speaks at the interfaith event in Atlanta.

518

If we send them now, they can seek political asylum and find work based on forged identity cards."

"How confident are you they will be granted asylum?"

"The situation in Yemen is dire. At the least they will be able to stay while a hearing is pending on their application, which will be more than enough time."

"And the identification cards are high quality?"

"The best. Hezbollah currently has operatives working in the US using the same type of documents while waiting for orders to strike appropriate targets. American employers are looking for cheap labor and aren't careful with background checks. Once in Atlanta, the Yemenites will find work at the hotel where the event is going to be held. That will give them easy access to carry out an attack."

"What sort of jobs will they try to get at the hotel?"

"Our preference would be food service, which would enable them to be in the large ballroom as part of their regular job duties."

"Will they use explosive vests?"

"Yes — and position themselves for maximum damage before detonating. Nails and ball bearings will be easy to purchase once they're in the US. The Americans would provide the explosive material."

"How?"

"From here," Khalil replied. "Our contractors working at Al Udeid can move about the facility. I've already performed reconnaissance while posing as a cleaning supervisor and know where blocks of C-4 are located. Because it is so powerful and stable, that is the best material to use. We will prepare a dummy block. I will return to the base and swap —"

"No," Rahal interrupted with a sharp wave of his hand. "The risk is too great. Find another source of explosives or give the Yemenites the funds to buy what they need once they reach the US. Trust me in this. My instincts have never failed me."

"The Yemenites are brave and willing to die in jihad. But they don't have the level of sophistication to do that without help."

"Surely they can purchase another type of material that is easier to buy in the US, perhaps something used in mining or clearing land."

"There is another way."

"What is it?"

Khalil took a deep breath. "I can go with them myself to oversee the operation."

After the dinner with Daud's mother and brothers, Hana and Daud returned to Avi's house. The art dealer had spent part of the day working on the arrangements to send the Ivanov artifacts to the US.

"Do you think there will be a problem?" Hana asked over a cup of tea.

"The documentation links Mr. Ivanov's claim all the way back to the Ottoman era. That should be sufficient."

Before going to bed, Daud and Hana spent another hour alone in the interior courtyard. It was as sweet as the previous time.

"I want to do this when we return to Atlanta," Hana said after Daud turned off the music and they sat quietly for several minutes immersed in the presence of the Lord.

"Then look for a courtyard in the middle of a house built with Jerusalem stone," Daud answered.

"That's not possible."

Daud smiled and didn't speak.

"Okay, okay," Hana continued. "The house in Abu Tor didn't have a courtyard either."

"But it had a rooftop."

When she woke in the middle of the night, Hana stayed in their bedroom and positioned a chair so she could look out the window at the neighborhood. She kept her thoughts and prayers silent and didn't write anything in her journal. Instead, she filled her heart with the peace she'd experienced in the room following the attack in Al-Bireh. That was the most important thing she could pack for the flight to Italy and take back with her to America.

The following morning they took a taxi to the airport. Once in Rome, Daud would stay behind at the hotel while Hana was at her meeting with the shipping company's risk management group. Armed with her laptop loaded with a PowerPoint presentation, Hana put on her most conservative business suit.

"How do I look?" she asked Daud.

"What do you want to accomplish?" Daud replied.

"To persuade a room full of men that they need to strike the right balance between risk and profit."

"You can do that regardless of your outfit."

Hana kissed Daud. After she left, he typed a detailed memo for himself about the attack near Al-Bireh while it was fresh in his mind. As part of the process, he transferred every text message and email between himself and the man who called himself Hosni Chatti to a secure file. The website for the plastics company in the UAE had been taken down. The business was a ruse with only one purpose — to lure him into a deadly trap.

Whether the Chechens were behind the attack was unclear. They always had the latest weapons and acted with a high degree of sophistication. Nevertheless, it still might have been a Chechen mission. The group had been significantly weakened as a result of Daud's efforts, and perhaps this had forced them to use more primitive weapons and tactics.

The other option was a connection between the Al-Bireh attack and what happened in Sharm el-Sheikh. The images captured at the seafood restaurant in Sharm el-Sheikh had blown Daud's cover. And anyone connected with the man he'd apprehended at the Kolisnyks' villa might be motivated by revenge. Daud paced back and forth across the hotel room. He should have handled the situation at the seafood restaurant differently. Stopping, he shook his head at the vanity of trying to undo the past. His focus needed to be on how to navigate the future.

He left the hotel for a long walk. He'd been in Rome before, and their hotel wasn't far from the Baroque-era Trevi Fountain. He mingled with the crowd and drank coffee at a sidewalk café before returning to the hotel for an aerobic workout in the exercise room. Hana had returned earlier than expected and was waiting for him in their room.

"How did it go?" Daud asked as he rubbed his head with a towel.

"Time will tell," Hana replied. "I pretended to be Mr. Lowenstein giving a PowerPoint presentation."

"Are you hungry?"

"Starving."

"Me too. I found a quiet restaurant not far from the hotel."

They enjoyed a leisurely meal capped off with a dessert of tartufo di pizzo, two flavors of ice cream molded together with cherries inside and covered with cocoa.

"This is delicious," Hana said after the second bite.

"Just like us," Daud replied. "Two flavors of ice cream pressed together into one piece with fruit in the middle and a sweet coating on the outside."

"Roma makes you a poet." Hana laughed. "Is our baby the sweet fruit in the middle?"

"However you want to interpret it. Once I release a metaphor, I don't try to control it."

The following morning they were up early for the return flight to New York, then on to Atlanta. Once on the ground, Hana checked her phone.

"Anything going on at the office?" Daud asked.

"No," she said, moving her fingers across the screen. "I was looking at the house on Berkdale Drive. It's still on the market."

"Any changes?"

Hana closed the screen. "Not that I can see. I was checking to see if it was built with Jerusalem stone and had a courtyard."

"No flat roof?"

"Or a view of the Old City wall."

"On fee simple land that would allow us to own it for generations."

Hana looked directly at him. "Why are we talking like this if we told Avi we weren't interested in the house in Abu Tor?"

It was a question Daud was ready to answer. He'd thought about it during his walk in Rome and on the flight over the Atlantic Ocean. He just didn't expect the issue would come up on an airplane a few minutes before they disembarked.

"Because we don't want the dream to die, but we know it may be a long time before it can become a reality."

"That's it," Hana said as she leaned back in her seat. "For now, America is our promised land."

Six weeks later Hana parked in front of the office for the real estate lawyer who was preparing the closing papers for the Berkdale Drive house. Daud hadn't arrived. He was coming from a meeting with the CEO and CFO of an Atlanta-based company interested in hiring him to help them open an office in Beersheba. The southern Israeli city in the Negev region was booming and growing at a rapid rate. An extra perk of the job would be the chance for Daud to spend time with his mother and brothers. He pulled up beside her and got out.

"Excited?" he asked.

"A little. But more importantly, I'm at peace. How did your meeting go?"

"They're going to hire me, which will pay four months of our new house payment."

"Is that how we're going to measure things from now on?"

"Until we start buying diapers and baby wipes."

Hana had been getting bigger so fast that she questioned the results of her initial sonogram, which revealed one baby, not two.

"Are you sure there isn't a second baby hiding behind the first one?" she'd asked the technician.

The woman had moved the wand over Hana's abdomen again. "Another baby wouldn't be able to hide from me without revealing an arm or leg. Based on what I'm seeing today, either you're going to have a big baby or you were pregnant earlier than you thought."

"My doctor has moved up the due date twice."

Daud was a solidly built man, and the idea of producing a child influenced by his gene pool was daunting.

"Everything looks great," the technician had continued. "The doctor will go over the details. Next time I see you, we'll likely be able to tell you whether you're having a boy or a girl."

Hana shifted her weight several times during the house closing, which was over in an efficient forty-two minutes.

"Congratulations, Mr. and Mrs. Hasan," the paralegal said when they finished and

527

she handed them a thick envelope containing their copies. "Enjoy your new home."

They left with the envelope and two sets
of keys.

"Do you want to swing by Jakob's office
for a few minutes?" Hana asked Daud. "It's
just around the corner."

"Sure, but I have something to show you
first."

Daud went to the rear of the Land Rover
and opened the gate. Lying on the carpet
was the original oil painting Avi Labensky
had given them as a companion to the print
he sent for their wedding gift.

"Do you like the frame?" Daud asked. "I
know it was a risk choosing it without your
input, but I wanted to surprise you."

He'd selected a tan frame with a raised
design.

"It looks like Jerusalem stone," she said.

"That's what I wanted. If we can't have
the real thing in our new house, at least we
can surround the painting with a good imi-
tation."

Hana held the painting at an angle so that
the natural light accentuated the sunlight in
the picture.

"I love it," she said. "And we need to find
a place to hang it so that the natural light
makes it come alive."

"In the master bedroom upstairs?"

"No, I want it downstairs where more people can see it and ask questions."

They arrived at Jakob's building. His office was on the second floor and took up a large space because he didn't have a full-time secretary or an administrative assistant.

"You look like you've been in court," Jakob said to Daud. "I hope you didn't get a traffic ticket."

Jakob led them to a corner where they could sit around a small conference table.

"We just came from the closing on the new house," Hana said. "The attorney was nearby."

"Congratulations. When can Emily and I come over?"

"As soon as we have a place for you to sit."

"We can bring camping chairs," Jakob replied.

"You might need to. We're going to take our time furnishing it. The down payment blew the top off our budget."

"Have you talked to Avi recently?" Daud asked Jakob.

"Yes, Vladimir came in yesterday, and we Skyped with Avi about the queen's head, the lamp, and the Bar Kokhba coin."

"Where are they now?"

"Vladimir has them. I told him to rent a safe-deposit box at a bank, but so far he hasn't followed through."

"That's not a good —" Daud started.

"I know," Jakob said. "But there is bigger news. Vladimir is willing to sell the queen's head to the Israeli government. Avi predicts a museum in Jerusalem will send someone over there to evaluate it, and we'll go from there. I've already organized the available paperwork on chain of title and provenance."

"What about the lamp and the Bar Kokhba coin?" Hana asked.

"Vladimir is going to keep those. He'll pay me from the sale of the queen's head. If the Israelis don't want to buy it, there will be plenty of other suitors."

"Suitors?" Daud asked.

Jakob explained the pun. "Museums all over the world will be interested."

"You're right," Hana said. "But I hope she's united with the king. That's the best result."

"And when I get paid, you'll get paid," Jakob continued. "You did more than I did to make this happen."

"Will it be enough to make a house payment?" Daud asked.

"Plus furnish a nursery," Jakob answered

with a smile.

They got up to leave. Jakob escorted them to the door, where he stopped. "Oh, I'm not going to be able to hear you speak at the interfaith forum. I put it on my calendar, but that's the same night as Emily's biggest recital of the year. She's going to have a solo in a string ensemble."

"If I had a choice, that's what I'd do too," Hana said. "I'd much rather hear Emily play the viola than listen to me talk."

"Do you know what you're going to say?"

"It's coming together. I'll begin with the story of my family, then transition to the substantive issues. I've also been studying the other participants on the panel so I can anticipate what they might emphasize. There are going to be lot of different ideas tossed out to the audience. I'm not sure how many friendly faces will be there, but Ben Neumann is going to bring Sadie. She's excited about picking out a new dress and staying up way past her bedtime."

Jakob opened the door for them. "Don't forget about the invitation to your house," he said. "Emily will want to come even if all we do is eat crackers and peanut butter while sitting on the floor."

CHAPTER 38

Khalil waited outside the hotel in a rental van. He'd meticulously coached the Yemenites on how to increase their chance of obtaining employment as either dishwashers or, better yet, servers. Their legal documents indicated they'd been in the US for over three years, not three weeks. The oldest of the men spoke English and could promise that he would make sure the others knew what to do. Khalil checked his watch. The longer the men stayed in the personnel office of the hotel, the better the chance they'd been hired and were filling out employment-related paperwork.

Entry into the US had been seamless. Using his Lebanese passport, Khalil arrived two days before the cousins and made arrangements for their housing at a week-to-week hotel. He camped out in a luxury suite at the Ritz-Carlton. The items needed for the attack were in a storage unit about five miles from the hotel. Khalil had located the law firm where Hasan's wife worked, and he had followed her one day to a nearby deli. Although unnecessary, Khalil ate lunch at a table within ten feet of her. He'd overheard snippets of her conversation in Arabic with a man in his fifties who either owned or managed the restaurant. The thoroughly Westernized and decadent woman was pregnant, and the Arab man gave her a free slice of baklava. Seeing her happiness hardened Khalil's resolve. Mustafa was dead at her husband's hand. Justice demanded retribution.

Khalil looked up as the Yemenites left the hotel. In handcuffs. They were accompanied by two uniformed immigration and customs agents. The agents led the cousins to an unmarked van parked not far from Khalil. One of the Yemenites glanced in Khalil's direction with a look of desperation in his eyes. Khalil slunk down in the driver's seat. In less than a minute they were gone, along with any hope that they would be able to carry out their mission.

Daud had become as familiar with the layout of the hotel as one of its maintenance men. Part of his plan required special scrutiny of men in their twenties or thirties who showed up at the event without a wife or family or as part of a mixed group of men and women. The assistant manager assigned to work with Daud had begun his career path in the hotel industry as a pastry cook but then jumped to the administrative side of the business. The interfaith convocation didn't include a sit-down meal but rather would feature heavy hors d'oeuvres and desserts.

"All our desserts will be made in-house," the manager said. "We have very strict quality control."

"Does that include running the cakes and pies through an x-ray machine before placing them on the serving tables?" Daud asked.

"No," the man replied, giving him a strange look. "We don't have an x-ray machine."

"We can either wand them with a metal detector before taking them out of the kitchen or precut the pieces."

"Oh, my preference would be to precut the pieces."

"And make them small. People can come back for seconds if they're hungry. I'll also want you to confirm the identity of all kitchen help and waitstaff and use only established workers," Daud continued. "No new hires."

"Not possible," the manager said and shook his head. "In a hotel of this size, we always have employees leaving and new ones coming in. And for an event of this size, there is a staffing agency I use to supply extra help for the night."

"Try to minimize the number of outside employees and provide me with background information on every person who will be working, including those from the staffing agency. Tell them you need the information two weeks in advance."

"I'm not sure that's —"

"Would you prefer I contact your human resources department and the staffing agency directly?"

"No, no. My boss has told me to work with you. That will make it look like I'm not doing my job."

"Then please get me what I need."

A week before the convocation, Daud collected the final background information from the assistant manager.

"There are a few more permanent employees working in the food and beverage areas. That will cut down on the number of outside workers coming in from the staffing agency," the man said. "I'll have a final list to you by the day after tomorrow, but there won't be any additions, only deletions."

Daud slipped the information into a leather case he carried with him. "The contractor setting up the screening stations will call you in the morning. And you'll have three cubicles ready nearby for us to use for private questioning, correct?"

"Yes," the manager said reluctantly. "People are going to get upset if they're dragged out of line."

"They're not going to be dragged. I think the correct term the people at the security firm taught me is 'escorted,' right?"

"Yes, but it's not going to matter what you call it."

Hana stayed late at the office working on the final touches to her presentation. Earlier that day she'd called Janet into her office to listen.

"What do you think?" Hana asked when she finished. "The opening is so important because it sets the tone for everything else that follows."

Janet pressed her lips together for a moment before responding. "You already know I believe you should begin with your family history. People like me want to know who someone is before hearing what they think. Your family has lived in the same area for four hundred years. That gives you the right to an opinion. All the historical facts and data you've researched are impressive, but you might want to slow down your delivery."

"I talk too fast when I'm nervous."

"Yeah, but it convinced me that you've done your homework. The Christian part makes sense to me, but I'm not sure how a room full of people from other faiths or with no faith at all are going to respond."

"Did I come across as too . . . aggressive?"

"I think the word you're looking for is 'preachy,' which is used to describe a person who tries to ram religion down someone's throat. But there's no point in beating around the bush. Come out and say what you believe and why."

"Was it a message of hope? That's what I want more than anything else."

"I'm not up-to-date on politics and the Middle East, but I've heard and read enough to know that there isn't much room for optimism. If hope is what you want to communicate, I think you still have some work to do."

"Any suggestions?"

"Let me think about that and get back to you," Janet answered.

"The event is this weekend."

"I know, I know. And I couldn't convince

Donnie to come. But I'll be there sitting in the cheap seats with Gladys Applewhite."

"I can move you up closer —"

"No," Janet responded as she held up her hand. "The rear of the room suits me fine. You do have a couple of intangible things going for you."

"What?"

"You're attractive. That will help with every man in the room and probably hurt with some of the women. But many of the women will be sympathetic because you're pregnant, which will also give you an excuse to be grumpy if needed."

Hana chuckled. "I'm not sure what to think about that."

"That it's a worthless comment. Here's what I think. Let the people in the room catch a glimpse of the person I've gotten to know and respect over the past three years. Speak as much from your heart as your mind. You're smart and beautiful, but it's your heart that makes you special. Do that and leave the results to the Lord."

"That's good," Hana said. "I need to relax and be natural, not try to impose my opinion."

"Exactly."

Hana was shutting down the computer on her desk when Mr. Lowenstein appeared in her doorway and asked for an update. Hana told him what Janet had said.

"That may be true," he replied slowly. "But this is going to be an intellectual crowd, so make sure you have plenty of facts, especially the kind of information that doesn't commonly show up in news reports. Misinformation is best discredited by showing that it's based on false assumptions. Expose the root and know the fruit."

"That's catchy. Did you come up with that?"

"No, I probably read it somewhere."

Hana summarized some of the data about higher levels of education among Christian Israeli Arabs than among those in the surrounding regions, and their participation in fields such as medicine, law, and business.

"The business run by my father and uncles shows that opportunities are there," she said.

Mr. Lowenstein nodded. "That sounds like an effective strategy."

"How is attendance lining up?"

"We've sold eighteen hundred tickets. There will be a flood of last-minute attendees, so I think we can expect around twenty-five hundred people to show up. Is Daud ready for that many?"

"He's been working a lot of hours. I know

he's feeling responsible for everyone's safety."

Leon greeted Hana with a friendly woof from his spot in the corner of the new kitchen. Since much of the dog's life revolved around eating, he'd quickly settled into a place within sight and sniffing distance of his metal food bowl. The kitchen was sparsely furnished with a foldable table and two chairs. For upstairs, they'd purchased a king-size bed and a large dresser. Daud had thrown together a bare-bones office in one of the guest bedrooms. Except for the Jerusalem painting that Avi gave them, the living room was as empty as the day they'd moved in. The only area in the house that looked complete was the sunroom; the previous owner sold them the existing furniture at a greatly reduced price.

"I'm home!" Hana called up the stairs.

She could hear Daud moving around. He was holding his cell phone to his ear as he descended the stairs.

"I want to hold a meeting with everybody scheduled to work the event at least two hours before it starts," he said. "Even if it means an hour extra on the payroll for some of them. Amanda Fletchall, the event planner, will modify the budget if that's what it takes."

The call ended as Daud reached the main floor of the house and kissed Hana.

"You sound more and more like an American," she said in English.

"The immersion process is making my brain hurt," Daud answered in Arabic. "But I know it's the most effective way to learn a language."

"Should we start talking in English at home?"

"No," Daud answered emphatically. "But it's okay if we use Hebrew from time to time. You speak it at work, but for me it's rarely needed."

"And you can practice Russian with Jakob."

"All he wants to talk about in Russian is football."

They went into the kitchen. It was Daud's turn to provide the meal.

"What's for supper?" Hana asked.

"It's in the oven."

Hana opened the oven door. "Pizza?" she asked.

"It's part of being an American. Do you know how many kinds of frozen pizza they have at the grocery store?"

"A lot." Hana eyed the circular pie skeptically. "But we always order pizza at a restaurant where they make it fresh."

"Which is why there's a bowl of salad in the refrigerator," Daud replied.

Hana opened the refrigerator and took out the salad. Daud had filled the bowl with fresh ingredients, including plenty of green and black olives, along with seedless cucumbers and tomatoes.

"You found purslane," Hana said.

"Supposedly it's organic. It wasn't as good as what we could get at home, but it's okay."

"Thanks," Hana replied as she placed the bowl on the counter. "And remember, this is our home."

CHAPTER 39

Khalil knew he should have checked in an hour earlier. Rahal would be getting anxious.

"Where are you?" Rahal barked.

"In New York about to get on a plane for Riyadh," Khalil answered. "My flight from Atlanta was delayed."

"You'll be out of the country before the attack takes place, right?"

"Of course. Three glorious martyrs are about to enter paradise. They are well prepared and resolute. Even if one is stopped, the other two can complete the mission."

"You were right to go to America." It was as close to an apology as Khalil would receive. "The Yemenites would not have been able to cope with the logistics on their own. But I'm relieved that you will be in the air over the ocean when the sword falls."

"And fall it will. Of that I am certain. I

need to board the plane."

Rahal spoke a blessing over Khalil. "I love you like a son of my own flesh," he concluded.

"That means much more than you know," Khalil replied, trying to hide the emotion in his voice.

After the call ended, Khalil went into the bathroom of his suite at the Ritz-Carlton to comb his hair. The Yemenites were still in the custody of the US immigration authorities based on discrepancies in the paperwork furnished by Khalil's contacts within Hezbollah. Fortunately, the jihadists were being treated as normal illegal aliens, not terrorist suspects. Their request for political asylum from their war-torn country might even be approved. But the cousins were no help to Khalil, who was wearing the uniform furnished by his new employer, the hotel where the interfaith convocation would take place later that evening. Beneath the white jacket worn by food service employees was a bomb vest filled with enough explosives and metal nails to shred any human flesh standing within fifty feet when it detonated. But the vest wouldn't be Khalil's primary means of bringing death and destruction. He wouldn't die until he'd seen the devastation caused by the bomb he'd assembled and concealed at the hotel over the past week. Once that exploded, Khalil wanted to look into the unbelieving eyes of those who remained alive and cry out, "Allahu Akbar!"

Hana had narrowed her outfit options to two choices, both expensive dresses that tried to straddle the line between maternity clothes and high fashion. Daud had raised his eyebrows when she'd come home with three dresses and told him how much she paid for them.

"Don't go there," she warned. "It's your fault my body is changing, and I need to feel confident when I'm standing in front of two thousand people."

Daud raised his hands in surrender. "Okay, okay. I'm sure you'll look fabulous whatever you decide to wear."

In the end, Hana selected a blue dress rather than a green one, partly because the blue one picked up on the colors of the Israeli flag. If she was going to stand up in public as an Arab and defend the nation of Israel, she might as well go all the way with her color choice too. Daud had left hours ago for the hotel, and she was putting the finishing touches on her makeup when her phone vibrated. It was Ben Neumann.

"Sorry to bother you since I know you're

getting ready," Ben said. "But Sadie has an upset stomach and won't be able to come tonight."

"I hope it's not too bad."

"I suspect it's a twenty-four-hour virus, but she really feels puny and doesn't want to get out of bed. She's very disappointed that she can't come."

"You should stay home with her."

"No, Laura is going to take care of her."

Over the past few months, Hana's optimism about Ben, Laura, and Sadie forming a new family unit had increased. In particular, Laura was making a consistent effort to connect with Sadie. They'd been cooking together often. Caring for the sick girl was another step.

"I really hope Sadie feels better soon."

"She'll bounce back. Things like this never keep her down for long. I'm going to let her wear her dress when we go out to dinner at a fancy restaurant. She made me promise to take a selfie with you tonight so she can see what you're wearing."

"She's almost grown up."

"I know, but let's not rush it."

"I agree. See you later."

Hana paused in her preparation when she felt the flutter of the baby moving within her. She and Ben might joke about keeping

546

Sadie a little girl, but Hana wanted her unborn child to grow quickly so she could meet him or her.

Arriving at the hotel, she showed the attendant a pass that allowed her to park in the VIP area. Another vehicle pulled in next to her. It was Mr. Lowenstein.

"Where's Mrs. Lowenstein?" Hana asked when they exited their vehicles.

"She's coming with friends," the senior partner answered. "How do you feel?"

"Pregnant and nervous."

"You look beautiful, and I'm looking forward to seeing you shine. Let me walk you to the speakers' room."

Daud had already shown Hana where to go and how to get there, but she was grateful for Mr. Lowenstein's company. On the way, they encountered several people the senior partner knew, and it was gratifying to hear the kind things he said about her when he introduced her to them. They reached the green room.

"Looks like you're the first one here," Mr. Lowenstein said. "Would you like me to wait with you?"

"No, that's not necessary. You have other responsibilities. I'll be fine."

"I'll be sitting to the left of the stage if at any point you need an encouraging face to focus on."

"Thanks."

Mr. Lowenstein left. Glad to be alone, Hana seized the opportunity of solitude to offer up some final prayers.

Standing in front of the stage that the speakers would occupy in a few hours, Daud finished his presentation to the hotel employees and extra workers brought in from the staffing agency. The assistant manager wasn't there. The staff had a surprising number of questions, which showed Daud they were taking their jobs seriously and didn't want there to be any problems.

Daud spent the next two hours finalizing procedures with the security personnel who would be checking the attendees as they arrived. He then returned to the kitchen and found the former pastry chef personally overseeing preparation of the desserts.

"Mr. Hasan, I'm very busy," the assistant manager said.

"And I'll let you go about your business in a moment." Daud reached into his coat pocket and took out a couple of sheets of paper. "There were two new hotel workers I had a question about. Both of them are in food service and you hired them. Can you tell me more about them?"

The manager quickly scanned the sheets of paper.

"Yes, I know them. Fahed's older brother worked for me a couple of years ago and sent him over to apply for a job. If he's anything like his brother, he's going to be an excellent worker. Based on his work history, Khalil is overqualified as a server but wanted a job here so he can be near the rehabilitation center where his father is recovering from a stroke. Even after the short time he's been here, I have him marked for a promotion."

"Did you check the references for both of them?"

"Of course. There's Fahed now."

A slightly overweight young man wearing glasses was pushing a cart containing pitchers of water toward the ballroom. Daud started to walk rapidly toward him but was interrupted when his walkie-talkie squawked.

"Mr. Hasan, we need you at the entrance, please."

Daud left the kitchen and went to the security checkpoint. The line was already beginning to lengthen. The man in charge approached Daud.

"We've had more people meet the criteria for extra questioning than we anticipated.

Can we abbreviate it or only pull aside every third person?"

As the man spoke, Daud saw a familiar face being ushered into a cubicle. He quickly stepped over to the area. It was Ben Neumann.

"There's no need to question him," Daud said to the woman who was escorting him. "I know him."

Ben saw him and smiled. They shook hands.

"Where's Sadie?" Daud asked.

"Sick. Why was I marked for special treatment?"

"You're a young male who's here alone."

"The young part makes me happy, but I wish I wasn't alone. I didn't want to miss the opportunity to support Hana."

"Thanks."

Ben moved forward. Daud turned to the man overseeing the checkpoint. "I'd rather shorten the questioning time than not identify people who pose a greater security risk. I'll stay here for a while and step in as necessary."

Over the next forty-five minutes, Daud personally dealt with eight irate men, one of whom began to curse him in Arabic and quit only when Daud spoke sharply to him in the same language. Another man complained under his breath in Hebrew and looked up in surprise when Daud answered. The program in the ballroom was already underway when Daud was finally able to pry himself away as the last stragglers were processed.

Because of her nerves, Hana didn't trust herself to eat anything. She would be the fourth of five people to speak. The woman serving as moderator of the event was an elegant Jewish lady in her forties who managed the Atlanta office of a New York investment bank. After welcoming the guests and recognizing the organizing committee, including Mr. Lowenstein, she asked how many people were surprised by the level of scrutiny at the security checkpoints. Virtually everyone in the room raised their hand. She then gave an explanation comparing what they'd experienced to everyday life in Israel and the West Bank where security posts existed at everything from bus stations to malls to restaurants.

"We are gathered tonight in recognition of the serious situation in the small strip of land between the Jordan River and the Mediterranean Sea and to hear from people who have differing ideas about those problems and the impact religious faith plays in the issues and possible solutions. There are note cards on the tables if you want to jot down a question for one of the speakers. We'll have time for that sort of interaction later in the evening."

The first speaker was a Muslim teacher currently working at a prep school in New England. He was as smooth as he'd been in the YouTube videos Hana had watched in preparation for the event. The second person was a Jewish woman from New York who had worked for five years in Israel for an NGO dedicated to bringing reconciliation to Jews and Arabs via dialogue for adults and sports camps for teenagers. Hana had heard about the group and viewed the woman as an ally for the evening. The third speaker was an Arab man who still lived in Hebron where he served in the municipal government. He adopted a more militant tone than the schoolteacher and quoted extensively from the Old and New Testaments about justice, righteousness, mercy, and how the presence of the State of Israel violated those tenets for the Palestinian people. He concluded with selected sections from the Qur'an that espoused similar sentiments. To someone with little knowledge of the region or how beliefs played out on the ground, it was a compelling presentation.

But the only logical conclusion to his words was that Israel had no right to exist. The final speaker would be an Israeli Jew who'd grown up in a religious settlement in the West Bank and ardently believed in the biblical promise of a homeland similar in size to what appeared in the back of most Bibles.

Hana stepped forward. Bright lights made it difficult to see the audience. Mr. Lowenstein was washed out in the glare, but when she looked down she saw Ben Neumann and the empty seat beside him. Even though Sadie was absent, Hana could imagine the encouragement the little girl would want to communicate to her.

"My name is Hana Abboud Hasan," she began. "My family has lived in the Nazareth area for over four hundred years. I'm a Christian Arab who is thankful that I grew up in the State of Israel. Here's why."

Daud stood to the side of the ballroom listening to Hana's presentation. She was relaxed yet passionate, humble yet confident. A smile of satisfaction and appreciation creased his lips. Whether a person agreed with his wife or not, no one could question her credibility or the integrity of her heart. The second in command of security at the entrance of the venue came up to him.

"We have a situation that needs your attention."

Daud hesitated. He wanted to listen to Hana.

"Sir," the man continued.

"Okay, okay."

Daud and the man circled back through a long hallway to the entrance area for the ballroom. Two of the workers were standing in front of a middle-aged Arab man who was gesturing to them.

"What's the problem?" Daud asked.

"Are you in charge?" the Arab man asked.

"Yes."

"I bought a ticket for the event, and they won't let me enter."

"He had this stuck down his pants," one of the security guards replied, handing Daud a folded-up piece of nylon fabric.

Daud immediately recognized what it was — a Palestinian flag.

"You can't take this into ballroom," Daud said. "No political disturbances are allowed."

"I'm not going to disturb anything. I demand admission!"

Daud turned to the supervisor. "Did you search him?"

"Yes, he's clean."

Daud knew that even if the man didn't unfurl his flag and wave it, he was likely to have another tactic to make his point.

"May I see your ticket?" Daud asked.

Based on the table number, the man's seat was toward the middle of the room. He returned the ticket to the man.

"Do you understand that audience members will not be allowed to speak and have to submit any questions in writing?"

"And I will not be insulted or lectured by a person like you!"

The man tore up his ticket and threw the pieces in Daud's face. One of the younger guards stepped forward, but Daud held out his hand. The man cursed Daud in Arabic with an Iraqi accent.

"That doesn't change anything," Daud replied in the same language. "And without a ticket, you will not be admitted to the event."

The man stormed off.

"What did he say to you?" the supervisor asked Daud.

"Nothing that I will translate and repeat."

"He makes number twelve of those who were offended by our procedures and left," the supervisor continued. "Eleven men and one woman."

"According to the moderator, we made our point," Daud said.

"Since we're done here, can I give the boys a snack?" the man asked.

"Only in shifts," Daud answered. "I want most of you to stay in this area in case someone like our friend with the flag causes problems inside the ballroom. Two of you can come with me to the kitchen."

Daud led the way to the kitchen. It was a hive of activity because most of the food and drinks would be consumed after the event concluded. The security supervisor and one of the guards picked up a couple of plates and began to load them with hors d'oeuvres. As a predominantly Jewish event, the kitchen had omitted shrimp, scallops, and bacon-inspired offerings, but there were plenty of seasoned meat pastries, spinach tidbits, glazed salmon, and a chicken liver crostini that Daud found delicious. He picked up another crostini to munch on.

At the other end of the kitchen, Daud saw a server leave the area pushing a cart covered with white linens. To enter the ballroom now would disrupt the program. Daud looked around for the assistant manager, but he wasn't in sight. No other carts were queued up yet to leave. Daud left the security personnel, who had moved on to a dessert table. Stepping into the long hallway that ran along the wall of the ballroom, he saw the server pushing the cart toward an entrance close to the front. The food tables were at the rear of the cavernous room. Daud started to call out, but the walls were thin, and his voice would possibly be heard inside the ballroom. He started walking rapidly toward the server and the cart. The server pushed the cart into the ballroom and turned away, leaving the cart and disappearing through a door that led back to the kitchen.

CHAPTER 40

Daud slipped into the ballroom. Hana was at the podium, and he paused to listen.

"My Christian faith wasn't imported from a distant country thousands of miles away," she said. "Jesus of Nazareth grew up five kilometers from where my parents live today and spent his entire earthly life between the Jordan and the Mediterranean. The Jewish presence in the land is even more ancient, dating back almost four thousand years to the patriarchs Abraham, Isaac, and Jacob. More than any other religions, Judaism and Christianity are native to the land of Israel, and their followers have a right to be nurtured and protected in the place of their origin."

The serving cart was completely covered by a white linen tablecloth. Daud lifted a corner of the cloth. Laid out in neat rows were several pitchers of water and empty glasses. He started to turn away when an unpleasant fragrance stopped him. He sniffed again. It smelled similar to road tar. Daud lifted the covering cloth again and the smell became more pronounced. No one wanted to drink water that smelled like runoff from a newly paved roadway. Perhaps that was why the server hadn't pushed the cart to the rear of the room. Daud leaned over so he could see the lower section of the cart. Positioned in the middle of the lower shelf was a large cardboard box wrapped in tape. He pulled the box to the edge of the cart. Taking out a small pocketknife, he cut the tape and opened the lid. The tar smell confirmed that the box was the source of the odd odor.

Inside were several blocks of claylike material wrapped in olive-colored plastic film. There were gaps between the blocks and they were surrounded by piles of nails mixed with razor blades. Extending from each end of the blocks were red-colored blasting caps. It was a bomb.

Daud grabbed the handle of the cart and pushed it out of the ballroom. The walls in the hallway were flimsy and would offer no protection in a significant explosion. In fact, the splintering material would join the nails and razor blades as deadly shards. Sprinting, he pushed the cart across the hallway and toward the kitchen.

"Get out!" he yelled at the top of his lungs as he burst through the swinging doors. "Bomb!"

Startled workers looked up and seconds later began to stampede toward the exit doors. Daud continued across the kitchen to a large walk-in cooler. Out of the corner of his eye, he saw the assistant manager flee toward the loading dock. Daud reached the cooler and flung open the heavy stainless steel door. Knowing the explosives would be triggered by detonation of the blasting caps and not by physical movement, he lifted the cart into the air and threw it into the cooler on top of boxes of frozen food, then slammed the door shut. There were still a few people in the kitchen. Less than a minute had passed since he'd left the ball-room.

"Go!" he yelled again to the workers. "Now!"

Daud sprinted from the kitchen toward the ballroom. Reentering the hallway, he collided with a man wearing a white server outfit. Both of them were knocked off balance by the impact and staggered backward. Daud caught a glimpse of the man's face. He looked eerily like the assassin sent to Sharm el-Sheikh. The identification pin on the man's jacket read "Khalil."

"You killed my brother!" Khalil shouted. "And today you will die!"

Khalil glanced upward for a second, then reached beneath his jacket. Daud lunged forward and knocked him to the floor. Landing on top of him, Daud pressed Khalil's face against the carpet. He could feel something wrapped around Khalil's chest. An explosive vest. Khalil squirmed and tried to force his right hand beneath his body. Daud grabbed the hand and with a sharp, powerful jerk twisted Khalil's wrist so that it snapped. He cried out in pain. Drops of sweat forming on his face, Daud brought both Khalil's hands together, but he didn't have anything to secure them.

At that instant the bomb in the cooler detonated.

Hana had seen Daud out of the corner of her eye standing next to a serving cart. When he suddenly pushed the cart from the room, she stared in his direction for a couple of seconds before continuing. Struggling to regain her train of thought, she stumbled through several sentences. Her next point had to do with contrasting the civil rights guaranteed all citizens in Israel with the laws of the surrounding nations,

561

including the area controlled by the Palestinian Authority.

A thunderous, deafening boom shook the walls of the ballroom.

She immediately looked to her left where the sound came from and where Daud had been seconds earlier. Screams and bedlam erupted as everyone realized something horrible was happening. People fled toward the exits. Stunned, Hana looked again at the small door where she'd last seen Daud. Where was he? Where was Daud?

"Hana!" a voice yelled out.

She looked down. Ben stood before her with his hand stretched out. The speaker from Hebron ran past Hana and jumped from the platform. Hana grabbed Ben's hand, and he helped her down to the floor. Still holding her hand, he dragged her toward the exits that were jammed with people.

"Daud!" she shouted in Ben's ear.

"Come on!" Ben kept pulling her forward.

In a few seconds they were swallowed up in the mob pushing through the exit doors. The doors were wide, and before long they popped out into the broad concourse outside the ballroom. Hana could hear police and fire sirens outside the building. Ben kept pulling her forward.

"But Daud's still in there!" she shouted.

Ben stopped and turned toward her with an anguished look on his face. Hana knew he was thinking about the helplessness he had felt when Gloria lay dying in Hurva Square, Jerusalem. He released her hand. Hana turned back and fought her way through the tide of people fleeing from the ballroom. By the time she reentered the room, it was empty. Fine dust from the nearby explosion floated in the air. Hana kicked off her shoes and ran across the ballroom to the doorway where she'd last seen Daud. Inside the hallway visibility was poor, and she coughed as dust attacked her lungs. Taking several steps, she saw two figures on the floor, one on top of the other. The man on top turned his head so that she could see his profile.

"Daud?" she called out as she took a couple of steps forward.

"Don't come any closer!" he shouted. "He's wearing a suicide vest! Get out of here! Now!"

Hana stood still. Daud was holding the man's hands behind his back. She stepped backward. Daud turned his head so that he could see her.

"Call for a bomb squad!"

Daud's command catapulted Hana into

action. She dashed from the hallway and across the ballroom. Once in the concourse, she desperately began looking for a police officer. One approached her waving his arms.

"Leave the area!" he ordered, pushing her toward the hotel exits.

Hana pointed toward the ballroom. "My husband is in there! He's holding down a man wearing a suicide vest!"

"The bomb squad is on their way," the officer said. "Move on!"

"They're in the hallway next to the ball-room!"

As Hana continued down the concourse, a large group of police officers wearing heavy protective gear approached and continued into the ballroom. Exiting the hotel, she stood barefoot on the sidewalk, surrounded by screaming sirens and flashing lights.

CHAPTER 41

Remembering the fighting skills of Khalil's brother in Sharm el-Sheikh, Daud made sure his grip on the suicide bomber was more secure. Khalil muttered something under his breath that Daud couldn't make out at first. He continued, and Daud picked up snippets from the Qur'an.

"I didn't kill your bother," Daud said in Arabic.

"Lying infidel."

"He was alive when I left him."

Daud heard the sound of men calling to one another in the adjacent ballroom.

"In here!" he yelled.

Moments later two officers in SWAT gear entered the hallway with their weapons drawn. "Move away and raise your hands!" one of the men ordered.

"This man is wearing a suicide vest!" Daud responded. "I can't release him."

Both of the SWAT officers immediately

backed away. Khalil moaned as Daud maintained the pressure on his wrists. The right one felt broken. Three officers returned to the hallway and cautiously approached Daud and the bomber. One of the officers placed the muzzle of his weapon close to Daud's neck.

"Get off with your hands in the air!" the officer said.

"The man is still a threat. He must be neutralized first. My name is Daud Hasan, and I was in charge of private security for the event."

"I don't care what your name is!" the officer barked. "Do as you're told."

"Check my identity badge!" Daud yelled in frustration.

The officer grabbed the lanyard around Daud's neck and lifted it over his head. The bomber muttered something in Arabic that Daud couldn't make out. A fourth officer joined the group. Daud glanced over his shoulder as the new arrival inspected the identity badge.

"Handcuff both of them, but the one on the bottom first," the fourth officer said.

"Secure his feet too," Daud added, motioning with his head toward the bomber. "I don't know the location of the triggering mechanism."

An officer knelt down to secure the bomber's hands. Daud maintained his grip until the cuffs clicked shut. Another officer put Daud in handcuffs, frisked him, removed the small knife from his front pocket, and confiscated his cell phone. An officer started to frisk the bomber.

"Stop!" Daud yelled at the officer. "You could accidentally detonate it!"

The officer lifted his hands and looked up at the others. "Yeah, up close I can tell that he's wearing some kind of vest beneath his uniform."

"Back off," said the officer who seemed to be in charge of the group.

Leaving Khalil in the hallway, one of the officers escorted Daud out of the hallway and across the ballroom. Daud started to protest but knew the man wouldn't release him until someone in charge authorized him to do so. They reached the concourse outside the ballroom. A man in civilian clothes with a badge affixed to his belt was talking to the private security officer who'd been in charge of the checkpoints. When Daud appeared, the private security officer looked at him in shock.

"You?" the man blurted out.

"No," Daud said and shook his head in exasperation. "I caught the bomber. He's

567

secured in a hallway to the side of the ballroom adjacent to the kitchen. He was wearing an explosive vest."

"Is that correct?" the detective asked the officer holding Daud's right arm.

"We found this man on top of a guy in the hallway. Officer Mitchell started to frisk the man on the floor but stopped because he may be wired."

"The bomb that exploded was on a serving cart," Daud said. "I discovered it and pushed it into a large cooler in the kitchen before it detonated."

"I don't know anything about a bomb in a cooler," the uniformed officer said.

The detective spoke into a communication device, listened to a response, and then turned to Daud. "One of our men in the kitchen area confirms that it appears to be the center of the explosion."

"Was anyone injured?" Daud asked.

"Unknown. We're just beginning to assess the situation. My name is Detective Swinney. We'll have to keep you in handcuffs until we can confirm what took place."

Outside the hotel, Hana didn't know what to do or where to go. She looked for a familiar face but couldn't find one. Then she heard someone call her name.

"Hana!"

Janet came running up to her with tears in her eyes. They hugged. Janet looked around when they parted.

"Where's Daud?"

Tears welled up in Hana's eyes. She managed to get out what she'd seen in the hallway near the ballroom. Janet covered her mouth with her hand and shook her head.

"I want to go back inside and make sure he's okay," Hana said when she finished.

Janet placed her hand on Hana's arm. "He'd want you to stay where it's safe."

"I know," Hana said. "But I'm going to be as close to the exit as they'll let me."

"I'll wait here with you."

"No, go home to be with your family. And I thought Gladys was here with you?"

"We drove separately, and Gladys already left. I called Donnie to tell him that I'm fine. He turned on the local news. They haven't even started reporting what happened."

The two women stayed side by side for half an hour. During that time they were ordered to move twice and ended up a block away from the exit through which Hana hoped Daud would emerge. Hana's purse was in the ballroom, and they used Janet's phone to make multiple calls and send several texts to Daud's cell phone. None elicited a response. Hana gave up.

"Why isn't he answering?" she asked in frustration.

"There he is!" Janet exclaimed, pointing.

Daud emerged from the hotel flanked by two uniformed police officers who were holding him by both arms. He was in handcuffs. News reporters rushed forward and started taking pictures and calling out questions. There was no way Hana could get close enough to find out what was going on or let Daud know she was there. The officers placed him in the rear seat of a patrol car that took off with its sirens flashing.

Janet turned to Hana. "Why would they arrest Daud?"

The first thought that flashed through Hana's mind was that her husband was an Arab man in the vicinity of a terrorist act.

"I guess I'll find out later when they give him a chance to make a phone call," she said, then sighed. "Let's go."

"Do you have your car keys?" Janet asked.

"No. My purse is in the ballroom."

"I'll take you home."

Janet had parked in an open lot a couple of blocks from the hotel. They made their way through a dense crowd of onlookers who'd assembled as news of the explosion spread.

"Why would people come out to see this?" Hana asked.

"Because it's exciting and they think the danger is gone," Janet answered.

"That's not always true. There can be second-level attacks."

"Then let's walk faster."

They reached Janet's car. Once she was in the passenger seat, Hana tried to call Mr. Lowenstein, but the call went to the senior partner's voice mail. In a shaky voice, she left a message telling him about Daud and asking if he could help. Less than a minute later Janet's phone vibrated. She answered it and handed the phone to Hana.

"It's Mr. Lowenstein."

"Where are you? Are you okay?" the senior partner asked.

Hana told him where she was and what had happened to Daud. Mr. Lowenstein didn't respond, and she thought the call had dropped.

"Are you there?" she asked.

"Yes. I'm still in shock."

"Can you try to help Daud?"

"I will try to find out what's going on. I spoke briefly with the general manager of the hotel. The sound we heard was a bomb detonating in the kitchen area. From where I was sitting, I didn't see Daud pushing a serving cart, but without a doubt, he saved our lives."

Tears burst from Hana's eyes. "Please help him," she managed.

Daud had enough experience with Israeli security and police forces that he knew the American authorities weren't going to quickly release him. He remained in handcuffs in the concourse outside the ballroom. Shortly after his conversation with Detective Swinney, an FBI agent interviewed him. Scores of people descended on the scene to completely secure it and began the investigation. Daud didn't see any injured people transported through the concourse, but he didn't know what had happened in the kitchen. It seemed everyone was fleeing toward an exit, but that didn't mean someone hadn't simply cowered down in paralyzing terror.

Daud's request to contact Hana and let her know that he was safe was denied. He didn't see her when he left the hotel. Instead of taking him to an Atlanta police precinct, the police car delivered him to the local FBI office. Daud was placed in a holding cell.

Forty-five minutes later the door to the cell opened.

"Mr. Hasan, we'd like to ask you some questions," an agent said. "Come with me."

Daud entered a conference room. Five people, three men and two women, were sitting around a polished wood table.

"May I let my wife know that I'm safe?" Daud asked as soon as he sat down.

"We already did," the woman sitting at the head of the table said. "She's aware that we need to hear from you before you can be released to return home."

The agents recorded Daud's account of the evening, occasionally interrupting to ask questions. As fatigue set in, his comfort level of communicating in English diminished. He didn't mention the connection between Khalil and the mission in Sharm el-Sheikh.

"It is hard for me to talk this long in English," he said.

"I understand," the woman in charge replied. "We're almost finished. Is there anything else you can tell us?"

Daud hesitated. "There's information I can't reveal about the bomber without knowing that you have the sufficient security clearance. I can give you my contact with the CIA."

The people around the table exchanged

surprised looks. Daud jotted down Charlie's direct number for the agent in charge. The room cleared except for a man who stayed with Daud. Half an hour later the woman who had headed the questioning returned.

"Someone from our Washington office will take over from here," she said. "The hotel parking lot is still closed, so one of our agents will drop you off at your home."

"What's the status of the suicide bomber?" Daud asked.

"He's in custody and receiving medical treatment. That's all I can say at this time."

"And the number of people injured in the explosion?"

"None with life-threatening injuries. A lot of people suffering from shock."

Relieved, Daud stood up.

"Thank you for what you did tonight," the woman continued.

"Are you going to issue a press release?" he asked.

"I'll report that a member of the security team at the event saved hundreds of lives."

"I need to keep a low profile for several reasons."

The agent paused.

"It's going to come out eventually, isn't it?" Daud continued.

"Yes."

"Okay, I'd rather it come from you. Please don't publicize my name or my connection to my wife as one of the speakers."

"The press will eventually dig it out, but I'm fine with making them work for it."

CHAPTER 42

Rahal was in the middle of his midday prayer ritual when there was a loud knock on the door. Before he could answer, five men burst into the room. Two of them grabbed Rahal by the arms and pulled him to his feet.

"Rahal Abaza, you are under arrest by order of His Royal Highness."

"Why?" Rahal asked in shock.

"Terroristic acts and theft of US government property."

"That's ridiculous," Rahal said, glancing around as if looking for a way of escape.

One of the men picked up the clay turbah from the floor. "Should I take this, sir?" he asked the man in charge.

"You're Shia?" the officer asked in surprise.

Rahal didn't answer. The man's face darkened.

One of the other men spoke. "The man

the Americans arrested is Shia too."

"Khalil?" Rahal blurted out.

"Yes," the officer replied. "We have video evidence of Khalil Morsi stealing explosives from the Americans at Al Udeid. Several hours ago, he was arrested and charged with terrorism in the United States."

Khalil had disobeyed a direct order not to steal C-4 explosive from the Americans and lied about being on a plane from New York to Riyadh. Rahal struggled to remain as confident as a man with his wealth and position should be. Wanting to maintain an appearance of ignorance, he asked a question.

"What sort of terroristic attack?"

"At a gathering of Jews in the US. A bomb exploded. There weren't any reports of casualties."

Rahal felt the life drain from his body. The attack had obviously failed. And now Khalil was in the hands of the Americans.

"I want to talk to my lawyer," Rahal managed.

"No," the officer replied.

The men dragged a slumped Rahal from the prayer room.

Hana fidgeted in the dark as she waited for Daud to return home. She'd tried to watch news coverage about the bombing on her computer, but it made her anxiety sky-rocket. It was after 3:00 a.m. when the front door finally opened. Seeing her husband's tired face unmarked by blood or injury burst the floodgates of Hana's emotions. They embraced just inside the door. Every cell in Hana's body needed reassurance that Daud was alive and well. Her tears quickly soaked a spot on his shirt near his shoulder. She pulled back her head.

"I'm so thankful," Hana said, wiping her eyes with the back of her hand.

Tears glistened in Daud's eyes as well. He took both of her hands in his, raised them to his lips, and kissed them.

"I know you want to take a shower and change," Hana continued. "Go upstairs and —"

"In a minute," Daud said. "What I need more than anything in the world right now is to be with you."

They sat at the table in their kitchen. Daud didn't let go of Hana's right hand. After a few moments he bowed his head and uttered a deep sigh. Hana reached over and stroked the back of his neck. Truly, there was no man on earth like him. When he lifted his head, Hana saw a new depth of strength and courage in Daud's eyes. Like one of King David's mighty men, Daud had emerged alive. Hana shared her thoughts. Daud smiled and shook his head. Hana reached out and touched his lips with her index finger.

"Don't disagree," she said. "I know what I saw, and it's true."

Daud took another deep breath. "I need to tell you what happened."

For Hana the interfaith convocation was already an event in the past. Much had happened since she stood on the platform in the middle of her presentation.

"There was a connection tonight with my mission for the CIA," Daud said. "And perhaps the attack on the car near Al-Bireh."

Daud told her about Sharm el-Sheikh. The cut on his arm had long since healed, but a faint scar remained. Now she knew why and how it occurred. Hana shuddered at the danger he'd been in and the risks he'd taken.

"All of the information about the mission in Sharm el-Sheikh is classified," Daud continued. "But riding home with the FBI agent, I knew I had to tell you everything. You're my wife."

"But you didn't kill Khalil's brother?"

"No. I suspect the Egyptians interrogated him and eliminated him. Khalil and whoever else he's connected with learned of the brother's death and blamed me."

"You don't think Khalil was acting alone? That means —" Hana stopped.

"I'm not sure," Daud answered. "But he's a jihadist looking for what he believes is a glorious way to die."

"You kept that from happening."

Daud told Hana about the press release coming from the FBI. "My role in what took place is going to come out eventually."

Images of TV cameras and reporters on their lawn flashed through Hana's mind. She ran her hand through her hair. "Our lives are going to be so chaotic," she said. "It makes me want to leave and go someplace else."

"I know where I'd like to go," Daud replied, looking directly into her eyes.

Hana's heart skipped a beat. "Jerusalem?" she whispered.

"But only if we believe it is God's will and that this is the right time," Daud continued. "Danger and threats don't respect national boundaries."

Hana glanced around the barely furnished kitchen. The new house suddenly felt temporary.

"Let's talk later," she managed. "Now that

you're home, I'll be able to rest knowing you're beside me."

Daud awakened to a slender ray of sunshine penetrating the interior shutters of their bedroom. Hana was still asleep. Daud lay on his back for a few minutes. His mind was like a computer rebooting all the data downloaded within the past twenty-four hours. Once complete, he experienced the joy reserved for those who've peered into the abyss of death without being cast down into it. He felt a touch on his arm and turned his head. Hana was looking at him with her eyes open.

"What were you thinking?" Hana asked.

"It's a new day," Daud replied.

"Yes, it is."

Daud turned on his side so that he faced Hana. He remained silent but looked into her eyes. She met his gaze, received it, and reciprocated. And in the following moments a level of connection took place between them beyond words and deeper than conscious thought. Neither looked away or spoke. They simply existed in the moment so that it could be what it was meant to be. Love flowed out of Daud because he sensed it coming into him from Hana. It wasn't the romantic attraction he'd felt when he saw her at the rear of the church on their wedding day. That was wonderful. But this was a love with strength, a love with hope, an unshakable love, a love forged in unity greater than any threatening power, a love that could face the future, a love that would last forever, a love with its origin in the throne room of heaven. Neither of them moved. Time was irrelevant. Then, suddenly, it lifted. Daud took Hana's hand in his.

"Speak it," she said.

Daud was used to Hana initiating a spiritual conversation. But he didn't hesitate to tell her what he sensed and believed had happened. Her eyes shone brightly.

"Yes," she said when he finished. "That was heaven coming to earth."

Peace accompanied them downstairs. The events and traumas and threats swirling around them remained real, but those things were no longer their greatest reality. They talked quietly while drinking tea.

"After our talk last night and what just happened between us, I'm free," Hana said, then paused to take a deep breath. "From fear."

Daud let her declaration linger in the atmosphere.

"Which means we can go and do whatever

we believe God wants us to do," she continued. "Not that there won't be other battles, inside and out, but you're right. This is a new day."

"Anwar said you would possess the promised land within."

"And the promised land without," Hana added. "I want to keep praying, but my heart is turned toward the eastern end of the Mediterranean."

After breakfast, Hana returned upstairs. Daud went into his office, turned on his computer, and began working on a written statement he knew someone within the US government would want. An hour later his phone vibrated.

"Mr. Hasan," a male voice said. "This is Charlie in Washington. I talked to the FBI about what went down in Atlanta last night. Sounds like you're a hero."

"Nobody died."

"Do you feel up to debriefing?"

"I was working on a written report when you called."

"Excellent. Let me fill you in on what we know so far. The bomber was a man named Khalil Morsi. He's originally from Lebanon but has been living for the past few years in Qatar. His bother Mustafa was the man who tried to kill the Kolisnyks in Sharm el-

Sheikh. The Morsi brothers worked for a wealthy individual in Qatar named Rahal Abaza. He financed the operation to assassinate Artem Kolisnyk in Sharm el-Sheikh and then refocused the group's efforts to eliminate you along with as many others as possible last night in Atlanta. The Qatari authorities arrested Rahal a few hours ago. We'd been closing in on them based on information obtained from Kolisnyk after he left Sharm el-Sheikh."

"How broad is the network?"

"We're not sure, but we think it is small. That should come out when the Qataris conduct their interrogation."

Daud could imagine what that would include.

"Khalil is also talking," Charlie continued, "but I can't reveal any specific details."

"Are you aware of the attempt to kill me near Al-Bireh in the West Bank?"

"No. Do you believe it's related?"

"Maybe."

Daud related the sequence of events.

"If you forward me the emails sent to you by the man purportedly from the UAE, I can have our internet forensics team check it out."

"Why would you do that?" Daud asked in surprise.

"Because we want you to come to work for us."

Charlie's offer stopped Daud in his tracks.

"I realize today isn't the optimal time to bring this up," the CIA official continued. "But you deserved an update, and I didn't want to miss the opportunity to float the idea. This would be completely different from working as a contractor. You'd be part of our team. We'll discuss it later after the dust settles. Obviously, anything I've passed along is off the record."

"After what happened last night, I told my wife about Sharm el-Sheikh."

Charlie was silent for a moment. "I think I understand why," the CIA officer said in a softer tone of voice. "We'll discuss future protocol if you're interested in considering my proposal."

"And I'm not sure how long I'll continue living in the US."

"That may not matter," Charlie responded. "In fact, depending on where you go, it might be a positive factor."

CHAPTER 43

Two months later Hana arrived early at work on a Friday morning. Her baby was in the middle of another growth spurt. Janet raised her eyebrows.

"Woman," the assistant said, "I'm not sure I want to be around you at full term. It will be painful to see."

"Come into my office for a minute and close the door," Hana said.

Hana sat behind her desk and waited for Janet.

"Am I in trouble?" the assistant asked.

"No, no. I was going to talk to you later today, but now is a good time. You don't need to worry about seeing me when I'm nine months pregnant."

"Of course," Janet said matter-of-factly. "You'll take some time off. I recommend at least a month before and two months after the baby is born. I wish I'd not rushed back to work so fast when my first —"

"You won't see me because I won't be working in Atlanta," Hana said. "Daud and I are going to sell our house and move back to Israel."

Janet's eyes widened, then teared up. She sniffled, and Hana quickly pushed a box of tissues across her desk.

Janet grabbed a couple. "You're not just a lawyer. I'm so wrapped up in your life that it will be like losing a member of my family."

"I'm not going to be lost," Hana replied quickly. "The senior partners have worked out a plan so I can work for the firm on a contract basis with our Israeli clients and hopefully develop new ones. You'll be my support person, which means I'm going to depend on you more than ever."

By this point fat tears were streaming down Janet's face. She shook her head and wiped them away with a tissue.

"It won't be the same," Hana continued, "but I'll come for visits."

Janet blew her nose before she spoke. "In the back of my mind I always knew this day would come, but I didn't think about it because it made me sad. But after what happened at the hotel —" Janet stopped.

"That moved up the timeline, but you're right. This has always been our future."

"Your family must be thrilled."

"Yes."

"Okay," Janet sighed. "I can't be selfish even though I want to be. When will this sad news become public knowledge at the firm?"

"At the end of the day. It will be a few more weeks before we move."

"Does Sadie know?"

"No," Hana said and shook her head. "And I'm not sure how to tell her."

Janet thought for a moment. "My advice is to give her something specific to look forward to. A possibility in the future for an eight-year-old girl won't cut it."

Daud, Hana, and Jakob were meeting for lunch at the Indian restaurant. Moving the base of operations for Daud's consulting business from the US to Israel had been fairly seamless. The big challenge would be traveling from Israel to other countries in the Middle East instead of departing from the US. That would mean more U-turn flights to Europe, since direct air travel from Ben Gurion Airport wasn't always possible. Daud would pass through London or Frankfurt. Like his previous work as a private investigator, the business was a cover for his real tasks. His new job working for the CIA included oversight of covert operatives in several Middle Eastern countries as well as coordination between the CIA and the Israeli Mossad.

"You'll be like me, only able to speak four languages," Charlie said when describing Daud's duties. "And to keep you out of trouble, we're tossing in a role as one of our liaisons with the Mossad."

Since accepting the position, Daud had spent several weeks in Washington that included meetings at CIA headquarters in Langley, Virginia. He'd found the Americans to be professional and serious, which meant the people he encountered were more like Charlie than Lynn. He'd not crossed paths again with the woman who cast him off onto the Red Sea beach with instructions to make his way home the best way he could. If he did encounter her again, he was prepared to be cordial but cautious.

Daud arrived early at the Indian restaurant and was able to hold a table. Five minutes later Hana and Jakob came in together.

Jakob looked surprised. "You're ganging up on me," he said to them.

"It's necessary," Hana answered. "If you separate us, you can get us to do anything you want."

"The only new thing on my plate is going

to be chilli paneer."

They returned to the table after everyone went through the buffet line.

"If it's okay, let me pray," Jakob said.

Hana and Daud glanced at each other and bowed their heads.

"Father, I thank you for my friends and this food. Bless them both. In Jesus' name, amen."

They opened their eyes.

"One other thing," Jakob said, closing his eyes again. "Forgive them for not asking my opinion about moving back to Israel. I'm not sure it's a sin against you, but it was definitely a sin against me. Amen again."

"Who told you?" Hana asked.

"I have confidential sources," Jakob answered slyly. "And that part about you sinning was meant as a joke. I'm not sure about humor in prayers, but I did read the other day in the Psalms that God laughs."

Daud chuckled. "I think that was in a different context."

"Possibly. Anyway, I'm not too upset. I'll have a permanent free place to stay. I hope you're going to settle in Jerusalem. My source didn't fill me in on that detail."

"You talked to Mr. Lowenstein," Hana said.

"Good guess. You know what great friends

we've become. I even mentioned joining Collins, Lowenstein, and Capella to take your place, but he reassured me that was impossible. He claims God only made one of you and after that he broke the mold."

"He didn't say that," Hana replied.

"In different words. But he mentioned you'd have a new role."

Hana explained the relationship she would have with the law firm. Daud focused on the lamb curry. He would miss the Indian restaurant. He didn't know of a comparable place in Jerusalem.

"And what about you?" Jakob asked Daud. "Are you going to be a house husband and take care of the baby so Hana can go to fancy dinners with prospective clients?"

"If she needs me to," Daud replied as he shifted his attention to a lamb-and-potato stew.

"Daud is going to continue his consulting business helping American companies open offices in the Middle East," Hana said.

"Will that keep you busy?" Jakob eyed Daud.

"If not, I can get a job as a clerk at Avi Labensky's shop."

"That's hard for me to imagine," Jakob answered. "But if you end up spending most of your time at home, remember that I like my coffee with one sugar and a dash of cream and prefer fresh pastries with fruit to anything sweet for breakfast."

"We'll prepare a menu and place it on your nightstand before you go to sleep." Hana smiled.

"Excellent. I like that."

At the conclusion of the meal, a waiter brought the check. Jakob pointed to Daud.

"Give it to him," he said. "If I hadn't convinced his wife to work with me on a case, they never would have met."

Daud grabbed the bill. "Yes, let me pay."

Hana talked to Ben on the phone about the best way to break the news to Sadie. They considered the ice cream parlor since that was one of Sadie's favorite places but settled instead on a private time at Ben and Sadie's townhome.

"We can fix supper together, then talk," Hana suggested.

"And I'll take Laura out for dinner so it will be just the two of you."

"Are you sure that's a good idea?"

"Yes," Ben replied. "And stay long enough to tuck Sadie into bed. She's always loved that."

Ben's words made a lump form in Hana's

throat. She was glad he couldn't see her face.

"Sounds good," she said, trying to sound lighthearted. "What evening works best for you? This is a priority for me, so I'm available anytime."

"Let's do Friday."

"Tell Sadie to plan the meal, and you can send me an email so I can supply the ingredients."

A couple days later Hana received a text from Ben letting her know they would be eating hummus, pizza, ice cream, and homemade cookies. Sadie didn't want Hana to bring anything except Leon. When Hana and Leon arrived at the townhome, Sadie patted Leon's head and greeted Hana with a hug.

"I can't come close to wrapping my arms around you," the girl said, pressing her face against Hana's abdomen.

"If Daud said that to me, I'd be upset," Hana replied. "But coming from you, I'll treat it as a compliment."

"Oh, it's a compliment. When I hugged you, I was hugging two people."

Ben appeared with his tie loosened around his neck. It had been over two months since he'd seen Hana. He raised his eyebrows.

"Don't hug her if you think she's fat,"

Sadie warned. "That will get you in trouble."

Ben lightly embraced Hana from the side. "She's not fat," he said. "She's been hard at work."

Sadie was leaning over rubbing Leon's head again. "I have a surprise for you," she announced as she stood up.

Ben adjusted his tie. "I'll be on my way to fight through traffic to pick up Laura. I'll text you when I'm on my way home."

He leaned over and kissed the top of Sadie's head.

"Have fun," she said.

"You too," he answered.

The door closed behind Ben.

Sadie turned to Hana. "I've been telling Daddy things I would like to hear myself. It's working pretty good. Also, Laura is nice, and she's trying really hard."

Curiosity urged Hana to ask a follow-up question about Laura, but discretion restrained her. She followed Sadie into the kitchen. They let Leon loose in the backyard to play. There was a large pot on the stove.

"Lift the lid," Sadie told Hana.

It was full of chickpeas.

"We're going to use dried chickpeas," Sadie announced. "They soaked in water all night in the fridge, and I've been cooking them for an hour. Mrs. Rosenstein says hummus made this way will be even better than what we made before."

While they worked, Sadie talked. It took only a single question every so often to produce another stream of words. Hana loved every syllable. At first she tried to remember nuggets to treasure, but there was so much that she gave up and immersed herself in the moment. Sadie remembered every ingredient Hana liked on her pizza.

"It's like I took a picture of it in my mind from the last time we made pizza at your old house and used it when Daddy took me to the store," Sadie said when Hana asked about it. "I almost forgot one kind of olive, but then I remembered it."

They cooked the pizzas, made the cookie dough, and snacked on hummus.

"This hummus is as good as what my mother makes," Hana said as she spread some on a pita chip.

"I'd like to eat your mother's hummus and see for myself," Sadie said.

Hana kept quiet.

"It's okay if everything doesn't come out of the oven at the same time," Sadie continued. "I like to let my pizza rest in my stomach for a few minutes before eating cookies. That way I get maximum enjoyment."

"I'm in favor of maximum enjoyment too."

Hana's greatest enjoyment came from watching Sadie confidently orchestrate the meal.

"I think your pizzas were better because you have that stone thing to cook them on," Sadie said after she'd eaten a couple of bites.

"This is just as good to me. I'll see if I can talk Daud into buying you a pizza stone."

Sadie was chewing a bite of pizza. "You can talk Daud into anything."

While the cookies baked, they went into the backyard to play with Leon. Hana hadn't realized how many dog toys Sadie had accumulated for his visits. They littered the yard. But the dog's favorite activity remained tug-of-war using a short, thick rope with a big knot on one end.

"He's getting stronger," Sadie grunted as she held on to the knot to keep the rope from slipping through her fingers.

"You are too," Hana said.

Inside, they each ate three cookies. Hana had been limiting her intake of sugar and savored every morsel.

Sadie took a final gulp of milk. "Let's go to my room," she said.

"Cleanup first."

"I knew you were going to say that," Sadie said and sighed. "I like cooking a lot more."

While they scrubbed and cleaned, Hana taught Sadie the first two lines of a classic Hebrew song. The girl had a high voice, even for a child, which was a big contrast from Hana's mellow alto.

"I'll sing it for my Hebrew teacher," Sadie said after she successfully sang it the third time without errors. "But not when other kids can hear me. Can you record it and send it to my daddy's phone so I can practice?"

"I have a better idea. Let's do it together and send it to him now."

They sat at the table and ran through it twice, selecting the best version to send to Ben. He quickly responded.

Laura and I love it!

"Laura can sing pretty good," Sadie said. "Not like you, but it doesn't hurt my ears."

Once the dishwasher was running, they went into Sadie's bedroom. Sadie took Fabia from her resting place in the drawer of the nightstand. The brown-skinned doll showed signs of much love. Her dark hair was a mess, and in addition to her wobbly head, her left leg hung down at such an odd angle that she looked like she needed a hip replacement. Fabia was wearing a green outfit and missing one shoe.

"What happened to her leg?" Hana asked as she wiggled it.

"One of my friends landed on her when she jumped off the bed. It stretched the rubber band that holds the leg in place, but I still take her out at night so she can sleep with me."

They sat on the carpeted floor and leaned against the bed.

"Would you like to meet the real Fabia?" Hana asked once they were settled.

"Yes." Sadie's eyes widened. "Is she going to visit you after you have your baby?"

"No, but maybe someday you could visit her."

"What do you mean?"

Hana took a deep breath. She watched the profile of Sadie's face as she spoke. "I've talked to your daddy, and he's willing to take you to Israel to visit Daud and me next summer. We're selling our house in Atlanta and moving to Jerusalem."

Sadie stared straight ahead and didn't move as she absorbed the news.

"Is that why you came over to see me?" she asked, glancing up with a sad look in her eyes. "To tell me you're moving away?"

Hana put her arm around the girl's shoulders and pulled her closer. Sadie didn't resist.

"I came to see you because I love you, will always love you, and wanted to share the news with you in person because you are so special to me."

Sadie remained quiet for a few moments. "Are you sure I'm going to come visit you? Adults say things like that but don't really mean it."

"I mean it or I wouldn't have said it."

"That helps a little bit." Sadie sighed. "Let's read a book."

Hana sensed Sadie didn't want to dwell on the move.

"Who reads first? You or me?"

"You go first," Sadie replied.

Back and forth they went. Hana could tell that Sadie wanted to squeeze in all her favorite stories. After that she took a shower, and Hana spent the time walking and praying through the house. She was confident angels watched over Sadie and Ben, but she wanted to make sure fresh requests for divine reinforcements rose up to heaven's throne.

"Your hair smells nice," Hana said when Sadie emerged from the bathroom wearing blue pajamas.

"It should. I'm using the shampoo you gave me."

Hana pulled back the covers, and Sadie crawled up into bed.

"You know what I want you to do now, don't you?" the girl asked.

"Yes. And once you go to sleep, I'll stay here with you until your daddy gets home."

Sadie closed her eyes. Hana sat beside her on the bed and began to hum softly. The hum transitioned to a few simple words that grew into thoughts, requests, dreams, and prayers. As was often the case with Sadie, the words were Hebrew, the ancient language of the girl's ancestors. Hana didn't rush. She made sure her heart released the full measure of affirmation and intercession that would follow Sadie Neumann all the days of her life. As her voice softened, Hana could tell Sadie had ridden the song into the land of dreams.

Hana placed her hand on Sadie's head and silently imparted every molecule of love and blessing stored up in her spirit.

EPILOGUE

Three Months Later

Hana and Daud stood in front of the glass case at the Israel Museum in Jerusalem. It was the first time they'd seen the two ceramic heads displayed side by side. The similarity in artistry and craftsmanship of the two pieces was even more apparent when they could be seen together. Hana rested her right hand on her greatly swollen abdomen.

"Do you think they really were a king and queen?" she asked.

"That's totally up to your imagination."

"Then I'll choose to believe they were." Hana pointed to a small sign at the bottom of the exhibit. "It's nice that the museum posted a notice about the connection between the queen's head and Vladimir Ivanov's family."

"Yes, I'm glad Jakob worked it out."

"With Avi's help."

601

"They have some new pieces in the Canaanite section," Daud said. "Do you want to see them?"

"No, this is why I came. And I'm feeling kind of strange."

"Strange?" Daud raised his eyebrows.

"Something's happening," she said. "I'm just not sure if it's the real thing."

They made their way to the exit. After buying the house in Abu Tor and moving to Jerusalem, Daud was prepared to sell his Land Rover in the US, but Hana insisted they ship the vehicle to Israel and pay the taxes assessed by the government.

"I'm not sure it makes financial sense," Daud argued.

"It makes heart sense," Hana responded. "The Land Rover reminds me how much I love you."

"Your face does that for me," Daud answered. "And it's a lot easier to import to Israel."

In the end, Hana won out. The fact that they were able to sell the house in Atlanta for a small profit after living there only a few months helped with relocation expenses.

Daud held open the door and steadied Hana's arm as she climbed into the vehicle.

"Oh," she said. "I really felt that one."

"Do you want to go to the hospital?"

"No, let's go home, and I'll see if the contractions become regular."

Daud smoothly navigated the city streets between the museum and the Abu Tor neighborhood. There was no place on earth like Israel; no city on earth like Jerusalem. At the beginning of the week, Hana had taken a leave of absence from her new position as Israeli counsel for Collins, Lowenstein, and Capella. So far the part-time job suited her perfectly. She'd been able to work with existing clients and generate new business. Daud's work phone buzzed, and he picked it up from its cradle in the console. He listened for a couple of seconds, then spoke in English.

"Yes, I will initiate secure contact with him later this evening and find out what he needs."

Hana didn't ask questions about the call. She was feeling more and more secure and at peace in Jerusalem. It helped that the Shin Bet had arrested the two men who had targeted Daud on the road near Al-Bireh, but the greatest change was the one inside her. The promised land within her soul had become conquered land, and those who lived in conquered land could be at peace. More than ever, Jesus was her Prince of Peace.

During the drive home, Hana had four more contractions, each one stronger than the last. They parked in the street next to the alley that led to their home. Daud came around the vehicle and opened the door. Hana, who was in the middle of another contraction, didn't budge.

"Maybe we should go to the hospital," she said through clenched teeth.

Daud's eyes widened, and he jogged back around to the driver's seat.

"Will you get my suitcase?" she asked.

"Yes, yes."

She watched Daud sprint down the alley. The suitcase was in the corner of their bedroom. Hana's love for the garden, the salon, and the rooftop had steadily increased. She especially enjoyed sitting on the roof in the starlight listening to the sounds of the night and the whispers of heaven.

"Ready," Daud said when he was back behind the wheel. "And I called Avi. He's going to check on Leon later this evening."

The route from Abu Tor to Hadassah Medical Center looped around the eastern part of the city to the west of the Mount of Olives. Hana's primary obstetrician was on call.

"Soon you're going to meet your boy," the

doctor announced after she examined her.

Seven hours later, and with Daud sitting beside her head, Hana pushed a final time, and the baby entered the world.

When the new family was alone in a hospital room, Hana brushed the baby's cheek with her index finger. Nothing in all creation could be more magnificent than the child in her arms. Daud looked both proud and in awe. They'd entered into a pact to pray and ask the Lord for their child's name without revealing it until he arrived.

"It's time," Hana said. "You're the father. What do you think we should name him?"

Daud gently laid his hand on his firstborn son's chest. "Yaqub."

The Arabic name for Jacob was common in previous generations, but less so now. Hana looked down at her son and repeated the name softly.

"What do you think?" Daud asked.

Hana glanced up with a mischievous smile. "Ilsrayiyl."

"Israel?" Daud's eyes widened. "That would be a challenge for him."

"I know," Hana replied. "I love Yaqub."

She kissed the baby on the top of his head and repeated his name three times.

"Yaqub and Ilsrayiyl were the same man,"

Daud said. "God changed his name."

Hana looked up and nodded. "You're right," she said. "And I believe our son will help bring the two worlds together."

ACKNOWLEDGMENTS

Many thanks to those who believed in and supported the writing of this novel. My wife, Kathy, is at the center of all I do. I appreciate the outstanding editorial input from Becky Monds, Jacob Whitlow, and Deborah Wiseman. Special thanks to the *mazkirim*. You know who you are.

DISCUSSION QUESTIONS

1. Hana's great-uncle spoke a prophetic word to Daud and Hana before their marriage. How does the conversation affect them later? Has anyone ever spoken prophetically to you? If so, how did it impact you?

2. Were you aware of the history of stolen artifacts and art collections during World War II? What do you think of Mrs. Zarkawi's decision to keep the coin and return the artifacts? Do you admire her integrity in giving back what had been taken, even though she was innocent? How responsible do you believe the current owners are to return the items to their original owners?

3. Do you think Hana was wise to agree to participate in the interfaith forum? In what ways do you think she's able to impact others based on her background? Have you ever been part of a group that

included people from different ethnic and religious backgrounds? How did that help to challenge and mature you?

4. Although Daud's occupation requires him to be secretive, do you think he's right in keeping significant details from Hana? In what ways does that impact their relationship?

5. Hana and Sadie have a very close relationship since Gloria died. How is their relationship beneficial for Sadie? In what ways might their closeness have negative consequences?

6. Daud is upset at how Lynn and the others handled his mission with Kolisnyk. Do you think he was right to be angry with them? Do you believe he was responsible for any of the fallout from the events in Sharm el-Sheikh?

7. The topic of profiling comes up during Daud and Mr. Lowenstein's conversation about security for the interfaith forum. This is a subject that is very controversial in our current culture. What do you think about profiling? Are there times when it's necessary? Is it possible to profile while still treating others with respect?

8. Daud chooses to make an unplanned detour to Abu Tor to look at a house to buy, while Hana moves forward with

purchasing a home in the US — neither of them consulting the other. Although they are able to work through it, how might things have turned out differently?

9. By traveling to Abu Tor, Daud not only deceived Hana but he put himself in harm's way by giving away his identity. Do you think he was justified in going, or were his actions careless and irresponsible?

10. Daud and Hana seem torn between living in the safety and security of the US and returning to the familiarity and culture of Jerusalem. Does their ultimate decision surprise you? In what ways do they sacrifice for each other in the process of coming to that decision?

ABOUT THE AUTHOR

Robert Whitlow is the bestselling author of legal novels set in the South and winner of the Christy Award for Contemporary Fiction for *The Trial*. He received his JD with honors from the University of Georgia School of Law where he served on the staff of the *Georgia Law Review*.

RobertWhitlow.com
Twitter: @WhitlowWriter
Facebook: RobertWhitlowBooks

The employees of Thorndike Press hope you have enjoyed this Large Print book. All our Thorndike, Wheeler, and Kennebec Large Print titles are designed for easy reading, and all our books are made to last. Other Thorndike Press Large Print books are available at your library, through selected bookstores, or directly from us.

For information about titles, please call:
    (800) 223-1244

or visit our website at:
    gale.com/thorndike

To share your comments, please write:
    Publisher
    Thorndike Press
    10 Water St., Suite 310
    Waterville, ME 04901